A Gathering of
SENTINELS

Novels by G. B. Holley

The Arklight Ancient Alien series:
Revelations
Recondite
Regulus

Quantum Arrow

A Gathering of
SENTINELS

A Holt and Dawson Ghost Sentinel Novel

G. B. HOLLEY

A Gathering of Sentinels

Spirit Owl Books, LLC.
P.O. Box 3547
Seminole, Fl 33772

First Edition: October, 2023

Library of Congress Control Number: 2023912314

Holley, G. B.
A Gathering of Sentinels

ISBN: 978-1-7356513-2-3 (e-book)
ISBN: 978-1-7356513-3-0 (paperback)
ISBN: 978-1-7356513-4-7 (hardback)

Printed in the United States of America

Interior Design and Formatting by: Jera Publishing, Roswell, Ga.
Book Cover Design by JohnEdgar.Design

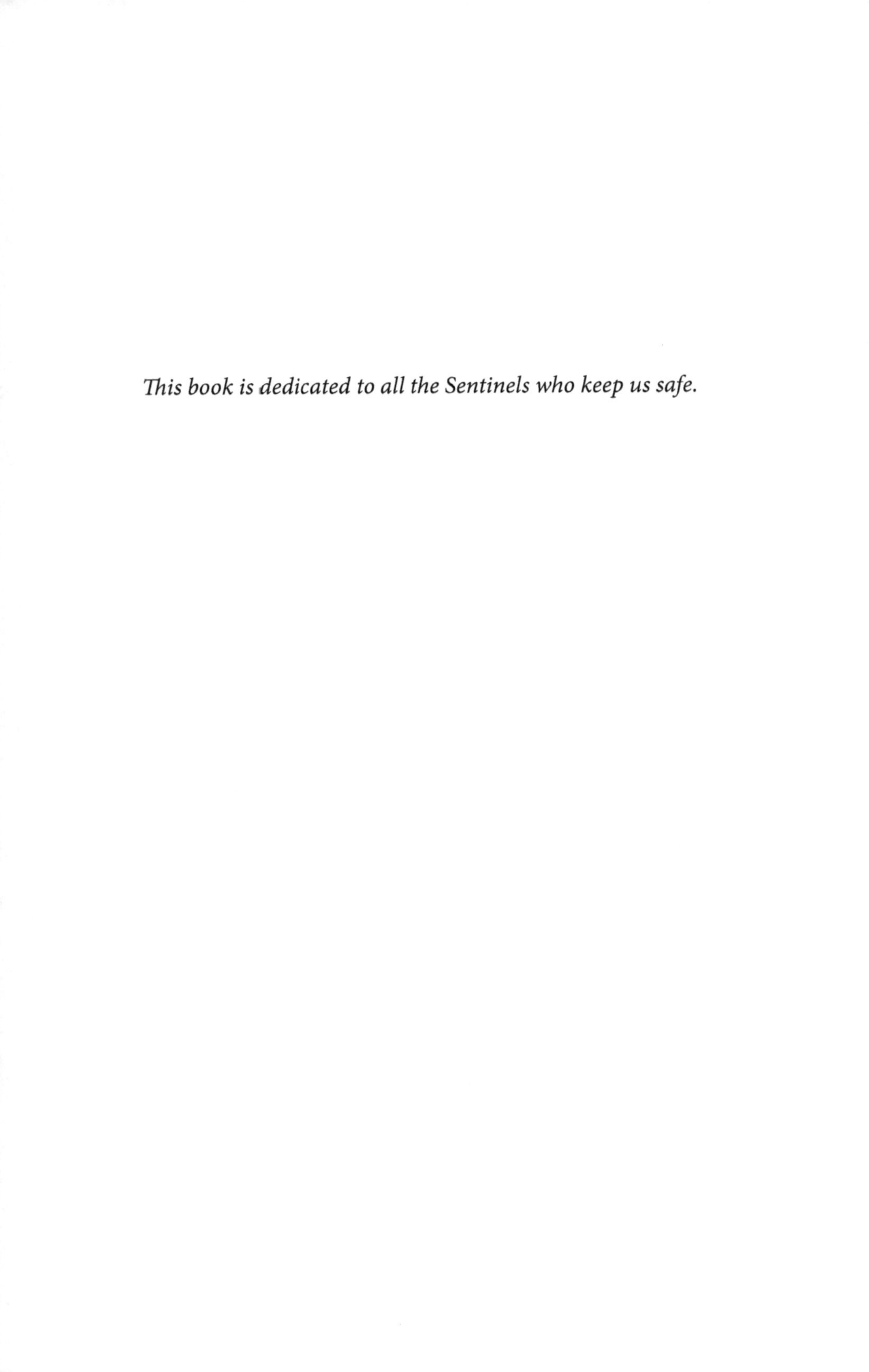

This book is dedicated to all the Sentinels who keep us safe.

What makes a true warrior is being
brave and having the courage in
the truth of what you believe.

Lakota Proverb

CHAPTER ONE

Asupersonic bullet whizzed past Special Agent Akicita Dawson's ear, driving her to the hard, root-covered ground. She rolled behind a large spruce tree just as another bullet hit where she'd been a second earlier. A third round struck to her left, blasting roots and dirt over her. The musty scent of damp soil permeated the early-morning air as the continued barrage of rifle reports echoed through the forest.

"Taking fire!" Aki shouted into her throat mic. She knew her body armor wouldn't stop the fifty-caliber rounds being fired at her.

A moment later, the tree bark above her head splintered.

"Aki, stay down," shouted her partner, Colin Chase.

"Really, Chase?" Aki replied, a sarcastic tone masking her fear.

"I'm moving up behind you."

"Chase, where the hell is our backup?"

"We're coming in from the north," Victor, the GSG 9 tactical team commander, responded over the radio in a heavy German accent. "I have a three-man tactical team flanking Dariya's position from the east."

"You *did* have a tactical team," a composed female voice taunted them over the radio in a Belarusian accent. "Agent Dawson, you realize that you will never capture me?"

Aki felt anger swell. "Listen up, you murdering psychopathic bitch! I'm going to put you away or take you out. You're nothing but a hired killer."

Laughter resonated from the radio, and then Dariya "Dar" Novikov replied, "You don't have what it takes to do either of those things—though your pursuit does keep me amused. I commend you on your detective work. Tracking me to my safe house took some skill, or maybe I just got careless."

"You won't be able to get away this time," Aki said. "You've just added GSG 9 officers to your list of homicides. The German Federal Police will hunt you down. Make it easy on yourself, and give up now."

"I didn't kill the tactical team. I only tranquilized them. They will be out for a few hours and wake up with a headache. I don't kill unsanctioned targets. Although highly trained, they aren't in my league, and neither are you."

"Apparently, you aren't a very good shot," Aki goaded.

"I wasn't trying to shoot you. I was just having a little fun scaring you. Agent Dawson, you are only doing your job, as were the other men, and none of you pose a real threat to me."

"You have standards? How professional of you. I guess we should thank you." Aki hoped she could keep Dar talking until Victor and the rest of his team could reach her sniper hide. Victor had to be close to it by now.

"Consider it a friendly warning," Dar said. "It's time for me to leave and for you to go home. Better luck next time."

Flash grenades detonated a hundred yards from Aki's position. She heard multiple rounds being fired. It sounded like suppressed MP5K submachine guns and Glock 17s.

"We are converging on her position now," Victor confirmed.

Aki stood, but she didn't move from behind her cover. She was in the assault team's field of fire, and she didn't need an errant round of friendly fire wrecking her day. She did several quick peeks around the tree trunk, hoping to see Dar being forced in her direction, but there was no movement in the dawning light invading the darkness beneath the trees, only elongated shadows.

All gunfire abruptly stopped. A stunning silence surrounded Aki. With an indrawn breath, she scanned the area to see if Dar was approaching.

"I've already breached your perimeter," Dar radioed. "Aki, if I encounter you again, it will be on my terms. Maybe someday, we'll sit down and have a cocktail."

"Victor, report!" Aki ordered, ignoring Dar's taunt.

"We found her hide. The area is secure. I have issued an alert. Air support will be on the scene in a few minutes. She won't get far."

Aki was dumbfounded as to how Dar could have eluded her net. Their intelligence was sound and Dar had been seen through an open curtain just before midnight. The German Federal Police had deployed their very best team for the capture. Aki wondered if air support should have been deployed sooner. However, the element of surprise would be less hazardous to the team and Victor had agreed. Aki didn't like being outfoxed.

"Victor, have the men Dar neutralized been located?"

"Yes. All three of them are alive, just unconscious."

Chase joined Aki, and they walked uphill toward the sniper hide. "Aki, how could she have taken out three GSG 9 operators?"

"Because she *is* that good."

"She had to have known we were coming and positioned herself accordingly."

"You think?" Aki pointed her flashlight at a tree branch high in the canopy. Her light reflected off a concealed remote camera. "That's the latest in security camera systems. It's Russian. I spotted it through my night scope just before she started shooting at me. She did see us coming and I can't help but wonder if she was tipped off, too. She was well prepared."

"Looks like expensive hardware," Chase commented.

"Very. I'm certain we'll find more of them, along with ground microphones and movement sensors." Aki shook the dirt from her long, black ponytail.

When Aki and Chase joined Victor and his team at the hide, Aki said, "Let me guess, she was using an LRT-3 sniper weapon system."

"You are correct," Victor said.

Aki pointed her flashlight into the hardened, camouflaged bunker and examined the fifty-caliber rifle equipped with a NightForce NXS tactical scope. The weapon was mounted on a motorized rotating platform.

"She was never here," Victor said. "The wiring for the weapon runs through a conduit toward the house. The breach team found monitors after they made entry into the residence. From what they've told me, she could fire the rifle from anywhere with a pad or a tablet."

"It's bolt-action," Aki said. "This is a very sophisticated remote firing system."

Victor kneeled and pointed at the automated bolt-action lever. "She could have fired several more rounds."

The radio crackled. *"Haus gesichert,"* a male voice announced over the radio.

"Sehr gut, Oxen," Victor replied. "Aki, the house has been deep-cleared and is secured."

Aki had met Oxen before the operation and knew that wasn't his real name. No GSG 9 operative is known by their real name outside the unit. They are known only by monikers. He was a large man, tall and bald, with a jovial personality. She didn't think he fit the stereotype of a hardened operative, which was why she'd taken an instant liking to him.

Oxen continued in German, "The housekeeper is the only one here. She looks a lot like the target, which is probably why she was hired. We found a room in the basement that has optical relays, which feed several cameras and are synched to three more automated weapons systems scattered around the property. Linked as they are, they provide a three hundred-sixty-degree field of fire capability. We have disabled them. She could have killed us all."

"Take the housekeeper into custody," Victor ordered.

Once Victor had translated Oxen's report, Aki said, "Dar allowed us to penetrate her perimeter and only targeted me with one of the weapons. She could be anywhere."

"I think she was playing with us," Victor said. He had a brief exchange in German over the radio, then said, "Medics report that my men were darted."

"If she darted them, then she'd have to have been close," Chase said. "She couldn't have gotten far."

"She has a good lead on us," Victor said. "I'm betting that she's slipped through our net."

After an extensive search without contact, Victor stated, "Let's go interrogate the housekeeper."

Hamburg – GSG 9 Headquarters – 0800 hours

A steel table and three chairs were positioned in the center of the gray-walled, soundproof interrogation room. Dar's housekeeper sat facing a two-way mirror. Oxen sat opposite her. The woman's shaking hands were shackled to the table. Aki didn't need Victor's translations to tell her what the house-keeper's body language was revealing.

"This is getting us nowhere," Aki said, watching from the observation room. "The woman is scared to death or she's a very good actress."

"I agree," Victor said, and spoke briefly to Oxen through the mic. Oxen immediately left the interrogation room.

Turning to Aki, Victor explained, "I've ordered a truth drug to be admin-istered, but I fear that she won't provide us with any additional details that will assist us in finding Dar. I think that she's what she claims—a live-in housekeeper and Dar's cook. We may as well get comfortable. This is going to take a while." Victor pulled a chair over to the window and sat down.

Aki admired his muscular build, penetrating blue eyes, and cropped blond hair. His crooked nose and the scar across his jaw only enhanced his warrior-like appearance. She was glad that he was on her side.

Aki knew that the GSG 9 tactical units in the German Federal Police had great latitude when dealing with combatants or suspected terrorists. They responded to kidnapping, hostage situations, and counterterrorist operations. Dariya Novikov was one of the best assassins in the world. She was an expert with weapons, explosives, and poisons, and because of her criminal activities and the collateral damage she left in her wake, she had been classified as a terrorist by several countries. She met all of the criteria for a GSG 9 deployment, which was why Aki and Chase had their support.

"Have your men recovered?" Aki asked.

"Yes. They're fine. Embarrassed and very fortunate that they're not dead. The team will learn from this experience."

"Your team has some of the best trained operatives in the world. I understand that only one in five complete the twenty-two-week training program."

"That is true." Victor gave her a hard stare. "Perhaps you failed to tell us something about our target."

"I told you that Dar is well trained." Aki decided to fill in the gaps she hadn't disclosed. "Dar was born in Minsk, Belarus. She joined the Belarusian military and became a special forces operator as a paratrooper. She was recruited by the State Security Committee of the Republic of Belarus and worked in counterterrorism assigned to the Alpha Group as an infiltration specialist and assassin. She was very good at her job. Dar's also a master of disguise and had a reputation as a skilled operator."

"This I know," Victor said.

"What you probably don't know is that she was romantically involved with her Alpha Group commander, Colonel Vasil Lesun, and she seemed to be on the fast track to the inner circle…until there was an incident."

"That I didn't know," Victor said. "What happened?"

"Dar assassinated the president's mistress, who she believed to be a CIA agent. Apparently, the president was in love with the woman. An investigation revealed that his mistress wasn't CIA and that Dar was responsible for the termination. Col. Lesun claimed it was an unsanctioned assassination to avoid any fallout. The president demanded Dar's head and she fled the country."

"How was she able to survive?"

"Col. Lesun actually orchestrated her escape by faking her death and providing Dar with the financial support and contacts for her new venture as a freelance assassin. I suspect that she threatened to kill him if he didn't help her."

"I can see that happening. How did she allegedly die?"

"Lesun ordered her termination. A week later, a body was discovered at a farm outside Minsk, following a staged standoff. The building was burned to the ground, the body found inside was unrecognizable, and the DNA comparison identified the woman as Dar. The file was closed until she surfaced two years ago in Russia. Dar killed a high-ranking oligarch who was rumored to have been creating problems for an oil industry consortium. As far as we know, this was her first assassination as a freelancer killer.

"All of her activities since then have fit a specific profile. The target is always a business or political target who is a problem for a power broker. She uses whatever means necessary to get the job done. She has many confirmed kills around the world, earning her a reputation as being a problem solver."

"Who do you really work for?" Victor asked, giving her a sly grin.

"As I told you, Homeland Security. I work in the International Operations Division, Special Projects."

"I had you pegged for CIA or DIA."

"Nope."

Victor snickered, then asked, "Wasn't there fallout for Colonel Lesun when Dar was resurrected from the dead?"

"Surprisingly, no. The DNA report supported his claim and there wasn't any evidence to link him to her escape. Our intelligence community thinks Dar has performed some missions for members of the Belarusian National Assembly and that they have turned a blind eye to her previous activities."

"So, the government may be protecting her so she can act on their behalf and they can deny any knowledge of her actions."

"Exactly."

"How do clients get in contact with Dar?" Victor asked.

"I wish I knew. Maybe it's similar to the dark web—you pay a fee and get access to a worldwide web of assassins and kidnappers."

Chase entered the room carrying three large mugs of coffee, his fingers laced through the handles. "I thought you both could use a jolt. I usually drink tea, but this smelled so good."

"The way you're carrying those mugs, I bet Victor could get you a job at a local *Hofbräuhaus*," Aki teased. She took one of the mugs and savored the fine aroma. "That smells good."

"We have the best coffee outside of Paris," Victor said with pride. "How long have you and Chase worked together?"

"Two years," Aki replied. "Chase, any updates from our people?"

"Nothing. All of our electronic traces are dark. The funds in her two Luxembourg accounts are also quiet, no money transfers. She's off the grid."

"Five million dollars is a lot of money to ignore while on the run," Aki said.

"I'm sure Dar's wondering if her last transfer to the Deutsche Bank in Hamburg is what led us to her," Chase said. "She's got to know we flagged those accounts by now."

"Is that how you found her?" Victor asked.

"It's what started us in this direction," Aki answered. "One of our intelligence analysts got a hit on a new alias Dar was using. She ran it down and found the two accounts that had been recently opened under that name. We put a trace on both accounts and got lucky."

"Finding her money and finding her home are two different things," Victor said. "How did you find the safe house?"

"I can only tell you that we have a high-level source within Deutsche Bank who helped us. We were able to monitor her real-time credit card usage and ATM withdrawals under one of her aliases. Several purchases and withdrawals were made around the Hittfeld and Seevetal areas. We were able to capture a photo of her vehicle from a security camera at one of the sites. The car was registered to Helga Swanson, an alias we didn't know about. From there we were able to locate her property, which is owned by a corporation registered in Bermuda. Helga Swanson is listed as one of the corporate officers. Don't ask me how we gained access to that information."

"Alright. But I'm sure that your NSA had something to do with it."

"They do have access to a very sophisticated electronic monitoring system," Aki said. "Chase and I set up surveillance around the access roads to her property, and once we verified that she was residing there, we asked for your assistance."

"I imagine Dar has money squirreled away," Chase said. "We're going to have to start from scratch again to catch up to her."

Aki took a sip of her coffee. "Let's see what the housekeeper has to say. If Dar doesn't surface before noon, we'll order a hack into the Luxembourg accounts and drain them. Victor, I'll see that GSG 9 receives half of the funds from her accounts to compensate the Bundespolizei for your effort. It may take a while to work through the red tape, but you'll see reimbursement for your time and expenditures."

"That is very generous. I am certain that my BPOL commander will be most appreciative."

When Oxen entered the room carrying a syringe, the housekeeper started yelling and attempted to pull away from the table. Oxen held her arm firmly as he administered the truth serum.

"It won't take long for the drug to take effect," Victor said.

An hour later, Aki had her next lead. The housekeeper told Oxen that two weeks ago she'd accompanied Dar to Travemünde, a borough of Lübeck, northeast of

Hamburg. She'd shopped for groceries for a special dinner Dar had requested, and Dar had taken her to lunch at a seafood restaurant along the Trave River. The housekeeper related that they seldom traveled anywhere together and never ate at restaurants, so this outing had been a special treat for her.

The housekeeper told them that during their lunch, Dar had received a cell phone call and she'd overheard her talking about a sailboat docked by the river near the ship *Passat*. Oxen asked her for the name of the restaurant, but she couldn't recall. She remembered it was near a lighthouse, that was also a maritime museum.

According to the housekeeper, Dar knew the owner of the restaurant and had asked if the sailboat was seaworthy, because she was planning a voyage. The owner had told her it was a good boat and recommended she purchase it before anyone else.

"Dar's planning to sail away," Aki said after hearing Victor's translation of the conversation. "We need to get assets to Travemünde and see if we can catch her before she leaves."

"I will see to it," Victor replied. "I'll also start a search of vessel-ownership transfers in the last month. With luck, the owner is local. I wish we had a description of the boat."

"We need to find the restaurant and talk to the owner," Aki said. "Do you know where the lighthouse and the *Passat* are located?"

"*Ja.* We did some maritime hostage-rescue training on the *Passat*. It's a four-masted barque and one of the last of the windjammers afloat. It's being used as a youth hostel and a museum, and it has large conference rooms for weddings and other functions. You can even take—"

"How far is it from here?" Aki interrupted.

"About an hour's drive."

"Can we get there any faster by helicopter?"

"The helicopter will take time to prepare for flight. It'll be faster if we drive."

"Shit. She already has a four-hour head start. Where can she go in a sailboat from there?"

"The Trave River feeds into the Baltic Sea," Victor replied. "She could go to Poland, Denmark, or any of the Scandinavian countries, even Russia. Or she could sail into the North Sea toward the UK or Ireland."

"So anywhere," Aki said. "We need to get people to the docks immediately."

"I'll send BPOL officers and have them start canvasing the restaurants," Victor said. "I will also have a helicopter available for us in Travemünde to help us search the tributaries and the sea."

"What about police boats?" Chase asked.

"I will alert the Küstenwache. They are not trained like your Coast Guard and are not equipped to deal with someone like Dar, but they can help us identify any sailboats in the area."

"Victor, is there a lot of sailboat traffic around there?" Aki asked.

"Depends on the weather. Today is a nice day, so there could be hundreds of boats."

"Great. Just great." Aki rubbed her temples, hoping to ease the pain of her tension headache. "She may have planned for her housekeeper to tell us about her conversation and the sailboat. It could be a ruse."

"It's possible," Chase said. "Victor, how far could she have gotten in a car by now?"

"She could be in Denmark, Poland, the Netherlands, or Belgium. We have people at the borders, but you said she was a master of disguise, so I don't think a cursory border check will find her. She could even have gone to ground right here in Hamburg."

"Let's concentrate on Travemünde," Aki said. "Victor, are there any problems with you continuing to work with us?"

"No. I was authorized to assist you until we are no longer needed. Dar is also a priority target for us, after what she did to my team in Hittfeld."

"Excellent. I need to advise my boss at HITEC and brief her while you get everything going here. Then we'll head for Travemünde. Maybe we'll get lucky."

Victor cocked his head, then asked, "What is HITEC? You hadn't mentioned that before."

"It's an acronym for Homeland Identities, Targeting, and Exploitation Center. They provide intelligence and analysis work for the special-projects teams, like the one Chase and I are on." She noticed his disbelieving expression. "Don't read anything into it."

"Whatever you say, Agent Dawson."

CHAPTER TWO

Devils Tower, Wyoming – May 20 – 0600 hours.

Graynger "Gray" Holt looked out from the front of his Forest River Georgetown RV at the magnificent Bear Lodge Butte, better known as Devils Tower, as he sipped his coffee. The massive butte towered twelve hundred feet above the Belle Fourche River, and the early-morning light cast an orange glow across the eastern face of the butte, giving it a mystical appearance. Taking in the beauty of the landscape around him, he understood why the butte was considered a sacred place by so many Native American tribes. He felt a deep spiritual connection to this place, and he'd only arrived last night.

After watching the movie *Close Encounters of the Third Kind* as a teenager, he'd promised himself that he'd visit Devils Tower National Monument someday. It was everything he'd imagined it would be. He planned to hike all five of the trails around its base, starting with the Tower Trail after breakfast and then the Red Beds and South Side Trail after lunch. He was going to save the other two trails for tomorrow.

He scanned the east face of the butte with his binoculars, admiring its sheer, rugged verticalness. He wished he was a little younger—then he'd have tried to climb to the top like so many others did during the summer.

Prior to driving his new home westward, he'd read some articles about Devils Tower and its connection to Native American culture. He knew that many Plains tribes conducted religious ceremonies there and that prayer ties, made of colorful cotton cloth and filled with tobacco, were often left in the trees and shrubs along the trails as offerings of gratitude.

He'd also learned that geologists were still debating how the stone pillar was formed. Most agreed it was a volcanic plug or had formed from the igneous intrusion of the remains of a now-extinct volcano, or possibly from rock being pushed up from the volcanic activity below it. In any event, it was a stunning sight.

Gray stretched. The campground was going to be his home for the next two days. He'd been lucky to reserve a great pull-through space for his RV. Rustic cabins lined the southern bank of the Belle Fourche River, and he appreciated the campground rule requiring quiet time for another two hours, so people could enjoy nature without the din from other campers. Large cottonwood trees were scattered throughout the property, and he listened to the chilly, forty-five-degree wind blowing through their robust green canopies. The tranquil setting was just what he'd needed to leave behind the turmoil of the last six months of his life.

He needed a fresh start and was looking forward to flying as an interagency pilot for the Office of Aviation Services, OAS, with the U.S. Department of the Interior. His position and nine other pilot positions were created as an experimental program designed to enhance aviation assets to multiple agencies in remote areas around the country. *The more remote, the better.*

He'd decided to leave Florida after the end of his twenty-year marriage. They'd parted amicably enough, and there were no custody issues since they had no children. His job at the Sheriff's Office had put a strain on their marriage over the years. She'd worried daily about whether he was coming home, especially when he left on high-risk callouts. She had wanted him to retire early, but he'd refused. The final straw had come when he and another deputy were wounded during a hostage standoff. He still had nightmares about that day.

The standoff involved a man holding a gun to his girlfriend's head, and when deputies arrived, he had thrown his phone out of the car window and threatened to kill her if they didn't leave. Gray and another negotiator had responded to try and convince the guy to give up. After being briefed and seeing where the man was located, Gray realized the only way to establish a meaningful dialogue would be to get close enough to talk with him without having to yell. It had been his decision not to use a tactical vehicle, fearing the sight of the armored vehicle would trigger a violent response. Gray and another negotiator had walked up to talk to the man, using handheld ballistic shields as cover.

After nearly two hours of negotiations, the man had agreed to release the woman. He'd allowed her to open the passenger door, and just as she stepped out, a SWAT member moved closer. The troubled man shot the woman and opened fire. When the firefight was over, the man and his hostage were dead, and he and his partner were wounded. As the negotiator team leader, his decision to forgo the armored vehicle haunted him. He knew the risk, and so did his partner. The outcome wasn't within his control, but his partner was left with a career-ending disability.

The incident had been bad enough, but the media had erred in their reporting of what actually happened. They claimed that Gray had fired at the troubled man first and that the woman had been killed during the subsequent exchange of gunfire. They also questioned why a lieutenant assigned to the flight unit was the negotiator commander. The new sheriff was image conscious and instead of issuing an immediate rebuke, met the accusations with only, "It's under investigation." It had taken days for the official internal review to be made public, but by then the damage was done and Gray was forced to resign from the team. The day after he was cleared of any wrongdoing, his wife moved out.

For the next few months, he tried to find solace in flying. Every time he left the ground, he was able to focus only on the mission and nothing else, and life seemed normal for a little while. But eventually he realized that the world had changed since he'd first become a deputy twenty years ago. He'd just turned twenty-one when he started with the Sheriff's Office and had worked his way up through the ranks, working in many different divisions. He'd worked as a patrol deputy, a detective, and had held several supervisory positions. Then, five years ago, he finally landed his dream job, command of the aviation unit. He loved it so much that he'd turned down a promotion to captain to keep the job.

Between the hostage incident, the change in the organizational culture, and his divorce, he decided to retire. A former commander of his had told him that he'd know when it was his time to leave, and that time had come when he found the Department of Interior pilot job posting. The grant position waived the age limit for new hires, and the pay was enough to make up for the pension deficit from his early retirement.

Law enforcement was his life, but flying was Gray's passion. After landing his OAS job, he purchased a five-acre spread near Custer, South Dakota, and bought his RV. The sale of his home near Orlando had covered the purchase price of both. His new property had power, a well, a septic system, and an RV pad.

His position required him to provide aerial support to the National Park Service, Forest Service, and other local and federal agencies, including the Bureau of Indian Affairs, BIA. His duties included search-and-rescue operations, aerial surveillance, cultural and natural resource management, and whatever else was required. He wasn't quite sure what he would be doing for the BIA, but he'd researched the history of the tribes around South Dakota and Wyoming. He liked being prepared. The closest reservation to his home base at Custer Airport was the Pine Ridge Reservation, home to the Oglala Lakota Nation.

The grant provided a Cessna 210 and an old military OH-58 helicopter from the National Guard. He figured that he was selected for the position because he was both a fixed-wing and rotor pilot. He had over two thousand hours as pilot in command in aircraft, but only fifteen hundred hours in a Bell 206, the civilian version of the OH-58. The natural resource grant allowed him to be the sole operator at the airport, which suited him just fine.

Gray was startled by a chilling child's scream as it echoed across the campground. He wasn't sure where the scream had come from, but he knew from the sound of the wail that a child was terrified. As he bolted from the RV, a second scream came from near the river, and Gray ran in that direction as additional shouts and gasps rolled past him. Emerging from between two rustic cabins, Gray spotted a man standing near the water's edge alongside a woman kneeling and embracing a sobbing child.

"I touched it," the little girl whimpered as Gray passed her. Then he saw a man facedown and suspended beneath the surface of the slow-moving river. When he got closer, he could see that the victim's left foot was missing, leaving the remnants of a mangled leg. The right foot was in a hiking boot and appeared intact. The man was clothed in long green pants and a long-sleeved khaki-colored shirt. His hair was cut short, and his skin was pale with a waxy sheen and appeared waterlogged. This wasn't a recent death. Gray knew that the river was cold enough to have slowed the decomposition process and that the body had been in the water for at least a week. People began surrounding him to take in the gruesome sight.

"I need everyone to stay back," Gray ordered. "Anyone with a phone, call the police."

Gray noted that the man's left leg had been taken by a predator. He wondered if this had been a bear attack. He knelt down for a closer inspection and saw a rope tied around the man's hands. *Definitely not a bear attack.*

"I have a park ranger on the phone," a woman yelled. "I told them someone had drowned. She said that we should get the body out of the water before it floats away."

Gray walked over to the woman, carefully checking to make sure he didn't step on anything that looked like possible evidence. "May I?" he asked, holding out his hand for her cell phone. The woman handed it over and stepped away. "This is Gray Holt. Who's this?"

"Park Ranger Sarah Goodson."

"Ranger Goodson, the body in the river is bound. I'm a retired deputy with homicide experience and this is either a homicide or suicide. I've secured the scene. I have no intention of moving the body. It appears to be snagged or tied to something under the surface."

"That changes things," Sarah said. "I'll be there in ten minutes. Don't let anyone leave."

"Understood."

Gray waved at Ranger Goodson as she got out of her National Park Service truck. She was a tall blond with an athletic build and looked to be in her mid-thirties. "Morning, Ranger Goodson. I'm Gray Holt."

"Morning. Where's the best place for me to approach so I don't disturb the crime scene?" Sarah asked, adjusting her Park Ranger campaign hat.

"Just keep walking straight ahead," Gray said, noting her confident command bearing. "The area had a number of people milling around before the scene was secured. I don't think this is the original site of the crime, anyway."

As they walked to the river bank, he caught a pleasant faint scent of jasmine with just a hint of lemon. She was only a few inches shorter than his six-foot-two height. "The body hasn't moved since we talked. It's snagged on some vegetation."

She stopped at the river's edge, knelt for a closer look, and said, "I see the ropes. Not an easy way to commit suicide."

"I agree. I believe the victim was killed and dropped in the river somewhere south of here. The current appears to be flowing north."

"It is. The Belle Fourche winds its way up from Campbell County, past Moorcroft and Devils Tower. It eventually joins the Cheyenne River in South Dakota. The largest body of water that feeds into the river is the Keyhole Reservoir, which would be a great place to dump a body."

"How far away is the reservoir?" Gray asked.

"About twenty miles. I don't see any obvious injuries, except for the missing foot. That was probably taken after he was dead. There aren't any wounds on his back."

"Hard to say if there's any other trauma without rolling him over. Ranger Goodson, is this going to be your case?"

"No, and call me Sarah. It's not on federal land. The Crook County Sheriff's Office will be responsible. I called them and they requested that I secure the scene. Their medical examiner will also be responding from Sundance. Rolling him over and removing the body will be their responsibility. We just need to keep the critters and looky-loos away."

"How large of an agency is Crook County SO?"

"They have ten deputies. I'm sure they'll ask for assistance from the Wyoming Division of Criminal Investigation. The DCI handles most of the major investigations and their forensic team will work the scene."

"How long until a deputy arrives?"

"Depending on where a deputy is, it could be thirty minutes to an hour," Sarah said. "The medical examiner may get here before the deputy. Do you have someplace you need to go?"

Gray shook his head. "No. I was just enjoying the sunrise when I heard a child scream and I ran to see what was happening. I have an RV in the campground. I'm on my way to my duty station in Custer."

"You're active military?" Sarah asked. "I thought you said you were a retired deputy."

"I was a deputy for twenty years and retired early to take a job flying for the Department of the Interior. I'm part of a new Office of Aviation Services program. I'll be working with a lot of different agencies, mostly in southwestern South Dakota and Wyoming. I thought I'd take in some sights on the way to my property before I start my job in a couple of weeks."

"You're a pilot?"

"Yes. Fixed wing and rotor."

"Nice, maybe you'll take me up sometime?" Sarah said. "Where's your property?"

"Near Red Canyon Rim, south of Custer."

"That's a pretty area."

"I thought so. That's why I bought it."

"This is a hell of way to start your new job," Sarah said.

"I'm not technically on the job yet. I officially report on the tenth of June. I have to complete an area orientation and a few more check rides in Rapid City before getting signed off to fly solo. Then I'll be flying out of Custer airport starting on the fifteenth. Fortunately, my home goes wherever I need to be."

"Well, I'm glad you're here. Will you be flying up this way?"

"I'll fly wherever I'm told." Gray looked down at the dead man and thought this was a strange conversation to be having at a crime scene. He glanced around and saw that most of the witnesses were standing near the cabins, watching. They probably thought that Sarah was questioning him.

"Are you going to be doing search and rescue?" Sarah asked.

"That's one of my jobs," Gray replied. He wanted to bring the conversation back to the crime. "Do you have many homicides around here?"

"No. It's very unusual. Though we did have three people go missing about three weeks ago. They disappeared in the Black Hills about sixty miles south of here near Newcastle. They work for a mining company and their vehicles were left at a sand and gravel company parking lot. After a week, the manager of the gravel company notified the Weston County Sheriff's Office and an alert was issued. They still haven't been found."

"What were they doing out there?"

"I'm not sure. Probably looking for new sites to dig for gold."

"Gold?" Gray said, surprised.

"Yes, gold. It's easy to get lost in the Hills. Forest Service, the Sheriff's Office and other agencies searched for two weeks. They appear to have just vanished. They could have been taken by a black bear."

"Are there lots of bears in the Black Hills?" Gray asked.

"They're making a comeback, so there's more now than a decade ago."

"You said Newcastle is south of here?"

"Yes. It's near the Wyoming and South Dakota border, at the southern edge of the Black Hills National Forest."

"Could this be one of the missing people?" Gray asked, pointing at the body.

"I don't think so. The body looks to be in too good of a condition. Besides, where would a bear get a rope?"

Gray chuckled. "Good point, but the water is pretty cold and it would preserve the body."

"True, but I think if it had been submerged for three weeks, fish and other predators wouldn't have left much. Plus, the river doesn't come anywhere near where those people were last seen. Spencer Reservoir is the only water near there and it doesn't connect with the Belle Fourche."

Sarah's cell phone rang. She answered, and after a brief conversation, she said, "Deputy Clay Gurley will be here in ten minutes. The medical examiner will arrive at about the same time. As I suspected, the DCI will be responsible for the investigation. Special Agent Roland Crawley will be coming up from Gillette." She rolled her eyes. "I'll stick around until he arrives."

"I take it you know Agent Crawley?"

"Unfortunately." Sarah didn't say anything else.

"I'll go let the folks know that it will be a little longer before they can leave."

"Thanks, Gray. Would you like to get a cup of coffee after Creepy Crawley is done interviewing us? I can give you a private tour of the butte, and maybe later we could have dinner, that is unless there's a wife or girlfriend waiting for you."

Gray was stunned by her directness, and a bit flattered. "No. There's no woman in my life right now. I'm recently divorced. A private tour and dinner sound good." An evening with Sarah seemed more interesting than the nightly viewing of *Close Encounters of the Third Kind* at the campground.

"Good. Then it's a date," Sarah said, with a sparkle in her green eyes.

There was a moment of awkward silence. Gray smiled, then left to talk to the other witnesses.

Ten minutes later, Crook County Deputy Clay Gurley parked his SUV next to Sarah's truck. The medical examiner's van pulled up and two people got out. Sarah waved them over. "Gray, that's Clay, Dr. Jack Beining, who is the medical examiner, and his new assistant, Joann Arnaut."

"Joann looks young," Gray said.

"She just graduated from college and is a very smart young lady. She's going to medical school in the fall."

"Has the body been moved?" Clay asked as he approached. He was wearing a tan uniform shirt, black pants, and black boots.

"The body hasn't been disturbed since I arrived," Sarah answered. "This is Gray Holt. He's a retired deputy and was present shortly after the body was discovered."

Clay nodded, then said, "I'm sure that Agent Crawley will want to talk to you."

"I would think so, Deputy Gurley," Gray responded.

"Just call me Clay, unless we're around Agent Crawley. He likes things formal."

"You going to wait for Crawley before you examine or move the body?" Sarah asked Clay.

"Yeah. I don't need any more problems with him," Clay responded. "Crawley radioed that he was a few minutes away. I was instructed to wait and not touch anything. What an ass."

Gray figured Agent Crawley must be a piece of work. He certainly wasn't liked by the local law enforcement.

Dr. Beining and Joann finished unloading their gear and joined the group. Introductions were made and Sarah pointed out the witnesses who had found the body. Gray noticed that the witnesses were growing impatient, and he couldn't blame them. Law enforcement personnel were on scene and it didn't appear as if anything was being done.

"You waiting for Crawley, too?" Sarah asked Beining.

"Yup."

A black Chevy Tahoe pulled up a few minutes later. An overweight man wearing a dark-gray suit and a black cowboy hat got out of the vehicle, and by the groans from Clay and Sarah, Gray figured he was Crawley. He was maybe five feet ten, and there was a swagger to his gait as he walked toward them. His black cowboy boots were shined and had silver-toed tips.

Gray leaned toward Sarah and said, "I know you don't like the guy, but is he a good investigator?"

"He's very good at his job. Just a pain to work with. He asked me out once and I turned him down. Since then, he's always making belittling comments about my job, like I'm not really in law enforcement. He gives me the creeps."

"Thus the name Creepy Crawley," Gray said.

"Correct. But don't let me influence what you think of him. If he doesn't like you, you'll know it. If you get in his way, he'll make your life miserable."

"Tell me what you really think of him," Gray said.

Sarah smiled at him, and said, "Oh, I will."

Crawley walked up and addressed Gray. "I'm Special Agent Roland Crawley with the Wyoming DCI. I know these people, but who are you and why are you standing in the middle of my crime scene?"

Gray gave a slight nod, then said, "I'm retired lieutenant Graynger Holt. I was a deputy in Florida. My friends call me Gray." Gray extended his hand and they shook. The overly tight squeeze Crawley gave him meant he was trying to establish that he was the alpha on the case.

"I don't care who you used to be, Graynger, why are you here?"

"I'm here because I responded to a child's scream and found the body. I secured the scene and your witnesses until Ranger Goodson arrived. If you like, I'll walk you through what I found, and when, so you can establish a timeline."

"You here on vacation?"

"No, I'm a pilot. I'll be starting work for the Office of Aviation Services in Custer soon."

Crawley took a deep breath, then asked, "You have any experience working homicides?"

"A little. I was a sergeant in charge of homicide investigations for four years."

Crawley nodded approvingly and gave him a quick smile. "Good enough. Start from the beginning."

Gray told Crawley what he knew and what Sarah and he had discussed. Sarah and the others remained silent while he briefed him.

"I've got what I need," Crawley said. "Appreciate your help. You're free to leave."

"Do you mind if I stick around? I'll stay out of your way."

"You can if you like," Crawley replied. "Just stand over there." He pointed to where the other witnesses were standing.

Gray gave a slight nod, then said, "Thanks."

Sarah accompanied Gray to the rear of a cabin and addressed the witnesses. "The special agent will be with you in a few minutes."

"Is he in charge?" a woman asked, pointing at Crawley. "I want to know when we can leave. We don't know anything and we want to go see Devils Tower."

Several other people voiced their desire to leave as well.

"He's the investigator you need to ask about leaving," Sarah said. "He is Special Agent Roland Crawley with the Wyoming DCI. You can't approach the scene. If you want to ask him anything, you'll have to do it from here."

The woman didn't waste a second before yelling, "Hey, special agent man, can my husband and I leave? We don't know anything."

Gray nearly broke out laughing. Sarah only raised her eyebrows at Crawley when he turned around. Crawley walked toward them with Clay in tow.

"This is going to be good," Sarah whispered to Gray.

"Ranger Goodson, didn't you explain to these people that they're witnesses in a homicide investigation and that they will have to stay until I interview them?"

"No, sir. I only informed them that you were in charge, and that only you could tell them when they could leave. If you want, I can take their names and contact information so you can work the scene."

"That isn't necessary. Deputy Gurley will handle that. Maybe you should get back to the park. Someone might need your help identifying a flower or want a Band-Aid for a blister."

"You're right. I do need to get back to my duties. Gray, would you like that coffee and tour now?"

"Sure, if I'm not needed here."

"I thought you wanted to stick around," Crawley said quickly. "I might want to get your opinion on something. Four years of homicide experience could prove helpful. I'd like you to stick around."

Gray was caught between the two rivals and looked at Sarah, hoping she'd see that he really did want to stay.

"Hey, I can show you around the area after dinner," Sarah said. "Agent Crawley needs all the support he can get. I'll swing by around five. Where's your RV parked?"

Gray caught a dagger-filled glare from Crawley. He believed Sarah had made her point. He also felt that the banter between them hadn't been the most professional exchange in front of the witnesses. He told Sarah where his RV was parked and she left.

"What can I help you with?" Gray asked Crawley.

"You can help Dr. Beining get the body out of the water. Then I want you to ride back to Sundance with him, relay any messages to me, and wait there until I arrive. I may have some more questions for you."

"I don't have a problem helping the doctor and I'm intrigued by what's happened here, but I'm not your gofer. Now, don't you want to wait on forensics before the body is moved?"

Crawley snorted. "You asked what you could do. I don't need forensics for this one. I'll take the photos and measurements. The scene is already contaminated." He motioned at all of the people standing around.

"There could be evidence on the body or around it," Gray cautioned.

Crawley bristled. "This is my investigation and I'll handle it the way I see fit. Once the body is out of the water, Dr. Beining's assistant will sift the river bottom and around the weeds. Deputy Gurley will handle the witness statements. Maybe you can give Beining's new assistant some pointers. Enjoy your ride back to Sundance." Crawley walked back to the river's edge.

Gray considered leaving, but something about the case compelled him to stay. A mystery needed to be solved.

CHAPTER THREE

Aki stared out of the H135 helicopter window at the calm and dark Baltic Sea. Victor was in front with the pilot, and Chase was busy scanning the area from the other passenger window through his binoculars. Aki had decided to use the helicopter as a last-ditch effort in attempting to find potential targets. She had no other options.

"We've checked the sailboats in the area, including those at the docks in the surrounding harbors, and nothing," Victor said. "There's no record of a vessel registered to her under any of the names you gave me. It's been two days—what do you want to do now?"

Aki was frustrated. They'd located and interviewed the owner of the restaurant yesterday. He had identified Dar from a photo, telling them her name was Helga, but he swore that he never had a conversation with her about a sailboat. "The restaurant owner was lying. He knows about the sailboat, but he's too afraid to talk. Probably because he knows that Dar will kill him if he says anything. Can you bring him in and use the truth serum?"

"No. I think Dar took the housekeeper with her to the restaurant so she would overhear the discussion about the sailboat," Victor offered. "She probably drove out of the country."

"Possibly." Aki took another look out the window. "We might as well head back to Travemünde."

The helicopter began a gradual turn. They'd spent the last hour flying a grid pattern several miles from shore, coordinating intercepts of potential targets. Aki couldn't believe how many sailboats and other pleasure craft were out on the open water. It was a pretty day and she wished that she was aboard one of those boats, just enjoying the late-afternoon weather and the smell of the sea.

Victor had been very thorough in coordinating the search of the marinas and intercepts at sea, but maybe they'd missed something. Aki pulled up a satellite map on her pad and looked at the waterways near Travemünde for the umpteenth time. Aki knew if Dar was on a sailboat, the assassin would have guessed they'd search for her over the Baltic and along the coast north of Lübeck as far as Rostock. Aki had a hunch that Dar had already sailed past Rostock. She looked over the map again, then said, "Victor, how long a flight is it to Stralsund?"

"Thirty minutes, maybe a little longer, but we'd be flying over the same area that we've already searched and we're getting low on fuel."

"If we have enough fuel to make Stralsund, let's go there."

Victor turned around and gave her a questioning look.

"Victor, I think she's past the areas we've already searched. Dar doesn't do anything without a plan, and I think she was setting up a safety net for an escape from Germany. We crashed the party before she was completely ready. I'm betting that she's headed for Belarus via Poland."

"If she is that far ahead of us, then the most logical place for her to sail would be Denmark," Victor said.

"She'd anticipate that we would search there."

"Okay, but why do you think she would go to Stralsund?"

"Dar wouldn't stop in Stralsund, but she could cut off some time sailing to Poland by using the inlet at Barhöft. We didn't search that far north."

"Possibly, but I've been in touch with our people in Stralsund and they haven't reported anything."

"If I'm reading this chart right, she could have made it to Stralsund before you issued the alert. She might have changed her mode of travel or just bypassed the marinas and sailed down the Warnow to any of the other tributaries."

"*If* she's on a boat, she would want to get as far from German waters as possible, then change transportation," Victor said. "On the other hand, Stralsund does offer ferry and rail service, and has an airport."

"She'd know that we would set a net for the transport hubs across Germany." Aki scrolled through the map again. "We've searched the Baltic as far into the open sea as she could have traveled since leaving Travemünde."

"We could have easily missed something. It's a big sea."

"True, but I think if she bypassed Stralsund, she'd have to sail around the northern tip of Germany and then down to Kröslin. From there she could work her way through the inland tributaries in the darkness and get into the Szczecin Lagoon, and then into Poland. Once she's in Poland, Dar knows that I lose GSG 9 help, and by the time I get authorization and assistance from the Polish authorities, she'll be halfway back to Belarus."

Victor nodded. "That's an interesting theory." He said something to the pilot, and the helicopter changed directions again.

Aki noticed Chase staring at her. "What?" she asked.

"I'm always amazed at your perseverance," Chase said. "That's why I like working with you."

Aki smiled.

"Let's see if your hunch is right," Victor said. "The inland waterways aren't that well traveled. I will make some calls and intensify our search along the tributaries and the border with Poland. I will also call a friend in the SPAP, the Polish counter-terrorism unit. It may save you some time getting authorization if she reaches Poland. But they will want proof that Dar is trying to enter Poland before committing the SPAP."

"Then that's what we need to find," Aki said.

To be on the safe side, the pilot had landed in Rostock for fuel. Aki watched the refueling with Chase as Victor checked in with the commander overseeing the search around Stralsund. Aki noted the frustrated expression on Victor's face when he rejoined them.

"I recommend we fly directly to Kröslin," Victor said.

"Why?" Aki asked.

"Since the alert went out, there's been a heavy Küstenwache presence around all of the marinas and harbors along the Northeast coast. No one fitting her description has been seen in Stralsund. To avoid Stralsund and contact with the Küstenwache, she'd have to take the long way around the northern tip of Germany by Putgarten. We're going to be losing daylight shortly and I feel that we'd be wasting our time searching any further around Stralsund. If we fly east to Kröslin, maybe we'll beat her there."

"Alright," Aki said. "It looks like the helo is fueled, so we better get going."

It was almost sunset when they landed in Kröslin. Aki knew if Dar was headed for Poland through the inland waterways, she would need a boat with a shallow draft. Victor had already ordered additional officers to check all sailboats that were at the docks around Kröslin.

Victor said, "If Dar beat us here, she could be anywhere. I think we should rest a bit before continuing."

Dar was close, Aki could feel it, but the pilot looked tired. They all were. "If she's not here, can we get another pilot and press on?" Aki asked Victor.

"We can, but night operations are not only more dangerous, but it's also far easier to miss something. I recommend that we eat a good meal and get a few hours of sleep and start again at dawn."

"Aki, listen to the man," Chase said. "We've been going nonstop for nearly forty-eight hours. We're all exhausted."

"Victor, when is first light?" Aki asked.

"Sunrise will be around six, but first light for operations would be an hour earlier."

Aki nodded. "Then let's find a place to eat and stay the night. We'll check the marinas after dinner."

"Why?" Chase asked. "Victor said that he had people doing that already."

"It doesn't hurt to look again. Do you know a place to stay for the night?"

"There are houseboat hotels in the marina as well as several great seafood restaurants," Victor said. "The houseboats will accommodate six to eight people. I would suggest we stay together."

"I agree," Aki said.

When Victor told Klaus, the pilot, that they were staying the night, he smiled and appeared relieved.

Aki convinced Victor that they should be airborne by four-thirty the next morning and start by searching the nearby tributaries. She had a feeling that they would find Dar tomorrow. Once they'd checked in at the houseboat, they freshened up and headed out for dinner.

After a deliciously fresh seafood dinner, they checked the docks. Aki didn't expect to find Dar, but stranger things had happened. Almost all of the boats were dark. They spoke to a few people who were liveaboards, but no recent sailboat arrivals had been seen. They had to have passed by at least a hundred sailboats by the time they'd made the rounds. At least that's how many Chase had claimed there were.

Sundance, Wyoming – Coroner's Office – 1500 hours MDT

Gray stood in the lobby of the medical examiner's office, waiting for Crawley to arrive. The autopsy had been prioritized, but Dr. Beining hadn't shared his findings. Gray had been kept out of the autopsy room, which suited him fine. Joann had checked on him a few times, but she had been equally tight-lipped.

In Gray's mind, the cause of death was pretty clear. When they rolled the body over, Gray had seen three large stab wounds in the chest. By the look of them, the wounds were probably from a large hunting knife. The rope used to tie the man's hands was a rough, braided lasso. The man had no wallet, watch, or jewelry. Once the body was loaded into the body bag and placed in the van, he'd used Dr. Beining's metal detector along the riverbank as Joann sifted the river. All he found were a few coins, a set of car keys, and a fork. They were tagged as evidence, but Gray didn't think they were related to the victim. Crawley had stood by and watched them, making suggestions as to where to look next. Crawley dismissed the DCI forensic team when they arrived, against both Gray's and Dr. Beining's advice.

He glanced out the office window and saw Crawley's Tahoe pull up, followed by Clay's SUV. "About time," Gray muttered.

When Crawley and Clay walked into the lobby, Crawley asked, "Has Dr. Beining completed the autopsy?"

"Yes," Gray replied. "I assumed that you would have wanted to be in attendance."

"I had other things to do at the crime scene, some calls to make, and none of what I was doing is any of your business. Besides, I hate autopsies, and I think we both know what killed him. Deputy, go find Dr. Beining."

"Yes, sir," Clay replied.

As soon as Clay had left, Crawley said, "I appreciated your help out there."

"No problem," Gray replied.

"What's going on between you and Sarah?"

"There's nothing going on between us," Gray replied, taken aback by the question. "I just met her at the scene and we talked while we were waiting for you to arrive."

"And you managed to get a date with her?"

Gray felt his anger rising. This guy was an ass. "That's really none of *your* business."

Crawley chuckled, then replied, "True. A word of warning about her. She'll lead you on, use you for what she can get, and then leave you flapping in the breeze."

"Is that what she did to you?"

"Nope. I've just heard things and I thought you may want to know what you're getting yourself into."

Gray stood silent, not wanting to engage in any further conversation about Sarah. Crawley must have sensed his reluctance and didn't ask him anything else.

Clay came back into the lobby with Dr. Beining and Joann in tow.

"Well, was the cause of death from stab wounds?" Crawley asked, wearing a goofy smirk.

"Yes," Dr. Beining replied. "The heart and liver were both punctured. I found no evidence of defensive wounds. Any of the wounds would have been fatal. I'd say our victim allowed his assailant to get close without putting up any resistance. He could have known his assailant, or been asleep, restrained, or drugged. I had little to work with for a drug screening, but I'm giving it a shot. I won't have any results for at least a week."

"What about the prints?"

"I used Thanatopractical processing on the finger pads and I was able to get prints from the fingers that hadn't been damaged by the aquatic life.

It's only the third time I've used this method for recovering fingerprints. Joann submitted them and his photo for facial recognition to the FBI Next Generation Identification System. I don't believe facial recognition will be much help. The facial features are too distorted from the prolonged submersion. I think the prints will be our best chance for identification. It'll also be faster than waiting for the DNA results or going through NCIC for a National Dental Image Repository comparison."

"What's the turnaround time on the NGI submission?"

"Normally, I get a response within an hour or so, but these may take longer because of the condition of the prints. I would think no later than tomorrow. I'll let you know when I receive the results. Just in case that doesn't give us his ID, I also submitted inquiries to the Wyoming Automated Biometric Identification System, and I've submitted additional requests to the Combined DNA Index System and the National DNA Index System. One way or another, we'll get the guy identified."

"My experience with CODIS was always positive, providing a sample was in the system," Gray said, "but the response times varied."

"Doc, any estimate on how long ago he was killed?" Crawley asked.

"At least a week, maybe longer. I did find something of interest concerning the murder weapon. The wounds were made with a large, non-serrated blade, probably a dull hunting knife. The blade used was about two inches wide and eight inches long. It's unusual that all three stab wounds were at the same angle and depth. I also found a small sliver of rawhide about a quarter of an inch long in one of the wounds. It looks as if it was torn off rather than cut by a blade. It could be from a coat sleeve or from an adornment on the knife. I'm having it analyzed."

"Anything else?" Crawley asked.

"The wounds came from violent thrusts. I can't say for sure which hand the weapon was in when it was used because the blade-penetration angle was straight on for all three wounds, which is unusual."

"What about the rope he was bound with?" Gray asked. "It looked to me like it was a lasso."

Dr. Beining said, "You're right. It's a nylon rope that's used on nearly every ranch around here. The rope is usually stiff, but the lasso loosened up after being submerged for so long. Something I think you already guessed the body was moved after death and dumped in the river."

"That's what Ranger Goodson and I thought," Gray said.

"Gray, what do you think was the motive for the killing?" Crawley asked.

"No wallet or jewelry on the victim, which could mean it was a robbery gone bad."

"Possibly, but I think otherwise," Crawley said. "Dr. Beining, could the knife have been Native American in origin?"

"Hard to say," Beining replied.

"Kind of a presumptive leap, thinking the perpetrator is Native American," Gray cautioned.

"Yes, it is. But I have a feeling he won't be the last victim we find. There's been some talk about mining companies having a renewed interest in mining gold from the Black Hills. I've heard rumors that the tribes, especially the Lakota at the Pine Ridge Indian Reservation, want to stop their exploratory efforts."

"Ranger Goodson told me that three people who worked for a mining company have been missing for a few weeks. Do you think the victim and the missing people are related?"

"I do. Dr. Beining, thank you for the update. Please email me the autopsy report. I'll be in touch. Gray, you better get back to your RV in time for your date. Sarah doesn't like to be kept waiting." Crawley walked out of the office before Gray could respond. Dr. Beining and his associate walked away without saying a word.

"Don't let him get to you," Clay said. "He's a bit of a dick. Sarah's good people."

"That's my impression, too. Is Crawley always like this?"

"He's had the same abrasive demeanor in every encounter I've had with him. I think he likes you, though."

"Is that good or bad?"

"Hard to say." Clay grinned.

"Any chance I can get you to drive me back to the campground?"

"Sure."

Devils Tower – 1700 hours

Gray showered and put on a pair of navy-blue slacks and a white long-sleeved dress shirt. He'd decided to wear his black loafers instead of boots. He heard the rumble of a pickup truck outside and went to the door. When he saw Sarah get out of the truck, he realized that he might have overdressed for the occasion. She was wearing blue jeans, hiking boots, and a red button-down blouse.

"You look all dressed up," Sarah remarked after greeting him.

"I wasn't sure where we were going, so I went with something that I thought would blend in anywhere."

"If you have a pair of jeans, that would be better. Hank's Steak House isn't all that fancy, but the food is really good. Don't tell me you're a vegetarian."

"No. I eat just about anything that's put in front of me. I'll change. Come on in."

Sarah stepped into the RV and looked around. "So, this is home?"

"It is until I get my house built."

"It's nice."

Gray went into the bedroom at the rear of the RV, shut the door, and changed into his jeans and Timberland boots. When he came out of the bedroom, Sarah was sitting on the sofa. He noticed she was wearing light makeup, although she didn't need any, and she smelled like the jasmine-and-lemon perfume that had caught his attention earlier. "Better?"

"Much. How'd the autopsy go?"

"Cause of death was three stab wounds to the chest, and any one of them would have been fatal. Body was moved after death, just as we thought." He filled her in on the rest of the discussion he'd had with Crawley and Beining. "The victim hasn't been identified yet."

"The rawhide in the wound is interesting," Sarah said. "Some of the tribes decorate their knives and sheaths with hides, but that doesn't mean it was someone from one of the reservations. People can buy those souvenir knives just about anywhere."

"I think Crawley made a bit of leap in suspecting a Native American at this point."

"He makes those leaps," Sarah said. "You hungry?"

"Starving."

"Let's get going, then. We'll take my truck."

"That would be good. Otherwise, I'll have to disconnect everything to take this beast. How far away is the restaurant?"

"About thirty minutes. It's down in Moorcroft, near where I live. I rent a small home just north of the city."

"Isn't there someplace closer for dinner? That seems like a long drive for you, since you'll need to bring me back."

Sarah smiled. "It's not a problem. Let's just enjoy the evening."

CHAPTER FOUR

Aki awoke to a commotion on the dock. She rolled out of bed and peered through a small window and saw Victor having an intense conversation with a uniformed officer. She checked the time. Three forty-five. *May as well get up.*

After quickly going through her morning ablutions, she donned her black fatigues and reluctantly stuffed yesterday's uniform in her backpack, fearing the smell of the dirty clothes would never come out. She threw it over her shoulder and did a quick check of the room to make sure she had everything.

Aki met Victor coming out of his cabin. "Lucky break," he said. "Late last night, a boater tried to help a woman who had run aground in shallow water near Wilhelmshof Usedom. She refused his assistance, which aroused his curiosity. Arriving at the marina, he mentioned the encounter to a uniformed officer. The man then identified Dar from the photo we circulated. She's on a twenty-eight-foot Alerion sailboat, navy-blue hull with a white deck."

"Where is Wilhelmshof Usedom?"

"About fifty kilometers east of here. It borders the Szczecin Lagoon."

"We need to alert everyone," Aki said.

"I already have, and I got Klaus headed for the airport. We're mobilizing every asset we have in the area to establish a perimeter. I need to alert the

SPAP and have them block the Polish side of the lagoon. I think we have enough proof to get them moving."

"Excellent."

Chase walked out of his room and asked, "What's all the ruckus?"

"Get dressed," Aki ordered. "We found Dar."

Wilhelmshof Usedom – 0600 hours

Their helicopter was quickly approaching Dar's last known location. Aki knew that the sound produced by the rotors of the H135 was announcing their approach. She looked through her binoculars and spotted a blue-hulled sailboat that was listing slightly, obviously aground. Aki's heart began to race with anticipation. There was a small motorboat tied alongside the sailboat, which meant Dar had a means of escape, if she hadn't left already.

"That's the sailboat," Aki said, pointing.

"I see it," Victor said. "Looks like she has a friend. Klaus, take us down and hold position. I want a closer look."

"I have movement in the cabin," Aki said, as they dropped closer to the sailboat. A second later, bullets perforated the side of the helicopter. "She's firing from the hatch!"

"Klaus, get us clear," Victor ordered in German.

Alarms sounded and indicator lights began flashing on the instrument panels. The bullets striking the aircraft continued in rapid succession. Several rounds blew through the floor and seat between Chase and Aki as the helicopter spun away from the boat.

"We are taking fire!" Victor shouted in German over the radio.

Klaus grunted and grabbed his leg, mumbling something Aki couldn't understand and Victor took the controls. The helicopter moved erratically but it was moving away from the incoming fire, and the barrage hitting the fuselage abated. Aki wondered if Victor knew how to fly and was taking evasive action or if he'd lost control. The helicopter had twin engines and was equipped with advanced technology, but that didn't mean it could land itself.

Aki saw a reddish-brown stain spreading across Klaus's right pants leg. Suddenly, a strong vibration resonated through the helicopter and it began to shake violently. Smoke poured into the cabin through the vents.

"Strap in tight!" Victor shouted. "We're going down. Open your doors before we hit the water."

Aki grabbed the handle above the door to brace herself as she pulled the passenger door open. The wind whipped through the cabin as the helicopter began to spin. She glanced at Chase and saw that his brown eyes were wide and his mouth was hanging open, as if he were caught in a scream without sound. "Chase!" Aki shouted.

He shook his head and pulled his door open.

"Brace!" Victor yelled as the helicopter flared up and canted to the right before it hit the water, the four composite blades cutting deep into the shallows, striking the bottom and breaking away. The crash wasn't as severe as Aki thought it would be, but the cabin was rapidly filling with cold water.

"Victor!" Aki shouted.

"Get out!" Victor commanded.

Aki jumped into the frigid water, the cold taking her breath away. Her feet sank into the muddy bottom until she was standing in chin-deep water. Chase landed next to her with a splash. Aki looked up and saw Victor struggling to get an unconscious Klaus free of his safety harness. She moved toward them just as the helicopter rolled onto its side and settled deeper. Steam filled the air around the engines and an acrid smell wafted across the dark brine as she watched a sheen of fuel spread across the water's surface. She hoped that the fuel wouldn't ignite as she pulled herself through the open door and back into the helicopter.

"I can't get the leverage I need to get Klaus clear," Victor said, frustration in his voice.

"I'll pull and you push," Aki said as she worked her way into the cockpit.

Aki and Victor struggled but managed to get Klaus positioned so that they could shove him out the door. When Klaus hit the water, he immediately slipped beneath the surface—they hadn't had time to put on life vests. Aki scrambled through the open door and jumped. She was able to grab the back of Klaus's flight suit and pull him up, then roll him over to keep his face out of the water. Chase joined her and grasped Klaus from the other side, and together they swam to shore and pulled him up the steep embankment.

"He's lost a lot of blood," Aki said.

Chase wrapped his belt just above Klaus's wound, while Aki applied pressure.

Victor came up next to them and said, "That's good. Keep the pressure on the wound. I got off a distress call before we crashed."

"That was the best crash I've ever been in," Aki joked through chattering teeth. She saw the motorboat speeding away from Dar's sailboat. "Victor, did you tell anyone that we found Dar, and about the other boat?"

"I was a little busy just trying to keep us in the air. I was lucky to get off the mayday call. I will tell them about the motorboat when a rescue team arrives. It won't be long."

Two hours later, Aki, Victor, and Chase were flying over the Szczecin Lagoon toward the Polish border in a H215 Super Puma helicopter. It was larger and faster than the H135, and armed. Klaus had been airlifted to a trauma center in Stralsund. The good news was that the bullet hadn't torn through the femoral artery and he was expected to survive.

"What did your friend at the SPAP say about securing the border?" Aki asked.

"They're deploying what they have, but he wasn't optimistic about finding her. We have received permission to fly into Polish airspace to search along the lagoon's coastline, but no further. We will start with the small bay at Altwarp along the border. Nowe Warpno and Podgrodzie are the nearest towns with vehicle access."

"She's got a big lead," Chase said.

"Yes. As fast as that motorboat looked, she could be as far as Szczecin in Poland or down any of the tributaries."

Aki peered through binoculars as they flew along the coastline. As they approached Altwarp, she started searching the docks for any sign of the motorboat. There were only a few boats around the docks and they didn't look anything like the one Dar had used in her escape.

"SPAP just advised that the getaway boat has been found!" Victor said, with excitement. "Dar wasn't aboard. One man is being detained. He actually called for help."

"Where is he?" Aki asked.

"At a dock in Trzebież. It's just over the border. We will be there in a few minutes. Their local police are trying to block the main roads out of the area."

"We need to interrogate the man that helped her," Aki said. "I'm sure your country will want to charge him with something."

Victor nodded and spoke to someone on a different radio channel for a few minutes. When he finished, he turned to Aki and Chase. "The owner of the boat is a resident of Trzebież. He has no prior record and is cooperating. He claims that he received a call around three this morning from a friend who asked him to go pick up a woman who was aground. The woman was willing to pay a thousand euros to use a fast boat. The boat owner said that he needed the money, so he went to get her."

"Who's his friend?" Chase asked.

"A ferryboat captain who also has a rescue vessel-towing business. He has a twenty-four-hour service. He claims he didn't want to make the trip because he'd had too much to drink. He's also cooperating."

"The owner of the boat left us and sped away," Aki said. "I'm not buying it."

"He claims the woman held a gun on him and forced him to take her to the coast near a small village about fifteen kilometers from here. She took his phone and disabled his radio after he dropped her off. He sped back to Trzebież and called the authorities. He reported the crash. Timing sounds right."

"Does the SPAP believe his story?"

"They do."

"Do you?"

Victor shrugged.

"I think they're both lying," Aki said. "Dar wouldn't reach out to someone she didn't trust."

"Possibly, but that will take time to determine," Victor said. "Aki, we cannot pursue her in Poland. If anything develops, I'll be notified. I want to head back to Stralsund and check on Klaus."

Aki looked out the window as the helicopter circled over the docks. She was irritated that she wouldn't get a chance to interrogate the charter-boat operator or the guy who picked up Dar. "Damn. We were so close. Victor, I guess we're done here."

Victor ordered the pilots to head for Stralsund.

"Did they find anything on the sailboat?" Aki asked.

"Just the AK47 she used to bring us down, lots of ammunition and explosives, food and water, but no documents."

"No surprise there."

Victor held up a finger to stop her from saying anything else. She listened to a lengthy, heated radio exchange between Victor and someone sounding like a superior. She didn't speak German, but she didn't have to in order to know that Victor had just been castigated.

When the conversation ended, Victor sighed. "I have been ordered back to Hamburg. So have you. Dar is no longer our concern. She's in Poland and they will have to deal with her for the time being."

"Why are we being recalled to Hamburg?" Aki asked, confused. "She just shot one of your pilots and downed a helicopter. I would think that the German Federal Police would want you to stay close to the action and near the border."

"I have been advised that two failures in three days warrants a review of my actions. I am no longer authorized to assist you in Dar's capture."

"You mean that you've been relieved pending an investigation?"

"Yes. And I was told that you are to call your director when we land. It appears that my commander spoke to her and expressed his displeasure."

"Well, that can't be good," Chase said.

"No, it's not," Aki said. She began formulating a strategy to convince Director Canton that she should be allowed to continue pursuing Dar into Poland, and beyond if necessary. She wasn't optimistic that she was going to be successful.

Hamburg, Germany – May 21 – 1130 hours

Aki sat in an office with Chase, speaking to Rebecca Canton on a secure video call.

"You will not pursue Dar into Poland," Canton ordered. "You and Chase will fly to Washington immediately. Am I clear?"

"Yes, but Director, you know that Chase and I can capture or eliminate Dar by tomorrow if I can get back on her trail," Aki said. "I have been in contact with the SPAP. They are willing to continue to help us." She neglected to tell Canton that there were some conditions attached in light of the German helicopter being shot down.

"I want to see both of you in my office tomorrow afternoon. Your hunt is over for now. I've got some bridges to mend with the GSG 9 and the Federal German Police. All of the assets we seized from Dar's Luxembourg accounts will go to the them as compensation for their losses."

"I understand. I already advised Victor that they would get some compensation. But why all of it?"

"Because it was all I could think of to placate them in the short term," Canton replied tersely. "We'll get another shot at Dar if the SPAP don't capture her first."

Aki was ready to argue the point but decided against it. She knew that Canton wasn't in the mood to debate the issue.

"Director, we'll leave Germany as soon as possible," Chase interjected.

"I know this doesn't sit well with either of you, especially under the circumstances, but I have no choice," Canton softened. "I'll explain everything when you get back."

Aki again held her tongue, then said, "I'll advise Victor and the SPAP that we are being pulled from the active investigation until further notice."

"You don't need to do that. I'll take care of it. Pack up your gear and get back here." The video screen was replaced with a Homeland Security emblem.

"I knew that she was going to recall us," Aki said. "Short-sighted—"

"Easy there," Chase said. "Let's go home. After the dust settles and Dar escapes the SPAP net, we'll try again."

"Let's go say goodbye to Victor."

Aki was surprised to find Victor waiting in the hallway just outside of the office.

"I take it you didn't convince your director to allow you to continue your pursuit?" Victor queried.

"We did not," Aki replied. "We have been ordered back to Washington."

Victor gave her a weak smile. "I thought as much. We gave it our best."

"Do I need to give a statement to anyone on your behalf?"

"Unnecessary. We have another GSG 9 team headed for Poland. I don't believe that they will have any luck finding her." Victor straightened and offered his hand. "It will be an honor to work with you again someday. Let me know how you make out."

"The same, Victor," Aki said, shaking his hand.

"Did you hear anything about Klaus?" Chase asked as they shook hands.

"He will make a full recovery and have stories to tell at the Hofbräuhaus. Until we meet again." Victor gave a slight bow of his head and walked away.

"Good guy," Chase said.

"He certainly is."

Devils Tower – May 21 – 0630 hours MDT

Gray slowly opened his eyes. He'd had a little too much to drink last night. His head was throbbing and his mouth tasted like…well, it wasn't pleasant. He rolled over and realized that he was on the pull-out sofa in the front section of the RV. Then he remembered that he'd not wanted Sarah driving home in her condition and had offered up his bed.

"Morning," Sarah said. She was standing at the kitchen sink dressed in a white t-shirt and pink panties. "I got the coffee going. How about I make us some eggs and bacon?"

Gray sat up and held his forehead. Her long, toned legs caught his attention. "How about some coffee first. Did you sleep well?"

"I did, thank you."

"Don't you have to get to work?" Gray asked, noting the time.

"I guess you want me to leave before everyone in the campground knows I spent the night."

"Not what I was thinking at all." He couldn't take his eyes off her legs.

"Well, I appreciate you being a gentleman last night. It was very sweet."

Not the words that he wanted to hear, but it had been the proper thing to do. "Do you need to head home for a uniform?"

"Nope. I have a clean one in the truck." She looked down. "I guess I should probably put some pants on before I make our breakfast."

"You don't have to on my account," Gray teased.

"Yes, I do." She walked over and stood in front of him. "I like you. Even though we've only known each other for a day, I can tell that you're a special man. I don't want to spoil anything. That didn't come out right."

Gray chuckled, once again surprised by her directness. "Well, I like you, too, and I agree. I think taking things slow is the responsible thing to do. I haven't been with a woman since my ex-wife, and we were married for twenty years. Dating is a bit foreign to me. I suppose I'm just an old-fashioned kind of guy."

"I like that quality in a man," Sarah replied. "Do you have any kids?"

"No. My ex and I focused on our careers. We married when we were twenty-one, just after I graduated from college and a few weeks before I started work at the Sheriff's Office. We never found a good time to start a family."

"I get that," Sarah said. "I'm also a career-oriented person. I joined the NPS right out of college. Never found a guy that held my interest for more than a few months, but I still have time to find Mr. Right. I'm only thirty-two."

"I'm a bit older than you," Gray said, wondering if a nine-year age difference was too great a gap between them for a meaningful relationship. He liked Sarah and wondered if his interest in her was a rebound thing. "Thanks for the guided tour of the butte last night."

"My pleasure. And you're not that old."

Gray watched as she walked toward the bedroom, wishing he wasn't a gentleman. He stretched, got out of bed, and poured a cup of coffee. He was wearing gray sweats and wondered when he'd put those on. The RV was a little chilly, but Sarah hadn't seemed to notice.

She came out of the bedroom wearing jeans. "I'll be right back. I need to grab my uniform."

"I'll pour you a cup. How do you like it?"

"Black with a touch of sugar."

"That's how I like mine, too. I'll start the eggs."

Sarah smiled at him and went outside.

His cell phone rang a moment later. He stirred in the sugar while ignoring the phone and let it go to voicemail. As Sarah came back into the RV, the cell phone rang again. He checked the caller ID. "It's Crawley I better get it," Gray said, handing her a cup of coffee.

She disappeared into the bedroom as Gray answered the call.

"This is Gray. This had better be important."

"It is," Crawley replied. "Your date still there?"

"Is that really why you're calling me at this time of the morning?"

"I'll assume she is. Another body has surfaced."

"What? Where?"

"In the river, about a half mile south of the Wind Circle Sculpture, where the Belle Fourche makes a big bend," Crawley answered. "Not on NPS land, but I figured that you and Ranger Goodson could get there faster than me. I need you to secure the scene and you need to keep the hiker who found the victim from leaving. A deputy is en route, but he's a good hour away. The hiker told me that the victim's hands are tied with a rope and that he has three stab wounds to the chest."

"He got that close to the body?" Gray said.

"Yeah. He jumped in the river, thinking the guy was drowning and pulled the body to the riverbank. He's waiting for you there."

"I'll get dressed and let Sarah know. I'll call you when we're on the scene. Does this mean that I'm officially working with the Wyoming DCI now?"

"No," Crawley said. The line went dead.

"I take it we have another victim," Sarah said, as she came out the bedroom tucking her uniform shirt into her unbuckled pants.

"Yup. I need to change."

"Where we headed?"

Gray told her as he brushed past her. She smelled good even without perfume.

Devils Tower – 0705 hours

Gray and Sarah found the hiker sitting on the side of the road about a quarter mile south of the monument. Sarah stopped the truck and Gray noted that the hiker was shivering and his clothing was still damp.

"Do you have a thermal blanket?" Gray asked. "He looks a bit chilled."

"I have several in my gear bag. I'll get him one and interview him in the truck. He'll appreciate the heat."

"I guess that leaves me to inspect the body."

"Yes, it does," Sarah replied. "Two bodies in two days, that's a new record. I hope this is the last victim we find."

"Me, too."

Gray checked the ground as he carefully navigated his way to the body on the riverbank. He knelt down and noticed the man looked to be in his forties. His brown hair was neatly trimmed above the ears. There were three stab wounds to the chest, and by the placement and appearance of the wounds, they were probably made by the same knife that had killed the first victim. The rope was the same type of lasso as well.

The victim was wearing blue jeans, a red flannel shirt, and hiking boots. There was no other trauma to the body that he could see, and he opted not to roll the man over until Crawley arrived. The man didn't appear to have been in the water as long as the prior victim, and the lasso wasn't as water-logged. He found no wallet or jewelry on the body and he appeared to be about the same age as the other victim, maybe a little younger.

Gray walked to the river's edge and scanned the banks on both sides, and then he walked south along the riverbank. There wasn't any sign of foot traffic in the tall grass and no evidence the man had been killed here.

"Find anything?" Sarah asked, joining him.

"As best I can tell, he wasn't killed here. He has three stab wounds in the same area of the chest as our other victim. No defensive wounds on this guy either."

"Do you think we're dealing with a serial killer?"

"I don't know what to think. I've worked many homicide cases and I have an unsettling feeling that this is going to be a bizarre one. This wasn't a crime of passion. It looks more ritualistic. Until the victims are identified, it's hard to draw any correlations or conclusions as to motive. I mean, were they friends that stumbled onto something? Are their deaths related to drug activity? So many possibilities. How's the hiker?"

"Writing down what he saw and did. He says he was walking along the river bank and came upon the guy. He thought the victim had fallen in and maybe hit his head. He jumped in to save him and realized that he'd been dead a while. I don't think he's involved. He seems rattled."

"Here comes the calvary," Gray said, pointing at Crawley's black Tahoe rapidly approaching.

"Oh, goodie," Sarah said, clapping her hands.

"I forgot to tell you, he wanted to know if you'd spent the night with me."

"What did you tell him?"

"I said it wasn't any of his business."

"Then he thinks we jumped each other," Sarah said, smiling at him. "I like it."

Agent Crawley exited his Tahoe, put on his black cowboy hat, and sauntered toward them. Gray noticed he was dressed similarly as the day before, his black, silver-toed boots clean and shined.

"Does he always wear the same thing?" Gray asked.

"Every time I've seen him, that's what he has on."

"Morning, you two," Crawley said, with a knowing grin.

"Good morning," Gray said.

Sarah nodded, then said, "The hiker is in my truck writing out a statement. Do you want to talk to him now?"

"Not yet," Crawley replied. "Gray, did you find anything of interest in the area?"

"Nothing. He wasn't killed here. Hands are tied with a lasso, like the one yesterday."

"I hate the weird ones," Crawley said. "Dr. Beining and Deputy Gurley will be here shortly. Gray, do you want to stick around for this one, or do you two have other plans?"

Before he could answer, Sarah said, "Gray, I have other things to do today. Why don't you stay and help this poor agent? I really enjoyed our time together last night. I'll see you again tonight."

"What time?" Gray asked, as she walked away.

"Same as yesterday," she replied over her shoulder. "We'll do dinner again." When she got back to her truck, she pointed out Crawley's Tahoe to the hiker, and he got out.

"Did she just tell him to go sit in *my* truck?" Crawley asked.

"I believe she did," Gray replied, trying not to laugh.

"Damn that woman."

"You want to examine the body?" Gray asked.

Crawley nodded.

Together, they rolled the body over. There were no additional wounds or marks on the back or sides. There were scratches on his arms, face, and hands, which could have been from being dragged along the bottom of the river by the current.

"I wonder if the two victims worked together," Gray said. "Are there any survey crews out here?"

"We have all kinds of people out here," Crawley said. "Mostly hikers. Some hunters, but the only thing in season now is black bear. Turkey season just ended. There are a number of panners that go up into the Black Hills looking for gold nuggets. Mining and oil companies send out surveyors and exploration people all the time. There are forestry and occasionally military units that train in the area. Then there's the archeologists, the cavers, the environmentalists, and the Native Americans. Do you want me to continue?"

"No…I only asked about survey crews, but I get the picture. Our victims could have been around here for any number of reasons."

"Exactly. Go tell the hiker he can leave if he's finished with his written statement."

"You don't want to interview him?" Gray asked.

"Not now. His statement will suffice. I'll talk to him if I need to later."

"Shouldn't we drop him off someplace?"

"No. He can walk. After all, he's a hiker."

Gray thought that was a pretty cold way for Crawley to handle it. When Gray met with the young man, he took the pad from him. He perused it, then asked, "You alright to continue hiking?"

"Yeah. I'm okay."

"Agent Roland Crawley will contact you if he has any further questions."

The hiker looked back at the body and then walked quickly towards Devils Tower.

A few minutes later, Dr. Beining and Joann arrived, and Clay was right behind them.

As Clay approached, he said, "Gray, you know, since you've been here things have gotten busy. Two bodies in two days. That's unheard of. Tell me that you'll be leaving the area soon."

Gray chuckled. "As a matter of fact, I have to report to Rapid City by the tenth of June. I was going to check out my property in Custer, then head up to the city. I'd planned to leave tomorrow, but with all the excitement, I think I'll stay another week."

"Then let's hope tomorrow doesn't start out like the last two days," Crawley said.

"We can certainly hope so," Dr. Beining added.

"Any word yet on who the first victim is?" Gray asked.

"Not yet," Beining said. "Hopefully, we'll know something later today… Well, at least we didn't have to fish this one out of the water. Agent Crawley, are you bringing in your forensics team?"

"No. They always seem to slow the process down. We know what killed him, and there isn't anything here to process. Let's load the victim up and get him back to Sundance."

Gray didn't say anything. *Maybe that's just how things are handled here.*

CHAPTER FIVE

Gray and Crawley sat in Dr. Beining's office waiting for him to finish the latest victim's autopsy. Gray noted the large collection of deer antlers adorning the walls, not his taste for office décor, but this was Wyoming. Crawley was typing on his iPad and Gray snuck a peek. It appeared to be a report.

"Until we know if the two victims knew each other, we could end up wasting time on determining motive," Gray said. "Ritualistic execution is the most likely motive for two people being killed in the same manner. The cause and manner of death appear to be identical, unless Dr. Beining finds something we aren't expecting. I'd say that they were killed at least a week apart."

Crawley turned the iPad off. "I agree. I think that we're dealing with a ritualistic serial killer or killers."

Dr. Beining and Joann entered the office and Beining sat down in the large brown leather chair behind his desk while Joann took a chair by the wall.

"We've completed the second victim's autopsy," Beining began. "The cause of death is self-evident. Just like the other victim, any of the stab wounds would have killed him. There wasn't anything found in the wounds this time. All of the wounds were strangely the same depth as found on the other victim. Did I heard you say you thought this might be a serial killing?"

"That's how I'm leaning," Crawley said. "Unless you have new evidence."

"No. We just received word about a missing person that was supposed to be in the area. The report was filed three days ago with the Custer County Sheriff's Office in South Dakota. The physical description of the missing man fits our most recent victim right down to the clothing he was last seen wearing."

"What's his name?" Crawley asked.

"Darren Waters. He's a professor from Brigham Young University. The woman who filed the report said he'd been periodically exploring the Black Hills for the past year looking for evidence of an undiscovered Native American civilization."

"Who's the woman?" Gray asked.

"A colleague of his. Let me see if Custer SO has forwarded the report." Beining opened his email and brought up an attachment. "Here it is. Dr. Angela Kingman, also with BYU. Dr. Darren Waters is a professor of anthropology and archeology. According to Dr. Kingman's statement, Dr. Waters was working on something that he thought could be a major historical discovery. She reported him missing after he failed to return or check in with her."

"Did she say exactly where he was working?" Crawley asked. "The Black Hills is only about a million square miles and is mostly in South Dakota."

Beining scratched his ear. "It's not in the report."

"We need to confirm that the dead guy is Dr. Waters," Crawley said.

"I already made the submission."

"Where's Dr. Kingman now? I want to interview her."

"Agent Crawley, now how would I know where she is at this moment?" Beining said, peering over the top of the glasses that hung low on his nose. "I'll print you a copy of the report and you can track her down. Isn't that your job?"

"Don't you get testy with me, Jack," Crawley replied.

Gray wondered if the two men bantered like this all the time, then asked, "Agent Crawley, are you going to need me for anything else today?"

"I'm not sure," Crawley said. "Oh, that's right, you have another hot date tonight with Ranger Sarah."

"I do."

Beining's phone rang. "This is Dr. Beining. Uh-huh. I see. Please forward the report to my email address. Yes, the one on file. Thank you." He hung up and looked at Crawley. "That was the FBI NGI lab. Victim number one has been identified."

"And?"

"I'll tell you more when I receive the report."

"Which will be when?" Crawley asked.

"In a minute or so," Beining replied, tilting back in his chair and folding his hands across his stomach.

They sat in silence until the receipt of an email delivery pinged on Beining's computer.

"Well?" Crawley asked impatiently.

After a moment, Beining looked up from the screen and said, "His name is Oliver Tanner. He's forty-eight, and he was a field exploration supervisor for the BHGM company in Rapid City. He was working in the same area where those three Universal Mining company employees went missing three weeks ago. You remember them, don't you?"

"Yes. I remember," Crawley said. "That is interesting. I also remember that their cars were found parked at the sand-and-gravel pit off Beaver Creek Road and US-16 near the South Dakota border. I'll need to let the Weston County sheriff know what we're working on. I may inherit those missing person cases from him."

"I imagine you will," Beining said. "I'll contact their medical examiner."

"I bet Tanner's car is still parked off one of the trail roads," Crawley said. "We need a description and a tag number."

"It's in the report."

"Any information about the professor's car?" Gray asked.

"Let me see." Beining scrolled back through the pages of the missing person report. "Dr. Kingman reported that Dr. Waters was driving a black GMC Sierra 1500 pickup truck. The Utah tag number is listed."

"When did the mining company guy disappear?" Crawley asked.

"Let's see. BHGM reported Tanner missing a few days ago. They provided his last known GPS coordinates, which put him in South Dakota. The report says that the company GPS tracker failed ten days ago."

"Why did they wait so long to report him missing, and where exactly in South Dakota?" Crawley asked.

"I'm not your secretary or a cartographer," Beining snapped. "I'll forward all of the reports to you and Deputy Gurley. You guys can figure this out. I will say that Tanner's body was probably submerged for at least a week to ten days."

"Thanks," Crawley said. "You've been a big help."

"What is BHGM?" Gray asked.

"Black Hills Gold Mining Company," Beining answered.

Crawley leaned forward in his chair and faced Gray. "You know Gray, I could use your expertise on this investigation."

"I'm not a certified law enforcement officer in Wyoming." Gray had an idea that Crawley was going to try to dump the gofer work on him, probably to keep him from seeing Sarah, and he wasn't going to let that happen.

"But you're still a certified law enforcement officer in Florida, right?"

"Yes. My certification is good for another two years."

"And you're working with the Department of the Interior."

"Not yet. Agent Crawley, I'm a pilot and I'll only be assisting law enforcement and other agencies in that capacity. Nothing more."

"Hmm, I might be able to get the Wyoming attorney general or the governor to give you a special appointment as a temporary agent working under my supervision. I know both of them personally. Hell, the governor and I hunt together. You could then investigate in an official capacity."

"Agent Crawley, I appreciate the offer, but I need to report to Rapid City on the tenth of June, and I'd like to check on my property in Custer before I do."

"This is going to be a major case. I can sense it. I'm giving you an opportunity to make a name for yourself out here."

Gray had a feeling he knew where this was headed. "I really don't need to make a name for myself. I'll be working under a federal grant and flying out of the Custer Airport in South Dakota. I don't mind helping you out, but I'm not going to do anything that will jeopardize my reporting for duty on time."

"How about you give me two weeks? I can have you sworn in by five o'clock this afternoon."

Gray sighed. He knew Crawley wasn't going to let this go, and he was intrigued and interested in solving the two homicides. If Crawley really knew the governor and others in political positions, Gray's helping the DCI on the case could lead to a full-time position when the DOI grant ran out. "Alright. Are you sure that your boss will want me involved? I'm sure that there are several other DCI agents that could assist."

"My regional supervisor will appreciate that I'm getting an expert homicide investigator to help for free. There are only thirty-six DCI agents in the state and we have a lot of cases. These weird ones tend to be time-suckers."

"For free?" Gray said, raising an eyebrow.

"You'll get the usual daily stipend of two hundred dollars, plus expenses, but you won't be on the DCI payroll. I'll also notify DOI that you're assisting me and provide some accolades when you're done."

"I'll need to make sure that they are okay with it."

"If there's any issues, I can get the governors of Wyoming and South Dakota to make some calls. If you're injured or killed in the line of duty, we'll cover the burial expenses. And I'll get the campground to let you stay there for free."

Crawley seemed well-connected and appeared to always get what he wanted, except for Sarah. "So, I'll be a special, special agent?" Gray joked.

"Don't get carried away. I'll get this approved, and then I'll need you to interview Dr. Kingman. Dr. Beining, Gray can have access to anything that you send me. Give him the contact information for Dr. Kingman and copies of all the reports."

"I'll see to it."

"I need to determine where the victims were killed," Crawley said. "These cases may end up being a South Dakota or federal case if they were killed on reservation or federal land. I have a feeling it's going to get complicated." Crawley looked at Gray and said, "You don't have a car, do you?"

"I do not. Just the RV."

"I have an idea that you may like. How about if I get Ranger Sarah assigned as a liaison. If my hunch is right, we're going to be stepping all over national park lands. The NPS has agents assigned to the Investigative Services Branch that will no doubt get involved if it turns out that these people were killed in the Black Hills national park. Sarah's familiar with how they operate and she's been on both homicide scenes. It could be a boost to her career as well, and she has a vehicle."

"Don't you think we should ask her if she wants to get involved before you do that?"

"I'll let you ask her over dinner tonight. In the meantime, I'll have Deputy Gurley chauffer you around and help us with the investigation. I'll call you when I have the authorization." Crawley abruptly stood and left the office.

"That's an interesting turn of events," Beining said.

"Yes, it is," Gray acknowledged. "Dr. Beining, I need a favor. I'd like to know if any other medical examiner or coroner has had unidentified victims in the last year where the manner of death was similar."

Beining smiled. "I figured Crawley would have asked for that to be done, so I had Joann submit search requests through the National Violent Death Reporting System for Wyoming, South Dakota, and Nebraska. Crawley told me earlier that he thought there may be a Native American component to this investigation, and some of the Native American reservations overlap state boundaries."

"I'm not sure about the Native American connection yet. Do you have access to a Violent Criminal Apprehension Program portal?"

"I do have a ViCAP link. But as you know, there aren't many small agencies submitting information. In fact, not many violent crimes are reported on the reservations. People disappear out here, probably victims of homicide, but no one reports them."

"I understand that Native Americans are often victims of violent crime, many based on bias and hate. It still wouldn't hurt to make an inquiry."

"Okay," Beining agreed. "I'll also search for any other death clusters. How wide of a net do you want?"

He wasn't all that familiar with the areas involved, but these two homicides and the three missing people all seemed to have disappeared while working in the same area. "I believe what you have selected for the NVDRS will suffice."

"Gray, Ranger Goodson is good people," Joann offered. "You should ask her advice and not just have her be a chauffeur."

"I second that," Beining added. "She has a lot of contacts and is well respected, even by Crawley, although he'd never admit it. That's probably why he wants her as a liaison and as part of the task force he's obviously putting together."

"I've only known Sarah a short time, but I agree, she is good people."

"I'll keep you posted, but I need your cell number," Beining said.

Gray wrote his number down and said, "Call anytime."

Crook County Sheriff's Office - 1515 hours

Gray decided to walk the two blocks to the Sheriff's Office to stretch his legs and save Clay the trip. It was a pretty afternoon and he took a deep breath of clean Wyoming air as he approached the two story, two-toned brown-and-tan structure. The Sheriff's Office, courthouse, and museum all shared the same building. He walked up the front steps to the Sheriff's Office and Clay greeted him at the door.

"I could have come and gotten you," Clay said.

"I appreciate that, but the walk allowed me some time to think. Crawley wants Sarah assigned to this case as a liaison. He wants me to break the news to her, and he's going to grant me special agent status later today."

"Well, isn't that special," Clay said.

"I'll fill you in on the latest information about the two victims," Gray said. "I need to call Sarah and let her know what Crawley wants her to do. And, he also volunteered you to assist us."

"That was nice of him," Clay said sardonically. "I don't think my sheriff is going to allow me to get involved."

"Crawley seems to get what he wants. Can I use one of your landlines? My cell hasn't been charged in a while."

"No problem. Follow me." After Gray updated him, Clay left to go speak to his sergeant.

Gray sat down behind a desk to call Harper Bartley, his OAS regional director, to make sure he could work with DCI. Bartley wasn't available, but his assistant informed him that he was approved for a two-week tour of duty with DCI. Apparently, Crawley wasn't just a name-dropper. He did have friends in high places, and they worked fast.

Next, he called Sarah, and she answered on the third ring. "Hey, it's Gray, and I need to tell you something."

"No, you don't. Jim Holden, my supervisor, just informed me that I was being assigned as a liaison to a DCI homicide task force, effective at 1800 hours today, and that the authorization had come from higher up."

"Are you okay with the assignment?"

"Absolutely. I might be able to wrangle an agent position out of this investigation. It'll leave the park rangers shorthanded until they find someone to temporarily fill my spot, but they'll handle it. What exactly is going on?"

"I've been drafted, pending approval, to be a DCI *special* special agent, and I'll be working with you for the next two weeks. I hope you don't mind."

"I like it. What are you going to be doing?"

"Consulting and gofer work, I think. Were you informed that your liaison position is not only to assist in the investigation, but also to be my chauffer?"

"No, but that sounds good to me. I guess I'll have to move in with you so I don't have to drive back and forth."

Gray didn't respond immediately. He wondered if that was a good idea, but he liked Sarah and didn't see any harm in her staying with him.

"You *are* okay with me living with you, aren't you?" Sarah asked after a long silence.

"Yes, of course," Gray finally answered. "Sarah, you may not like living in tight quarters with me. So feel free to tell me if it isn't working."

"I don't think that'll be an issue. I hope it won't be for you."

"It'll be fun. Sarah, I have a feeling that this case is going to grow tentacles and become a complex investigation. I'm not sure it will be completed before I need to report to Rapid City, so that will leave you working with Crawley and Clay."

"Crawley roped Clay into this?"

"Yup. He's the local muscle. Just so you know, the victims have been identified. The one the hiker fished out of the water is Darren Waters. He was a professor at BYU. I need to speak to his colleague, Dr. Angela Kingman, who reported him missing, and I'd like you to sit in on the interview."

"Be happy to," Sarah said.

"The other victim is Oliver Tanner, an employee of Black Hills Gold Mining. I'll need to get some additional background on him."

"BHGM has been around for years. They have a reputation for being aggressive in their pursuits and don't mind stepping on toes or ruining the environment to make a profit. Maybe someone decided that they'd had enough of their business practices."

"But that doesn't explain the professor's killing," Gray said. "No, these murders are linked and I get the impression that they were not done out of revenge. We can talk strategy after I fill you in on the rest at dinner tonight, if we're still on?"

"Of course. Do you know what Crawley wants from me, besides being a chauffeur?"

"You'll be a liaison and make introductions with NPS investigators, the local environmentalists, and I have a feeling the Native Americans on the reservations. Some travel will be involved. You okay with driving me around?"

"I'm looking forward to it."

"Where do you want to go for dinner?"

"You still in Sundance?" Sarah asked.

"Yes. I'm at the Sheriff's Office with Clay."

"How about we do dinner in the city. I know a place you might like. I can pick you up there around 1830 hours."

"I'll have to see what Crawley has in store for me, but that sounds like a plan for now."

"See you soon, partner."

Gray hung up and leaned back in the chair. Clay poked his head over the cubicle partition and Gray asked, "What'd your sergeant say?"

"Actually, my sheriff caught me in the hallway and told me that I've been assigned to a DCI homicide task force. He said that the governor had called him and that Crawley had requested that I be assigned to these *sensitive cases* so that 'the criminal or criminals could be brought to justice in an expeditious manner.' His words, not mine. I'm to assist you and Crawley whenever and wherever required. The sheriff wants me to learn as much as I can about homicide investigations, which can only mean good things for my future."

Gray said, "I believe Crawley has assembled his team."

"For better or for worse, I'm excited about it."

"I'll answer any questions that arise about the investigative process." Gray's cell phone rang, and seeing it was Crawley, he answered, "This is the most special agent, Graynger Holt, of the Wyoming DCI at your service."

"Knock off that shit," Crawley barked. "I have authorization to make you a temporary agent. I also got Ranger Sarah and Deputy Gurley authorized to assist in the investigation, and the governor should be making the calls."

"They've already been notified."

"Good. Your paperwork is being faxed to the Crook County Sheriff's Office by the Wyoming State Attorney General's Office. You'll need to fill out the forms, sign them, and then fax them back in the next thirty minutes."

"Why is the attorney general involved?"

"The DCI is under the Attorney General's Office."

"I didn't know that. Will I get a car?"

"No, you won't need one. Goodson and Gurley will drive you wherever you need to go. Plus, I don't want you doing anything without backup. Once you get the paperwork back to the AGO, they'll notify me, and I'll call you so you can start interviewing people. If Dr. Kingman is staying nearby, I want you to go talk to her."

"I'll give her a call and determine her location," Gray said. "I'll see if we need to talk to her in person or if it can be done over the phone."

"Pushing the boundaries already. I'll make the decisions on this case. You tell me what she says, and I'll decide what needs to be done. Are we clear?"

"Yes, sir. I think that we're going to have to work out what I can act on without checking with you first." Gray smiled when he heard Crawley sigh.

"Just fill out the damn paperwork and we'll discuss this later."

Gray clipped his cell phone to his belt and looked at Clay. "This is going to be a fun adventure."

Clay grinned and said, "Well, it might be, for some of us."

"Crawley said he's having paperwork faxed here. Do you know where I can find the fax machine?"

"Faxing it? That's old school. Follow me."

Crook County Sheriff's Office – 1710 hours

Gray had faxed his paperwork back to the AG's office and was looking over the reports that Dr. Beining had texted him. Darren Waters had an ex-wife and two teenage daughters who were living in Salt Lake. They'd been notified of his death and Gray believed it would be best to give them a bit more time to grieve before he interviewed them.

The information he'd received from BYU was just basic HR information. Waters had been with the university for fifteen years. Good reviews and no threats on his life had been reported. Gray remembered a homicide case he'd worked years ago where a professor had been stabbed to death by one his grad students over a grade. He couldn't rule out a student connection, a jealous colleague, or other associates being involved, but it didn't fit with the other homicide. If Crawley was worth his salt, he'd still want to go through the motions of ruling out all other possibilities.

Gray looked at Dr. Angela Kingman's file. She'd been an associate professor of archeology at BYU for five years with stellar performance reviews. She was thirty years old, unmarried, and her employment application indicated that she earned her Ph.D. in anthropological archeology from the School of Human Evolution and Social Change at Arizona State University. Gray raised an eyebrow. He wondered why she hadn't been in the field with Dr. Waters. Her academic background would make her well suited to working with him. *Was she an academic competitor?* He'd mention it to Crawley.

According to the missing person's report, Dr. Kingman was staying at a motel in Custer with Dr. Waters when she filed the report. *Could they have been more than colleagues?* It was imperative that he and Sarah speak to her in person before she left for Utah. The case had been assigned to Lieutenant Takoda White Owl and he would need to contact him to follow up.

Clay cleared his throat, startling Gray, and said, "Crawley's on the line for you. He said you weren't answering your cell. He didn't sound pleased."

"He's a hard man to please." Gray followed Clay to an office and answered, "This is Gray."

"Your cell phone keeps going to voicemail," Crawley growled.

"Sorry about that. I had put it in Do Not Disturb while I went through the reports that Dr. Beining forwarded."

"Don't do that anymore. I want you available at all times of the day and night. Don't even turn it off."

"I understand."

"Anyway, your appointment is official. I'm in Gillette picking up your credentials. You're now Assistant Special Agent Graynger Holt. It's going to be late before I'm done here, so I'm not driving back to Sundance today. I'll get your creds to you in the morning. I still have some work to do and I need to follow up with the sheriff in Weston County, then check in with Beining. You are officially cleared to call Dr. Kingman and let me know what she had to say."

"I reviewed the missing person's report on Dr. Waters," Gray said. "When Kingman filed it, she was staying at a motel in Custer with him. We should interview her in person, if you approve."

"I approve. You going there tonight?"

"Let me see what she has to say first, then I'll decide if it can wait until tomorrow."

"You wouldn't be putting off driving to Custer because you have another date with Sarah?"

"That isn't a factor."

"Okay. Let me know what she says." Crawley hung up before Gray could respond.

Clay ambled up and asked, "Are you official?"

"Yes. I'm now Assistant Special Agent Holt."

"Whoopie."

"I need to see if I can reach Dr. Kingman," Gray said. "I'd like you to listen in."

"My first official assignment from a special agent," Clay quipped. "How thrilling."

"Be nice," Gray cautioned, "or I'll make you drive me to South Dakota tonight."

Clay chuckled, then said, "Let me get a cup of coffee and I'll meet you back in your cubicle. Do you want a cup?"

"No thanks." Gray went back to the desk he'd been using earlier and found Dr. Kingman's contact number. He jotted down some questions and when Clay joined him, he dialed her number.

"Hello," a woman answered in a shaky voice.

"Is this Dr. Angela Kingman?"

"Yes. Who's this?" Her voice grew stronger.

"I'm Wyoming DCI Special Agent Gray Holt. I'm assisting in the death investigation of Dr. Darren Waters." He decided not to say, *his murder.* "I'm sorry for your loss."

"Thank you. He was a good friend."

"Are you up to answering a few questions?"

"Yes. I was told that Darren was found in Wyoming," Angela said. "Is that true?"

"Yes. Who told you that?"

"Lt. White Owl called me and said that he'd been murdered and that his body had been found near Devils Tower. Am I a suspect?"

Her question caught Gray by surprise. Most innocent people didn't ask that question so soon in an interview. "No ma'am. Are you still in Custer?"

"Yes. Is Darren's…"

Gray heard her whimper and knew what she was going to ask. "His body is here in Sundance, Wyoming. Was he staying with you at the hotel in Custer?"

"Yes."

"Do you have his belongings?"

"Yes." Another soft sob.

"Dr. Kingman, we know that he was working in the Black Hills, but we don't know where exactly. Did he leave any journals, notebooks, maps, or anything that can help us pinpoint where he most likely had been?"

"Darren left a journal in our room. I went through it, but I didn't find anything indicating where he was working." Angela paused. "He told me that he'd made a discovery of some magnitude, but he refused to talk about it. He said it might be dangerous and he didn't want me in the field with him."

Gray found that last bit of information interesting as it wasn't in the report. "Did he tell you why it was dangerous?"

"No. He only said that he'd seen some things that he couldn't explain. I should have been with him."

Gray listened as she wept. When she finally stopped, he asked, "Do you have any idea what he was referring to?"

"No, he refused to talk about it," Angela replied.

"When are you planning to return to Utah?"

"Soon. There's nothing else for me here. I imagine that his ex-wife will be the one to make the funeral arrangements."

"That all depends. They're divorced and he may have made other arrangements. Do you know if he had a will?"

"He does. He changed it after the divorce. He told me that everything he had left after the divorce, he'd willed to his daughters. I feel so sorry for them."

"Dr. Kingman, Dr. Jack Beining is the medical examiner here in Crook County, and he can tell you what arrangements have been made." Gray provided her with the number, then asked, "This may be insensitive, but it seems like your relationship with Dr. Waters was more than just friendship?"

There was a slight pause. "Yes. We were very close."

"I'd like to stop by your motel before you leave for Utah."

"I'm not up to it today," Angela said. "Can I meet you somewhere on my way home tomorrow? Where is Sundance?"

"It's just east of Devils Tower."

"Okay, that's not too far out of the way. I'll come there. Where would you like to meet?"

Gray gave her the address and directions to the Sheriff's Office, then added, "Please bring the journal and his personal belongings. I'd like to examine them to determine if there's anything that may have bearing on the investigation. It'll take you about an hour and a half to get here, so what time would you like to meet?"

"I'm an early riser, but I need to pack and check out. Let's make it nine."

"I'll see you then." Gray hung up. *What had Waters encountered that he thought was so dangerous?*

"Do you still need a ride to Custer?" Clay asked.

"No. As you heard, Dr. Kingman will be here tomorrow at nine, so I'll need an interview room."

"That I can do."

"Sarah's going to meet me here at 1830. I have a few more calls to make, so you can head home if you like. Are you married?"

"No, and no girlfriend either," Clay said. "I can't leave until you do. I have my orders."

"Alright then. Give me ten minutes to call Custer County SO. Then I need to contact the Black Hills Gold Mining Company, but I doubt anyone will be able to answer my questions about Oliver Tanner at this late hour."

"Probably not."

"I'll make the calls fast." Gray contacted the Custer Sheriff's Office and left word with the duty deputy that Dr. Kingman was leaving Custer tomorrow morning, and left his contact number for Lt. White Owl to call him. Then he called the BHGM corporate headquarters in Rapid City, and as expected, the offices were closed. He'd have to try again in the morning. Then he called Crawley and gave him a synopsis of his conversation with Dr. Kingman.

"I'll meet you at the Sheriff's Office at eight-thirty," Crawley said. "I want to be there for the interview and take custody of that journal."

"If you have other things to do, I can handle the interview," Gray said.

"I'm sure that you can, but I want to speak with her."

"She's pretty distraught."

"I really don't care. She's a witness in a homicide investigation and she may be able to tell us what personal items Waters might have had with him. We didn't find anything on either victim, so if he wore a watch or ring, they could turn up in a pawn shop. If something is missing, I'll have you run down those leads."

"I figured as much," Gray said.

"I'll see you in the morning."

"Wait, I have another question," Gray said.

"What is it?"

"Were you able to get the GPS coordinates from Tanner's tracker?"

"Yes. I'll tell you about it later."

The line went dead.

"That guy is just plain rude," Gray muttered. He packed up his notes and found Clay watching the news on an old television.

"You done?" Clay asked.

"Yup. You can escort me out. I'll see you here in the morning at eight."

"You won't need a ride in?" Clay asked, with a knowing smile.

"If I do, I'll call you."

CHAPTER SIX

Noel Ketterhorn was looking out of the floor-to-ceiling glass windows of his office at The Forks, where the Red River and Assiniboine River joined in the center of the city. The early-morning sun, blocked by the skyscrapers, cast shadows across the busy roadways. He adjusted his Italian bespoke suit coat and smoothed down his tie. It was a habit before every meeting.

As the CEO of Universal Mining, he occupied the most spacious and luxurious office on the twenty-eighth floor of the Progress building. He was waiting for the other three members of the Mázazi mining alliance to connect via video conference in the adjoining conference room. All of them were mining giants in their own right, and their latest joint endeavor was supposed to have been an easy business venture, but it had turned into a fiasco.

He considered alliance member Mark Santos, the president and CEO of BHGM, to be the only trustworthy member of the group. Santos was headquartered in Rapid City, South Dakota, and had been instrumental in getting mining permits for the alliance in sensitive areas throughout the western United States. Santos had boasted of his strong political connections in several states where the Mázazi alliance had mining interests, and that had been proven true on numerous occasions.

The shadiest partner, and Ketterhorn's least favorite member, was Dragos Marcu, the owner of DTOS Mining in Romania. Ketterhorn didn't care for the man's complete lack of ethics, but Marcu had access to undisclosed financial resources, and he didn't mind bending the rules to succeed in the industry.

The latest member to join the alliance was William Ossa of the Pelion Mining Company, headquartered in Greece. Ketterhorn saw him as a bit of a whiner, but he had deep family ties in the mining industry, with banking and investor connections throughout the Mediterranean that were of value.

Ketterhorn wasn't pleased with the latest developments involving their gold exploration in the Black Hills, along the Wyoming and South Dakota border. The project was consuming more of his time than expected, and so far, all he had to show for it was missing employees. A multispectral analysis from the latest Terra satellite indicated that a potentially vast gold deposit existed in the southwestern Black Hills. It was a source of extreme frustration that the satellite hadn't provided enough detailed information to confirm the deposit. They needed this confirmation before submitting claims and making requests to start test-drilling in the sensitive area, which he knew would inevitably lead to a fight with the environmentalists and Native Americans. The alliance had sent eco-biologists and mining and geological engineers to determine if they should proceed.

If the large deposit was confirmed, the alliance stood to make nearly ninety billion American dollars, maybe more, over the next ten years. Ketterhorn had wanted to keep the circle tight on the find to avoid any negative press. Too many mines in the Black Hills had already closed, been converted to scientific research facilities, or had been turned over to the government for cleanup. Environmental interests remained a public relations concern, but Santos had assured him that his political friends would squelch any issues.

Santos had called last night and given him the distressing news that Oliver Tanner, a missing BHGM exploration supervisor, had been found murdered in Wyoming. Ketterhorn feared that the three missing members from his company might have suffered the same fate.

Santos also told him that two days ago, two more field explorers had gone quiet: Tucker Ryan, another exploration manager for BHGM, and Tyra

Stathopoulos, a geologist with Pelion Mining. They'd both been working in the same area where Tanner's GPS tracker had stopped transmitting. His own employees' trackers had failed in the exact same location.

Ketterhorn wondered if someone was targeting the alliance's field teams.

His office door opened and his assistant said, "Mr. Ketterhorn, everyone has connected on the conference call and they are waiting for you to join them."

"Thank you," he replied.

Ketterhorn strolled into the conference room and sat down in front of the multiscreen monitor. After pleasantries were exchanged, he asked Santos to update them about what he knew about Tanner's death and the disappearances.

When Santos had finished, Ossa appeared distressed by the news. He ran his hand through his thick salt-and-pepper hair and wiped the sweat from his upper lip.

"William, you look concerned," Ketterhorn said.

"I am very concerned. I didn't tell any of you, but Tyra Stathopoulos is my niece. Mark, I sent her to you so she could to gain field experience. I thought she'd be safe there. I don't know how I'm going to tell my sister that she's missing. We need to find her before I have to make that call."

"We will do everything we can to find her," Santos said.

"No one has seen or heard from her for two days?" Ossa said.

"Correct," Santos replied.

"Then something has happened to her. You need to report her missing to the authorities immediately and start an extensive search of the area."

"Sometimes accidents happen," Marcu said, in a deep Romania accent. He was chewing on something while he scratched his bald head, appearing indifferent, almost bored. "You Greeks are so passionate and emotional when it comes to family. Phone or satellite service could be out. There could be many reasons why contact was lost."

"I wonder if you would be so cavalier if a member of your family was missing," Ossa snapped venomously.

"Before this becomes unproductive, let me say that I agree with William," Ketterhorn said. "We'll report them missing immediately and begin search operations. But William, two days is not a long time to go without reporting in. We often have GPS failures. That's why I didn't report my three people missing for over a week."

"I don't care how you handled your missing people. I'm talking about my niece."

"I care about all of my employees," Ketterhorn emphasized.

"How did Tanner die?" Ossa asked.

"They wouldn't tell me," Santos replied. "All they said was that he'd been murdered. Tanner's GPS tracker was found fifty miles away from his last-known GPS upload."

"You have Tyra's last coordinates?" Ossa asked.

"Yes," Santos replied. "We were alerted when it stopped reporting. We'll start the search there. William, cell phone service in the Black Hills is sporadic. Like Noel said, two days without contact is not unusual."

"Why did all of these trackers fail in the same area?" Marcu asked. "Do you think we are looking at industrial espionage or a conspiracy to beat us to our claim? Maybe someone leaked the location and they know about the potential yield."

"Possibly," Ketterhorn said. "William, Mark will need you to provide him with as much personal information as you can on Tyra, including her latest photo."

"I will forward everything we have," Ossa said.

"Maybe we should provide our exploration teams with an armed escort," Ketterhorn offered.

"Will the Americans allow it?" Marcu asked, sounding intrigued.

"It wouldn't be a problem," Santos answered. "Though, I'm hesitant to send any additional staff into the Black Hills until we find the missing, even with an armed escort. We don't know what or who we're up against. We could be dealing with a violent environmental group or drug traffickers."

"Or nothing at all," Marcu said.

"What matters now is finding our people," Ketterhorn said. "What else can we do to help the authorities in their search?"

"I'll contact my senator friends and get the feds involved," Santos said. "The locals are good, but the more eyes and aircraft we have in the area, the faster we'll find them. In light of Tanner being killed, I expect a more intensive search."

Ossa said, "My niece is a very special woman. I hope that one day she may become the CEO of Pelion." His voice cracked.

"Does anyone have any other suggestions on what we can do?" Ketterhorn asked.

"I know someone who may be able to assist us," Marcu said, with a sly smirk.

"Who?" Ketterhorn said, feeling his dislike for the man grow.

"I hired a contract operative about a year ago to help me with an issue at one of my mines here in Romania. A competitor had hired brutal Russian mercenaries to disrupt my mining operations. Several employees were threatened, a few were beaten, and one was never found. I was forced to shut down operations. A few days after she arrived, the problem went away and I was back in business."

"A woman?" Ossa questioned.

"Yes. A very skilled and well-trained woman. The mercenaries were never seen again and my competitor suffered a near-fatal accident. Gentlemen, understand that she doesn't play by the rules and she isn't afraid to get bloody. If a competitor is responsible for your missing people, we need to do more than just search for them. I can tell you that she is effective but not cheap."

"What would it cost us?" Ketterhorn asked.

"I'm not sure. My problem set me back ten million US dollars, but it was worth it."

"I don't like where this conversation is going," Santos said. "How can a hired gun help us find our people? Don't forget, I live here and I can't be tied to a killer."

"It won't be an issue," Marcu said. "We will not be linked to her actions. She's discreet and prefers not to make contact with her clients. In fact, I don't even know her name. She did her job and I wired her payment to a numbered account."

"How did you learn about her?" Ketterhorn asked.

"I have a friend who knew about my problem and he contacted her. She sent me an encrypted email asking what I needed done. I sent her the specifics and she provided a quote and an estimate of how long it would take to resolve the problem."

"I say we make an inquiry," Ossa said. "I need to find my niece, and I'm willing to take whatever action is needed to get her home safe."

"I agree," Ketterhorn said. "We need to get this resolved."

"Dragos, you're certain that there won't be any blowback?" Santos asked.

"Positive," he replied. "I'll tell her what we know and see what she can do for us. If we don't like her terms, we won't move forward."

"Alright, make the call," Santos said.

"I will let you know when I've made contact. I have to go through my friend, so it could take a few days."

"A few days!" Ossa bellowed.

"Calm yourself," Marcu stated. "I will emphasize that our needs are time sensitive. In all likelihood, it will only take a day."

"Call me as soon as arrangements have been made," Ketterhorn said.

"I will," Marcu said.

"I believe our business for today is complete," Ketterhorn declared and signed off.

DHS Field Office, Fairfax, Virginia – May 22 – 0900

Aki sat calmly in Director Rebecca Canton's office while Chase paced nervously. Canton was late for their meeting, and Aki felt that it was probably on purpose.

"How much shit are we in?" Chase asked.

"Let's just see what the director has to say," Aki replied. "She didn't sound that upset on the conference call yesterday. Relax."

A minute later, Rebecca Canton entered her office and said, "Did you enjoy your trip?"

"It could have been better," Aki replied.

"Chase, sit down," Canton ordered.

Chase took the chair next to Aki, while Canton continued standing by her desk. "I know you did your best, but what a mess. I've been getting heat from Under Secretary Bassett, who's getting it from the Germans, and this morning the Polish government called to express their displeasure. The

Germans are demanding an internal review of your actions. In other words, they want heads to roll so they can save face. What went wrong over there?"

"Nothing that could have been foreseen," Aki replied. "The GSG 9 team was the best I've worked with and Dar still managed to neutralize three of their men with tranquilizer darts as we approached. She had a very sophisticated surveillance and defensive system we didn't know about, but I suspect she knew we were coming before we launched the raid."

"Why do you say that?"

"She was too well prepared and chose a tranquilizer gun to clear an escape route. She had to have known we were coming and was waiting for us even before we set the perimeter." Aki continued with a detailed report of what had transpired up until they located Dar's sailboat.

"And that's when she shot your helicopter down," Canton said.

"That's correct. Victor had the helicopter descend so we could get a better look at the boat. We needed confirmation that she was still onboard. The pilot was hit in the leg and Victor tried to fly us out of danger, but the helicopter was too badly damaged and crashed. Later, we learned that Dar used a motorboat to flee into Poland. We were in pursuit when Victor was relieved of his command and *you recalled us*." Aki emphasized the last few words with obvious disdain for the order back to Washington.

"Careful there, Aki," Canton cautioned. "This is a debrief to determine if a formal review is warranted. You both need to understand that I have a responsibility that exceeds your capturing Dar."

"I apologize for my tone," Aki said.

"Is that it?"

"Yes," Aki replied. "It's detailed in my report. I forwarded it to you this morning."

"I read it, but I prefer to hear things firsthand."

"Why is the Polish government upset with us?" Chase asked.

"The Polish SPAP tracked Dar to Szczecin. They ended up in a gun battle trying to apprehend her and she escaped. The SPAP claims that they weren't properly briefed on the level of danger that Dar posed, and asserted that if they had known, they would have deployed additional resources to deal with her."

"That's a bunch of crap," Aki said. "Someone's covering their ass. The SPAP knew exactly how dangerous she was because Victor briefed his contact there. Was anyone injured in the firefight?"

"No, thank goodness, but there are now bullet-ridden cars, boats, and buildings across the city and harbor."

"So, the SPAP also needs a scapegoat and we're it," Chase said.

Canton settled behind her desk and leaned back in her chair. "Correct. If I'd allowed you to pursue Dar into Poland, it would have ended with you being in yet another firefight with more collateral damage. At least this time, you weren't in the mix."

Aki took a deep breath to keep from saying what she wanted to say. "So, what do we do now? Are we under investigation?"

"No. I believe that you acted properly, but you are both being transferred."

"What!" Aki cried, leaning forward in her chair.

Canton smiled. "Relax. I'm assigning you and Chase to a new TCT unit that I was authorized to create a few years ago. Aki, you'll be the team leader and report directly to me. Chase, you'll be second-in-command. The unit will be small with only four support personnel. I've authorized you to have an intelligence and threat assessment analyst, an electronics intercept specialist, a counterterrorism specialist, and an executive support assistant. Aki, you'll need to staff those positions."

Aki was stunned. "I don't know what to say. I'm honored, but confused."

"As am I," Chase said. "What does TCT stand for?"

"Target, Capture or Terminate." Canton sighed, then continued, "We've experienced an increase in compromised investigations within Special Projects, including your failed mission. Several other joint investigations within the intelligence community have also failed. Up until the last six months, our track record had been exceptional. I believe we have an internal leak."

"So, I'm not being paranoid," Aki said.

"No, you're not. I need people I can trust and who can operate outside of the scope of normal operational parameters and constraints. TCT will be completely autonomous."

Aki felt a sense of excitement.

"We're going dark?" Chase asked.

"Yes, but you won't be undercover, per se. You will still be under DHS, but no one within Homeland will know about your assignments except for me and Secretary Evans. Even POTUS will be on a need-to-know basis. Under Secretary Bassett won't be in the loop either, unless Director Evans thinks it's necessary. I'm also moving your offices to a new location."

Aki frowned and said, "I have several questions."

"I thought you might."

"How broad is our operational authority to target and pursue threats? If we're autonomous, are you saying that we can operate outside of legal constraints? And how are we funded without someone knowing about us?"

"TCT is fully sanctioned to operate under a presidential secret powers executive order. I'll provide you with your missions, but that doesn't mean you can't conduct your own investigations into potential threats. I just need to be kept aware of them so that there's no overlap or conflicts with other operations. As to your legal constraints, you have presidential authority to take *whatever* action is required to fulfill your missions. Your operational funding is hidden within intelligence community black funds."

"And our first mission is to find the leak?" Chase inquired.

"I haven't decided yet. The mole must have a high clearance level, with access to our mission files."

"It could be a techie," Chase said.

"I don't think so. I've already had someone look into that possibility and there wasn't any correlation. One of the reasons I'm moving your offices is to eliminate any chance that your activities are discovered. Aki, you will only share information with other agencies as is necessary to complete your missions. Keep as much as you can compartmentalized."

"I understand."

"Your relentless pursuit of targets, even when faced with the most difficult setbacks, convinced me that you were the people I needed to lead the new unit. You may find that your transfer from Special Projects will be interpreted as a disciplinary action."

"Which affords you the opportunity to tell the SPAP, GSG 9 and Bassett that we've been properly castigated."

"Correct, and I won't be lying when I tell Bassett that I've moved you both to a new location and given you new responsibilities."

"What about Dar?" Chase asked.

"Dar is still a target—just let the dust settle for a while before you start after her again. I'll forward a list of current targets that I'd like you to develop operational action plans for once you've assembled your team."

"Understood," Aki replied.

"If I need help identifying the mole, I'll let you know."

"We're here to serve," Aki said. Her mind was reeling at what this new assignment would bring.

Canton appeared to relax a little. "Akicita. Your parents blessed you with a Lakota name that befits you. You are a warrior and I need that spirit to make this unit successful."

"Thank you, but Akicita was not my birthname. It was the name I was given by my father and the tribal elders when I reached adulthood. They thought 'Akicita' was appropriate considering my tendency to get into altercations."

"What was your birthname?" Canton asked.

"Mahpiha, which means sky. My mother told me as a baby I would try to grab the clouds. When I was a teenager, I was called Weeko. Which I didn't care for and was probably one of the reasons I was always getting into fights."

"What does that mean?" Chase asked.

"Pretty girl."

Chase chuckled. "What other names do you have?"

"I have a spirit name that is only known by the Medicine Man. I think that's enough personal history for now."

"Why were you always getting into fights?" Chase asked.

Aki sighed. "You aren't going to let this go, are you?"

"Nope."

"There were several young men on the reservation who enjoyed teasing me and the other girls. Sometimes they got physical with us and I gained a reputation for protecting those who were weak. The small scar above my right eyebrow is from a rather nasty fight I had with a large bully. He outweighed me by almost two hundred pounds and he was over a foot taller. He was a giant of a man."

"You mean that you picked a fight with a six foot eight- or nine-inch-tall guy who weighed over three hundred and fifty pounds?" Chase said. "What happened?"

"I don't like to talk about it."

"You've made us curious," Canton said, leaning forward in her chair. "Tell us."

"His name is Mato. In Lakota, it means 'the bear.'" Aki took a deep breath. "He was taunting a girlfriend of mine in front of a group of men. They had her surrounded and wouldn't let her pass. Mato kept reaching out to try and a grab her braid. I walked over to the group, grabbed one of the men by the back of his hair, and threw him to the ground. The men knew me and backed away when I challenged Mato. It was a dumb thing for me to do."

"Did you beat him?" Chase asked.

"No. I got my butt kicked. I did land the first punch and it felt like I'd hit a stone wall, but it was game on, so I came at him with everything I could muster. The harder I fought, the harder he punched back. I soon realized that he was just toying with me. I couldn't say how many times he knocked me to the ground. My nose was bleeding, I ached, and he just stood there smiling at me.

"I was so angry that I grabbed a fist-sized rock, got up, and charged him. I managed to hit him in the face with the rock, which knocked him backwards. After he swiped the blood from his face, the look he gave me is something that I hope never to see again. He took one big step, swung, and knocked me out."

"And that's how you got the scar," Chase said.

"Yes. When I came to, Mato was kneeling over me with a concerned look on his face. Blood was still dripping from his cheek. When he saw that I was alive, he got up, grunted, and walked away. The other men said that after he'd knocked me out, that he was the first one to check on me. I think he thought that he'd killed me. Mato has a nasty scar across his left cheek to remember me by, and I have mine."

"Did he ever bother you again?" Canton asked.

"No. Mato respects strength and we eventually became friends. He told me that standing up to him had been the right thing to do. He said it taught him to respect those weaker than him and he became a defender of the weak."

"Sounds like he might be a little like Dar," Chase said. "She respects strength and uses only the force necessary to keep from losing."

"Don't compare Mato to Dar," Aki admonished. "Director, I'm willing to bet that Dar has returned to Belarus. I'm sure that she has funds and safe houses there."

"You aren't going to let the dust settle, are you? Alright, once you've assembled your team, have one of them initiate inquiries, but I don't want the two of you mentioned by name in any of them."

"Yes, ma'am. Where are our new offices?"

Canton pulled a large packet from her top desk drawer and handed it to her. "They're in Springfield, Virginia, at a secure location. Everything you need to know is in the packet, including your identification badges and parking passes. I've included your initial passwords for the terminals and encrypted lines. Once you gain access, change them. I believe that you'll enjoy the campus. We should be able to communicate through secure video calls, but if we need to meet in person, I'll set the place and time. There's a cell number in the packet that no one else has for our calls. Your team will not disclose what you are working on to anyone unless authorized by me. Are we clear?"

"Yes, ma'am," Aki and Chase answered.

"Good luck. I'll be in touch. Go check out your new offices."

Aki and Chase stayed silent as they walked down the hallway. Once outside the building, Aki said, "I can't believe our luck."

CHAPTER SEVEN

Sarah and Gray pulled into the small parking lot behind the Sheriff's Office, and Sarah said, "Strange, Crawley's not here yet. He usually likes to arrive early for interviews."

"He said he'd be here at eight-thirty. He's bringing my credentials. I guess I'll have to *ooh* and *ahh* over them."

Sarah snickered. "Don't you dare become his toady."

"It's Crawley, how could I possibly? Thank you for dinner last night. I'd like to pick up the check next time."

"Hey, I invited you. Thanks for letting me crash at your place again."

"No problem. I like the company."

"Maybe we should start sharing the bed. The pullout can't be comfortable."

"What happened to the 'take it slow' plan?'" Gray asked.

"Slow is one thing. Glacial is another. Do you think Dr. Kingman will show?"

"I hope so, but you never know." Gray stepped from Sarah's truck just as Crawley and Clay pulled in and parked next to them.

"Told you he liked arriving early," Sarah said, as she joined Gray. "I wonder what snide innuendo he'll toss at us this morning."

"Who cares?" Gray noticed Crawley was carrying a small box in one hand and a notepad in the other.

"Morning, you two," Crawley said. "Did you both have a nice evening?"

"Yes," Sarah replied with a sweet smile, then added, "very nice."

"Well, that's good. Gray, did you get us an interview room?"

"Actually, Clay reserved it for us yesterday."

"Good," Crawley said. "I guess you all are acquainted well enough to dispense with the formalities of addressing each other by titles when in private."

"It would be easier," Gray said. "May I call you Roland?"

Crawley pursed his lips, then said, "No."

"Okay. Agent Crawley, Sarah and I put together some questions that we want to ask Dr. Kingman. Do you want to look them over?"

"Not necessary because I've decided to take the lead in the interview," Crawley announced. "The homicide cases and the missing people are now our priority. The governor and the AG want them solved quickly, which is what we're going to do. I've had all of my open cases reassigned to other agents.

"Sarah, I want you to call Dr. Waters' ex-wife and see if she knows anything about where or what her former husband may have been working on in the Black Hills. See if he told her anything about a new discovery. Get her to be as specific as you can. I want to cover all the bases. Can you handle that?"

"Certainly. I'll see what I can get out of her."

Crawley handed Gray the box he'd been holding. "Your badge and creds are in there. Respect and honor what they represent. Go ahead, open it."

Inside the box was a seven-pointed gold star with *Special Agent* engraved across the top. The star was affixed to the front of the badge case. He opened the case and admired his credentials. "Wow. Very nice. Do I get to keep them as a souvenir when we're done?"

"No. Now—I need to swear you in." He looked around the parking lot, then said, "I guess this is as good a place as any." He pointed at Sarah and Clay. "You two can be witnesses. Gray, raise your right hand."

After Gray took the oath, Clay said, "Congratulations, Agent Holt."

"Yeah, congrats," Sarah added.

"Agent Crawley, Sarah and I were thinking of driving up to Rapid City after the Kingman interview. The missing person's report filed by BHGM lacked details and we thought we could get more information if we paid the CEO a visit."

"That's a good idea. Deputy Gurley and I will head south and meet with Sheriff Lyons in Weston County after the interview. I want to take a look at the recovered vehicles, drive out to where they were left, and ask around about the missing mining employees. Then I thought Deputy Gurley and I would go for a hike. I hope that you're up for a walk in the woods?"

"Always," Clay replied.

"Good. Grab your gear. You'll ride with me."

"Is there any current intelligence on the local environmental or tribal activists?" Gray asked.

"I haven't heard of any new developments. Let's go inside and I'll make a few calls. Sarah, contact Mrs. Waters."

Twenty minutes later, Gray left the interview room and nearly walked into Sarah. She smiled and asked, "Going somewhere?"

"Coming to see you. There are no active threats toward any of the mining companies. Crawley arranged for us to have access to all the databases we'll need for the investigation. He doesn't think the interview with Kingman will take very long, so we can be in Rapid City before noon. Can you call BHGM and set up our interview with the CEO and whoever knows the most about Tanner's disappearance?"

"Sure. I spoke to the ex-Mrs. Waters. First I'd like to brief you on what she said."

"Great, go on in and have a seat. I need to use the restroom."

A few minutes later, Gray entered the interview room and noted how cramped it was with four people around the table.

"I'll make this brief," Sarah began. "As expected, Mrs. Waters didn't know anything about her late husband's work. I mean absolutely nothing. She wasn't aware that he was even in the Black Hills. She also didn't ask any questions about his murder. However, she did ask if Dr. Kingman had been with him on the excursion and if she was also dead. It seems that Dr. Kingman's intimate relationship with Dr. Waters was the reason for their divorce."

"The confirmation that Dr. Kingman was involved with Dr. Waters is helpful," Crawley said. "When was the last time Mrs. Waters saw or spoke to the victim?"

"She claims it's been several weeks. She did say that her daughters had mentioned that they hadn't heard from their dad lately, which was unusual. What struck me as odd was just how cold she sounded after hearing the father of her children was dead. When I told her that she needed to contact Dr. Beining in Sundance, she was surprised to hear that his body was in Wyoming. She also sounded put out that she might have to make funeral arrangements. I think she may have a change of heart after she gives her daughters the news."

"That is interesting," Crawley said, as he strummed his fingers on the table. "You and Gray will need to speak to her in person at some point."

"That's what I thought," Sarah said.

"Does she have an alibi for the past few weeks?" Crawley asked.

"Yes, but I'll need to verify it. She said that she's been at work during the day and at home with the kids in the evening. That's all I have. I'll go make that call to BHGM."

"Thank you, Sarah," Crawley said. "Deputy, why don't you go with her and make arrangements with Weston County for our visit." He added. "It's too cramped and stuffy in here. Couldn't you have found us an office or a bigger room?"

"This is the only interview room we have," Clay replied.

"We'll just have to suffer through then."

Sarah and Clay left the room, leaving the door open.

"How do you want to work the interview?" Gray asked.

"I'll ask my questions first. If you have anything that you think we need answered, then you can have a shot. Do not ask her anything until I'm through. Clear?"

"Yes."

"Good. I'll be curious to see what you think of her reactions to my questions. So pay attention to her body language."

"I will watch her every movement."

Crook County SO – 0900 hours MDT

"Your witness is here," Sarah announced, sticking her head into the interview room. "I'll go fetch her."

"How'd your call to BHGM go?" Gray asked.

"Still waiting on a callback."

A few minutes later, Sarah escorted Dr. Kingman into the interview room and directed her to a chair at the table across from Crawley, then closed the door as she left.

Dr. Angela Kingman wasn't what Gray had pictured. She was tall, about six feet, with a thin build and long, braided red hair. Gray noticed a small circular tattoo on her right wrist. She appeared attentive as her piercing blue eyes scanned the room and settled on Crawley. Gray knew that Crawley wasn't expecting her to be such a stunner. Her Utah driver's license photo didn't do her justice.

"Dr. Kingman, we appreciate you taking the time to drive to meet with us. I'm Agent Graynger Holt—we spoke on the phone—and this is Special Agent Roland Crawley with the Wyoming Division of Criminal Investigations. He's in charge of the investigation."

"I thought you were in charge," Angela said.

"No. He's the senior agent."

Crawley leaned forward, rested his elbows on the table, and gave Kingman a hard stare for longer than was necessary, then said, "I understand that you're an associate professor of archeology at BYU, and you've been in that position for five years."

"That's correct."

"Do you plan to continue teaching at BYU?"

"Yes."

Gray noticed a quizzical look cross her face. She obviously wasn't expecting that question.

"And to make full professor, does someone have to retire or die for that to happen?"

"No. I believe they want to see me publish more and gain further recognition before they offer me a full professorship."

Gray was surprised by Crawley's confrontational questions so early in the interview.

"By 'further recognition,' you mean discovering something that would be groundbreaking and of importance in your field of study?" Crawley asked. "Would that expedite you making professor and gaining tenure?"

"Yes, publishing something that was groundbreaking would carry weight in speeding that process along. What are you getting at?"

"Do you know where Dr. Waters was working or the importance of what he had found?"

"Like I told Agent Holt, I don't know exactly where he was working, only that it was in the southern part of the Black Hills. I know he thought he'd made an important discovery. This was his second trip back to explore the area further and he wanted me to stay behind because he didn't think it was safe."

"Hmm. Did that trouble you?"

"Of course. I really didn't want him to be out there alone, but he insisted. I told Agent Holt this before."

"Were you with him the last time he was here?"

"No. He came alone."

"When was that?"

"About a month ago."

"Dr. Kingman, will you be able to follow up on his work?" Crawley asked.

"I don't understand," Angela replied.

"I mean, can you publish and take credit for his discovery now that he's dead?"

"You think I killed him?" Angela turned to glower at Gray. "Agent Holt, I thought you said I wasn't a suspect?"

Gray glanced at Crawley. He couldn't believe Crawley was continuing the hard approach.

Crawley leaned back and huffed. "You're not a suspect. I'm just trying to understand the academic world. Why are you so defensive?"

Angela bristled and said, "I am not being defensive. You're insinuating that I could profit from Darren's death."

"Could you?" Crawley asked callously.

"I don't like where this is going."

"I don't care. Could you continue his work and get credit?"

"If I knew what it was, possibly. But I would never take sole credit for his discovery."

"Do you know where he was killed?" Crawley asked.

"No!" Angela exclaimed. "As I've explained, I don't know where he was working. I'd like to know how he ended up in Wyoming."

"Good question," Crawley replied, then rubbed his forehead. "Dr. Kingman, I asked if you knew where he was killed, not where he was working."

"I assumed that was where it happened."

Gray noticed her hands were shaking, perhaps from nervousness or anger.

Crawley sat quietly for a moment, then said, "Did Dr. Waters drink?"

"A little. Usually beer or wine." Angela shook her head. "What does that have to do with Darren's death?"

"Maybe he went to a bar, got drunk, and pissed off the wrong cowboy."

"Darren doesn't go to bars," Angela insisted.

"You're sure?"

"Yes. We spent all of our time together, except this time when he was in the field. For some reason he wanted to keep everything secret."

"How did that make you feel?" Crawley said, leaning in.

"None of your damn business. You're really pissing me off. Do I need an attorney?"

"Not unless you have something to hide," Crawley replied, smirking. "Are you willing to continue?"

"I want whoever killed Darren found, and if answering these inane questions helps, then, yes."

"Good. Did you and Dr. Waters drive to Custer together?"

"No. I followed him up so we'd both have a vehicle while he was working."

"I see. You share the same field of study, but he wouldn't tell you where or what he was working on? Why? Was he worried that you might steal it?"

Angela snorted. "Look. I already said that he believed there was an element of risk and he wanted me safe. I would never steal his research. If you're going to keep asking me the same stupid questions, it will get you no closer to finding Darren's killer."

"Just answer the question," Crawley said.

"As far as our sharing an academic field, well, that we did, but our research areas were different. Our commonality involved Native American history and cultures. He was interested in discovering ancient sites and his academic concentration was physical and biological anthropology, and archeology. He was more of a post-processualist. My specialization is comparative cross-cultural anthropology with a focus on indigenous archeology."

"I see. That doesn't sound all that different."

"It is in many respects."

"How so?" Crawley asked.

"First of all, in my work, rather than digging with heavy equipment to discover artifacts at suspected sites, I believe that ethical consideration must be given to the indigenous people who lived on the land. There are multiple tools available that don't require the use of invasive excavation.

"We can discover past cultural practices and customs by analyzing Native American oral traditions. They tell us about their movement across their ancestorial lands, how they lived, where they lived, what they ate, their beliefs, and how they interacted with other indigenous people—all without anyone having to dig holes in the ground. We study what the Hopi call 'footprints.'"

"Footprints, huh?"

Angela rocked her jaw. "Yes, footprints. I spoke briefly with Ranger Goodson before she brought me to the interview room. She can tell you about the efforts of the National Parks Service to work with scientists in helping to preserve the sacred lands of the indigenous people. I support that measure and have been consulted on several sites found on federal lands."

"That's why I asked her to join the investigative team," Crawley bragged. "She works at Devils Tower and has a great rapport with the Native American people that visit there. Did she tell you that she was at the scene when Dr. Waters was found?"

"I didn't know that. Does Darren's death have anything to do with the tribes in the area?"

"Let me ask you this. Did Dr. Waters carry a knife when he was in the field?"

Angela sat back in her chair and paled. "Yes. He carries an original bear-tooth-handled knife. It's over a hundred years old. He's quite proud of it. I don't know where he got it, but he said it had Lakota origins."

"Describe the knife for me."

"It's about seven, maybe eight inches long. The top part of the handle is a bear tooth. I think the rest of the handle is from an antler. It's a bit stained and there's a strip of buffalo hide tied to the handle."

"What's the sheath look like?"

"Dark brown with red and blue beads on it," Angela replied.

"Any idea what the sheath is made of?"

"Darren said it was buffalo hide."

"Is it true that you two were romantically involved?" Crawley asked.

Angela stiffened and her brow knitted. "If you're asking if we had a sexual relationship, the answer is, yes. I loved Darren, but I don't think he loved me the same way. He was divorced because of our relationship and it caused his family a great deal of pain, for which I am sorry. He needed time to deal with his family issues before our relationship could progress any further. His daughters hate me and they were his life. I understood all of that and didn't want to push him into something that would make things worse." Her eyes welled with tears.

"I see. Did you bring his journal?"

Angela took a brown leather journal from her purse and put it on the table. "I've been through it several times. I don't see anything in there about where he was working or exactly what he'd discovered."

"Do you think that this discovery would enhance his credibility in the academic community?" Crawley asked.

"He said that what he'd found could be a potential link to an unknown ancient civilization. If that proved true, then it would have cemented him as one of the best in his field."

"But he wouldn't share any details about the discovery?"

"No. How many times do I have to tell you that? It's not unusual to make a discovery and keep it secret until the preliminary work is complete. You don't want to make a grand statement about a find and have it turn out to be nothing."

"I see." Crawley paused, then handed Gray the journal. "Why don't you look through that and see if anything jumps out at you."

Gray took the journal, unwrapped the leather ribbon wraparounds, and opened it. The first page was nearly full, with notations in the margin in a spidery-looking handwriting.

"Dr. Kingman, I'm sorry if I sound a bit callous," Crawley said. "It's my job to determine who killed Dr. Waters and I have to look at all possible motives for why he was killed."

"I understand," Angela said.

"I guess I'm just having a problem grasping why a professor who makes an important discovery chooses not to tell the person he's closest to about it. Did you ask him about the ancient link and what it meant?"

"Of course I did. He said he would tell me once he'd put all of the pieces together. You'd have to know Darren to understand. He was very guarded and private about his work."

"Did he have any other notebooks or journals with him?"

"He had several that he took with him into the field. They were in his backpack. And before you ask, I never read any of those journals."

"What color is his backpack?"

"Black."

"Why do you think he left the one journal behind? Isn't that odd?"

"Not if it wasn't needed for his work. It would just be extra weight. The journal had only a few blank pages left."

"Gray, did you find anything of interest in the journal?"

Gray looked at him and said, "If you're asking if there's a map with an X marking the place where he was working in the first three pages, the answer is no."

"Well, keep looking." Crawley took a deep, calming breath as Kingman cracked a small smile for the first time. "Dr. Kingman, how long have you known Dr. Waters?"

"About five years. We hit it off when I started at BYU. We didn't become romantically involved until about a year ago."

"Could his ex-wife have hired someone to kill him?"

"No. She'd hire someone to kill me, but not Darren. She wouldn't deprive her daughters of their father."

"Tell me more about your research."

"Most recently, I've been doing work on the cross-cultural and religious aspects of the Plains tribes. Specifically, those in the Sioux Nation, including the seven tribes of the Lakota, the four bands of the Dakota, and the three bands of the Nakota. I also speak Lakota."

"How did you come to learn the language?" Crawley asked, crossing his arms.

"I did field work on the Pine Ridge Reservation while working on my doctorate. I befriended a Lakota woman, Makawee, who was attending the Oglala Lakota College in Pine Ridge, where she was working on her Master's degree in Lakota leadership. We've talked at length about their religion, rituals, legends, and myths over the last six years. She taught me the language and even the Sun Dance, although I didn't do the ceremonial skewering of my arms. Instead, I opted for a tattoo." She pointed to her wrist.

"I see. Do you speak any other Native American languages?"

Some. I've found understanding languages and their origins helpful in my research on the Plains tribes. I'm also considered an expert on Native American folklore and myths."

"Do you ever get your hands dirty digging for artifacts and such?" Crawley asked.

"Yes. But like I said, it's surgical in nature."

"Hmm. Why haven't you asked me how Dr. Waters was killed?"

Angela flushed. "I guess because I figured that you'd tell me what had happened when it was time."

Crawley leaned across the table and said, "You also haven't asked if we've found Darren's truck or any of his other personal belongings, including his knife that you described in detail? Why is that?"

"Again, I figured that you would tell me eventually."

"Most people want to know how their loved ones met their demise," Crawley said. "Unless they already know."

"I don't know how he was killed or where," Angela snapped. "Will you tell me?"

"No," Crawley replied, leaning back. "Did you bring everything from the motel? His suitcase? Yours?"

"Yes."

Gray noticed her hands were shaking again.

"Will you consent to us looking through your personal belongings and his suitcase?" Crawley asked.

"I most certainly will not."

"Why not?" Crawley gave her a hard stare.

"Because I don't like being treated like a suspect. We are done here!" Angela stood.

"Agent Holt, doesn't she seem defensive?" Crawley asked, as he gave him a slight nod.

"Dr. Kingman, please sit down," Gray said in a calm voice. "This is just routine questioning." He looked at Crawley and said, "I'd like to tell her about the manner and cause of death."

"Go ahead."

Gray was direct. "Dr. Waters was stabbed to death and his body was found in the Belle Fourch River, not far from Devils Tower."

Angela's reaction was what he'd expected. She sat, put her head down, and sobbed. He waited until she stopped. Angela looked through her purse, took out a tissue, wiped her eyes, and blew her nose.

Gray hadn't thought to bring a Kleenex. It would have been a good way to establish a rapport with her, he reflected. After a moment, he continued. "We didn't find his knife or any personal belongings when we recovered his body. We'd like to know if the knife was in his possession before he was killed, or if he wore a watch or ring. It's always possible that whoever killed him could have pawned them."

Angela took a deep breath and wiped her cheeks. "Like I said, he always carried the knife with him in the field. Is that what he was stabbed with?"

"I can't say," Gray replied.

"Darren also wore a black-banded Citizens watch with an orange face. I bought it for him several months ago."

"Any other jewelry?"

"No. He stopped wearing his wedding ring after the divorce."

"Dr. Kingman, it would really help the investigation if one of us could look through the suitcases, briefcases, or whatever else you brought with you," Gray said. "You may have not noticed something that was packed away, or he could have hidden something in one of your bags. If you'd feel more comfortable, I can have Ranger Goodson go through them with you."

"There's nothing in his suitcase but clothes. But if you think it will help, I have no objection to you or the ranger looking, but not him," Angela said, pointing a finger at Crawley.

"Thank you," Gray replied. "That's very helpful. Do you have a photo of the knife or the watch?"

"I have a picture of him holding the knife at a site we worked together about six months ago. You might be able to enhance it. There's nothing special about the watch."

"Any engravings on the back?"

"No."

"How about the knife sheath?" Gray asked.

"I'm sure that I have a photo of it on my cell phone." She looked through her purse, then said, "I must have put my cell it my backpack. It's in the car. Can I go get it?"

"Certainly—I think a quick break might be in order," Gray said. "If you agree, Agent Crawley."

"I think that's a great idea. Agent Holt, I have to follow up with Sheriff Lyons in Weston County on another matter. Dr. Kingman, we're also searching for three people who have gone missing in the Black Hills, and their disappearance might be related to both murders."

Angela shot Crawley and Gray a puzzled look. "Wait, both murders?"

"Another homicide victim was found in the river near where we found Dr. Waters," Gray told her. He wasn't sure why Crawley had mentioned the missing mining employees or the other homicide, but since he'd opened the door, Gray added, "Both victims' cause and manner of death are identical."

"I don't understand," Angela said. "Who was the other victim?"

"We'll get to that later," Crawley interrupted. "Dr. Kingman, your work with the Native Americans in the area may be of help to us in the future. I hope that you'll assist us if called upon." Crawley stood and walked out of the room before she could respond.

Gray was actually embarrassed by the way Crawley had left the interview. He looked at her and said, "He's a good investigator, but he can be a braying ass at times."

"You think?"

CHAPTER EIGHT

Sarah, Gray, and Kingman were standing on the sidewalk in front of the Sheriff's Office as Crawley drove past without any acknowledgement. Clay gave a half-hearted wave from the passenger seat, already looking miserable.

"Crawley's not a social person," Gray said.

"No, he's not," Sarah said. "Dr. Kingman, which car is yours?"

"It's the green Range Rover at the end of the block."

As they neared Kingman's car, Sarah said, "Nice ride."

"Yes, it is. I got it as a part of my divorce settlement six years ago. It still looks and runs like new."

"I didn't know you were divorced," Gray said, wondering why he'd missed that detail in his background research.

"The marriage only lasted a few months. I found out that my ex-husband wasn't the monogamous type. He gave me the Range Rover to atone for his numerous affairs and to avoid paying alimony."

"Where did you meet Dr. Waters?" Sarah asked.

"I met Darren at BYU." She swallowed hard, but she didn't tear up. "I'm responsible for stealing him away from his family, so I guess I'm no better than my ex-husband."

"Dr. Kingman, we're eventually going to have to search his home," Gray said. "I think it would be best if you accompanied us when we do."

"Certainly."

She unlocked her car and stood back while Sarah and Gray went through Dr. Waters' luggage.

"May I look through your backpack and field pack?" Sarah asked.

"Sure, but there's nothing to see. Grab my cell for me."

When they finished the search, Gray said, "Let's go back inside."

"Agent Holt, is there anything more you can tell me about how Darren died?" Angela said as she took her seat in the interview room. Tears glistened in her eyes.

Gray knew that grief had a way of sneaking up on you when you least expected it. "Like I told you, he was stabbed."

"That's why you were so interested in Darren's knife. Agent Holt, do you still need to see a picture of it?"

"Yes."

Angela took out her cell phone and looked through the photos, then handed it to Gray. "That's the best picture I have of the knife."

After a moment, Gray said, "I don't believe it was the murder weapon."

"Why not?" Angela asked.

"The size of the knife blade doesn't match the wounds." Gray realized his mistake as soon as the words left his mouth.

"He was stabbed more than once?" Angela cried.

"Yes."

"How many times?"

"I'm not going to tell you. What I will tell you is that both victims were stabbed in the same area of the body, the same number of times, but their deaths were days apart. The method of the killing appears ritualistic in nature." Gray paused for a moment as she processed the news.

"Ritualistic? You mean someone butchered Darren?"

"No. His death was quick. I can't go into any more details. What I can tell you is that Agent Crawley feels that there may be a Native American connection based on some evidence that was found on the first victim. We're exploring the possibility that we're dealing with a serial killer or killers who prey on people in the Black Hills. We're still putting the pieces together. Like Agent Crawley said, your knowledge and connections with the local tribes could be of help as the investigation unfolds."

"I don't know how, but I'll be glad to assist you any way I can. I could introduce you to Makawee. She may be able to help you with anything related to the Pine Ridge reservation."

"Makawee?" Sarah said, questioningly.

"A Lakota friend of hers that she met years ago," Gray answered.

"I know a Makawee," Sarah said. "She teaches at the Oglala College in Pine Ridge. We talk when she brings students to Devils Tower. Is that her?"

"Yes," Angela replied. "Small world. Her name means 'Earth Maiden.'"

"I didn't know that."

Gray picked up Darren's journal from the table as Sarah and Kingman talked about Makawee. He looked more closely at the leather ribbon wraparounds, which had a carved wooden ball on the end. There was an engraving on the side of the ball. It looked like a symbol, but he didn't recognize it. The binding and cover of the journal were well worn. He flipped through the pages until he found where he'd left off. Something was tugging on his intuition.

The notes in the journal didn't mention any discovery. It was mostly about research paper ideas, some interest in the Wind and Jewel cave systems, observation notes at different sites, and a few notes near the back of the journal about places he wanted to explore, including a cave in the Yucatan. There were general notations about cave and cliff sites.

What caught his interest were the strange U-shaped symbols over some of the notations. A few of the U's were inverted, others were on their sides. At the end of the last notation in the journal there was a large double-lined U with a caret symbol over it.

"Excuse me, Dr. Kingman, what do these symbols mean?" Gray said, interrupting as he showed her a page with a notation.

"Darren sometimes used a form of cryptic shorthand when he did research," Angela said after she looked at them.

"Can you read his shorthand?"

"Some of it, if I know the context."

"He's referenced several cliffs across Wyoming, South Dakota, and Montana. What is that all about?"

"A little over a year ago, Darren proposed a theory that three thousand years ago, an advanced, ancient cave-dwelling civilization built an empire across the plains area. He thought that their culture and beliefs had been passed to the indigenous people found in the Four Corners area. He speculated that the civilization was very advanced for the era and that the civilization had come to an abrupt end."

"Like the Anasazi?" Gray said.

"Yes. But this civilization predated the Anasazi. Darren believed that this previously undiscovered civilization had been larger than that of the Mayans, and had reached its apex around 750 BC. He thought it was possible that trade routes had once extended south into Mexico, connecting many societies. Perhaps they traded goods, exchanged beliefs, rituals, farming and cultivation techniques, customs, and possibly even writing. He was trying to connect them and thought that the caves in the Black Hills might hold some evidence."

"You mean some of the ancient cliff-dwelling people in the Four Corners area were descendants of that original civilization?" Sarah asked.

"Yes, and more. He surmised that the remnants of the ancient civilization had scattered when their empire disintegrated and that possibly all of the Native Americans living across the western states from Arizona to Canada and as far east as the Ohio Valley were descended from the ancient civilization."

"That would be a tremendous discovery," Sarah said.

"Yes, it would be."

"Do you think he found the connection?" Gray asked. "Could that be what he was investigating on this trip?"

"He hadn't mentioned the theory for a while, so I don't know. Darren was always working on a number of projects at the same time."

"I saw that he'd made notations about the Register Cliff," Gray said. "Any idea what that's about?"

"The Register Cliff is located along the old Oregon Trail in southwestern Wyoming. He was probably looking for evidence of dwellings around the limestone cliffs."

"In his notes about the Wind Cave and the Jewel Cave, he uses a U-shaped symbol next to a double-lined U for his last notation, and then there's a caret symbol over it." Gray handed her the open journal. "What does that mean?"

Kingman took a moment to read the notes, then passed the journal back to him. "In set theory, the U means union and the double-lined U means the universal set of all possible values. The caret symbol in programming language is a string concatenation or a primitive notion. Darren was probably indicating there was a connection between the two cave systems."

"Is it possible that he found a new cave in the Black Hills that would substantiate his advanced-civilization connection?" Gray asked.

"Anything is possible, but if he did, he never mentioned it to me."

Gray flipped back a few pages. "He also made a notation about limestone and granite with a sideways U and a line through it."

"Let me see that again." Kingman took the journal from him, read a few pages, then said, "That would mean one set is not a subset of the other. Darren probably meant there was no connection between the Register Cliff and the caves in the Black Hills."

"Dr. Kingman, how old are the cave systems in the Black Hills?" Gray asked.

"I'm not sure exactly."

"The Black Hills were formed about three hundred million years ago by a geological uplift," Sarah stated. "New caves are being found there all the time."

Gray gave Sarah a quizzical look, then asked her, "Do you know anything about the Jewel and the Wind Cave?"

"I know a lot about those cave systems and many others."

"Really?" Gray said, leaning back in his chair.

"Yes, really. Both of those caves are a part of the National Park Service. The Wind Cave is north of Hot Springs and was formed over seventy million years ago. Most caves are formed by water eroding limestone, sandstone, and shale, creating passageways. The Wind Cave is still developing and changing. Over one hundred and fifty miles of passageways have been mapped.

"The Jewel Cave is even larger. It's about twenty miles northwest of the Wind Cave. It was created about the same time, although a geologist I spoke to said he thought the passages were formed around fifty million years ago. Interestingly, the Jewel Cave is the third-longest cave in the world. Over two hundred miles of it have been mapped. I actually helped map some of the passages. Gray, do you know why it's called Jewel Cave?"

"Is it because jewels were found there?"

"No. It's called Jewel Cave because the people who explored it back in the early 1900s thought the calcite crystals looked like jewels. It's really incredible to see."

"How do you know all of this?" Gray asked. He was truly impressed.

"I was trained in cave-rescue operations and I've explored a lot of the cave systems around here. I know them well."

"Since the two cave systems are so large and close together, I have to wonder if they're connected?"

"I wouldn't be surprised if they were," Sarah replied. "Caves fascinate me."

"I can tell," Gray said. "Dr. Kingman, do you think that the local tribes' ancestors lived in the caves in the Black Hills like Dr. Waters suspected?"

"There are many myths and legends about the Lakota, Cheyenne, and many of the other tribes concerning the caves in the area. Some of the caves are considered sacred. It's believed that humans emerged from the *Tunkan Tipi* or the spirit lodge, which is a cave, to start life on the Earth."

Gray raised an eyebrow.

Angela continued, "The Lakota believe there was another world before this one. When the Great Spirit became displeased, he destroyed that world in a flood and created a new one. People were forced to live underground and were warned not to come back to the surface until it was allowed. One story claims that the Creator became displeased when some of the people didn't listen to Tokahe's warning and followed the wolf from the Tunkan Tipi onto the surface."

"Who's Tokahe?" Gray asked.

"The First One."

"Like Adam and Eve, and the wolf would represent the tempting serpent like in the Bible," Sarah offered.

"There are many similarities in ancient creationist lore around the world," Angela said. "When the people who followed the wolf emerged, they suffered in the elements, and eventually the Creator turned them into bison as punishment for disobeying him. Then later, Tokahe received word that the world was ready for people to live on the surface again, and he led them through long cave passages to stand upon the land. To ensure that the people learned to live on the surface, the Creator closed the cave entrance so the people couldn't return."

"An interesting story," Sarah said. "Makawee told me about a myth involving a female serpent called Unhcegila, who was evil and was responsible for people disappearing or being killed. Unhcegila was always shrouded in a mist, had eyes that burned, and iron claws. Whoever looked into her eyes would go blind."

"There are several versions of that story," Angela said. "I think the most interesting one is how Unhcegila caused the primordial flood and was slain by the Wakinyan Tanka, the Great Thunderbird."

"Floods again," Gray said. "How did Wakinyan slay the serpent?"

"He shot lightning from his eyes and destroyed her red crystal heart," Angela replied, crossing her arms and leaning back.

Letting Kingman talk about her field of expertise was helping him normalize her response patterns. He wasn't completely convinced that she wasn't hiding something. He'd always found that by letting a subject talk about anything other than the crime, that you'd develop a bond and learn more from them.

"Darren and I would often discuss and compare Native American cultures and myths, looking for patterns," Angela said.

"Did you find any?" Gray asked.

"There are parallels. Both the Maya and many of the Native American tribes lived in caves during the same period."

"Dr. Kingman, I think it would be natural for people to want to find a protected shelter from the elements and other threats," Gray said.

"True, but it's the level of sophistication the ancient cultures achieved to dwell there, and how big a role the caves played in their religions. For example, the Mayan were polytheistic, worshipping over two hundred and fifty deities. One Mayan cave system contains eleven temples which are connected by well-constructed stone roads. Similarly, most Native American tribes, including the Lakota, are polytheistic in their spiritual beliefs. The Mayan also had a feathered serpent in their myths, while the Lakota had Wakinyan."

"If Darren found something in the Black Hills that would confirm his theory, it would be historic to say the least," Gray said. "Which could be a motive for him being killed. Who else in your academic field knew about Darren's theory?"

"No one that I'm aware of. Like I said earlier, Darren kept things secret while he worked on his projects."

"Is it possible he reached out to someone other than you while doing his research?"

"Certainly, but I don't know of anyone."

Gray picked up the journal and went to wrap the straps around it, when the wooden ball at the end slipped from his hand and struck the table hard, making a hollow wooden sound. The ball separated from the leather strap and rolled onto the floor. "Oh, I am sorry."

He reached under the table and as he rose, he noticed the end of the ball was ajar and a piece of white paper was rolled up inside. "Well, this is interesting. Dr. Kingman, did you know this came apart?"

"No."

"There's a piece of paper inside."

"Let me see," Angela said.

As she examined it, Gray glanced at his watch, then said, "Sarah, when do we need to be in Rapid City?"

"I haven't received a confirmation callback yet. I'll check when we're done here."

"Agent Holt, do you have a pair of tweezers or a paper clip?" Angela asked. "I can't get a grip on the paper."

Gray looked around and Sarah handed him a paper clip. "Let me see it," Gray said.

He worked the paper clip around in the hole until a sliver reached the edge, and then he pulled it out and slowly unfurled it. It was a larger piece of paper than he thought could have fit in the small ball.

"What does it say?" Sarah asked, with excitement.

"It doesn't really say anything," Gray replied. "It's just a bunch of strange-looking marks and symbols in and around a flat hourglass symbol."

"May I?" Angela said, leaning across the table.

Gray handed her the paper, and asked, "Is that Darren's handwriting?"

"Yes, but this is strange." Angela paused. "The triangular hourglass symbol is a Kapemni. It represents the relationship among the stars, the sun, and the Earth. The center where the lines cross represents the connection between them. This is a powerful symbol in the Lakota culture. Translated, it means 'twisting,' which is how the Lakota viewed the stars. They even used it hundreds of years ago to map the stars in order to locate places on the ground."

"It's a map?" Gray asked.

"It can be used as a map. They didn't have grids or coordinates back then, but they used it to know when to move the tribe to different hunting grounds, and it was used to locate sacred sites."

"How?"

"The position of the stars and the sun moves in relation to the Earth's shifting axis. They tracked the movement and used reference points on the ground to guide them. Think of it as a sextant."

"Is there anything else that's special about the symbol?" Gray asked.

"The upper triangle represents the stars and sun, or the spirit world. The bottom is the Earth or the physical world. This symbol can be found on Lakota tepees, in their art, and as a focal point for religious reasons. It is depicted as a two-dimensional figure on paper, rocks, and clothing, but it's really two three-dimensional cones that are connected. Tepees are fashioned after the lower cone."

"That's something I haven't heard before," Sarah said.

"The Lakota believe that Black Elk Peak in the center of the Black Hills is where the Earth's heart is located. They used this symbol to find it."

"Did they use other types of maps?" Sarah asked.

"Yes. My understanding is that there are star maps that are held sacred and kept secret from all but a few Lakota. Makawee told me that the star maps and the Paha Sapa have been protected for thousands of years."

"What's the Paha Sapa?" Gray asked.

"The Black Hills, which are considered sacred land."

"What about the other symbols—lines and dots around the outside and inside of the Kapemni?" Gray asked. "Some of those markings look like cuneiform."

Angela sat in silence for a few minutes as she examined the paper, turning it in different directions. Then she put the paper down and said, "I think Darren left this behind in case anything happened to him."

"Why do you think that?" Sarah asked.

"Darren was adamant that I stay at the motel the morning he disappeared. I knew something wasn't right."

"Do you know what any of these symbols mean?" Gray asked.

"Yes. I have a background in ancient languages. As you suspected, some of them are cuneiform. The dots and horizontal lines are Mayan. They represent numbers."

"Why would he use both types of symbols to write numbers?"

"I don't know, but Darren may have left this behind because he knew that I'd be able to decipher the message if anything happened to him." Angela paused for a moment, her grief overwhelming her again. "I'm sorry."

"We understand," Gray said. "What are the numbers?"

"I need a notepad," Angela said, wiping a tear from her cheek.

Sarah gave her the one she'd been using.

"I'll start with the numbers on the outside first and then interpret the inside, moving from the top left to the right and then down. Both languages are read left to right. The shell symbol means zero in Mayan, and the double challis-looking mark is a placeholder for zero in Sumerian. The Sumerians didn't use zero in their math as a value, but the Mayans did."

"I counted twenty characters," Gray said.

"Yes. Give me a moment." Angela scribbled numbers on the pad as she checked each symbol. "There are actually seventeen numbers, two space holders, and I don't know what this bar means. Mayan numerology five-count bars are written horizontally like these. This bar is vertical. It could mean any number of things. What I find interesting is that two of the placeholders have a line through them, which would mean 'not zero,' but that doesn't make sense."

"Could Darren have been using set theory to indicate those two placeholders meant something other than zero?" Gray asked.

"Possibly." Angela paused. "I wonder if they're decimal points."

"May I take a look?" Gray took the pad and wrote the numbers Angela had deciphered and added decimals. "It reads 43.921024, then the vertical bar, followed by 104.054510." He paused for a moment as he realized what they could mean. "I think these are latitude and longitude coordinates. Sarah, can you see if there's a map around here?"

"I don't need to. Those numbers are close to here. Devils Tower is at 44.59 north and 104.71west." Sarah took the pad from Gray and typed the coordinates into the GPS application on her cell phone. "It looks like it's on the Wyoming and South Dakota border in Weston County." She turned her phone around.

Gray looked at the satellite image of the area. "Remote, and it looks like those coordinates are surrounded by ravines. Good place for a cave."

"Yes, it would be," Sarah said. "It's also the area where the three other employees from Universal Mining went missing."

"This can't be a coincidence." Gray turned and asked, "Dr. Kingman, do you know this area?"

"No. I've not been in that particular part of the Black Hills."

"Sarah, we need to check this area."

Sarah said, "Crawley and Clay are near there."

"Let me call Crawley and see if he wants us to go to Rapid City, or if he'd prefer that we join him for a nature hike."

National Geospatial-Intelligence Agency Building – 1100 hours EDT

Aki and Chase drove along GEOINT Drive toward two nine-story glass-and-steel buildings.

"Have you ever been here before?" Aki asked.

"No. I've only driven by it."

"It's a spectacular work of architecture."

"I'd say. According to the info packet, the NGA Campus East, or NCE, is the third largest facility in the DC area and is the eastern headquarters for the National Geospatial-Intelligence Agency. A five-hundred-foot-long, eight-story atrium separates the north and south towers. Did you know that over eight thousand people work at the NCE?"

"Fascinating—you'll make a great tour guide," Aki teased.

They stopped at the checkpoint, showed their ID's and parking permit, and were directed to the third floor of the parking garage.

"It's nice that we have a spot in the garage," Chase said.

"We actually have six reserved spaces." Aki pulled in and parked, then said, "Let's use the main entrance. I believe that you'll want to pass under the circular 'eye' in the main lobby."

They cleared security and walked through the lobby toward the bank of elevators.

"This is probably the nicest office building I've ever seen," Chase said.

"We're on the fourth floor of the south tower. I believe we go this way."

They found their office and used a passkey to enter. Aki noted there was also an additional Bioscan entry option. "We'll need to get that activated," Aki said.

She was stunned by the size of the office area and the view from the windows that looked out over a reflection pond. Aki went to the floor-to-ceiling, bullet-resistant glass window and gazed out on the creek and concrete spillover that abutted the building. "Amazing. I could get used to this."

"Maybe we should cause problems more often," Chase jested.

There were five offices and a conference room behind a reception partition. Three of the offices were on one side of an open space and faced the other two offices and conference room.

Aki looked in the conference room and observed a long table with eight chairs. Eight monitor screens were mounted on the wall, four on each side. "That should be enough space for our meetings."

"And then some," Chase added, sticking his head through the door.

All of the offices were spacious, with high-quality furniture, and every desk was equipped with tri-monitor computer screens.

"Chase, which office do you want?"

"I'll take one with a view," Chase quickly said. "I've always wanted a window."

"Then I'll take the other outside office. Let's put our intelligence-and-threat-assessment analyst next to me. The counterterrorism specialist and the electronics intercept officer will be on your side. The executive support assistant will occupy the reception desk."

"I suppose if we need additional people, we can use the conference room, or we can get the director to pull some strings and get us more space."

"I don't think we're going to need that for a while. Let's see if we're linked to the intelligence community."

Thirty minutes later, they had logged into their systems, changed their passwords, and secured a connection to DHS with access to all of their files.

"I need a cup of tea," Chase said. "I saw a Starbucks sign on the first floor. I think I'll go explore. Do you want to join me?"

"No. Remember, we're hiding in plain sight."

"I know."

"I need to find someone who can activate the Bioscan access system and let the director know that we've settled in. We're going to need access to HR files so we can start looking for our teammates. I have someone in mind to fill the threat-assessment analyst spot, but I need to call her and see if she'd even be interested."

"Who is it?" Chase asked.

"Sharon Madison."

"I don't know if she'll want to give up her position with CETC. I understand that she may be getting promoted to a supervisory position in a few months."

"Possibly, but her work at the Current and Emerging Threats Center is being underutilized and I think she's ready for a change," Aki said. "Her analysis is always spot-on and from what I've heard, she wants to become more involved in operational activities. Working with us, she can do what she does best, and be more engaged."

"I think that she'd be a good fit. I'll head down while you make your calls. Can I bring you back a bagel and a cup of coffee?"

"That sounds good. Thanks."

CHAPTER NINE

Mark Santos had just finished a lengthy discussion with Noel Ketterhorn. In addition to other business matters, he'd related his reporting Tucker and Tyra missing to local law enforcement agencies and that he'd spoken with both of his senator friends, who had assured him that they would get the FBI involved.

In addition, he'd told Ketterhorn about NPS Ranger Sarah Goodson wanting to meet with him and Ketterhorn had recommended that he take the meeting. Ketterhorn had also said that he was having second thoughts about hiring Marcu's problem solver. Santos had agreed and hoped at least that troubling concern would go away.

After speaking to Ketterhorn, Santos stretched, then dialed Ranger Goodson's number.

"Goodson," Sarah answered.

"Good morning. This is Mark Santos. I'm the president and CEO of Black Hills Gold Mining. I understand you wish to speak to me."

"Yes, thank you for returning my call. My partner and I need to meet you to discuss Mr. Tanner's homicide. We were planning to drive up today."

"I can't meet you today," Santos said. "How exactly is the National Park Service involved in the investigation?"

"The NPS has assigned me to work with a Wyoming DCI task force on the investigation, since I was one of the investigators who found Mr. Tanner.

We're also investigating another homicide that may be related and we're looking for the three missing employees from Universal Mining."

"I see. What about the other two employees who I just reported missing?"

"What other employees?" Sarah replied.

Santos told her about Tucker Ryan and Tyra Stathopoulos, and added, "I hope that we can keep this from going public until the case is solved and the missing employees are found."

"I'm certain that while the investigation is active, it won't be made public. I'll need everything you have on the other missing employees forwarded to me as soon as possible, including photos."

"I'll see that they are sent," Santos said.

Sarah provided her email address, then said, "Do you know exactly where they were working?"

"I'll have their last-known GPS coordinates sent to you as well. Their trackers went dark, just like the others." He needed to emphasize the urgency of the investigation. "Ranger Goodson, I've spoken to my two senators and they are expecting this horrible business to be resolved quickly. They're requesting the FBI get involved. Would my contacting the Wyoming governor and your state senators help get your task force additional resources?"

"The Wyoming governor is already aware of the situation, which is why the task force was formed. Once I receive the coordinates, I'll contact Forestry and have them begin an aerial search of the area."

"Excellent," Santos replied. "Was the other victim from another mining company?"

"I can't provide any details while it's under investigation. Mr. Santos, how often do the GPS trackers transmit?"

"It depends on how they are set. They can ping every thirty minutes to once every six hours."

"What are all of your people doing in the Black Hills?"

"Ranger Goodson, we're in the mining business. What do you think they were doing there?"

Sarah didn't respond to the barb, but asked, "Is there a direct number where I can reach you? I'll need to schedule a meeting and it may be on short notice."

"Just call the main number and they will connect you. Where can I reach you?"

"It's the number you called."

"Please keep me updated on any developments," Santos said.

After he disconnected, Santos instructed his assistant to forward all of the information they had on the missing employees to Ranger Goodson and gave her the contact information. Then he called Ketterhorn and gave him an update.

Crook County SO – May 22 – 1110 hours MDT

Sarah walked back into the interview room, sat down next to Angela, and dropped three deli sandwiches on the table. "What did Crawley have to say?" Sarah asked Gray.

"He wants us to meet them at the Weston County Sheriff's Office," Gray replied. "He thinks we should check out the area around the coordinates. I hope you didn't make an appointment with anyone at BHGM, because we've been ordered to get down there 'ASAP!' Crawley requested that Dr. Kingman join us, and she's agreed. Where'd you get the sandwiches?"

"From Fred's Deli," Sarah replied. "I thought you all might be hungry. I know that I am."

"What did you get us?"

"Roast beef on whole wheat with mustard. I hope that's okay. Dr. Kingman, you're not a vegetarian, are you?"

"No," she replied.

"I spoke to Mark Santos, the CEO of BHGM, and he said that he couldn't meet today anyway. He also told me that two more employees have gone missing in the same area."

"Two more people!" Angela exclaimed. "What did Darren stumble into?"

Gray asked, "What did Santos tell you about them?"

Sarah opened her sandwich, took a bite, and motioned for the others to start eating.

While Sarah told them what she knew between bites, her phone beeped. "It looks like the information on the two missing people has arrived." She opened the email on her phone and noted several attachments. "Santos has also provided the GPS coordinates up until they stopped transmitting. It shows the location fixes were set at six-hour intervals. We'll have to figure out where these are exactly. He also sent contact numbers for Noel Ketterhorn, the CEO at Universal Mining, and William Ossa from Pelion Mining. Oh, and he made a point of telling me that he's already contacted both of South Dakota's U.S. senators, who will be contacting the FBI. He asked to be kept informed of any developments."

"Big money brings influence," Gray said. "We really need to avoid a media circus."

Sarah nodded in agreement. "I don't think that will be an issue. Santos made it clear that he doesn't want this going public."

"I wonder why?" Angela said. "I would think that they'd want as many eyes as possible looking for these people."

"Sarah, didn't they delay reporting the first group of missing employees?" Gray asked.

"That's my understanding," Sarah replied. "Maybe they didn't want people knowing where they were looking for gold or other deposits."

"What else did he send?" Gray asked.

"Looks like personnel files." She opened the first file. "Tucker Ryan, thirty-two, is a ten-year employee. He's an exploration manager, a geologist and chemist." She opened Tyra's file. "She's twenty-seven, Greek, and has worked for Pelion for three years. I guess that's why he sent the contact information on Ossa. She's a geologist." She turned the cell around so Gray and Kingman could see their pictures.

"Pretty girl," Angela said.

"You said that the GPS tracker transmitted a location once every six hours?" Gray asked.

"Yes." Sarah scrolled through the information. "Interesting."

"You do realize that we don't know what you're looking at, right?" Gray said.

"Sorry. Okay, Tucker's and Tyra's units went offline at the same time two days ago, close to the coordinates that Darren hid in the journal. It looks like they turned the trackers on at a campground in Pennington County,

South Dakota, about three miles northeast of their last-known location, and then spent some time working in the area before they disappeared."

"All of the evidence points to those coordinates as the center of activity," Gray said.

"Yes, it does," Sarah replied. "It appears that Lt. White Owl is our point of contact at the Custer Sheriff's Office. Neither the Pennington County Sheriff's Office nor the Rapid City PD have assigned anyone yet."

"Probably because none of the victims were found there. Sarah, do you know anyone at Pennington County SO?"

"Not really."

"Call Lt. White Owl and make sure he has the new information. Maybe he can run by the campground and check on the cars. Also, give him the coordinates of where we are going to be searching. Why did Santos wait to report these people missing until today?"

"That's a follow-up question we'll need to ask him." She scrolled further. "I need to contact Forestry with the new info for their aerial search. Gray, it's too bad you haven't been checked out in the helicopter yet. You could fly us over the area."

"That would have been helpful. I need to call Crawley and brief him on the new information."

Angela asked, "Why would the GPS trackers stop working at the same time?"

"I don't know," Sarah replied. "Gray, you may as well give Crawley their vehicle descriptions while you're at it. I'll send you all of the files."

"How long a drive is it to Newcastle?" Gray asked.

"About an hour. Dr. Kingman, are you going to ride with us?"

"Yes. Is it alright to leave my car here?"

"Shouldn't be a problem," Sarah replied. "We'll tell the sergeant that you're going with us."

"Dr. Kingman, we may be down in Newcastle for a while," Gray said. "Are you sure that you don't want to follow us?"

"I'm sure. I'll go where you go. Unless there isn't room."

"My truck is an extended cab, so you'll have room," Sarah said. "I'll just need to put some things in the back."

"I hope I can be of some help," Angela said.

Kingman's resolve had hardened over the last hour. Sarah believed that she seemed genuinely interested in helping them.

"I may as well send Crawley all of the files," Gray said. "He isn't going to be happy that we haven't left yet."

"He doesn't seem like a happy person anyway," Angela replied.

"No, he's not usually," Sarah said. "I'll go get the truck ready."

Angela listened to Gray's conversation with Crawley. It was obvious that Crawley was giving him a hard time.

"If you're done, we need to get a move on," Gray said after the call. "Do you need to change your clothes?"

"I'm good. I'll grab my hiking boots and field pack from the car on the way out in case we have an extended stay. I'm prepared for any event and enjoy camping in the woods."

"You're sure you're up for this?" Gray asked.

"Don't worry about me. I'll be fine. I think helping you find Darren's killer will be better than sitting in a motel room or at home."

When they reached the lobby, Sarah said, "I gave Forestry the GPS coordinates. We should get there about the same time their chopper arrives. I have their radio channels, so we can communicate with them."

"Dr. Kingman needs to grab her field pack before we leave," Gray said.

"I think we can dispense with the formalities," Angela said. "Please call me Angela."

"Angela, it is. Call me Gray."

"Sarah's fine by me. I also think we need to stop and pick up some extra food, water, and camping gear just in case this turns into a protracted search. I'm certain Crawley and Clay aren't prepared for an overnight excursion."

A few minutes later, they climbed into Sarah's truck and headed south.

GEOINT Building – May 22 – 1330 hours EDT

Aki and Chase had selected their team members quickly. Sharon Madison had accepted the threat assessment-and-analyst position as Aki had expected, and she would report tomorrow.

Brian McFee was a preeminent electronic intercept specialist and cryptologist who had also jumped at the chance to work with them. Aki had worked with him on several assignments over the years and knew his background. After Brian had separated from the Air Force, he'd landed a job at NSA, and worked there for a few years before coming to Homeland. Officially, he'd left the NSA for personal reasons, but Aki knew the real reason was because he'd made the NSA's politically well-connected rising stars and their supervisors look foolish too many times, and his advancement opportunities had become nonexistent.

Brian was incredibly intelligent and had a tendency to speak his mind, which wasn't a good fit at NSA. He had a number of colleagues who appreciated his candor. Brian had a network of contacts throughout the intelligence community and Aki figured that those connections would allow him to pull intel from other agencies before the official information was filtered and passed along.

Omar David would be their counterterrorism specialist. He was former CIA and spent two years working there until the CIA learned that his uncle was an operative in the Israeli Kidon. The Kidon was a specialized unit within the Mossad that was responsible for conducting assassinations. Omar didn't disclose his uncle's affiliation with Mossad because he hadn't been aware of it, but that hadn't mattered. The CIA felt that Omar was a security risk even though he'd been subjected to numerous polygraphs and had passed them all. The problem was that the rumors and innuendo had spread through his department, and his loyalty and integrity were being questioned. Omar had sought employment at DHS, with full disclosure about his uncle, and had come to Director Canton's attention. In considering Omar's degree in homeland security and solid track record at the CIA, Canton told Aki that she felt the connection with Mossad was an asset. Aki agreed with Canton's assessment. She'd attended a number of Omar's briefings over the last six months and Aki liked his direct and professional manner, his work ethic, and his attitude toward mission accomplishment.

The executive assistant position was to be filled by Traci Long, at Chase's insistence. Traci had been with DHS for two years and she was more than qualified. She spoke Spanish, French, and Italian, was a graduate of the Elliot School of International Affairs at George Washington University, and had exemplary reviews. Aki liked what she saw when they interviewed her by video chat, but she needed to address a concern with Chase before she made an official offer.

"Chase," Aki said. "Sharon starts tomorrow. Omar and Brian will start the following day."

"That's great news. What about Traci?"

Aki spoke in a serious tone. "Chase, as your boss, I have to ask you a question about Traci."

"Okay."

"You told me that Traci has a great work ethic and is well-educated and intelligent, which she appears to be, but are those the only reasons you thought she'd be an asset to the team? There were other candidates that had more time with DHS and were just as qualified."

"She's a nice person and will work well with us."

"You know what I'm asking, so don't play dumb."

"I must confess, I was attracted to her at one time," Chase admitted. "We went out a few times, but she's involved with someone now and I think it's pretty serious. Our relationship will be purely professional."

"I don't need any office drama."

"It won't be a problem," Chase assured her.

Aki decided to let it drop. "Okay. I'll offer her the position."

"Great."

"Chase, I want Sharon working to find Dar first thing tomorrow, before any other projects find their way onto our agenda. When she contacts the SPAP counterterrorism unit in Poland, make sure she tells them that she's doing a follow-up review for the Current and Emerging Threats Center. Remember, we've gone dark and we aren't to be mentioned by name."

"I'll see to it," Chase said.

CHAPTER TEN

Newcastle – May 22 – 1330 MDT

Sarah pulled into the nearly empty rear parking lot of the Weston County Law Enforcement Center and parked beside Crawley's Tahoe.

"Looks like a quiet little town," Gray said.

"It is," Sarah said. "Here comes Crawley."

"He looks angry," Angela observed.

"Yes, he does," Sarah replied. "But his bark is worse than his bite. Don't let him get to you."

Gray had just walked around the rear of Sarah's truck when Crawley bellowed, "About damn time."

"We got here as soon as we could," Gray said. "We stopped to pick up camping gear, figuring we might have to spend the night in the woods."

Crawley huffed, then said, "It just might be an overnighter. Did you bring supplies and gear for us?"

"We did," Gray replied.

"Good. Is that Dr. Kingman in the truck?"

"Yes," Sarah answered as she joined them.

"Did you have a chance to look at the mining company vehicles?" Gray asked Crawley.

"We did. They're in an unsecured impound lot south of town. Deputy Gurley and I went through them. Nothing of evidentiary value. No notebooks or maps. All three vehicles are registered to Universal Mining, which we already knew. I called Universal while I was waiting and told them where they could retrieve them. Sheriff Lyons agreed that there wasn't any reason to hold them any longer."

"You don't think that we should have forensics process them?" Gray asked.

"Sheriff Lyons had his people do that already. They found nothing of interest."

"How are we going to get into the search area?" Sarah asked.

"Sheriff Lyons suggested that we take Beaver Creek Road north past the cutoff. The coordinates you gave me put our target area about seven to eight miles north of here and about two miles east of the road. Lyons told me that we'll have to cross some private property, but he assured me no one will even notice us. I asked him not to tell anyone what we were doing up there."

"How close can we get to the coordinates by vehicle?" Gray asked.

"Well, we have two options," Crawley began. "We can go in on the South Dakota side and follow Summit Spring Road, which would get us to less than a mile from the coordinates. But it's a rough trek through heavy foliage and trees, and a longer drive. Or we can take Beaver Creek like Lyons recommended, staying in Wyoming up to an old fire trail that's across from the Martin Thompson Reservoir. That'll get us to within about a mile of the coordinates and the terrain looks a lot easier to negotiate, although it'll be a steep climb, so I say we stay in Wyoming and come in from the north."

"I'll call Lt. White Owl and let him know," Sarah said. "He can cover Summit Spring Road on the east side. Maybe he'll have an update on the other missing cars. How soon will we be in the area?"

"We should be there in about forty-five minutes," Crawley replied. "Just one thing that you need to work out with him. We may end up in Pennington County in South Dakota. Make sure he's still okay with working with us there."

"Will do."

"Gray, where is Dr. Kingman going to stay while we go on our nature hike?" Crawley asked.

"She wants to stay with us."

"That's fine, just tell her to keep her mouth shut. By the way, nice work on the interview. I figured you'd get more information out of her using some sweet talk after I opened the door with the stick. Deputy Gurley, I have a special assignment for you."

"Yes, sir."

"I want you to babysit Dr. Kingman on our walk in the woods. Make sure she doesn't get in my way."

"Yes, sir."

"Lt. White Owl will meet us out at the location in a little over an hour," Sarah said, clipping her cell phone back on her belt. "He wanted to know why we were looking out here, so I told him about the coded message. He's going to contact Pennington SO and see if they want to send a deputy."

"Good," Crawley replied. "Something else that may be of interest. Sheriff Lyons said that some of the folks that live up that way have mentioned seeing strange lights at night near the area where we're headed. We need to be alert. There could be a drug-grow operation up there. Which means boobytraps."

"Have they had drug problems in the area?" Gray asked Crawley.

"None have been reported, but there's always a first time. Gray, I want you to take my shotgun and load it with slugs. We might run into bears."

"Bears?" Gray asked.

"Yes. Bears. They live in the woods."

"Is Sheriff Lyons going to give us any support?" Gray asked.

"He can't spare the deputies right now," Crawley replied. "They have some big event at the fairgrounds for the next three days. If we find something, I'll call him. Deputy Gurley, you're with me. We'll lead the way. Let's get going."

Sarah and Gray got back in the truck. Crawley drove out of the parking lot, kicking up a cloud of dust. Sarah had to punch it to catch up with them.

"Where are they going in such a hurry?" Angela asked.

Gray turned to her and said, "The same place we are. We should be about a mile from the coordinates when we stop."

"The downside is that we'll be at over six thousand feet in elevation and the walk is uphill," Sarah said.

"An easy hike," Angela said. "I was expecting it to be further away from a road."

"So was I," Gray said. "There's a fire trail that runs off the main road that will provide us access to the area. Lt. White Owl from Custer SO is going to come in from the South Dakota side. I believe that you spoke to him."

"I did."

"Angela, two more things," Gray began. "First, stay out of Crawley's way. He's assigned Clay to be your escort. Second, if we encounter hostiles, you stick close to Clay and don't run off into the woods on your own. If there's gunfire, find a tree to hide behind."

"I don't believe I saw those warnings in the brochure," Angela joked. "Don't worry about me. I've been in some real shithole areas before."

When they passed a sand-and-gravel company entrance off Beaver Creek Road, Sarah pointed and said, "Angela, that's where three of the missing mining employees' vehicles were left."

"Seems like a long way from Darren's coordinates," Angela said.

"It's about six miles away," Gray said. "The coordinates may not be relevant to their disappearance. In fact, Darren might not have disappeared from there either."

"The terrain looks rugged to the east," Angela said. "Lots of trees, ravines, and rocky hills."

"It's a place you can get lost in," Sarah said.

A few minutes later, Crawley radioed, "The reservoir and turnoff are just ahead. I don't see the helicopter anywhere."

"I'll check," Sarah replied.

Sarah was unable to raise anyone on the Forestry radio channel, so she called the main number on her cell and after a brief conversation said, "Well, that sucks. We aren't getting any air support." She picked up her radio and said, "Agent Crawley, our air support isn't going to make it today."

"Not surprising," Crawley responded. "Here's our cutoff." He made a sudden turn onto a bumpy dirt trail.

"This isn't much of a road," Gray muttered as he bounced around in his seat.

"It's a fire trail," Sarah said. "Good thing we have the truck."

The trail wound through dense forest, and Gray noticed that they'd been gradually going uphill for the last few minutes. Crawley's brake lights lit up and he pulled onto a flat grassy area.

"It appears that we're here," Gray said, relieved that the jarring ride had ended.

After Sarah parked behind Crawley, Gray got out, stepped into the high grass, and looked around. The hike was going to be up a steep slope through a dense wooded area.

"Well, that doesn't look very inviting," Gray said.

Angela walked up beside him and said, "I've seen worse."

Sarah yelled, "Hey, Agent Crawley, do you want us to unload everything?"

"May as well. It'll save us a hike back."

"Even the solar panels? They're bulky."

"Then leave them." Crawley opened the liftgate, took off his black sport coat, and pulled out a brown soft rifle case. "Gray, this is yours."

Gray went to the Tahoe and unzipped the case. Inside was a Mossberg 590 tactical shotgun. Two boxes of shells were in the side pouch, all slugs. He worked the pump-action, and a round flew out.

"Didn't I tell you it was loaded?" Crawley said.

"No." Gray picked up the shell and reloaded it into the eight-round extended magazine, then put a box of shells in his new pack.

"You aren't taking the case?" Crawley said.

"If we need it, I won't have time to get it out," Gray replied.

Crawley smiled. "Suit yourself, but you'll need to clean it when we get back." He turned to Sarah and said, "Ranger Goodson, you'll take the lead and blaze us a trail. I'll follow you, then Gray, Dr. Kingman, and Deputy Gurley. I want us to stay in single file just in case there are any surprises. Gather up your gear and let's get going."

"What kind of surprises?" Angela asked.

Crawley stared at her for a moment, then looked at Gray. "Explain it to her. There'll be no talking as we approach the area unless there's a threat or you see something of importance. Got it?"

Everyone nodded.

"Angela, drug dealers set up grow operations in desolate locations," Gray said. "They're known to set boobytraps to discourage people from trespassing."

"Again, not in the brochure. I'll just follow you."

Sarah said, "The GPS app on my cell is okay for now. Cell reception is poor and it will only get worse as we move into the woods. I've reconfigured the app so if the cell service dies, we still have navigation capability. I've also taken a compass reading and identified some landmarks as best I can in case the battery dies."

"That's why I have you taking point," Crawley said. "You have all that ranger survival training."

"It looks like we have about a quarter mile of dense woods, followed by a rock-strewn brushy area for another quarter mile while going uphill, then back into the woods," Sarah said. "It gets really dense as we approach the site. Watch out for prairie rattlesnakes in case I miss seeing one."

"Won't we hear them rattle?" Angela asked.

"Not always. Sometimes they strike, then rattle, and sometimes they just strike. The good news is that it's the only venomous snake out here and there aren't that many of them. We just need to leave them alone. Follow me."

Gray slung the shotgun over his shoulder and adjusted the straps to his pack. He checked on Angela and saw that she looked comfortable with her field pack. He noticed that Clay was trying to get his pack situated. He was carrying the most weight—Crawley had made him the water bearer. "Deputy, if that water gets too heavy on the climb, I'll spell you," Gray said.

"Thanks. It's not that bad. I left some water behind in the truck. If we need it, I'll hike back and get it."

"Let's go," Crawley ordered.

They moved deeper into the woods, which were densly covered with ponderosa pine. Gray noted that saplings seemed to be everywhere, creating additional obstructions and making it hard to remain quiet. He caught the scent of butterscotch and vanilla that emanated from the pinesap seeping from the reddish bark. The ground was covered in common juniper, and the slender stems and light-pink flowers of mountain ninebark and other shrubs seemed to be everywhere. This was going to be a tough hike, but it appeared that Sarah was finding the easiest route.

Twenty minutes later, they walked out of the woods and continued their climb across the rocky hillside. There wasn't an easy path to take.

Small stones shifted and rolled down the hill announcing their presence. Up ahead was another line of ponderosa pines and bur oaks.

When they reached the edge of the tree line, Crawley said, "Let's take a break." He took off his cowboy hat and wiped the sweat from his balding head with his sleeve.

Gray knew Crawley had underestimated the hike. Crawley was only five foot ten and weighed well over two hundred pounds. It was obvious that he didn't exercise regularly and wasn't in condition for moving through this type of terrain. Angela didn't even look winded, and Sarah had disappeared into the shadows of the trees up ahead.

Gray moved back to where Clay was standing and asked quietly, "Do you want me to take some of that weight?"

"Nope, I'm good. But thanks for the offer."

When Sarah returned, she motioned for everyone to huddle up, then whispered, "There's what looks like an old trail that leads in the direction we're headed. It doesn't look like it's been used for a long time. The canopy is thicker, with less light. Crawley, I don't think there's any illegal plants being grown in there."

"That's good news."

"There's an open meadow that skirts the heavier woods to the north that would make for easier traveling, although the grade is steeper and it will be a longer hike. If we go that way, we'll still be about a hundred yards from the coordinates, and we'll need to work our way through some dense brush and trees. Either way will be difficult."

"Let me see the satellite image on your cell," Crawley directed, holding out his hand. He looked at the satellite map, then said, "Let's take the trail through the woods. That meadow looks like a good campsite if we need to stay. We can come back out that way."

"As you wish," Sarah said, turning and setting off.

After fifteen minutes of walking through the dense shrubs, Sarah raised her fist slowly and knelt. Gray saw that she was focused on something up ahead. He motioned for Clay and Angela to kneel. He glanced behind him and saw that Clay had drawn his Glock 21 and was scanning the trail behind them for any threats. Gray pulled the shotgun from his shoulder, moved slowly past Crawley, and knelt beside Sarah.

He didn't see or hear anything, but Sarah was definitely on alert. She pointed directly ahead and made a walking-man motion with her fingers. Gray nodded. Then he heard the snap of a twig and small rocks shifting. Someone was definitely ahead of them.

A radio crackled with static and Gray caught sight of a tan long-sleeve shirt with a sheriff's patch on the shoulder. Gray relaxed, then whispered, "I think Lt. White Owl beat us here."

"Lt. White Owl!" Sarah called.

"Yes."

"Stay where you are. We'll come to you."

When they met, Gray noted that Lt. White Owl was a formidable-looking man. He stood six feet and had a muscular build, with braided black hair and dark-brown eyes.

"Have you been here long?" Sarah asked, after she'd introduced everyone.

"I just arrived. It was one hell of trek through that dense brush."

"Any issue with you working with us?" Crawley asked.

"No. I spoke to Captain Cecelia Hunt at the Pennington County Sheriff's Office and she advised that they would send a deputy out if we found anything. She's aware of the other two missing mining employees and appreciated my help. My sheriff didn't have an issue with me working outside the county."

"Excellent," Crawley said.

"Dr. Kingman, I'm sorry to hear about Dr. Waters," White Owl offered.

"Thank you."

"Where did you all park?" White Owl asked.

"About a mile to the north."

"I'm parked up on the ridgeline to the east. I have to say that the first hundred feet coming down wasn't bad, then it turned into this crap." He pointed at the brush.

"Lt. White Owl, did you see anything that looked like someone had parked along the road recently?" Crawley asked.

"No. It doesn't look like anyone has been out this way for a long time."

Crawley looked around, then grumbled, "There's nothing here. I think we're wasting our time."

"Why don't we check the area anyway?" Gray said. "Dr. Waters didn't leave a hidden coded message pointing to this spot without a reason. There has to be something here."

"I agree," Angela said.

"We're here, we may as well search the area," Sarah urged.

"Alright," Crawley said. "Gray, where and how do you suggest we start?"

"Form up into two-person teams. I think Dr. Kingman can help us set up a search grid."

"I'd be happy to help," Angela said.

"Perfect," Crawley scoffed, shaking his head.

"Look for marks on the stones or on the trees or for anything that doesn't look like it belongs in nature or has been disturbed," Gray said. "Sarah, are we close enough to the coordinates?"

"We're right on them."

"Let's use this location as our datum point," Angela said. "We'll search in quadrants and mark the areas we clear. That way we don't miss anything."

"And how will we know that we've searched an area completely?" Crawley asked.

Angela put her pack on the ground and removed two rolls of string and several orange flags from a zippered pocket. "We'll use these as a guide. Normally, I'd have more with me on a dig, but we can still use the flags as bearing markers. We'll cut the string in twenty-five-foot lengths. That way there'll be less chance of it getting tangled. Let's try going out fifty feet at first. As thick as this foliage is, I'll lose sight of you after that."

"It sounds like you've done this before," Crawley said.

"A few times." Angela pulled out a notebook. "I'll sketch the area and map each segment as we go."

"I'll work with Lt. White Owl," Crawley announced. "Gray, you're with Ranger Goodson. Deputy Gurley stays with Dr. Kingman."

"How do you want us to start?" Sarah asked Angela.

"I'll use compass headings to map the X and Y axis of each quadrant. Sarah, you and Gray take a line and I'll guide your track. Start south, two abreast and an arm's length apart. When you reach twenty-five feet, put a flag in the ground, then move a few feet to the west and start back. Agent Crawley, you'll start where Sarah and Gray stop, go another twenty-five feet, then follow their line back." Angela planted a small flag in the ground and opened her compass, then took out a tape measure and cut two strings to length.

"Very thorough," Crawley said.

"Was that a compliment?" Angela asked.

"Just an observation."

They dropped their gear in a pile by the flag and Gray handed Clay the shotgun.

Angela pointed at a tree and said, "That tree is nearly due south. Use it as a guide. In the dense areas, just lay the string across the top of the brush."

Sarah said, "Let's go, partner."

"Slowly," Angela cautioned. "Like you're watching for a boobytrap or a snake. If Darren left any marks, they would be in chalk."

Gray walked up on Sarah's right. "Wouldn't chalk wash away in the rain?" he asked Angela.

"The chalk we use lasts a while."

The terrain was uneven, so going slow was the only way they could make headway. Gray couldn't believe just how many plants and different-colored rocks there were in the area. He used his boot to brush aside the bushes so he could look beneath them. "This is going to take a long time," he whispered to Sarah.

"Yup. It's a good thing we brought the camping gear."

Four hours later, they'd finished searching one hundred feet away from their datum point and had covered four of the eight quadrants, but nothing of interest had been found.

"I don't believe this area has ever been searched so thoroughly," Gray said. "I'm not sure anyone has ever been here before. I didn't even find a piece of trash."

"It's getting late," Crawley said, wiping the sweat from his brow with an old red bandana. "I really didn't think we'd find anything, but it was worth a shot."

"We still have the area to the north to search," Gray said.

"You really want to continue?" Crawley asked.

"Yes. We can camp and start early in the morning."

"Or, we could head back to Newcastle and stay at a motel."

"If we stay here, we might see or hear something," Gray said.

"I'm with Gray," Sarah said.

Crawley frowned. "Well, I'm filthy and need a shower. You can stay if you like. I'll be back in the morning. Deputy Gurley, you're riding with me. Dr. Kingman, what's your preference?"

"I'm with them." Angela answered.

"Suit yourself," Crawley said. "Is there anything you need me to bring back? More flags, rope or string?"

"If you can find some flags and string, that would be helpful," Angela replied.

"Are you sure you guys will be okay out here?" Clay asked. "You may want to have another set of eyes and some additional firepower just to be safe."

"I see where this is going," Crawley said. "Alright, you can stay. I'll leave the keys to my Tahoe with you just in case. Lt. White Owl, I'll need to ride with you."

"Certainly. Why don't you stay in Custer for the evening? I'll help you find the items you need at a hardware store in town, then we can grab a bite to eat."

"Thank you. I'll take you up on that." Crawley threw Clay his keys. "I assume you all will be camping in the meadow?"

"That looks like the best place," Gray replied.

"Lt. White Owl, we'll need to be back out here by nine," Crawley said.

"Not a problem," White Owl said.

"We should complete the grid search by noon tomorrow if we start early," Angela said. "If we don't find anything, we need to decide how we're going to expand the search."

"You mean if *I* decide to continue the search," Crawley corrected.

"Agent Crawley, I think we should continue the search even if we don't find anything tomorrow," Gray said. "These coordinates mean something. I'll be happy to stay another night if you need to get back to follow other leads."

Crawley nodded. "I appreciate the offer. Let's just see what we find tomorrow. Lt. White Owl, let's go."

Crawley and White Owl went up the slope and disappeared into the thick brush. Crawley's profane comments drifted down to them.

"I bet he wishes that he'd stayed with us," Sarah said. "Angela, do we just leave the flags for now?"

"Yes. If Crawley can't find any more, then we'll just use the ones marking the interior grids."

"Let's go set up camp," Gray said. "The sun's going to set soon."

Sarah said, "It should be a pretty night."

"Just to be on the safe side, we may want to set security watches," Clay suggested.

"That's a good idea," Gray acknowledged. "How about three-hour shifts? Sarah, you can take the first one. I'll take the second from one to four, and Clay, you have the last one."

"I can stand a watch," Angela said.

"I appreciate it, but I think Sarah, Clay and I can handle it."

"So, what's on the menu for dinner?" Clay asked.

"There's a delicious selection of Mountain House meals for you to choose from," Sarah said. "I like the beef stroganoff the best."

"Oh, yummy," Clay said.

CHAPTER ELEVEN

Dar drove from Poland to Brno, Czechia, changed cars and identities, stopped, then drove through Austria and Switzerland to her safe house in Nice, France. She'd avoided Germany, fearing that since she'd shot down a German police helicopter, crossing that border wouldn't be wise, even in disguise.

She discovered that the funds in her Luxembourg accounts had already been seized. It was a setback, but not crippling. Fortunately, she had other funds in numerous banks around the world, including Monaco, which was a short thirty-minute drive from her safe house.

Dar stared out of the large, bulletproof window of her home, which was atop a hill with a view of the city and the Mediterranean Sea. She'd purchased it long ago under another alias. The old two-story was surrounded by a six-foot concrete wall that was painted a light yellow to match the house. The wall followed the contour of the steep hill down the southern embankment to the abutting property which was owned by wealthy businessman, Laurent Bastin. As with all of her homes, it had a state-of-the-art security system. The only drawback with the location was the limited exit options. The Avenue de Fabron, a narrow two-lane road, offered the only way out by car, but she didn't plan to stay at the house for very long, and she doubted that anyone would find her, even Agent Dawson.

Dar caught movement by Laurent's pool. It appeared that he was entertaining a very attractive young lady who looked to be half his age. She shook her head as the young woman disrobed and jumped into the pool. *This may be entertaining*, she thought. Just then her laptop chimed an alert with a priority message.

Dar took one last look at Laurent's naked, handsome physique as he jumped into the pool, and then she went to check the message. She typed in the decryption code and connected to the secure server. It appeared that she wasn't going to have to wait very long for a new operation.

She smiled, seeing that Dragos Marcu had another job for her, and that as usual, it was time sensitive. Normally, she wouldn't work with the same client twice, but for some reason she trusted Marcu. Besides, she'd fleeced him out of ten million dollars to resolve a problem that hadn't required much effort. She'd just had to get her hands a little bloody and Marcu was pleased with the outcome. In light of her Luxemburg funds being seized, she could use the work, and she decided to make an exception providing the money was right.

Dar acknowledged receipt and provided a secure email address. Then she made a perfect vodka martini and went back to the window. It had been a long time since she'd been with someone. Vasil was the last man she'd loved and he had left her out in the cold. She'd persuaded him to help her disappear or she would have killed him.

A few minutes later, the alert chime sounded again. "That was fast," she muttered. She took a sip of her martini, walked to the table, and opened the new file on her laptop. It appeared that her services were needed in the United States. *Not my favorite place to work.* After reviewing the information, she decided to contact Marcu directly. She retrieved a clean cell phone that was equipped with a voice-masking app and dialed his number.

"*Yiasou*," Marcu answered in Greek.

"Speak in English or German," Dar commanded.

"Who is this?" Marcu responded in English. "And how did you get my private number?"

"This is your problem solver. I know how to reach people. Why did you answer in Greek?"

"I was expecting a call from an associate. I didn't think you made direct contact."

Dar thought he sounded arrogant. "I usually don't, but for you, I made an exception. Your message indicated the operation was time sensitive. There weren't sufficient details for me to make an assessment. Explain further."

Marcu told her what he knew about the missing people and the murders, and who was conducting the search and the investigations.

"No FBI involvement?"

"Not as of yet, although one of my business partners has requested their assistance."

"So, this is a rescue or recovery mission, and you need whoever is responsible to be eliminated."

"Yes, and nothing can be linked to me or my associates."

"Of course. I accept the assignment, if you agree to my fee."

"What will this cost us?" Marcu asked.

"From what you've explained, this will require a great deal of preparation and I will be operating in a hostile environment. I will also have to avoid American law enforcement while there." Dar paused, then said, "Twenty-five million euros. Twenty-five percent up-front and the rest upon completion. I will forward a new account number for the first wire transfer when you agree."

"Twenty-five million euros is a great deal of money."

"Take it or leave it. I do not negotiate," Dar said.

"I'll need to consult my associates before agreeing to your fee. How do I contact you?"

"You don't. I'll call you back in an hour. If you decide not to accept, never make another request." Dar disconnected and went back to watching Laurent and his young friend.

Exactly an hour and two martinis later, Dar called Marcu back.

"*Buna,*" he answered in Romanian.

"Well?" Dar said, in English.

"We accept. The funds will come from four different sources. I will cover the first twenty-five percent and coordinate the transfers from my associates later."

"I hope you explained to your associates what will happen if they don't pay."

"They are aware. They also have a condition."

Dar didn't like having anyone making demands. "What is it?"

"If any of the mining company employees are found alive, they need to be protected and returned to an associate in Rapid City prior to them speaking to law enforcement."

"The ones that went missing three weeks ago are dead."

"How would you know that?" Marcu asked.

"From experience. No one would hide and feed them for that long. Whoever took those employees will have gotten the information they wanted and disposed of them."

"Do you think that the last two to go missing are still alive?" Marcu asked.

"Maybe. If I find them, I'll take them to your associate in Rapid City. Unless those responsible are stupid, they won't be with the two employees. It'll take time to track them down regardless."

"Tyra Stathopoulos is the niece of one of my associates. She is a priority."

"That explains the Greek connection," Dar said. "Once I receive confirmation of your deposit, I'll make the necessary arrangements. Additional account-transfer information and instructions will follow."

"Should anything change, how do I contact you?"

"I'll include an email address that only I can access," Dar replied. "Do not give it to anyone and do not use any of your current electronic devices to send the information."

"I understand. My colleagues want to know when you will be in South Dakota."

"I'm not sure exactly. It's a long flight. Probably tomorrow evening."

"Like I said, time is critical. The sooner the better."

"Planes only travel so fast," Dar said. "Understand that this assignment will require some finesse to investigate, and I will need to engage local resources to assist me, possibly even law enforcement who are open to financial enticements. I don't know exactly how long that will take, so tell your associates that it will be done on my schedule."

"This needs to remain a covert operation. Local law-enforcement involvement may be risky."

"Everything I do is risky," Dar said. "If I need anything further, I will contact you. I expect the rest of my fee to be wired within twenty-four hours of notification that the assignment is complete."

"It will be done."

Dar disconnected, then removed the battery from the phone and tucked the phone in her pack. She'd dispose of it later.

Nice, France – May 22 - 2330 hours CEST

After Dar received confirmation that Marcu had deposited over six million euros in her Monaco account, she booked a charter flight on a G650ER long-range jet to Winnipeg, Canada. The aircraft had a top speed just below Mach one, which meant it would be a nine-hour flight. It was a beautiful aircraft capable of circumnavigating the earth with only one fuel stop and could carry fifteen passengers. On this trip, she'd be the only one aboard. The aircraft was far more luxurious than she required, but it fit her needs and time schedule.

Marcu had forwarded updates as requested and she felt that this assignment would be an interesting one. No group had claimed responsibility for the murders and abductions, but based on the number of people missing, she believed that there had to be more than one assailant involved.

Dar's flight was leaving in a few hours and she needed to get into disguise. To become Cora Zemanski, she needed to dye her hair and eyebrows blond, add some hair extensions, and wear blue contact lenses. High heels would give her some additional height and the darker outfit she planned to wear would slim her stocky build. It was a disguise that she'd used in the past when traveling through Canada. Her passport and driver's license photo would match her disguise, and all of her credit cards and other identification were in Cora Zemanski's name.

She'd obtained both a United States ATF permit and a Canadian permit to bring weapons into those countries months ago, and she was pleased to see that her permits were still valid. She planned to take a scoped Remington 700, which was a good hunting rifle and legal in France, and her favorite Glock 26 pistol. She had both of them stored in the gun safe in the basement, along with many other weapons, explosives, and poisons. Transporting firearms across borders was always tricky, but for this assignment she'd be legal. Obtaining weapons in the United States would not be difficult, but she preferred using ones that she'd used in the past.

She planned to rent a small plane in Winnipeg and fly across the border into the United States, landing at the secluded Peace Garden airport in North Dakota. The airport was only a few hundred yards from the border, had a small customs office, and only a few aircraft landed there daily. Her paperwork was in order and she didn't anticipate any problems going through customs, but in the remote chance that she needed to escape from the US authorities, she could easily disappear into the heavily wooded area just across the Canadian border. Dar had also rented a four-wheel-drive Jeep, which would be at the airport when she arrived.

Dar yawned and wondered if Agent Dawson would come after her if she was discovered entering the United States. Definitely. *This will make for an interesting game. I think I will leave her a clue.* "Let's see how good you really are," she said aloud.

Camp Site – 2200 hours

Gray and Sarah sat together by a small fire. Angela and Clay had settled on a blanket across from them.

"Beautiful night," Sarah said. "Gray, you may want to turn in and get some sleep."

"I will in a bit," Gray replied. "I'm enjoying looking at all of the stars. It's been a while since I actually camped."

"What about the RV?" Sarah asked.

"The RV doesn't really count as camping. Does anyone else have sore legs?"

Sarah snickered. "Going up and down rugged terrain will do that to you if you're not conditioned for it. And yes, mine are sore. I have some Tylenol in my pack."

"Thanks."

"It's incredibly quiet," Angela said. "Does that strike anyone as odd?"

"I hadn't thought about it," Sarah said. "But now that you mention it, yes, it does."

"I've camped around the world and there are always noises at night," Angela said. "A squirrel rustling through the trees, critters foraging or hunting. Since we entered the search area, I haven't even seen or heard an insect."

Gray sat forward and listened. "You're right. No birds or animal sounds at all."

"Okay, is this some kind of prank to freak me out?" Clay asked. "Because it's working."

Sarah stood and walked into the darkened field. When she returned, she said, "I could hear something moving in the woods toward where we parked, but there's nothing to the south of us. It is odd."

Gray stood and looked toward the search area. It was complete blackness beyond the first row of trees. "I think I'll take a short hike."

"I'll go with you," Sarah said. "You two stay here."

"You guys are really serious?" Clay asked.

"Yes, this is weird," Gray replied, picking up a flashlight. "I just want to check things out. Clay, I'll leave you the shotgun."

Clay nodded. "We'll stay put. If you need us, check in on channel three."

Sarah picked up the walkie and strapped it to her gun belt. "We won't be long."

Gray led the way into the thick woods. "Sarah, I'm going to leave the light off for a bit to let our eyes adjust. The campfire diminished my night vision."

"Same here. Let's just listen for a minute."

Gray stopped and scanned the total blackness ahead of him. The orange glow from the campfire behind him seemed to be getting brighter, which told him that his eyes were adjusting to the dark. "Let's move a little deeper in," he whispered.

They walked for another few minutes, trying not to make any noise. The darkness surrounding them was complete. Even the stars had disappeared from view under the heavy tree canopy. He listened to Sarah breathing as she walked slowly next to him, her silhouette a dark shadow. He took her hand and pulled her to a stop.

"What is it?" Sarah whispered.

"To our left, in the eleven o'clock position," Gray replied. "I see a faint blue glow through the trees above that rise."

"I see it now. Wait, it's gone."

"Mark our position and take a bearing with your GPS app. I'd say the glow was near the search area."

"Distance is hard to measure at night without a reference point." The GPS monitor illuminated when Sarah turned it on and she quickly covered the light with her hand. "You're right, the glow was coming from the center of our search area."

"Right where the coordinates said there was something."

"Do you want to check it out?" Sarah asked.

"I think we need to wait until daylight. We know that there's someone up there, and I don't think we have the firepower or the advantage to risk approaching now. We need to report this to Crawley."

"You are a cautious one," Sarah said. "We came out here to find something or someone. I think we should push on and see who's there."

Gray shook his head. "No. We need support."

"I'll call Clay on the radio."

"No. They'd never find us in the dark, and I don't want to risk giving our position away. Your GPS app lit us up pretty good already."

"Then let's go back and get Clay and Angela."

Gray sighed. "Let's just sit here and listen a minute and see what happens."

"Gray, what if someone else is about to be killed? We have to prevent it."

"Shhh. Look over there."

"Where?"

"Ten o'clock. It looks like a red light moving through the trees. It's headed toward where the blue light was glowing a moment ago."

"I see it. Red lens on a flashlight makes for better night vision. Someone is walking toward the source. We need to follow."

"The light isn't wobbling," Gray said. "It looks like it's floating." Just then the red light blinked out. A minute later, the blue glow reappeared for a moment and then went out again. "I didn't see any movement, just the lights. Very strange. Go ahead and radio Clay and let him know what we've seen."

Sarah attempted to raise him on the radio without success. "Comms are sketchy out here."

"I guess we should check it out, but be ready for anything."

They moved quickly and silently up the slope to where the light had been, but there was nothing there.

"Okay, this is very weird," Sarah said, after a few minutes of searching the area. "I know this is where we saw the light."

"I agree."

"I think we should head back down and get Clay and Angela to help us search the area," Sarah said.

Gray stayed still and listened for a moment, but there was no sound. "Alright, let's go."

"Angela, do you want something else to eat?" Clay asked. "I got the munchies."

"Probably because you know that you can't just go to the fridge and get what you want. I'm fine."

"It's bad enough that we don't have any beer, but—"

There was a thud and Angela felt a presence behind her, and then a hand covered her mouth and face. It felt like a large, powerful animal had clamped onto her. She managed to turn her head slightly and saw Clay on the ground holding his head, moaning in pain. She hadn't seen or heard her attacker, but she knew that there had to be a second one behind her because her attacker's grip never wavered as her hands were bound behind her. The rope chafed her skin as it was tightened. Then a cloth that smelled like a dead animal was placed over her mouth.

A man wearing buffalo hides bound Clay's hands and gagged him. He was lifted effortlessly from the ground. Someone else wearing hides walked in front of her. His face was covered. Only dark, soulless eyes peered out from the eye slits in the hide, and then for the briefest second, she caught the glint of a red reflection in his eyes. She glanced up and saw a red orb hovering above them, and then it disappeared. No words were spoken between the men.

She felt her feet leave the ground as she was thrown over the man's shoulder and carried away from the campsite. *This can't be happening. Is this how Darren died?*

It was unnatural, how fast they were moving across the rocky terrain and without making a sound. Her fear rose and she squirmed in the strong, vise-like grip. She managed to loosen the gag by rubbing her mouth against her shoulder. Then she screamed.

They were almost back to the campsite when Gray suddenly stopped at the tree line. He knelt and pulled Sarah down with him. He could see the fire, but he didn't see Clay or Angela.

"What's wrong with you?" Sarah asked.

"I got a bad feeling. Something isn't right. The shotgun is lying on the ground."

Angela's scream resonated through the trees.

"To our right," Gray said. "Move!"

They both ran along the tree line in the direction of the scream. Sarah stumbled and landed hard.

Gray stopped. "You alright?"

"Shit. No. I twisted my ankle. Go!"

Gray took off at a slower pace, using the trees as cover. The ground was becoming more uneven, and it was covered with loose rocks and boulders. Then he saw shadowy movement ahead. He stopped and drew his Glock. He crept closer and stooped behind a tree, took out his flashlight, and sighted on the figures with the Glock.

When he turned the flashlight on, it took him a moment to grasp what he was seeing. Clay and Angela were bound, and they were being held off the ground by three very tall and heavyset figures dressed in hides.

"Freeze!" he shouted. "Wyoming DCI."

The three subjects turned briefly, and then one of them pulled a rifle from his shoulder and fired at him several times. Gray returned fire and the subject went down, his rifle hitting the rocks with a clatter. Gray heard movement behind him and he rolled back to challenge the new threat. It was Sarah, limping toward him with her gun pointed at the subjects.

"You are all under arrest!" Sarah shouted. "Drop your weapons. Do it now!"

"Sarah, get down!" Gray ordered. He rolled and took aim on the subjects again.

Clay and Angela were tossed to the ground and the men disappeared into the darkness faster than Gray thought was humanly possible.

"Stay here," Gray said to Sarah. "I'm going after Clay and Angela." He moved quickly over the rocky terrain, stumbling a few times before reaching them. "Stay down," he ordered, seeing that they were trying to get to their knees.

Gray realized they were out in the open, but there was nothing he could do about it. He removed the cloth gags, pulled a knife from his pocket, and cut the ropes that were binding their hands. The ropes felt coarse, like a lasso. He tossed them to the ground to mark the location. He'd retrieve them later for comparison against the lassos that were found on the homicide victims.

"Can you both walk?" Gray asked.

"Yes-s-s," Clay stuttered weakly.

"I can walk," Angela replied.

"Then let's move back to Sarah's position."

As Clay stood, he swayed. Gray grabbed him before he fell.

"He was hit in the head," Angela advised.

"I gotcha, Clay," Gray said. "Sarah, cover us."

They walked slowly back to her, and then they all took cover in the trees.

Sarah shined her light on Clay and said, "You don't look so good."

"I don't feel so great either."

"Angela, let's have a look at you," Sarah said, shining a light on her.

"Clay, sit here." Gray directed him to a large rock. "Sarah, let's not light ourselves up again. They may come back."

"Right." Sarah turned her flashlight off.

"We need to get some support out here, including medical," Gray said. "I also need to protect the crime scene and the body of the one I killed. Sarah, see if you can reach Crawley or anyone else."

"Cell phones aren't working out here," Clay offered. "I tried earlier. I think we're too close to the ridge. Try the radio."

"I did when I tried to reach you," Sarah said. "I don't think we have the range to reach anyone with the walkies."

"I'll hike down to the truck and drive until I have service," Gray said. "Sarah, I don't like the idea of leaving you guys, but I don't think Clay or you are going to be up for a hike in the dark."

"Probably not," Clay said. "My head is swimming."

"Gray, I think it would be better if we all stayed together," Sarah said.

"Good point," Gray said. "But I want to see who we encountered. You guys stay put. Sarah, cover me."

"I'm not going anywhere," Clay muttered.

Gray walked cautiously back to where he'd last seen the man he'd shot. After a few minutes of searching without success, he risked turning on his flashlight. He briefly scanned the area, but the cloaked subject was gone. "I can't believe this… bodies don't get up and walk away," he mumbled.

The other two subjects must have returned and retrieved their accomplice and his weapon. Gray found the lassos and gags where he'd left them and picked them up. He looked around a little longer, but found nothing. *They could have finished us all off. So why didn't they?*

Gray rejoined the others and said, "The guy I shot is gone. So's his rifle."

"That isn't possible," Sarah said. "You just didn't see them or you were looking in the wrong place."

"I wasn't," Gray replied. "I found the lassos and gags right where they should have been. There may be some blood-splatter on the rocks or some other evidence, but we'll have to wait for daylight to do a thorough search. Angela, you've been very quiet. Are you sure that you're okay?"

"Yes. Those must have been the same men who killed Darren."

"I would say that's a good possibility."

"Let's get back to camp and decide on our next move," Sarah said.

They took it slow going back to camp, and when they got there, Sarah found the first-aid kit and opened an instant cold pack. She gave it to Clay for him to hold against the lump on his head. She opened another cold pack and pressed it to her left ankle. Angela sat quietly on the blanket, staring at the remains of the fire.

Gray scouted the perimeter of the camp and found no sign that anyone had walked into the camp. "They didn't take the shotgun. That's a bit strange. Angela, what exactly happened?"

She looked up and said, "I've never felt so helpless. The guy that grabbed me was incredibly strong."

"What did he look like?" Sarah asked.

"I couldn't tell you. They were all masked and covered in buffalo hides. You saw them."

"Yeah, but not up close," Sarah said. "You're sure it was buffalo?"

"Yes, I know what buffalo smells like."

"Were they Native American?" Sarah asked.

"I told you they were masked, so how would I know?" Angela replied tersely. "They never said a word. I could see their hands, but it was too dark to determine a race."

"What about the masks?" Gray asked.

"They were also made of buffalo hide, with eye slits. The one who gagged me had eyes as dark as night, and for the briefest moment, I saw red light reflect in the eyes. I looked up and saw a red orb in the sky, which disappeared. It was very strange. We'd be dead if you two hadn't come back when you did."

"You're sure it was a man?" Sarah asked. "You said they didn't speak."

"I've never seen a woman that large. In fact, I haven't seen many men that big either."

"Clay, you need to stay awake," Sarah said, noticing he was about to nod off. "You may have a concussion."

"I doubt it," Clay said. "I have a thick skull. At least that's what I've been told. I'm just really drained."

Sarah stood and limped over to Gray. "I know you want to call for help, but I really think that the best thing would be for us to stay here until dawn."

"Clay, it's your head," Gray said. "What do you think?"

"I'm alright."

"I think we need to move to the tree line," Gray said. "We're out in the open here."

Sarah said, "I think moving the camp into the trees will only give our adversaries an opportunity to sneak up on us. At least here we'll see them coming."

"You may be right," Gray acknowledged.

"I don't know about that," Angela said. "They made no noise. I didn't hear a thing until they grabbed us."

"We need to put the ropes and gags in evidence bags," Gray said.

"I'll get them," Sarah said.

"I'll keep watch," Gray said. "You guys get some rest."

CHAPTER TWELVE

Aki and Chase had just finished giving Sharon Madison a tour of the facility and were back in their office.

"What do you think?" Aki asked.

"This is a beautiful campus," Sharon said. "Everything in the office is state of the art. I'm very pleased."

"I'm glad to hear it," Aki said.

Sharon took a sip of her coffee. "The coffee from the cafe downstairs is quite good, but I think we'll need our own machine and the option to make tea."

"I agree," Chase said. "A cup of English breakfast tea in the morning is always a good way to start the day."

"When do you want me to start work on finding Dar?"

"As soon as you get settled."

"I'll start with my European contacts and see if they have any information," Sharon said.

"Just don't mention our names to GSG 9 or SPAP. Remember, you're conducting a follow-up assessment for CETC. Nothing more."

"I understand. Is it true Dar shot you down in Germany?"

"That's true," Aki replied, not really wanting to think about it again. "Then she shot up a town in Poland during her escape from the SPAP. The SPAP and GSG 9 needed to save face and we became the scapegoats. Take a look at the after-action reports before you make your calls. You have access to all of our files. If you have any questions, just ask."

A phone rang in the reception area and Chase answered it. "Hang on a minute. Aki, it's Brian McFee. He has something for us. I'll put him on hold and you pick it up in the conference room."

The three of them went into the conference room and sat in the new chairs. Aki put the call on speaker. "Hey, Brian, we have you on speaker."

"Hey, everyone," Brian said. "I know I don't officially start until tomorrow, but I came across an interesting bit of information that was logged by NSA an hour ago that I thought you would want immediately. It would take a few days through normal channels to reach you. It concerns an alert on an NSA net that you cast last year."

"Can you be a little more specific?" Aki asked.

"A voice-recognition hit on signals traffic from a flagged number originating in Romania to an unknown number in Belarus was intercepted yesterday afternoon. There was an annotation that the parties were linked to Dariya Novikov."

"You have my attention," Aki said. "But before we go any further, do we need a more secure connection?"

"No one can intercept this call. I verified that all of our GEOINT office phones are tied to a hard-lined encrypted system and my end is secure."

"Do I want to know how you got the information from NSA?" Aki asked.

"Let's just say that I still have connections, and I think that my skill set in this area is why you selected me for the job."

"You're right. Go ahead."

"Colonel Vasil Lesun and Dragos Marcu, a Romanian mining mogul, discussed contacting someone known as 'the problem solver' who had helped Marcu in the past."

"Is Dar the problem solver?" Sharon asked.

"Yes," Aki replied. "Colonel Lesun was Dar's superior and love interest when she worked for the Alpha Group, so I had NSA set up a net hoping to get a lead on her. Several calls were intercepted between Marcu and Lesun over a few days, but Dar was never mentioned by name. We later determined that a woman matching Dar's physical description eliminated several well-trained mercenaries at one of Marcu's mines and his competitor suffered a near-fatal accident."

"Problem solved," Brian said.

"Exactly," Aki said. "I thought it was odd that Marcu even knew Lesun or how to reach him, so I requested an intercept net with voice recognition because Lesun changes numbers frequently. This is the first time that the two men have spoken since then. Their relationship must be closer than I thought if Marcu has his latest contact number."

Chase added, "For background, Lesun is the one who ordered Dar killed after she assassinated the president's mistress. Later, he was responsible for faking Dar's death. We're pretty sure that he's acting as a go-between for Dar and potential clients."

"And now Marcu needs her help again," Brian said.

"It sounds like it," Aki said. "Brian, that's great work."

"Thanks."

"Brian, I'd like you to determine if DTOS Mining or Marcu have made any large fund transfers over the last forty-eight hours," Aki said.

"I still have a few things to finalize before I'm officially yours," Brian said. "I also have to exit clear. I won't get to it until later today."

"Time is critical," Aki said. "The last time, Marcu's company sent ten million US dollars in two payments to a private bank account in Greece. We tracked a money transfer to a bank in Venezuela, where the trail went cold. All of the accounts were closed following the transaction. Maybe we can get ahead of the curve this time."

"Alright, forward the account information and I'll start working on it."

"Welcome to TCT," Aki said. "Swing by the campus after you exit clear. We'll be here until late tonight."

"See you this evening."

"Should we notify Director Canton?" Chase asked.

"Not yet," Aki replied. "Let's see where this leads us."

GEOINT – May 23 – 0830 hours EDT

Aki was deep in thought when her phone rang. "Agent Dawson," she answered.

"Hey boss," Brian said. "I stumbled across something when I linked one of those accounts you gave me to a seldom-used DTOS Mining account."

"That was fast."

"I thought I'd further impress my new boss."

"Stop calling me that."

"Anyway, Marcu transferred a little over six million euros to a bank in Nice, France. The BNP Paribas bank confirmed receipt of the funds late yesterday evening. It went into a confidential numbered account belonging to Adrianna Chastain."

"How did you get that information?"

"Like I said before, I have connections," Brian replied cagily.

"The bank was open that late?"

"For special customers and for large money transfers, they will conduct business at any time. The interesting thing is that Marcu received two calls an hour apart just before the money was transferred."

"You're earning your salary today," Aki said. "Who called him?"

"That I don't know. The call originated in southern France from an unregistered cell phone. The phone went silent immediately after the second call. There's no way to track it. I've flagged the number just in case it goes active again."

"Excellent work. I'll have Sharon start working up a profile on Adrianna Chastain. I have a feeling there won't be much on her."

"I also learned that four million of the transferred funds were immediately forwarded to a bank in Venezuela for a substantial banking fee. You know how unfriendly Venezuela is when it comes to our inquiries."

"I do," Aki said. Brian had been an excellent choice. "Can your friend do more snooping?"

"I already asked and the answer is no. Those funds could have been split and forwarded to any number of accounts under many different names. I'm betting the Venezuelan account will be closed soon. French banks are more cooperative when you mention the transactions are related to terrorist funds."

"I think I see how your friend got cooperation. Where'd did the other two million go?"

"It hasn't moved yet."

"Dar's preparing to do some work for Marcu," Aki said. "Forward the account information to Sharon. She may be able to monitor the other two million."

"Will do," Brian replied. "Later."

"Sharon! Chase!" Aki shouted.

Sharon walked hurriedly into her office. "You bellowed?"

"I did. Chase!"

"I'm coming. Give me a second."

When Chase entered the office, Aki said, "Sharon, Brian will be sending you bank-account information concerning Adrianna Chastain. I'm certain that is another of Dar's aliases. The bank in France is the one we need to monitor in real time if possible."

"So, Dar's in France?" Chase said.

"I'm not sure where she is, now that she's been paid for whatever she's up to next. Chase, let Sharon follow the money from now on and I want you to contact your buddy in the Directorate-General for External Security in France. Let's see if we can get more information from them."

"My friend with the DGSE may not be available. When we last spoke, he said that he was thinking of leaving the intelligence service."

"Maybe he changed his mind. Once this work gets in your blood, it's hard to stop. Call and find out."

"I'm on it."

Chase and Sharon left her office and Aki took a moment to gaze out the window. *What are you up to, Dar?*

Black Hills – May 23 – 0630 hours MDT

None of them had managed to get much sleep. Gray was keeping a close watch on the tree line, looking for any movement.

Sarah joined him and said, "Gray, you look beat."

"I am. How's your ankle?"

"Better. Still a little swollen and stiff, but nothing permanent."

"I want to have another look around the area, and then I think we need to make the trek down to the trucks. How's Clay?"

"I checked the lump on his head and the swelling is almost gone. I don't think he has a concussion. Angela is still in her tent. I thought I'd let her sleep a while longer."

Gray nodded. "I'll take Clay with me and scout the area."

"Stay where I can see you," Sarah said. "Don't go off into the woods. Take some evidence bags and the good camera."

"Why don't you try the cell phone and radio again?"

"I already did. Still no reception."

Gray walked over to Clay and asked, "You up for a walk?"

"Sure."

"I checked the area around the camp again," Gray said. "There's no sign anyone was here last night except for us. The only footprints I can find are the ones we've made."

"As big as those guys were, they should have left impressions on the ground," Clay said. "It doesn't make any sense. Gray, they didn't make any noise, even when moving across the rocks."

"Let's see what we can find. There should be blood splatter on the ground and three shell casings from the rounds that were fired at me."

Gray and Clay scoured the rocky terrain for twenty minutes without finding any blood. Gray did find two 44-40 Winchester shell casings and several of his own shell casings, which he photographed and placed in evidence bags.

"This is bizarre," Clay finally said. "There's no blood anywhere."

"Clay, do you know what kind of rifle uses 44-40 ammunition?"

"The only one I know of is the lever-action Winchester model 1873. It was reintroduced a few years ago and is a popular rifle around here."

"Lever action means one casing could still be in the rifle," Gray said.

"That's true. Gray, Crawley isn't going to believe the guy you shot just got up and walked away."

"We have the shell casings, lasso, and gags as proof of our encounter."

When they got back to the camp, Angela was awake and sitting quietly on a blanket by the remains of the fire. Sarah was sitting across from her.

"Anything?" Sarah asked.

"We only found shell casings," Gray said. "No blood."

"But I saw you shoot one of them and I saw him fall," Angela said emphatically. "There has to be blood somewhere."

"Perhaps he was wearing a bulletproof vest," Sarah offered. "He dropped from the bullet's impact, recovered, and moved off. There'd be no blood and he could have retrieved his rifle and made a quiet escape."

"Maybe," Gray said. "All of them did appear to be very thick around the chest. I'm going to walk down to the truck to call Crawley."

Angela stood and said, "I'd like to search the site again before this place turns into a zoo. You and Sarah said that you saw blue and red lights, and I saw a red light in the sky that disappeared. There's got to be an explanation. I believe that there has to be a cave or something hidden underground and the entrance is nearby. That has to be what Darren found and why we aren't finding anything."

"That was my thought, too," Clay added. "Crawley is going to be here in a few hours. Let's search the site before he gets here. Maybe we'll find something."

"I agree with Clay and Angela," Sarah said. "I don't think we need to worry about the buffalo guys returning. If they'd wanted to finish us off, they would have last night."

"Instead of continuing the grid search, let's concentrate on the area where you saw the light," Angela recommended. "It'll be faster with four of us searching the area. Besides, you're armed and we won't be surprised again if someone does come looking."

"She has a point," Clay said. "Crawley isn't going to be thrilled, hearing about what happened last night. Maybe we'll solve this case before he arrives, which would really piss him off."

Sarah said, "If we do solve it, he'll still take credit."

"Alright," Gray said. "Let's go find where the light came from."

Black Hills - 0800 hours MDT

Gray felt as if he'd been walking over the same piece of ground for the last ten minutes. The rocks, shrubs, and trees all looked the same. Sarah, Clay and Angela were only feet away from him as they traversed the rocky slope. He stopped and said, "The blue glow was coming from right in this area. I'm sure of it, but there's nothing here."

Angela looked around, then asked, "Could the lights have been a reflection from a car up on the road, which created an optical illusion?"

"I don't think so," Gray said, shaking his head. "Sarah and I saw the blue glow twice. It was as if a door opened and closed. The red light was only visible for a short period of time and then it disappeared."

"What do you want to do now?" Clay asked Gray.

"We keep searching until Crawley arrives."

"Let's move more to the east," Sarah said, "and spread out a little more."

"If we're searching that area again, let's do this so we maintain continuity of the grid pattern," Angela said.

Gray really appreciated Angela's attention to detail. "Alright."

It wasn't long until Clay shouted, "I found something."

"Clay, stay there," Angela directed. "Sarah, you and Gray go to him."

"Isn't that the area that Crawley and Lt. White Owl searched yesterday?" Sarah asked.

"It's close to the grid line," Angela answered. "They may not have searched that exact spot."

Gray reached Clay first. Clay pointed at the ground and said, "I tripped over that rock. It looks like there's a watchband under it."

Gray noticed a weathered black band protruding from under the rock. Only a small part of it was visible. "Sarah, I need you to take a picture before we move the rock. Angela, give Sarah a flag to mark the spot. Then I want a hands-and-knees search, turning over every rock around this one, and we need to look under every bush within ten feet."

Sarah took several photos and placed the flag next to the watchband.

"Clay, you have good eyes," Angela said.

"Thank you, and let's not forget my big feet. I can see how this could have been missed."

Gray took an evidence bag from his pocket and held it open. "Clay, it's your find. You have the honors." Sarah handed Clay a pair of gloves.

After Clay turned over the rock, he said, "The watch isn't the only thing here. There's a wooden box in a hole."

Gray knelt next to him. "The lid has something carved into it. Hard to tell what, it's encased in dirt. Sarah, take a picture."

"I wonder why the watchband was dislodged from the box?" Sarah said.

"I don't' know," Gray replied. "Lucky break for us, though. Clay, pull the box out of there."

"Wait!" Sarah exclaimed. "It could be boobytrapped. Maybe they wanted to attract our attention."

"I doubt that," Gray said. "I think someone got sloppy and didn't notice that the watchband was hanging out of the box when they put the rock back."

Clay said, "What if Sarah's right?"

"The watchband was under the rock, so it wasn't left that way to attract our attention," Gray replied. "But to be safe, I'll get it out of the hole." He grabbed the box by the partially open lid and pulled it up before anyone could object.

"Do you have a death wish?" Sarah asked.

Gray knew that she was both relieved that nothing had happened and angry. He opened the lid fully. "It looks like a collection of watches and rings."

"Could be a trophy collection from the buffalo guys' serial killings," Sarah said.

Angela moved closer to see the contents, gasped, and stepped back.

"What is it?" Gray asked.

"That's Darren's watch," Angela said, pointing. "He had a black-banded Citizens watch with an orange face."

"You're certain?" Gray asked.

Angela nodded. "Yes. I bought it for him. Is his knife in there?"

"No," Gray said. "Let's get some photos of the items. We're also going to need metal detectors up here. There could be more evidence buried around the area." He peered into the hole, then felt around in the dirt. "There's nothing else here."

"Gray, may I keep Darren's watch?" Angela asked.

"I'm sorry, but it's evidence. I'm certain in time, you'll get it back."

"I only have three evidence bags left," Clay said after looking through his pack.

"We'll need more evidence bags and a lot more people to search the area properly," Sarah said. "Crawley and White Owl should be here any time now. White Owl probably carries an evidence kit in his cruiser."

"Do we continue to search while we wait?" Clay asked.

"I think that's a good idea," Gray said. "Forensically speaking, any viable evidence, like DNA, will have been washed away or lost to exposure, but you never know. Let's secure the box in a bag for now."

They searched ten feet out in all directions, turning over one rock at a time, without finding anything else.

"The hole you found looks like it was dug just for the box, but I don't understand why these items were left out here," Gray said. He picked up the box and examined it more closely. "There's an engraving on the lid. Angela, do these symbols mean anything to you?"

She scrutinized the lid through the clear plastic bag. "Hard to tell. The lid is too encrusted in dirt."

Gray put on a glove and removed the box from the evidence bag, brushing some of the dirt back into the bag to preserve any possible evidence. "It appears that the engraving is a circle with a cross in the center, and there's a feather engraved next to it. It looks like it may be painted. It must be old, the paint's faded."

Angela drew closer. "That's a Lakota medicine circle symbol."

"You're sure?" Sarah asked.

"Yes. The circle represents the knowledge of the universe and is symbolic of the cycle of life and death. Where the vertical and horizontal lines intersect is where one would stand to pray if this symbol were inscribed on the ground. It represents the center of the Earth."

"And the feather?" Gray asked.

"It's the sign of Wakan Tanka, the Great Spirit, who has power over everything. The faded colors are red, yellow, black, and white. Each carries a different meaning. It's definitely Lakota. The yellow color is symbolic of bringing light to all creation like the Morning Star rising in the east. The red represents the north and is used to represent finding the wisdom to walk a better path." Angela paused, then added, "It's also symbolic of the home of the Buffalo People."

"Interesting," Gray said. Angela always seemed to be in teaching mode when she explained things. "What about the other two colors?"

"The white symbolizes the connection to life after death. Life begins in the south. It's there to help guide a person to the next phase."

"So, black represents the west?" Gray said.

"Yes. The color black can represent honor and respect. It can also symbolize the Thunderbird, which brings the power of the rain and wind. The Thunderbird stands against evil and ensures the respect of others. Do you remember if the box was oriented so that the colors matched the compass?"

Gray visualized how the box had been orientated. "I believe they did. Could this have been left as a tribute to the victims?"

"Possibly," Angela said. "The attackers were dressed in buffalo hides and maybe believed that they were guiding their victims to the next life. Didn't you tell me that all of the victims were found in water?"

"Yes," Gray answered.

"Water is used in purification rituals. That could be a clue."

"Even if all of these events are related, it still doesn't give us a motive," Sarah said.

"No, and I hate to say it, but Crawley might be right. There's a Native American connection."

"Don't tell him that right away—it'll only swell his head," Sarah said.

Gray heard a noise coming from the bushes and Clay took aim with his shotgun. Men's voices carried through the trees.

"That's Crawley," Sarah said. "I'd know that grumbling anywhere."

"Crawley, we're over here," Gray shouted. "Keep coming down the slope. Just be careful where you step. We've found some evidence. Is Lt. White Owl with you?"

"I'm here," White Owl responded.

"We're going to need additional evidence bags, a metal detector, and an evidence kit if you have one."

"Wish you had told me that before I humped my butt through the brush," White Owl said. "I'll head back up."

"Sorry about that," Gray replied, "but the radios and cell phones aren't working."

Crawley walked out of the dense brush and stopped. "What did you find that requires all that gear?"

"An assorted stash of watches and other jewelry," Gray responded. "Angela has identified Darren's watch."

"We have a few other things to tell you about as well," Sarah added to goad him.

"Where's the outer edge of the crime scene?" Crawley asked.

"The flag marks where we found the evidence," Gray said. "We've searched outward ten feet from there in all directions and found nothing else."

"I'll walk to you, checking the ground as I go. Who found the property?"

"I did," Clay said proudly.

"Good work," Crawley said. "I thought we checked this area yesterday?"

"You did," Gray said. "But we started again this morning after the events of last night."

"What events?"

"We saw strange lights and what I guess what you would call a buffalo-warrior attack and attempted kidnapping," Gray replied.

"Don't forget to tell him about the warrior you shot, who then disappeared into thin air," Sarah added.

"Oh, yeah," Gray said coyly. He wasn't even ashamed that he was enjoying baiting Crawley.

"What!" Crawley exclaimed. "Why the hell didn't you call me?"

"Like Gray said, we had no communication capability, and Deputy Gurley and I weren't able to travel because of our injuries," Sarah answered.

"We'll tell you the whole story as soon as White Owl gets back," Gray said, knowing that Crawley was ready to explode. "He's going to need to hear this as well. We're going to have to call the Pennington Sheriff's Office for support. This is their jurisdiction."

"I'll decide if they're needed," Crawley barked.

After Gray had finished relating the events of the previous evening, Crawley looked at White Owl and asked, "What do you think?"

White Owl shook his head and replied, "An interesting story, but that doesn't explain the missing body and lack of blood. The mysterious lights are curious. The evidence does support an encounter."

"The lassos that were used to bind Deputy Gurley and Dr. Kingman are like the ones used on the other victims," Crawley said. "The gags look like deer hide. Gray, the shell casings you found may or may not be from whoever shot at you. Lt. White Owl, have you heard any rumors about men wearing buffalo hides on the reservation?"

"No."

"The Lakota people are known to be members of the Buffalo Nation," Angela said. "Wi represents the solar spirit of the Bison. The attackers could be dressing in buffalo hides as a homage to Wi."

"So, you think we could be dealing with a group of Lakota serial killers emulating a mythological deity," Crawley stated.

"I don't know," Angela replied. "I was just giving you some background. They may not be Native American but want you to think they're from one of the tribes. It's even possible that they're spirit warriors or misguided warriors influenced by Tatankan Gnaskiyan, the Crazy Buffalo Spirit."

"What the hell are you talking about?" Crawley asked.

White Owl said, "Tatankan Gnaskiyan is a part of Lakota lore and is supposed to be responsible for forcing people to commit murders."

"I see. Dr. Kingman, you're an expert on Native American cultures, correct?"

"Yes."

Crawley smiled. "Have you ever seen one of these deities or spirit warriors?"

"Maybe last night. Many indigenous people believe they exist, and if they were spirit warriors, it would explain why they didn't leave any footprints behind. Like ghosts, they moved easily over the rocky landscape without making a sound and had unbelievable strength. They picked Clay up as if he didn't weigh a thing."

"Dr. Kingman, you want me to believe that spirit warriors or a demonic spirit forced men to dress in buffalo hides and made them commit these crimes?" Crawley asked incredulously. "I'm not buying any of this. The Pine Ridge Reservation isn't that far from here and the box found with the recovered property is Lakota. I would say that's a good place to start looking for the suspects, not in the spirit world. Don't you agree, Lt. White Owl?"

"The Lakota believe in living in harmony with others, but I can't deny that the evidence points to a Lakota connection. I grew up on the reservation and know many of the families living there. I've not heard anything about the killings or kidnappings on the reservation."

"We were shot at last night, and Gray shot one of them," Sarah said.

"Maybe the guy just tripped and fell or Gray missed him, or he was wearing a ballistic vest," Crawley stated. "If they were spirit warriors, why would they fall after being shot? Wouldn't a bullet just pass through them?"

"Agent Crawley, what we've told you is true," Gray said. He was growing tired of Crawley's condescension.

"Agent Crawley, what I find interesting about the description of the attackers is the height of the warriors and the glowing lights that were seen," White Owl said, in an obvious attempt to reduce the tension between Crawley and the others. "Dr. Kingman is correct. There are many legends about spirit warriors wearing buffalo hides, and it is said that they are known to disappear like ghosts into shrouded forests without making a sound."

"You're buying this load of crap?" Crawley said.

"That's enough," Gray cried. "You need to listen to what we're telling you."

White Owl cleared his throat. "Agent Crawley, I can tell you that a blue light is associated with Skan, the spirit of the universe. Wi's spirit color is red. Both lights were seen together. There's no sign of any light source, so perhaps what they saw was Wi's spirit or others entering the universal spirit lodge through a portal of some kind."

"Seriously?" Crawley said, his disbelief obvious. "I've entered the Twilight Zone. I'm surprised at you, lieutenant."

"These are the Black Hills, and I know from experience that strange things happen out here," White Owl replied.

Sarah said, "Agent Crawley, Sheriff Lyons told you about people seeing strange lights out here. Remember?"

"Yes. What we have here are three men, probably Lakota, who are serial killers or are on some quest to rid the Black Hills of trespassers they perceive to be a danger to the land." He pointed at the evidence bags. "There's our proof that it's connected to this world, not spirits. A spirit wouldn't keep trophies and shoot at you with a rifle."

"Why not?" Angela asked.

"I'm not going to justify that with a response," Crawley spat.

"You're an idiot," Angela said.

"Agent Crawley, we're all tired and just want to find answers," Gray said. "A level of civility would be appreciated by all of us."

"Agent Holt, you had better watch your tone," Crawley said. "We have a crime scene to work. It's possible that the lights you saw came from a cave or underground facility that's camouflaged. If there is such an area, then it is certainly not being entered through a mystical portal by a spirit warrior. This has nothing to do with spirits. Is that clear?"

No one replied.

"Let's focus on what we know and follow the evidence and leave the fables out of the discussion. Lt. White Owl, where's that metal detector?"

"Still in the car. I'm not a pack mule. I couldn't carry everything through the brush. I'll go get it."

Gray knew White Owl was also growing tired of dealing with Crawley.

"Thank you. Let's get the jewelry that Deputy Gurley stumbled upon *properly* bagged and tagged."

"We could use some additional help searching the area," Gray said. "If we plan on staying out here again tonight, it would be prudent to have additional support."

"I'll decide if we need more people and whether we're staying the night," Crawley replied. "If I come off as being *uncivil*, well, that's too bad. I'm just turning over every stone, literally, in a homicide investigation and trying to point out that we need to stay grounded in the real world. Ghosts and spirits have no place here. We're hunting human killers. Let's get to it and see if we can find more tangible evidence."

GEOINT – May 23 – 1600 hours EDT

Aki entered Sharon's office and asked, "Any updates on the money trail?"

"Once the funds hit Venezuela, they vanished into dark accounts. No names, only dummy corporate accounts with coded account numbers which are scattered across the globe."

"How was it distributed?"

"A few hundred thousand went to Laos, a half million to Vietnam, a million to Columbia, the same to the Cayman Islands. A half million remained in Venezuela. The rest went to Switzerland. I'm trying to follow the trail from those banks."

"What about the funds in France?" Aki asked.

"Still there."

"Keep on it."

Chase entered Sharon's office. His brown eyes were filled with excitement. "You guys need to see what I just received. Now!"

"Okay," Aki said. "What is it?"

"My old friend did leave the DGSE, but he hooked me up with an active agent. She just called and told me that she'd discovered a surveillance clip from the BNP Paribas bank from a few months ago when Adrianna Chastain opened the account. I sent the clip to Sharon."

"Your friend must be important to get someone to work this late in France," Sharon said as she opened the file.

Aki moved behind Sharon to watch the video. "Have you seen this?" she asked Chase.

"Of course. It's not the best quality."

"No, it's not," Aki replied, as it played. "Stop it there." She leaned in closer to the monitor and studied it for a moment. "That's definitely Dar."

"Yes, it is," Chase said. "Open the other file I sent you."

Sharon keyed it up and said, "It looks like a security camera captured a plane at a gate."

"It is," Chase said. "They were able to connect this video via facial recognition. It's a private terminal at the airport in Nice, France. The DGSE received a tip that a woman was departing for Winnipeg, Canada on a jet that normally carries fifteen people and she had paid cash for the flight. The person making the report thought it was suspicious, especially in light of the rifle case she was carrying."

"And?" Aki said.

"Keep watching." A moment later, a blond woman walked from the terminal to a large private jet. Just before entering the jet, the woman turned back, looked at the security camera, and smiled.

"Zoom in!" Aki ordered. There was no mistaking the face even with the enhanced cheekbones. "That's her. Blond or not, I'd still know her in any disguise. Chase, where's the plane now?"

"It landed in Winnipeg early this morning. She's using a Canadian passport under the name of Cora Zemanski."

"Dar wants us to know she's coming this way, but why?" Aki said.

"She's playing with us," Chase replied. "Just like she did in the woods in Germany."

Sharon asked, "Do you want me to alert the Canadian Security Intelligence Service?"

"No," Aki replied. "I don't want to spook her or have them draw fire and turn this into another Poland. Sharon, check everything under the new alias. Let's see if we can find out where she is or where she's going."

"Looks like a late night tonight," Sharon said.

Brian McFee entered the office just at that moment and said, "Late nights are always fun."

"Happy to see you could make it," Aki said. "You know Chase, and you've probably crossed paths with Sharon."

"Yes, Sharon and I have worked together on projects before. Good to see you again."

"Glad you've joined the team," Sharon said.

"I thought that you'd be here earlier," Aki said.

"I had a few more things to finish up than I thought. I received an unexpected call just before I left that has bearing on Dar's Romanian contact."

"Dar's not in Europe," Chase interrupted. "We just learned that she's in Winnipeg, Canada."

"Interesting," Brian said.

"What's interesting?" Aki asked.

"Dragos Marcu has made a number of calls to several mining-company CEOs over the last two days. One of the people he called was Noel Ketterhorn, the CEO of Universal Mining Corporation. The corporate headquarters is in Winnipeg."

"That *is* interesting," Aki said. "I wonder if Marcu is having a problem with Ketterhorn?"

"I don't think so," Brian replied. "Marcu, Ketterhorn, and two others—Mark Santos of Black Hills Gold Mining, headquartered in South Dakota, and William Ossa of Pelion Mining in Greece—have a business association. The conglomerate is called the Mázazi mining alliance. They work together on speculative projects."

"Let's find out what we can about the mining company CEOs and see if we can track Dar in Canada," Aki directed. "I wouldn't be surprised if she changed to a new alias once she landed."

"I'm on it," Sharon said. "Aki, when is Omar arriving?"

"I spoke to him earlier. He has HUMINT assets that he needs to hand off to new handlers. He'll be working late tonight, so I told him to start tomorrow morning."

"I'll help Sharon if someone will show me which office is mine," Brian said.

CHAPTER THIRTEEN

Black Hills – May 23 –1930 MDT

"Tired?" Gray asked Sarah.

"Not so much tired as that the throbbing pain in my ankle has returned."

"Why don't we take a break?"

"We don't have too much of this grid left to search. The sun's going to set in another hour. Crawley still hasn't said whether we're going to get additional help tonight and I'm not comfortable with his lack of concern."

"Yeah, that bothers me, too," Gray said. He moved the metal detector around the base of another large cluster of plants with yellow blooms. It was the second time he'd checked the area with negative results. "We should just take a weed eater to this undergrowth. It would speed things up."

Sarah chuckled. "You know that plant you're standing by is edible if you're hungry. It's called the arrowleaf balsamroot. The bright-yellow flowers give them their nickname, Oregon Sunflower."

"Thanks, I'll pass."

"They're actually pretty tasty with a little salad dressing and croutons on top."

"Stop talking about food. I'm starving, and for future reference, I prefer my food cooked."

"Good to know," Sarah said. "I have a power bar I saved. Be happy to share."

Gray nodded. "That would be good, thanks."

Taking off her work gloves, Sarah pulled the bar from her cargo pocket and unwrapped it. "You just want to take a bite, or do you want me to break it?"

"Just break it in half. I'm in need of a shower and you may not want to get too close to me."

She snapped the bar and tossed half of it to him. "I'm a bit ripe myself."

"Gray, are you two taking a break?" Crawley shouted, from his search area fifty feet away. "We're losing daylight. Let's get this done."

Gray stuffed the power bar into his mouth. It was easier than biting his tongue. Crawley was really pissing him off. He and White Owl hadn't covered half the ground that he and Sarah had, and they'd taken many more breaks. Gray considered throwing his shiny new badge at him and walking off the hill.

"What a dick," Sarah muttered.

An hour later, exhausted, Sarah and Gray had finished their grid search. They'd found nothing.

"Angela, we're coming back to you," Gray announced, putting the metal detector on his shoulder.

"You finished the search?" Crawley asked.

"What do you think?" Gray replied. He couldn't help himself.

"Attitude check, Assistant Special Agent Holt," Crawley said.

"Kiss my ass, Agent Crawley," Gray retorted.

Everyone broke up laughing, even Crawley.

Sarah and Gray met Angela and Clay at the hub of the search area where they had all started. Crawley and White Owl walked up. Everyone was covered in dirt and grime.

"I suggest we retire for the evening," Crawley said.

"You going to call in some relief?" Gray asked.

"Not necessary. Lt. White Owl, I'd like to camp here tonight. What are your thoughts?"

"I have my gear in the car. I'll go get it. I have additional supplies, ammunition, and weapons, but I'll need a little help bringing them back."

"The smart-ass and Deputy Gurley can help you," Crawley said. "Sarah's ankle is still bothering her and I'm too tired to climb that damn hill again. Besides, someone needs to stand guard until you all get back."

"Lieutenant, I'll be glad to give you a hand," Gray said. "And thanks for staying. We may need the extra firepower if the buffalo warriors return."

"I hope they do," White Owl said. "I'd like to see them."

"I think you're in the minority on that point," Angela said. "I'd just as soon never encounter them again."

"Well, I hope I get to see them and the eerie lights," Crawley said, making a waving motion with his hands. "I want to figure out what you all saw, and if they do come back, I'll arrest the bastards."

"But aren't you out of your jurisdiction?" Angela asked.

"Not by much. I'll hold them until Pennington SO arrives or drag them across the border into Wyoming."

"Let's get up this hill and get the gear and supplies back to the campsite before it gets dark," Gray said to White Owl. "I want to be ready."

Two hours later, everyone had eaten, cleaned up as best that they could, and were seated around a small campfire.

"We need to douse the fire and the lights soon," Gray said. "Our eyes need to adjust to the dark."

"The witching hour approaches," Crawley joked. "Gray, I want you to take Lt. White Owl and me back to where you saw the blue and red lights."

"It might be better if we all go," Gray said.

"Alright."

"Sarah, are you up for it?" Gray asked.

"I've eaten and taken two Tylenols. I'm good to go. I suggest we take all the weapons with us. If the buffalo warriors hit the camp again, we don't need them arming themselves further."

"Good point," Gray said.

"Dr. Kingman, how proficient are you with a rifle?" Crawley asked.

"I've only fired shotguns and pistols at the range."

"Okay. Gray, give her the shotgun. Perhaps if your buffalo warriors return, they may think twice about attacking if we're all armed. Dr. Kingman, do not shoot at anything unless they shoot at us first. Got it?"

"I understand," Angela said. "Agent Crawley, I guess this means that you finally believe that I wasn't involved in Darren's murder?"

"I never really thought that you were."

"I'll bring the camera," Sarah said.

"I brought my night vision binoculars," Lt. White Owl said. "They should be helpful."

"You could have told us that you had those earlier," Crawley growled.

"I suppose I could have, but it didn't cross my mind."

"Let's move up the hill and get into position," Gray said.

When they reached the place where the lights had appeared, Gray assigned them positions that kept each of them within eyesight. He was surprised that Crawley didn't object to him making the assignments.

Black Hills – May 24 – Midnight

Gray listened to the wind whistling through the treetops. He looked up through the thick canopy and saw a few stars twinkling in the clear, crisp night sky. He was sitting against a tree on the west side of the perimeter, and he could see the others in the moonlight. White Owl was kneeling behind a bush on the southernmost edge of the perimeter, scanning the area with his night-vision binoculars. Angela was on alert next to Clay. They were watching the north approach in the direction of their camp. Crawley was sitting on a large rock in the middle of the group, while Sarah was prone on the east side. They had a tight defensive circle, and Gray knew no one could sneak up on them.

A hazy blue glow illuminated the trees about twenty yards up the slope in front of White Owl's position. Its sudden appearance had likely blinded the lieutenant, because he jerked the binoculars away from his face. Gray was stunned when Crawley stood up, unholstered his weapon, and aimed it in the direction of the light as he walked several yards past White Owl.

"Who's there?" Crawley shouted. "Wyoming DCI, show yourselves."

The light immediately blinked out.

"Crawley, get down," Gray shouted, but his warning came too late.

The blue glow lit up the slope again and a small red orb materialized from within it. The orb flew over Crawley and illuminated him with a red beam of light. Crawley stood frozen as it hovered just above his head. The orb's light grew more intense, casting a reddish brilliance across the entire area, illuminating all of them. A moment later, four large figures dressed in buffalo hides emerged from the darkness in front of Crawley. It was as if they'd just materialized from the trees. Their eyes glowed red.

No matter how hard he tried, Gray wasn't able to pull his sidearm. He was frozen in place as well.

The buffalo warriors lifted Crawley and took him toward the blue light. The red orb extinguished its paralyzing beam and followed. They made no sound as they moved over the rocky terrain. Their figures cast fast-moving shadows within the ethereal glow amongst the trees. A moment later, Crawley's pain-filled, terror-stricken scream echoed through the trees, and both lights winked out.

It had taken only a few seconds for the warriors to grab Crawley. Gray wasn't really sure what he'd just witnessed, but Crawley was gone. "Crawley!" he yelled, when he was finally able to move.

"Gray, I couldn't move," Sarah said.

"Me either," Clay added.

"Movement!" White Owl shouted, adjusting his binoculars.

"Where?" Gray asked, as he quickly moved up and knelt next to White Owl.

"I count five more of them further up the slope, just past where the lights went out. They're moving this way. Damn, they're big, and they're also covered in buffalo hides."

"White Owl, any sign of Crawley?" Gray asked.

"No."

"Everyone, pull back and find better cover," Gray ordered.

"What about Crawley?" Clay asked.

"He's gone," Gray announced.

White Owl moved down the slope and joined Clay and Angela just as rifle fire exploded from where the five advancing warriors were moving through the trees. Then more rifle shots rang out from the east.

"They're trying to flank us!" White Owl cried. "There are seven more of them to the east," he added as he continued scanning the area.

"Shit!" Sarah exclaimed as she fired at the new threat.

Gray shouted, "Sarah, you and I will provide cover fire. The rest of you head for the camp and get ready to run for the trucks. Sarah, you cover the east flank. I'll take the threat from the south."

"No way we're leaving you!" Clay cried.

"Then we'll have to shoot and move back down the slope together!" Gray yelled. He didn't have time to argue. "Sarah, move now."

When Sarah and Gray reached White Owl's position, all of them fired at the advancing warriors. The distinctive boom of the shotgun told Gray that Angela had engaged the threat, too.

"Gray, there are more of them further up the slope behind the first group," White Owl said. "Where did they all come from?"

"Head down the hill," Gray commanded.

White Owl led the way down the rocky slope with Angela and Clay right behind him, while Sarah and Gray provided covering fire.

Gray stopped firing and quickly reloaded, and then he and Sarah moved to where White Owl had stopped his retreat.

"Sarah, we don't have the ammunition for a prolonged withdrawal," Gray said.

"Yeah, I know. We better make them count."

"I see several subjects on the ground to the east and in front of us," White Owl announced after a quick check of the area. "We've hit some of them."

The cacophony of gunfire in front of them seemed to be abating.

"Now might be a good time for us to get the hell out of here," Clay said.

"Angela, Clay, rapid retreat to camp, now!" Gray shouted.

Sarah fired several rounds, then moved past Gray to new cover and said, "Gray, move."

Sarah, White Owl, and Gray continued firing for nearly another minute as they quickly moved down the hill. Then the gunfire in front of them suddenly stopped.

Gray asked, "White Owl, any activity to the north?"

"I only see Clay and Angela running toward camp." He scanned the trees to the south and east. "What the hell?"

"What's wrong?" Gray asked.

"The fallen warriors just got up and walked away."

"That's not possible," Sarah said, breathing heavily.

"It might be time to hasten our retreat while our luck holds," White Owl said. "I can't believe what I just saw."

"I'm amazed none of us were shot," Sarah added. "I could hear the bullets whizzing over our heads."

"Since they aren't advancing, Sarah and I will hold position here," Gray said. "You go catch up to Clay and Angela. Can I use your binoculars?"

"You saw the red eyes on the ones that took Crawley, didn't you?" White Owl asked, handing the binoculars over.

"Yes," Gray replied. "They looked like they were floating above the ground."

"That's what I thought," White Owl said.

"Get back to camp."

A moment later, a brilliant flash of blue light lit up the woods. It was brighter than ever before. Then a red orb rose quickly above the trees and vanished as it shot into the western sky. The blue light flashed twice more, then winked out.

Gray scanned the woods with the binoculars. "I don't see anyone."

"We need to go find Crawley," Sarah said. "He may be injured."

"We need more ammunition before we go back into the hot zone. I'm nearly out. They may be waiting for us."

"You don't think Crawley's alive, do you?" Sarah said.

Gray didn't hesitate in his response. "No, I don't." Crawley's scream had sent chills through him.

"Those warriors just appeared out of nowhere," Sarah said. "And how did they move so fast? And why were we unable to move? This is crazy."

"I know. Let's get back to camp. I'll have Angela and Clay go back to the truck to call for help."

After a short hike, they approached the edge of the tree line and White Owl appeared from the shadows, startling Sarah.

"It's not a good idea to sneak up on us like that," Sarah said, lowering her weapon. "I nearly shot you."

"I'm sorry," White Owl replied. "Clay and Angela are back in the camp. I decided to wait here just in case you needed cover fire."

"They've all gone," Gray said. "We need more ammunition before we head back to look for Crawley."

"Is your curiosity satisfied now that you've seen the buffalo warriors?" Sarah asked.

"Yes," White Owl replied. "The way they moved matched a story that my father told me when I was a child. He claimed to have seen spirit warriors once when he was out hunting. He said they flew through the woods like ghosts and that their red eyes glistened in the darkness as they passed him. My father believes they left him alone because he was Lakota. He said that he watched the warriors until a blue light appeared and swallowed them back into the Earth. All this time, I thought that he was just trying to scare me with an old tale to keep me from going into the woods alone at night, but now I know what he told me was true."

"Being Lakota made no difference tonight," Sarah said. "They shot at you, too."

White Owl rubbed his chin as if in thought, then replied, "Not the ones with red eyes who took Agent Crawley. They weren't carrying any rifles. Only the ones who came after they had taken Crawley fired at us."

"They were all wearing buffalo hides," Sarah said.

"Yes, but the ones who came later moved slower, like men."

Gray said, "Let's get back to camp."

They walked from the tree line and Gray saw that Clay and Angela had already placed the remaining ammunition, a first-aid kit, some power bars, and water bottles together in front of a tent.

"I'm afraid there's not much ammo left," Clay announced.

"It'll have to do," Gray replied. "Angela, I want you and Clay to head down to the truck and call in the calvary. No need for all of us to go back up the hill."

"I'm not going anywhere," Angela said defiantly. "If you find Crawley, you'll need our help to bring him back."

"She has a point," Clay said.

"My cruiser is at the top of the ridge," White Owl said. "If we find him, it would be closer to take him up there. If he's injured, rescue units can reach us faster, and there's a trauma center in Custer."

"That's if we get past the buffalo warriors defending the high ground," Gray said. He wondered if going back for Crawley was the smart thing to do, but if Crawley was miraculously alive, he couldn't just leave him. "Alright then, grab what you need and let's get back up there."

"I've seen some strange things in my life, but nothing like what I've witnessed the last two nights," Angela said.

"I think they're aliens," Clay claimed.

"And they dressed up in buffalo hides and fired rifles instead of ray guns?" Sarah quipped. "I think that hit to your head is clouding your judgement."

"Then how do you explain what just happened?" Clay replied defensively.

"They were Wakanpi," White Owl said quietly.

"Spirit warriors," Angela said.

"Those weren't spirits," Clay refuted. "They're alien beings hiding their form under buffalo hides. They looked like the ones that took Angela and me, but the ones who grabbed Crawley moved so much faster. And that red orb froze us in place."

"We'll piece this together after we search for Crawley," Gray said.

They left camp and worked their way slowly up the ridge. Gray took point while White Owl walked slightly behind him, scanning the area through his binoculars. When they arrived at the scene, they quickly searched the area and found no sign of Crawley, and thankfully no one else.

"I believe that they've left and taken Crawley with them," White Owl said.

"Where would they take him?" Sarah asked.

"Into the Earth," White Owl answered.

"White Owl, you and Clay go call for help so we can secure this area. We need to widen our search just to be sure Crawley isn't here."

"And if we encounter any aliens on the way, I'll yell," Clay stated.

Gray stared at him without replying, then shook his head.

White Owl and Clay started up the slope toward the top of the ridge and disappeared into the woods. The sound of their boots moving across the stones reminded Gray that there had been no sound from the warriors who had taken Crawley. *They should have made noise as they moved through the brush.*

"Don't forget, we have a crime scene to protect," Sarah said. "I've located some shell casings on the ground." Sarah let the beam of her flashlight reflect off several of them that were scattered among the rocks a few feet away. "Pretty easy to see. Some of them are ours."

Gray turned on his flashlight, scanned the woods, and shivered. He felt like someone, or something, was watching him. "Sarah, do you see anything out there?"

"No, but I got a funny feeling we're being stalked," Sarah replied, coming to stand next to him. "I had this same sense once when a grizzly was watching me." She scanned the woods with her flashlight. "I don't see anything. Gray, do you believe we were attacked by spirit warriors?"

"I don't know what to think." He wanted to stay grounded in reality. There had to be a better explanation than aliens or spirit warriors, but he couldn't think of one.

"They're not ethereal beings, at least not like I would imagine a spirit to be," Sarah replied, pushing a strand of hair behind her ear. "Crawley, Angela and Clay were held in their grasp."

Angela joined them and said, "I hate to say this, but I'm starting to think that either White Owl or Clay may be right. Whatever attacked us wasn't human."

"I have to admit that I'm starting to lean that way myself," Sarah said.

Gray checked the area again while Sarah and Angela kept watch. He found more shell casings and noticed the splintered tree bark from where their rounds had hit. Scanning the ground with his flashlight, he found no sign of blood where he knew the warriors had fallen. There were quite a number of 44-40 casings on the ground. He left them where they were and wandered back to the north, checking for any damage to the rocks and trees they'd used for cover. After a few minutes, he said, "I don't see any evidence that their rounds hit anything near where we were standing."

"Maybe we'll find more evidence when the sun comes up," Sarah said. "The rounds sounded like they were above us."

"That's what I thought." Gray saw a shadow behind a bush. Drawing his sidearm quickly, he shined his light and walked slowly toward it.

"What is it?" Sarah asked, hurrying toward him, firearm at the ready.

"I found Crawley's hat," Gray replied as he holstered. He knelt down and saw that small droplets of blood were splattered across the underside of the brim.

"Is that blood?" Sarah asked.

"Yes," Gray replied. "Spread out. He has to be nearby."

Clay sounded like a large animal as he stumbled through the brush on his way back down the steep slope. "It's just me," he shouted.

"We hear you coming," Gray said.

When Clay walked out of the thick brush, he said, "No human could get through that without making some kind of noise."

"I agree," Gray said. "Did Lt. White Owl get through to anyone?"

"Yes. We'll have support from Pennington and Custer SO in about forty minutes. He also contacted Wyoming DCI and explained what happened. They're sending a bunch of people, and so is Sheriff Lyons from Weston County. The FBI and assorted other local and federal agencies have also been notified. White Owl stayed up by his cruiser so he could lead them down to us."

"What about air support?" Sarah asked.

"Both air support and K-9 will be coming. The Oglala Sioux Tribe Department of Public Safety on the reservation has also been advised, but they aren't sending anyone."

"What did you all tell them happened to Crawley?" Sarah asked.

"Just that we were ambushed while working a homicide case, that Crawley had been kidnapped by four large men wearing buffalo hides, and that we'd been involved in a firefight." Clay looked at Gray and added, "We didn't mention aliens, strange lights, or spirit warriors."

"Probably good that you didn't," Gray said. "We found Crawley's hat and there's blood on it."

"That's not good."

"We also haven't found any sign of warrior blood," Sarah added.

"Maybe they don't bleed," Clay replied.

"We never found blood from the one I shot yesterday either," Gray said. *What are we dealing with here?*

GEOINT - May 24 – 0200 hours EDT

"I found her," Sharon shouted from her office.

Aki hurried to Sharon's office, with Brian and Chase following.

"Where is she?" Aki asked.

"You aren't going to believe this. She landed in North Dakota at the International Peace Garden Airport four hours ago."

"Under what alias?" Chase asked.

"Cora Zemanski. She used her Canadian passport and has cleared customs already."

"I know that airport," Aki said. "It's small and only a few hundred yards from the border. She must have chartered a small aircraft from Winnipeg."

"She did," Sharon said. "A Cessna 182 that's registered to a flight school at St. Andrews Airport in Canada. It has already flown back over the border."

"Crap," Aki snapped. "She could be anywhere by now."

"It gets better," Sharon said. "She declared a Remington 700 rifle with scope, and a Glock 26 semiautomatic."

"How the hell did she get those through customs?" Chase asked.

"She had all of the proper permits," Sharon replied.

"I wonder if she's headed for a meeting with the CEO from the Black Hills Gold Mining company?" Brian asked.

"Dar could have met with Ketterhorn in Winnipeg before crossing the border," Sharon added.

"She doesn't meet clients in person," Aki said, sounding puzzled. "Brian, I want all signals traffic between those two companies over the last week analyzed, then cross reference all of those numbers to any of Dar's numbers. I want to know who Ketterhorn and Santos have been talking to even if wasn't her."

"I'll have to call in a big favor," Brian said, "and the data dump will be huge."

"Then you better get to it," Aki said. "Sharon, send me everything you have so far on all of the Mázazi-affiliated companies."

"I'll do it right away."

After noticing Sharon's bloodshot eyes, Aki said, "Sorry for the late night or early start, but we have a chance to find Dar on our turf."

"No need to apologize, I'm enjoying every minute."

"In that case, find out the pilot's name that flew Dar into the States and how she paid for the charter. If she used a credit card, we can track or freeze her card."

"I'm betting that the pilot and aircraft charter are random," Sharon said. "The credit card could be under another alias."

"Possibly. Contact the pilot and see if he has a return trip scheduled with her, but don't spook him. See if Dar told him anything about what she was going to be doing here."

"I'm on it."

"Sharon, also check hotel and motel reservations under all of her known aliases in and around Rapid City when you have a chance."

Sharon snickered as her fingers flew over the computer keys. "I love this job."

"Should we issue an alert?" Chase asked.

"Not yet. Let me see what the customs agent at Peace Garden has to say. Chase, I want you to start searching for any current conflicts or issues that Black Hills Gold Mining has with any environmental or Native American group. Check police reports and media, especially around the Pine Ridge Reservation. You know the drill."

"That's where you grew up," Chase said.

"Yes." Aki didn't say anything else.

Chase nodded and left the office.

"Aki, are you Lakota?" Sharon asked, not taking her eyes off of her monitor.

"Yes." Aki went back to her office and sat at her desk. *Does Dar know that I'm Lakota?*

She picked up a pen and began drawing circles on her pad as she thought about what they needed to do next. *Dar is definitely leaving a trail, but why? Is she targeting a Lakota or another Native American group over mining rights and she wants to draw me into the fight? Why does she want me to know what weapons she has with her?* Aki rubbed her forehead, then found the number for the Peace Gardens Customs office and dialed.

"CBP Peace Garden, Officer Gordon Osborne speaking."

"Officer Osborne, this is Agent Akicita Dawson with Homeland Security. I need some information."

"What can I do for you?"

"You had a small plane land about four hours ago, and Cora Zemanski cleared customs there at 2010 hours your time."

"Yes. She wasn't on any alerts. Is she wanted?"

"Just someone of interest," Aki replied.

"I know what that means."

"Was she with anyone?" Aki asked.

"No, she deboarded the plane alone and we cleared her. The plane left immediately for Canada. She had some bags and two weapons, which were permitted. Is there a problem?"

"I know about the weapons," Aki replied. "Tell me what she looked like."

"Blond hair, maybe five feet ten. Blue eyes and attractive. She had on blue jeans, a long-sleeve black shirt, and black tactical boots. She said she was going to be doing some hunting in the area over the next few weeks. I can send you our video and photos."

Aki knew that she'd ditch that disguise shortly, but having her current photo might prove helpful. "Thanks." She gave him an email address. "Did you talk to her?"

"Yes. She told me she was looking forward to hunting and spending time in the woods. She didn't strike me as the hunter type. She did mention that she was going to meet some other hunters."

"I can assure you that she is a hunter," Aki said. "Did she say where she was going to meet the others or how many of them there were?"

"No."

"How did she leave the area?"

"A green Jeep was delivered earlier in the day. I didn't see anyone else with her when she drove away."

"What rental company?" Aki asked.

"I don't know."

Aki was having to pry everything from Osborne and was getting frustrated. "How many bags or suitcases? Tell me everything you can remember about your encounter with her, no matter how insignificant you think it might be."

"Not much more to tell. She had a rifle case, a handgun case, and two matching teal hardcase suitcases. I inspected them. She had clothes, including camouflage clothing, shoes, more boots, and assorted other personal items in the suitcases. She had a box of 9mm ammo for the Glock and a box of .308 for the rifle, an iPad, and two cell phones. That's all that I can remember."

"Two phones?"

"Yeah. I asked her about them and she said one was personal and the other was for business."

"Did you get the numbers?" Aki asked.

"I did not."

Aki knew that would have been too easy. "Which direction did she go when she left?"

"She drove south from the airport. She never said where she was headed."

"Okay. Thank you for the information. Is there anything else you can tell me? Anything unusual?"

"No. She was very pleasant and cooperative. Now I have a question for you."

Aki rocked back in her chair, wondering if she should just hang up. "Go ahead."

"If she returns, do I detain her?"

"Absolutely not. Any dialogue with her needs to be routine. Do not post any information about her or discuss our conversation with anyone. Clear?"

"Clear. I assume you'll want me to contact you if she does come back through here."

"Yes." Aki gave him her office number.

"I'm by nature curious. Why is she of interest to Homeland?"

"Don't be curious. Thank you again for the information." Aki hung up before he could ask any more questions. She hoped he'd gotten the message. "Chase!"

"You bellowed, Boss?" Chase shouted, from his office.

"Get in here. It's time to call Director Canton. We're going to take a little trip."

"Where to?" he asked, as he stepped through the doorway.

"We're going to Rapid City unless the director says otherwise. Sharon! Brian!"

"Yes, Boss," they both answered.

"Please, will everyone stop calling me that. I want you all present when I contact the director. Once the jet is ready, Chase and I will be flying out. So, you'll have to catch Omar up."

"Providing the director approves," Chase qualified. "Or we can just not tell her where we're going and see what our operational limits really are."

"I think it best we feed her this intel. We may need support. All of you sit down." Aki dialed Director Canton's secure cell.

A groggy voice answered after two rings. "Yes, Aki."

"How'd you know it was me?"

"You're the only person who has this number," Canton replied. "What is it?"

"I have you on speaker. Chase, Brian, and Sharon are listening. May I continue?"

"Yes. Good morning, all."

"Director, first, sorry for the early call, but I wanted to let you know that we've tracked Dar down. She crossed the Canadian border under an alias and we believe she's headed for Rapid City, South Dakota."

"That was fast work," Canton replied.

"I have a great team. With your permission, Chase and I want to try and intercept her."

"You don't need my permission. Do what you need to do."

"She brought two weapons through customs, a rifle and a handgun. I spoke to the customs and border protection officer. Dar told him she was going to be doing some hunting."

"I bet she is. How did you track her down?"

Aki explained it, then added, "I think she wants us to know she's here."

"From what you've told me, I believe you're correct. Which means she'll be prepared to engage you and that makes her even more dangerous."

"We're still trying to determine her target," Aki said. "The rest of the team will be working on that while Chase and I are en route. How do you want to handle the reporting updates?" There was long silence on the line. "Director?"

"Aki, it's your operation. Keep all intel tight. Does your team understand?"

"Yes. They know what's expected. No information will leave the office."

"Good. Call me when you have Dar in custody or she's dead. If you create a mess, it's your mess to clean up."

"Understood," Aki said.

"Good luck."

Aki looked at the others in the office. "We're on our own. Chase, I want to be wheels-up in less than an hour. Dar said that she was going hunting. Let's make sure we take a long-range sniper rifle with us. If we need gear for an extended stay in the woods, we'll buy it out there."

She and Chase kept an assortment of weapons and ready-go bags in their vehicles for rapid response.

"We'll send you updates on what we find while you're headed west," Sharon said.

"Thanks. I want you to be our relay. I don't want everyone calling us. Brian, you and Omar will funnel your intel through Sharon. If it's time sensitive, obviously forward it immediately by the quickest means."

"Stay safe," Brian said.

"Plan to," Aki replied.

CHAPTER FOURTEEN

As soon as Aki and Chase landed at Rapid City Regional Airport, Aki's cell phone rang.

"Yes, Sharon," Aki answered, putting the cell on speaker.

"There's a massive manhunt underway in the southern part of the Black Hills. A Wyoming DCI agent was kidnapped during a gun battle last night. The chatter indicates multiple local, state, and federal agencies are involved in the search. Details are still sketchy."

"I doubt that Dar's involved," Aki said. "She just got here."

"It may be why she's there," Sharon replied. "DCI is working two homicides. One of the victims recovered was an exploration supervisor for Black Hills Gold Mining in Rapid City. There are several other missing employees from three of the four mining companies associated with the Mázazi conglomerate."

"Okay, that's interesting. What else?"

"Both homicide victims were found near Devils Tower, Wyoming, but they were last seen in the Black Hills. The Wyoming DCI agent who's missing was in charge of the investigation, and members of his task force were involved a firefight last night with those who took him."

"That explains why the Wyoming DCI agent was in South Dakota," Chase said.

The small jet rocked slightly as it transitioned to the taxiway, forcing Chase to grab the back of a seat.

"Careful, Chase," Aki cautioned.

"Everything alright?" Sharon asked.

"Yes. Chase just lost his balance when the plane jostled. Continue."

"All of the missing mining personnel were scouting the Black Hills. For some unknown reason, the employees weren't reported missing right away. The companies were also vague about the exact location they were exploring. Of interest, and probably why Dar was called, is that one of the people missing is William Ossa's niece. He's the CEO of Pelion Mining."

"It sounds like the companies didn't want what they found or any of their troubles to be made public," Chase said. "Instead, they called Dar to find their people and eliminate the problem."

"It won't stay quiet for long now that a DCI agent is missing," Aki said. "The area will be crawling with law enforcement. Whatever is going on there must be big if the bad guys were willing to engage in a firefight and kidnap a DCI agent. Sharon, did you find any information on environmental or Native American confrontations of late?"

"Nothing recent. I found numerous references to long-standing legal battles between a number of mining companies—including BHGM—and the Lakota and other tribes over damage to the environment and infringement on Native lands. Probably the same ones that Chase found."

"Chase and I will stop by the reservation and see if anything is brewing," Aki said. "The mining of the Black Hills has been destroying our sacred land for over a century. Politicians receive substantial political funding from the mining companies and often pass legislation to support their interests on Native lands. That usually results in water-table contamination for the Lakota and other nations. The Mázazi companies may have found something they want to claim and have pissed off one of the tribes."

"I'll take a look and see what else I can find," Sharon said. "I just learned that *Mázazi* means 'gold' in Lakota…?"

"Yes, it does, and thanks for the update." Aki signed off.

"I think we should pay an unannounced visit to Mark Santos' office," Chase said. "If Dar contacted Noel Ketterhorn in Winnipeg, she might be meeting with Santos."

"It doesn't make sense that she would want a face-to-face with any of the mining execs."

"Do you think this assignment is too big for Dar to handle alone?"

"You read my mind," Aki said. "She might be forced to work with the security teams from the Mázazi alliance."

"There's a lot of area to search, and trying to find who's responsible will be a monumental task."

Aki thought for a minute, then said, "Dar's always been a lone wolf, but we can't rule out that she may have to use their people. Santos may be willing to cooperate with us, given the right incentive."

"Are you going to activate a response team?"

Aki smiled. "I already requested a DHS rapid response team. They're supposed to be en route to the Camp Rapid National Guard facility. They'll stage there until we have something definite on Dar's location. Air support will also be available. If we can locate her, the team will be on-station within an hour."

"I have a feeling that we're going to catch the bitch this time," Chase said.

Black Hills – 0630 hours

Gray rubbed the tension knot on the back of his neck as he stood watching the forensic teams painstakingly working the site. So far, they'd found shell casings and some footprints. He was sleep deprived and in a foul mood, and now he'd been summoned to meet Wyoming DCI Director George Sutton and both of the Wyoming DCI regional commanders. They were waiting for him at the new command post on the top of the ridge. He wasn't looking forward to the steep climb and then having to repeat the same story he'd already told investigators. His head was pounding.

"You look like I feel," Sarah said, joining him and putting her hand on his shoulder.

"Gee, thanks. I don't think anyone believes our story."

She handed him a cup of coffee. "I know they don't."

"Where'd you get the coffee?"

"At the new mess tent," Sarah replied. "At least someone thought ahead and brought food and drinks and a few portable toilets. Law-enforcement personnel are streaming in from all over Wyoming and South Dakota, and several mobile command buses and trailers have also arrived. We wouldn't be in this situation if Crawley had just called in some help before this turned into such a Charlie Foxtrot."

Gray took a sip of his coffee. It was lukewarm but better than nothing. "He did what he thought was right at the time."

"You're defending him?" Sarah asked, giving him a quizzical look.

"No." Gray looked up as a helicopter flew over. "I'm just saying that hindsight is always clearer."

"He still should have listened to us. I think he didn't call in support because it was what we requested and he wanted us to know that he was in charge."

Gray couldn't disagree. "I guess I better go talk to my temporary bosses." Gray drained the cup. "Wish me luck."

"G'luck."

Gray worked his way up the slope, avoiding the large crime-scene area that had been taped off. As he passed by two investigators, he heard them complaining about the lack of cell reception and radio communications. *Welcome to our world.*

When he reached the top of the ridge, he saw Lt. White Owl speaking with three men by a newly erected, large mess tent. He noted White Owl's face appeared hardened and his jaw was clenched.

"Here he is now," White Owl said, nodding in Gray's direction. "You know where to find me if you have any further questions." Then he turned and walked away.

A tall, heavyset man walked toward him. His dyed jet-black hair matched his horseshoe mustache, and his black cowboy hat and suit. He looked to be in his late fifties and he reminded Gray of a character from an old Western movie. The other two younger men who fell in behind him were dressed similarly. Gray figured that they must have all shopped at the same store as Crawley.

"Agent Holt, I'm DCI Director George Sutton. This is Regional Commander Justin Littlejohn, who's Agent Crawley's immediate super-visor, and this is Regional Commander Luke Windward from Cheyenne."

No one offered to shake his hand. Gray felt this was going to be about as much fun as a prostate exam. "Nice to meet you gentlemen."

"Agent Holt, I wasn't in favor of your DCI assignment, even temporarily, but I was overridden by both the governor and the attorney general," Sutton stated.

"I appreciate your candor. I wasn't really interested in the assignment at first either, but Agent Crawley was persuasive. I'll be starting my new job with the Office of Aviation Services under the Department of Interior in a couple of weeks. I'm a pilot."

"I was briefed on your future assignment," Sutton said dismissively, then locked eyes with Gray.

The tension knot in Gray's neck tightened.

"Agent Crawley has a way of getting what he wants and doesn't care much for the chain of command unless it serves his needs," Littlejohn said.

"Commander Littlejohn, how long has Agent Crawley worked for you?" Gray asked. He'd never heard Crawley even mention having a supervisor.

"A number of years." There was a touch of emotion in his voice. "He was a good man."

"He still is a good man," Sutton corrected. "We don't know that he's dead, unless temporary Special Agent Holt knows something we don't."

"I told the investigators what I know," Gray said. "And I don't appreciate the insinuation."

"I don't really care," Sutton replied. "I was told that you have homicide experience."

"That's correct."

Sutton continued his hard stare, then said, "Lt. White Owl told us what happened and we've been briefed about your statements and those of the others who were with Agent Crawley last night. Quite frankly, I find it hard to believe this was perpetrated by mysterious lights and buffalo-spirit warriors. What aren't you telling us? Did one of you shoot Agent Crawley?"

And now I know where Crawley learned his interview skills, Gray mused. He understood Sutton questioning their story. "Agent Crawley wasn't shot by any of us. He was carried away by what can only be described as spirit warriors. Lt. White Owl told me that they fit the description of the legends of such warriors, which was corroborated by Dr. Kingman, who is a professor and expert in Native American culture."

"So I've heard," Sutton said, taking a half step toward Gray. "I want you to tell me what really happened."

Gray didn't give ground. He spent the next few minutes relating the events.

"So, you contend that you all saw a flash of blue light followed by a mystical red orb that flew over Agent Crawley," Sutton said. "Then warriors magically appeared out of nowhere and ferreted Agent Crawley away while none of you did a damn thing to stop them because you were frozen in place by the red light."

"That *is* what happened," Gray said.

"And you're certain it was Agent Crawley you heard scream?"

"Yes."

"That's a bunch of crap," Sutton spat, taking another step closer. "I want you to tell me where you buried Agent Crawley's body and the 44-40 caliber rifle. Right now!"

Gray bristled. He wasn't going to let Sutton's absurd accusation go unchallenged. He stepped forward, forcing Sutton back. Littlejohn and Windward closed ranks.

"We didn't kill him!" Gray stated firmly. "It's ludicrous for you to think that we'd concoct a bizarre story to cover up for someone having shot him. We don't even know each other that well."

"Bizarre is right," Sutton said. "Lt. White Owl claimed the spirit warriors had red eyes, but you didn't mention that detail just now."

"Listen up," Gray began. "Everything I've told you is true. And yes, the spirit warriors had red eyes. Director Sutton, I've been shot at by two different adversaries over the last two days, I'm tired, and I forgot that detail. As for the rifle casings, the same caliber casings were found after both encounters."

"Uh huh. The shell casings we've collected, other than yours, all look weathered and could have been out here for years. There's no physical evidence to corroborate that you shot anyone, and what's even harder to believe is that they all got up at the same time and walked or floated away."

"I don't have an explanation for what we saw."

"Why the hell are you in South Dakota?" Sutton barked.

"We followed a lead left by one of the victims. The coordinates pointed to this location. Lt. White Owl was our South Dakota liaison. If you want physical evidence of our encounter with the spirit warriors, look at the back of Deputy Gurley's head. He was struck during our first encounter and should have a bruise on his scalp."

"So I was informed. Amazing that you were able to rescue him and Dr. Kingman. Why do you think they took their time carrying them away and not freezing you in place?"

"I don't have a clue."

"Why didn't Agent Crawley notify us of your first armed encounter?" Sutton asked. "He should have, considering you supposedly shot someone."

"I don't think that Agent Crawley believed our account. If he did, I can only surmise that he thought we'd encountered people wearing bulletproof vests and that it didn't warrant reporting anything until he concluded the investigation. There's physical evidence from that encounter, just no blood."

"Quite a coincidence that all these people were shot and there's not a drop of blood anywhere," Sutton said.

"Look, we asked Agent Crawley to bring in additional personnel for security and to help with the first crime scene, but he didn't think we needed support and refused."

"That does sound like him," Littlejohn interjected. "He has a particular way of conducting investigations and doesn't like having too many investigators in the mix."

"I noticed that on the homicide investigations," Gray said. "We also found some other items in a box buried under a rock. A watch found in the box was identified as belonging to one of the homicide victims, and we believe the other items belong to the people who are missing. The box had Lakota markings on the lid. We wouldn't have found that evidence if we hadn't crossed into South Dakota."

"So I was informed." Sutton paused a moment. "Maybe you can tell me why Dr. Kingman, a civilian, was shooting a shotgun."

"Agent Crawley gave her the weapon and told her to only use it to protect herself if she was fired upon."

"Agent Crawley gave her the shotgun?" Sutton scoffed. "None of what you're telling me or the investigators makes any sense."

"I can't be any clearer," Gray replied, fighting to keep his temper in check.

Sutton adjusted his belt and pushed his hat back off of his forehead. "I really don't know what to think. You seem sincere. Will you submit to a polygraph?"

"Certainly."

A DCI agent hurried up to them. "Sorry to interrupt, Director Sutton, but the forensic team has found something that I thought you would want to see immediately."

"Why didn't you just call me?"

"Phones aren't working."

"Well, what is it?" Sutton asked.

The agent handed him his phone.

Sutton looked at the photo displayed on the screen. "It's a boot. What's it doing in a tree?"

"I don't know. One of the searchers looked up and noticed it. I'd say it's about fifteen feet off the ground."

"Where was it found?" Littlejohn asked.

"It's about a half mile west of here near Kinney Canyon. It hasn't been moved and K-9 is searching the area. I'm pretty sure that boot belonged to Agent Crawley. I remember he wore that style." The agent looked at Gray. "You saw him last. Was he wearing them?"

Sutton raised his hand before Gray could respond and said, "I'll ask the questions." He enlarged the photo on the screen, then showed Littlejohn the photo. "What do you think?"

"I think that's Agent Crawley's left boot," Littlejohn said. "He always wears Laredo Brentwoods. He keeps a shined pair at the office."

"Agent Holt, was he wearing these out here yesterday?" Sutton asked, showing him the photo.

"Yes, sir. I didn't understand why he wanted to wear them in this terrain, but he did, and they were pretty scuffed up, just like that one. The silver toe and heel are distinctive."

Sutton gave the phone back to the agent, then said, "Get one of those choppers over that area and have more K-9 units respond."

"Yes, sir," the agent replied, and left.

"Damn, this just gets weirder and weirder," Sutton mumbled.

"Director, there's nothing further that I can tell you," Gray said. "I'd like to get some rest."

"I want you and the others involved to remain close to the command area. Commander Windward, I want tents and cots set up for all personnel. We're going to be here for the duration. I also want food trucks and whatever else you think needs to be brought in for support. You can coordinate with Captain Hunt from Pennington SO. They're sending their mobile-command unit and the Pennington County search-and-rescue team. As the other South Dakota agencies arrive, I want you to liaison with them and the feds."

"Yes, sir," Commander Windward replied, then hurried away.

"Gray, I'll have your friends join you in few minutes," Sutton said. "The command bus has a shower and facilities if you want to get cleaned up, which I recommend. No offense, but you reek."

"No offense taken."

Sutton's tone softened. "I'm still not sure that I believe you."

"If I hadn't experienced it, I may not have believed it either."

"When did you last sleep?"

"It's been a while for all of us," Gray answered.

"Commander Littlejohn, see that they all get something to eat and some shut-eye. When forensics is done with their camp, have their tents and gear brought here."

"Yes, sir," Littlejohn replied.

Rapid City – May 24 – 0830 hours

Dar sat in her newly rented maroon Toyota Sequoia, sipping a weak cup of coffee while watching the entrance to the BHGM building. *Americans have no idea how to brew coffee.* She took a bite of her cinnamon bagel to wash away the bitter taste. She hoped that Aki had put the pieces of the puzzle together and would be paying Mark Santos a visit this morning. She needed to confirm that her adversary had taken the bait and to determine what kind of support she had with her. She yawned and took another sip of the coffee.

She'd broken a cardinal rule last night when she'd contacted Santos directly. Dar needed help and had to make contact if she wanted to find the hostages, or more likely the victims. The area she needed to search was too vast to do it alone. She was going to have Wayne Hagans, the chief of security for BHGM, do some snooping for her. Santos had approved. She'd provided Hagans with some grunt work, just to test the waters and see if he drew Aki's attention.

Dar had also hired a local private investigator, Carlton Safir, as an independent intelligence gatherer. She wanted someone who could conduct interviews and not be linked to her or the mining companies. There weren't that many investigative agencies in Rapid City, and the Discreet Investigations website posted no photographs of Carlton or his staff, which was smart. Carlton claimed to have sources on the reservation and in several of the law-enforcement departments around the Black Hills. He asserted that he could get her answers to anything she needed to know.

She wasn't completely sold that he'd deliver what he claimed, but Dar felt that he'd do just about anything for the right amount of money. She'd paid him for three full-time investigators, plus expenses upfront, for two weeks. Dar felt that would get his undivided attention. And if he didn't deliver as promised, Dar would make sure that she was his last client.

Dar was having second thoughts about having told Santos that he would be visited by Homeland Security agents today. That information had sent him into a tirade about how Marcu had assured him that the mining consortium wouldn't be tied to any of her activity. He'd voiced his displeasure about being questioned by Homeland agents. When he finally calmed down, she'd instructed him to call her after the agents left and told him to meet her at a local café off St. James Street to discuss the operation further.

Of course, she wouldn't be meeting him. The café wasn't far from his office and she could watch both locations from where she was parked. If Aki was here, Aki would follow Santos when he left. That was when she'd get a better idea of how many operatives were with her and what they were driving. Dar planned to wait until noon. She had nothing else to do until Carlton turned up something.

Dar didn't have to wait that long. Aki and Chase pulled up and parked in front of the BHGM building in a red Ford Explorer.

"Well, well," Dar said, focusing her high-powered binoculars on the BHGM entrance. "Aki, you're so predictable." She scanned the area to see who else was with them, but it appeared that they had come alone. *Odd, they didn't bring a team.*

Dar watched as they sat in their car for several minutes. Aki finally got out of the SUV and looked around, and then Chase pulled away. Dar continued observing Aki as she stood near the front entrance. She figured Chase was checking the area for her Jeep. After a few minutes, Chase returned and parked.

It's time to have some fun.

CHAPTER FIFTEEN

"No sign of Dar or the Jeep," Chase said, getting out of the Explorer. "She probably changed cars."

Aki took another minute to scan the parking lots near the building. She sensed Dar was close. "Let's go see Mr. Santos."

The double glass doors opened automatically as they approached. When they entered the large lobby, Aki noticed an elegantly dressed, pretty blond receptionist seated behind a long slate-topped counter. The BHGM company logo of crossed mining picks beneath a golden sun hung on the wall. The lobby was impressive.

"Good morning, how may I assist you?" the receptionist asked.

Aki showed her Homeland Security identification, then said, "We're here to speak with your president and CEO, Mark Santos."

"Do you have an appointment?" The receptionist's tone was distinctively less pleasant.

"No," Aki replied. "He'll want to speak with us. It's concerning your missing personnel."

The receptionist nodded and dialed a number. After a brief conversation, she said, "His secretary advised that he's been expecting you. Security will need to escort you up. It's a secure floor. Please wait by the elevator. It won't be long."

As Aki walked with Chase to the elevator, she quietly said, "He's been expecting us? That's interesting."

The elevator door pinged and a muscular security guard stepped off. "I need to see your identification."

Aki and Chase provided their credentials.

"Are you armed?"

"Always," Aki replied.

"You'll need to check your weapons and cell phones over there." He pointed at a bank of lockboxes that were nestled between two plastic ficus plants.

"We aren't checking our weapons or our phones," Aki said. "We're federal agents."

"I can't take you to see Mr. Santos unless you comply. It's company policy."

"Very well. I'll call in my HSI response team to cover all the exits. We'll wait for him outside and question him when he leaves." Aki crossed her arms.

The security guard backed into the elevator and closed the doors.

"Well, he's either calling your bluff or going to talk to his boss," Chase said.

"Yup. Let's head for the door and see what happens. The security cameras will capture me making a call." Aki took out her cell phone and held it to her ear.

Chase smiled at the receptionist and said, "We'll be outside waiting for the rest of our team."

They went to the Explorer and donned their blue HSI raid jackets.

"Not really covert now, are we?" Chase said.

"Whatever gets the job done," Aki replied. She stared up at the security camera that hung over the front entrance. She knew that Santos wouldn't want them standing there drawing attention.

A few moments later, the security guard they'd spoken to at the elevator hurried through the front doors and said, "Mr. Santos will see you now. He requests that you leave your jackets in the car."

"That's a reasonable request," Aki replied.

They put their jackets back in the SUV, and then she pretended to call off the response team as they walked back into the building. The guard followed and rode up in the elevator with them without saying a word.

When the elevator doors opened on the top floor, two more security guards were waiting in the spacious office-reception area, and a few people stopped working to look at them.

"This way," the guard said.

Ornate double doors electronically opened as they approached an office. A short, balding, overweight man in an expensive gray suit stood waiting to greet them. Aki recognized Santos from a picture she'd seen of him, which had obviously been taken years before when he was younger and had more hair.

"Mr. Santos, thank you for seeing us," Aki said, extending her hand. "I'm Special Agent Akicita Dawson, and this is Special Agent Colin Chase. We're with Homeland Security."

"Yes, I know. I was told that this visit was related to our missing personnel. Did you find them?"

"No. We're here on a matter of national security, which may be related." Aki looked at the guard still standing in the open doorway. "We need to discuss this in private."

Santos dismissed the guard, then said, "National security? I don't understand."

"May we sit?"

"Yes, please." He motioned to the chairs by the round, highly polished mahogany conference table. "What's this all about?"

After they were seated, Aki leaned forward, placed both hands together on the table, and said, "Mark, you have a problem." She waited for his reaction and was rewarded with a small eyelid twitch, followed by his breaking eye contact.

"Please explain."

"The person you hired to help investigate the missing personnel from the Mázazi mining alliance is a terrorist and a hired assassin," Aki stated.

"And we're here to capture her," Chase added. "So, we need to know where she's staying, about any contacts you've had with her, what was discussed during those contacts, if and when you plan to meet with her, and everything else related to why she was hired."

A small film of sweat formed on his brow. "I didn't know she was a terrorist when we hired her. One of our associates recommended her. She's supposed to be very good at resolving issues. He thought that she'd be able to find our personnel quicker and with less publicity than the local law enforcement."

"She wasn't only hired to find your employees, was she?" Aki inquired, in a knowing tone.

"I don't know what you mean."

"Dragos Marcu hired her and has already paid his share of her fee. We're also aware of the previous work that she did for him."

"How could you possibly know that?"

"We know many things," Aki replied cryptically. "Let's not play games. Have you met with her?"

"No. I spoke with her by phone."

"Have you forwarded any payments to her in the last eight hours?"

"No, I've not paid her anything. Dragos made all of the arrangements and he's supposed to provide me with an account number when she finds our employees. That's all I know." Santos paused, removed his glasses, and wiped the perspiration from his forehead with a monogrammed handkerchief. "I knew this was a bad idea from the start."

Aki casually leaned back and asked, "How did you know we were coming?"

"She told me to expect you."

"We'll need the numbered account when you get it. What name did she use?"

Santos appeared puzzled by the question, then replied, "Cora Zemanski."

"Have you agreed to provide her with any assistance?" Chase asked.

Santos didn't answer immediately, then said, "I'm going to get one of our attorneys to join us." He used the phone on the table, and after a brief conversation, he hung up and said, "We'll wait for him before we go any further. You're questioning me like I'm a criminal."

"We're just doing our job," Chase said.

"You know, I have very influential friends in the senate and several governors who won't take kindly to me being treated this way. I'm sure that they know your boss. Threatening me with a raid was outrageous. You should tread lightly."

Aki smirked. "Mark, I don't care who you know."

"You will address me as Mr. Santos."

Aki shook her head, then said, "We aren't here about mining rights or any of your shady business dealings or infringements on Native American lands. We're hunting a killer who poses a threat to this country and others. Make sure you tell that to your senator friends when you speak with them. Now answer the question. Are you providing her with any assistance?"

"We'll wait for my attorney before we continue," Santos repeated firmly.

A moment later, there was a knock at the door. Santos went to his desk, pressed a button next to the phone, and the doors opened. A tall elderly man sauntered into the room. The muscular guard waited at the door.

"Mr. Santos, you don't need to answer any more questions," the attorney said, without introducing himself. "Agents, this interview is over."

"Wow," Chase said. "I think you're overreacting a bit. You haven't even heard the questions yet. What are you all afraid of? Oh, that's right, BHGM's association with a known terrorist."

"You heard my attorney," Santos said angrily. "Leave."

"I suggest you speak with us now before it's too late," Chase said.

"I said, this interview is over," the attorney uttered, more forcefully.

"If you have offered her assistance, you need to tell us before she starts killing people—and she will," Aki said. "As I'm sure Dragos told you, that's how she solves problems."

"And when she kills someone, you and your associates will be accessories to murder and a whole bunch of other charges," Chase added.

"Get out!" the attorney bellowed. He turned to the security guard at the door. "Escort them out. Now!"

"Mark, you're about to have a big problem," Aki said. "We'll see you again, soon."

"No, you won't," the attorney said. "Not unless you have a warrant or a subpoena."

Aki stood and faced the attorney. "You need to take a hard look in the mirror, because the person we're hunting will strike again and the blood of those killed will be on your hands." Aki walked past the guard and out of the office.

As Chase walked past the attorney, he said, "Big mistake." He followed Aki to the elevator, and the security guard rode down with them to the first floor.

Once out of the building, Aki said, "I think that went well. Get Brian on the phone. Let's find out who Santos calls first."

"I'm on it."

"Give me the keys. I'll drive," Aki said. "We'll park down the street and see if he leaves the office in a hurry."

Forty minutes later, Santos left the building, alone. He looked up and down the street, then walked to a black Lincoln Aviator that was parked in his reserved space.

"Game time," Aki said.

"I was starting to think we were wasting our time," Chase said.

Santos pulled onto the road, drove two blocks, and parked in front of a café.

Aki had just pulled out to follow but had to quickly pull back to the curb.

"That was a short trip," Chase said.

"Yes, it was."

When Santos exited the car, he looked around again, then went into a café.

"He has to be meeting someone," Chase said. "He's not there for breakfast or the coffee. He had quite an assortment of food and drink at his office."

"I agree," Aki said. "Let's wait ten minutes and see who joins him. If no one shows, we'll go grab a bite in the café and make him nervous while we eat. I'm hungry."

"What if Dar's already there?"

"We won't get that lucky. If anyone's there, it'll be someone doing her bidding."

As they waited, a maroon Toyota Sequoia passed slowly by as if looking for a parking space, then sped off.

"Did that seem suspicious to you?" Chase asked.

"A little."

"That couldn't have been Dar?"

"Unlikely," Aki replied. "Remember, she told Santos to expect us. She wouldn't be joining him for breakfast knowing that we're nearby. Maybe it was someone from BHGM security. Screw it. Let's go talk to Santos and rattle his cage."

Aki drove up in front of the café and parked. When they entered the café, Aki noted that Santos was seated at a booth in the back of the restaurant next to an exit door. He was typing on his cell phone and didn't notice their approach until Chase slid in next to him, forcing him to move over. Aki sat down across from him.

Santos concealed his phone and said, "What the hell?"

"Hello again," Aki said. "Is this a good place to grab a bite? I missed breakfast and I'm starved." She picked up a menu that was on the table in front of her. "Expecting a guest to join you?"

"I'm not saying a word and I'll be filing a complaint," Santos threatened.

"Complain away," Chase said.

A waitress stopped at the table and said, "Looks like your party has arrived. I'll get another menu."

"No need," Chase said. "A coffee and tea would be great. Mr. Santos, do you want anything?"

Santos just glared at Chase. The waitress left quickly, sensing the tension at the table.

Aki said, "*Mark*, I feel bad just barging in on you like that this morning, but you did say that you knew we were coming, which tells me that you'd spoken to Cora."

Santos didn't respond.

When the waitress retuned with their coffee and tea, Aki and Chase ordered omelets with bacon on the side. Santos continued to stay mute.

Aki said, "Cora isn't coming." Santos' eyelid twitched and he broke eye contact. "You know, I can appreciate you wanting to hire the best to find Mr. Ossa's niece and the others. I really can."

Santos said, "You know about his niece?"

"Like I told you earlier, we know everything about you and your partners. We also know that Cora is nearby and that she told you to meet her here. Something else you should know about her is that she doesn't take personal meetings, so this was probably arranged to see if we were following you."

"Were you just texting her?" Chase asked. "Let me see your phone."

Santos slid to the wall and kept a tight grip on his cell phone.

"Just give me the phone," Chase said.

Santos didn't move.

"I don't think you realize how dangerous she is," Aki said. "She's shot at us several times and even shot down our helicopter. Help us capture her before there are more casualties. Tell us what you know, and what she's asked of you and the other members of the Mázazi mining alliance."

Santos swallowed hard, then sighed and said, "I'm not accustomed to being in this type of situation or being treated with such disrespect."

"I'm certain that in the mining industry, you're considered a powerful man and have a lot of influence over your interests and political allies," Aki said, "but you have stepped into something that is way out of your league. If your people are still alive, we'll find them. Law enforcement is crawling all over that area right now. You don't need Dar, if that's what's keeping you from cooperating with us."

"Who's Dar?"

"That's Cora's real name," Aki answered.

Just then Santos's phone pinged.

"Let me get that for you," Chase said, reaching for the phone.

Santos didn't resist this time and Chase took his phone.

"Well, that's different," Chase said, after reading the text. "It's from Dar, but the message is for us. She'd like us to call her."

"Let me have that," Aki said, taking the phone. "Get Brian working on triangulating her location while I talk to her."

Chase called Brian as Aki scrolled through the text messages between Santos and Dar. "Interesting," she said. "It seems that you are providing support. I believe that Mr. Hagans is your chief of security." Aki looked up from the phone. "Does he drive a maroon Sequoia?"

"No," Santos said, in a defeated tone. "Chief Hagans hasn't done anything."

"We'll need to speak with him," Aki said, "and without the attorney. Oh, and we'll be hanging on to your cell phone."

Chase said, "Brian asked us to give him a few minutes to get everything ready. They'll ping the cell towers while you talk."

A few minutes later, Chase received a call from Brian telling him that he was ready, and Aki dialed Dar's number from Santos's phone and put it on speaker.

"Hello, Aki," Dar said, sounding like they were the best of friends.

"Hello, Dar," Aki replied, turning the volume down.

"I see that Chase is with you on this excursion."

"Yes. Why don't you stop by the café? We can have a little chat. Mr. Santos was disappointed that you stood him up. I'll even buy you breakfast."

Dar chuckled. "Now, where's the sport in my just giving up? You know that we're actually working toward the same goal. If I stop now, more people could die. I couldn't live with myself if that happened, not to mention the blemish on my reputation."

"I imagine that Dragos Marcu's money transfer was just a down payment?"

"Yes."

"I'm not sure that the other partners are going to send you the rest of your fee now that they know who you are and how you operate."

"They *will* pay me when I find their people," Dar replied threateningly.

Santos stiffened.

It was the reaction Aki had hoped Santos would have when she had baited Dar. "I don't see how you're going to complete this assignment. Your primary search area is crawling with law enforcement. They'll find those people before you do. Looks like you're going to have to write this one off."

Chase nodded excitedly at her, then scribbled on a napkin, *She's within a quarter mile.*

Dar gave a snort. "It's just means that it will be more of a challenge. I'm surprised that you and Agent Chase came alone. At least you weren't in a helicopter this time."

"Dar, let's stop this inane bantering. You know that we're here to take you in and we aren't going to stop until we do. So, save us all some time and effort, and let's do this peacefully. I don't want this to end badly for you or any other innocent civilians. You really made a mess in Poland."

"Poland was unavoidable." There was a pause. "Agent Dawson, I'm not going to let you arrest me. I suppose if it comes down to it, we'll have to see if you can kill me before I kill you. You know that I could have killed you several times already, but I really do like you. I enjoy watching you come up with different ways to pursue me. I also think that you enjoy pursuing me. So, let's keep playing the game."

"It's not a game," Aki said. She really wanted to put a bullet in Dar's head.

"You need to realize that I'll always be a step ahead of you. Who knows, maybe in time, we will become friends. I'd still like to buy you that drink."

"That isn't going to happen."

"Well, that's too bad," Dar replied. "You know that I'm near the café. Chase looked excited when he received word of my location."

Aki turned and looked out the front window. The maroon Sequoia that had drawn their attention earlier was parked across the street.

"Yes, Aki. I'm in the Toyota. I'll be seeing you." Dar pulled up in front of the café, rolled down the window, waved at her, and then sped away.

"Shit!" Aki tore out the café, but Dar was nowhere in sight when she reached the road.

Chase ran up to her. "I'll get the car."

"We won't catch her, she's in the wind," Aki said. "Let's go see if we can get any more information out of Santos and his security chief."

"Aki, she can't be that far ahead of us. Maybe Brian can track her phone."

"I'm certain that she had her escape route planned before she taunted us, and the phone is probably lying on the side of the road. Our paths will cross again. She's going to continue looking for the missing mining employees, and so are we."

"Seriously?" Chase said. "We're going to assist in the search?"

"We'll be following the same leads that Dar will follow. We'll be in the same area as her and I know that she's not going to give up on this assignment. I believe that we can add a layer to our investigation by helping the locals, and in turn, they just might help us. If we find the missing agent and the others before she does, Dar will have failed, and that won't sit well with her."

"Okay, but our interaction with other agencies will draw attention."

"I can live with that. I'll alert Director Canton in case anyone inquires."

"I'll call Sharon and let her know we're looking into the homicide and missing persons investigations and see what she can dig up. I'm sure she won't mind adding a few more things to her list."

"Make sure she knows that she can delegate," Aki said. "We're also going to need topographical maps of the area. It's been a while since I was in the Black Hills. And, see if we can get access to a high-altitude drone for aerial surveillance on short notice."

"What about Mr. Santos?"

"Let's go see what else he has to say and finish our breakfast. He'll need time to get his chief of security briefed before we get back to the BHGM building."

BHGM Headquarters – May 24 –1215 hours

Aki's and Chase's interview with Santos and Security Chief Wayne Hagans hadn't revealed any actionable information. Santos confirmed that Dar was hired to eliminate those responsible for the kidnappings and killings. He adamantly professed that he was opposed to hiring her, but he'd been overruled by the board.

"Santos didn't tell us everything," Aki said, as they left the BHGM headquarters.

"Yeah, cooperating fully, my ass," Chase replied. "I don't think Security Chief Hagans held anything back."

"I agree. He hadn't run any of her requests down yet, and he's not going to do anything for her now. I got the impression he wanted nothing to do with her."

They got back in the Explorer and Chase checked in with Sharon.

"Sharon says that the contact number Dar gave Hagans and Santos isn't in service," Chase advised. "You were right, she killed the phone."

"Not surprising. Dar would have anticipated us questioning Hagans and that he wouldn't be able to do her legwork. But she's still going to need help running down investigative leads. Which means she has to have assets in the field helping her. The question is, who?"

"Maybe someone from the law-enforcement community needed extra cash," Chase offered. "They could run down leads for her not even knowing who she is."

"Or people on the reservation who know the area and are desperate for money."

"At least Santos provided the last-known coordinates of the missing people when their GPS tracking monitors failed," Chase said. "He said that he gave Dar the coordinates, so that will be a good place to look for her. It's strange how all of those trackers failed, some of them at the same time."

"Yes, it is," Aki said. "And all of them were within a few miles of the search area where the DCI agent was kidnapped."

"There's a lot of agencies working the area, and with the right disguise and credentials, Dar could infiltrate the search scene and no one would be the wiser."

"That's another reason we need to check the scene." Aki looked out the window in thought. "Santos said that he'd spoken to Park Ranger Sarah Goodson. I think we'll start by speaking to her and the others that Sharon said are assigned to that homicide task force. From the reports Sharon forwarded, there appears to be a Lakota connection."

"Do you want to check in with the police on the reservation first?"

"That can wait. I'm sure federal agents are already on the reservation asking questions. I doubt that they'll learn anything. There's a long-standing distrust of the government and I don't want us to get lumped in with them."

"Is the trust issue related to the mining?"

"That, and for many other reasons going back over a century," Aki said. "The confidential investigative FBI files that Brian intercepted indicate that strange events and lights were reported by the task-force members. What do you make of that?"

"It seemed a bit out there."

"I'd like to get a firsthand accounting. Let's head to the scene."

Black Hills – May 24 – 1320 hours

Gray awoke with a start from a vivid and disturbing dream. As he recalled the events, it was as if he were reliving the firefight from last night, but this time it was far worse. Sarah had been shot and buffalo-clad warriors surrounded them. He remembered being on the ground as a warrior stood over him. Hatred burned in the warrior's eyes as he aimed his rifle at him. The warrior's face was covered in blue, white, and black lightning-bolt stripes of war paint from forehead to chin, and his buffalo hides were covered with strange symbols. The shot Gray expected never came, and then the dream had changed.

There was a beautiful but fierce-looking woman sitting atop a brown-and-white horse. A black braid fell over her shoulder, and her brown eyes had flakes of copper in them that were ablaze in the sunlight. There was a small scar over her right eyebrow, her cheeks were adorned with streaks of blue and white ceremonial paint, and a wide vertical blue stripe covered her chin. She was dressed in a tan buckskin dress and leggings, with a long knife secured in an ornate sheath at her waist. The lever-action Winchester rifle in her hand looked weathered and old.

He couldn't believe how much detail he was remembering. She'd spoken to him in Lakota, and somehow he'd understood her. She'd said that the Paha Sapa was watched over by the Waawanyanka, and that those trespassing would be vanquished by the Wakanpi and the Wakinyan if they did not leave. Then she rode away and the warriors followed her.

The warning from the woman warrior and intensity of the dream lingered, making it feel very real. Maybe Angela could explain what the dream meant. He sat up and swung his legs off the cot. He rubbed his eyes and saw that Sarah and Angela were still asleep at the back of the tan, ten-person military-style tent. The cots belonging to Clay and White Owl were empty, the sheets and blankets piled in a heap on top of their pillows. He hated to wake Angela, but he wanted to talk to her about the dream before it faded.

The five of them had chosen to stay together in the tent, which had been erected under a cluster of ponderosa pines to offer some shade. The fresh-canvas smell of the tent was a refreshing change for Gray. He'd spent many nights in old moldy tents as a child camping with his parents.

He checked his watch, noted the time, and took a deep breath. At least his utter exhaustion had abated. He stood and stretched, hoping to alleviate the aches and stiffness. His hips and back hurt from sleeping on a cot that wasn't designed for his older frame. At least the shower and change of clothes had made him less malodorous.

He glanced at the front of the tent. There was a lot of noise around the command site, but he wanted to talk to Angela before he investigated what was going on. He shook Angela's shoulder and she slapped his hand away, causing her long red hair to fall across her face. Gray shook her a little more vigorously, and she awoke.

"What is it?" she asked. "Is everything alright?"

"Yes. I need to talk to you about a dream I had before I forget the details."

"You woke me up to ask me about a dream?" She ran her hand through her hair and pulled the mussed strands behind her ears as she sat up. "This had better be good."

After providing the details of the dream, he asked, "What do you think it means?"

"That you had a bad dream."

"But what about the fact that I could understand the woman warrior when she spoke Lakota?"

"You probably only thought that you understood what she was saying. I told you about the Paha Sapa and the Wakinyan a few days ago. You're tired and your mind was probably subconsciously processing what has happened over the last few days. I'm going back to sleep." She lay back down and pulled the blanket up to her chin.

"I'm sorry I woke you up."

She waved a hand at him weakly, then quickly sat back up. "Wait a second. What were the designs and colors of the war paint again?"

"Blue, white, and black lightning bolts on the warrior, and blue and white stripes on the woman."

"Hmm. The color blue is considered the most sacred of all colors by the Lakota. It's associated with the Great Spirit, Wakan Tanka, who created the Earth."

"I thought you said that the carved feather on the box represented the Wakan Tanka."

"They both do," Angela replied. "The black stripes could represent the Wakinyan, and the white would exemplify life. You said the woman mentioned Waawanyanka?"

"Yes."

"It's odd, the way you said she used it. I don't remember mentioning the Waawanyanka to you. Do you know what it means?"

"I do, but I don't know why," Gray replied. "It means 'the guardian spirit.'"

"That's right." She bit her lower lip and then her eyes widened in excitement. "I don't think you had a dream. I think you had a vision. The details of the war paint didn't come from any events we experienced and certainly nothing I've told you about, and you knowing what *Waawanyanka* means is extraordinary."

"Why would I have a vision? I'm not Native American."

"You could have Lakota ancestors that you don't even know about. Over a century ago, thousands of children were removed from their families and sent to boarding schools to be taught the ways of the white man. Many families who adopted the children chose to hide their lineage."

"I've never traced my ancestral tree," Gray said. "Angela, why would a woman be wearing war paint? I thought that was a guy thing."

"There's a lot more to war paint than the stereotypical belief. Women often wear it. War paint is more about ceremony than just preparing for battle. It's used to signify membership in exclusive factions within the tribes, for ceremonial rituals and for beautification." Angela paused, then said, "I wonder if the lightning bolt could represent a faction that's affiliated with the thunder beings. I know that the great Lakota war chief Tasunka Witko painted himself before battles with a red lightning bolt that went from his forehead to his chin."

"Who?" Gray asked.

"Crazy Horse. The colors and the materials used, and the way the paint is applied, all have meaning. Ceremonial paint is used mostly to call upon spiritual power and for protection. There are over five hundred different tribes in the United States, all with their own cultural beliefs, and almost all of the indigenous people apply ceremonial paint. Some of the painted designs represent what came to a person during a vision." She paused, then added, "The Lakota are a very spiritual people. I think the woman warrior you described is very interesting."

"Why?"

"She kept a warrior from killing you and provided a warning to keep you out of further danger. She was there to protect you. Was Sarah dead or just shot in your vision?"

"Just shot and needed my help, but I couldn't get to her," Gray replied, reliving the frustration he'd felt at not being able to help her.

"Hmm. Perhaps the woman warrior's intervention saved both of you. The Lakota believe that all things are connected. I think your vision serves as a harbinger of things to come. Our intrusion onto this site has brought forth the Wakanpi to protect this land." Angela paused for a moment. "I'm glad you woke me up. We need to share your vision with White Owl and the others. Where *are* Clay and White Owl?"

"I'm not sure," Gray replied. "They were gone when I woke up."

"I'm going to reach out to Makawee and get her interpretation."

"Let's keep this quiet. We don't need any more issues."

"Makawee is my friend from the reservation. She's an expert on myths and the protection of the Paha Sapa. Relax, I trust her and Sarah knows her. I believe that she can provide insight."

"Makawee's the one who told you about the sacred star maps."

"That's her. In the meantime, I think someone needs to tell the mining companies that they need to stop their exploration and all of us should leave this area as soon as possible. I'll also see if Makawee can help get us an appointment with the chairman of the tribal council."

"Leaving isn't an option," Gray said, wishing it were. "Let's consult with White Owl before contacting anyone on the tribal council. No offense, but he may have more influence in getting us an appointment."

"Good point," Angela replied.

Clay walked into the tent, shook his head, and sat down on his cot.

"What's up?" Gray asked.

"Still nothing new about Crawley. Multiple agencies from Wyoming and South Dakota are combing every inch of the area that we already checked, and no surprise, they aren't finding anything. The K-9 units are searching the remote areas to the south and west. The FBI has arrived and has set up a command center. They appear to be taking over the investigation. Director Sutton and his people have already been embroiled in heated discussions with them, which was entertaining.

"I also let my sheriff know what was happening. He wasn't pleased that I hadn't called sooner. He gave me permission to stay until we find Crawley."

"Did you get any sleep?" Angela asked.

"Not enough. I woke up when Commander Windward came into the tent and talked to White Owl. The FBI wants access-control records kept of everyone coming through the checkpoints. The Custer and Pennington SO deputies have that responsibility, and White Owl was asked to coordinate."

"That sounds like a smart idea," Gray said.

"A National Parks Service command bus arrived a few minutes ago. What were you two talking about?"

"I had a dream last night," Gray replied.

"He had a vision," Angela corrected.

"About what?" Clay asked.

After Gray told him about the dream, Clay said, "Okay, I just got goosebumps. That's a lot of detail to remember from a dream. I think Angela is right. You had a vision."

"What the hell are you all talking about?" Sarah cried. "I'm trying to sleep."

"Sorry," Gray said. "Since you're awake, did you have any dreams last night?"

"No," Sarah said, getting up. "Why would you ask me that?"

"That's what we were discussing," Angela answered. "I think Gray had a vision last night. You were in it and had been shot. A woman warrior told Gray that we needed to leave the area. Then she rode away."

"You can't be serious," Sarah said as she moved closer.

"Yes, I am, and I want to have Makawee and White Owl give me their opinions on what the vision might mean."

"What does it matter?" Sarah asked. "A dream is just a dream. And don't you have to go on a vision quest to have a vision?"

Angela looked as if she was in thought, then replied, "Most of the time, but not always. That's one of the reasons I want to have White Owl and Makawee weigh in on the matter. Gray doesn't want this getting out."

"I can appreciate that," Sarah said. "What is all that noise outside?"

"The feds have moved in, including NPS," Clay replied.

Gray said, "I need to brush my teeth and get a cup of coffee. No more discussion about my dream. Please."

"I'll go with you," Sarah said. "What time is it?"

Gray checked his watch again, then replied, "One forty-five."

"I need more sleep," Sarah whined.

"Don't we all," Gray said.

CHAPTER SIXTEEN

"Good afternoon," Aki said to the deputy at the checkpoint. "Afternoon…no one is being allowed through here."

"We know, but we're with Homeland Security."

"I need to see your identification." The deputy looked at their credentials and wrote their names in the log, then said, "You're the first Homeland agents I've seen. Can you tell me what's going on up there?"

"Sorry, no," Aki replied.

"Any more agents from DHS coming?"

"Couldn't say. Is this the last checkpoint before we reach the command site? We've already passed through two."

"This is the last one," the deputy replied. "Security is tight and we're double-checking everyone who passes. The scene isn't that far from here, just another mile or so up the ridge." The deputy motioned to another deputy in one of the marked units blocking the road to back up.

"Thanks," Aki said as she drove past, then said to Chase, "There may be a number of security checks, but they haven't been very thorough."

"Nope. Dar could get through any of them with fake ID."

Aki drove along a winding, two-lane road through wooded terrain. "I'd forgotten just how beautiful it is here," she said. "I might just retire here."

"It certainly offers some majestic scenery."

When they arrived at the command site, Aki was amazed by the large law enforcement presence. She knew the FBI was on scene from the signal intercepts Brian was capturing. The supposedly secure communication between the command bus and the FBI Crisis Operations Team in the Strategic Information & Operations Center in Washington wasn't all that secure.

Three more mobile-command vehicles representing Wyoming DCI, the National Parks Service, and the Pennington Sheriff's Office were parked behind the FBI command bus in the middle of the road. Several large green-and-tan military-style, air-conditioned tents had been erected, while additional vehicles were parked in the grass and along both sides of the road. It looked more like a military base than a crime scene.

"I guess Santos wasn't kidding when he said that he had influence with the governors and senators," Chase said.

"It appears that way," Aki said. "I'm glad I had Brian start monitoring signals traffic from here earlier. Getting the information in real time will give us an edge."

"Looks like the FBI Evidence Response team is busy processing something," Chase said as they passed by their black truck. Its back doors were open and there were several ERT technicians working intently.

Aki noticed additional tents and facility trailers parked near a copse of trees on the south side of the road, and dozens of cars were parked in a small field. She decided that was where they would park and she pulled up next to a marked unit.

Chase said, "I'm not sure Dar will want to be in the middle of this, even if she gets past the checkpoints."

"Maybe not in the middle, but certainly nearby," Aki replied. "Let's find Ranger Goodson. We'll start at the NPS command bus."

They donned their blue HSI raid jackets and walked over to the NPS bus. Aki knocked on the door and was greeted by a petite young woman dressed in an NPS uniform.

"Hi, we're with Homeland Security," Aki said, offering her credentials. "We'd like to speak to one of your rangers. Do you happen to know where we can find Sarah Goodson?"

"Why do you want to talk to Ranger Goodson?" the woman asked, sounding surprised.

"That will be between us," Aki replied. "We also need to speak to the other DCI homicide task-force members."

A man with a deep voice said, "I'll talk to them."

A moment later, Aki stepped back as a muscular man with braided black hair dressed in a Custer County Sheriff's Office uniform stepped from the bus.

"I'm Lieutenant Takoda White Owl. What's this all about?"

Believing that he was Lakota, she greeted him with, "*Aŋpétu wašté*, Lt. White Owl. I'm Special Agent Akicita Dawson and this is Agent Colin Chase."

"Good day to you both," White Owl replied. "We've already been interviewed and I'm tired of answering questions in any language. Do us a favor and check with the FBI or the DCI over by the buses. They have already taken our statements and can fill you in." White Owl went to get back on the bus.

"Lt. White Owl," Aki began, "what we have to discuss with the task-force members has national security implications which supersede the search for Agent Crawley."

White Owl turned and gave her a quizzical look. "How so?"

"We're tracking an international terrorist who's been hired to find the missing mining employees," Aki replied. "Agent Chase and I flew here from Virginia last night to capture her. Since the investigations intersect, we can offer assistance in your search for Agent Crawley with resources that other agencies don't have, and I'm hoping that in return all of you can help us in our investigation."

White Owl stepped toward her and asked, "Where did you grow up?"

"I lived on the Pine Ridge Reservation until I was sixteen. My parents walked on after being struck by a drunk driver. The driver was so impaired that he didn't even know that he'd hit anyone."

White Owl nodded and said, "I'm sorry for your loss, but their journey continues in the Land of the Winds."

"Yes, it does."

White Owl nodded, then asked, "How did you end up at Homeland Security?"

"After the Keeping of the Soul ceremony for my parents, I went to live with my great aunt in Virginia. She left the reservation after the second Wounded Knee incident in 1973 and married outside of the tribe. I finished high school in Virginia, and was recruited by Homeland Security after graduating from college."

"Who were your parents?"

"Chatan and Zitkala Enapay. We are True Oglala."

"And your aunt?" White Owl asked.

"Kimimela Cox."

White Owl nodded. "Come inside."

"How did I not know that about your parents?" Chase asked. "I gather that 'walking on' means they passed away?"

"Yes. Alcohol and drugs are a big problem on the reservation. Even though it's illegal to possess alcohol there, you can still purchase it just off the reservation."

Aki sat down in a padded, well-worn swivel chair in the center of the bus next to White Owl. Chase took a seat at the dinette table.

"Dawn, I'll listen to the radios and the phones," White Owl said to the woman who had greeted Aki. "Go get a bite to eat."

"I could use a snack, thanks."

Once Dawn had left the bus, White Owl asked, "What do you wish to know?"

"I understand that you and the other task-force members encountered what's been described as buffalo-spirit warriors."

"Yes. A red orb flew above us and we were frozen in place as the four warriors took Agent Crawley away, and then we were attacked by twelve other warriors." He described in detail what had transpired.

"That is most interesting," Aki said. "Especially the lights."

"Can I assume that is another national-security layer in your investigation?" White Owl asked.

"Yes," Aki replied. "I know the others are tired, but we'd really like to hear their accounting of the events."

White Owl simply nodded, then called Gray. "They'll be here in a few minutes. Now, I have a few questions. It seems a bit odd that the mining companies would hire a terrorist to find their missing people."

"I agree. She's an assassin and one of her objectives is to kill those responsible."

"She's deadly, extremely well-trained, is a master of disguise, and is wanted in many countries," Chase added. "She shot our helicopter down a few days ago when we tried to capture her in Germany."

"She's out of her element here and she'll need to recruit help," Aki said. "She's well funded for this operation and could bribe law enforcement to gain information or access to the area."

"And you believe that she'll come here?" White Owl said.

"She *is* here," Aki said. "We saw her in Rapid City earlier today but were unable to pursue." She showed White Owl numerous photos of Dar in different disguises from her cell phone.

"I have not seen her, but I'll keep an eye out."

"Don't try to apprehend her if you come in contact, just call us and observe as best you can from a safe distance."

"Okay."

"Just so that you're aware, we already have a number of specialists working on Agent Crawley's disappearance, mostly through classified channels," Aki said. "If we discover anything, we'll tell you first."

"I appreciate it." White Owl leaned back, crossed his arms, and gave her a playful smile. "It just came to me. Akicita, you're the one who gave Mato the scar on his face."

Aki was taken aback at hearing him mention Mato. "Yes, I was fifteen when we fought. He left me with this scar." She pointed to her right eyebrow. "How did you hear about that?"

"Mato has told the story about your fight many times, but you don't look anything like the beast he described."

Aki cocked her head. "How does he describe me?"

"You're supposed to be eight feet tall, as strong as three bears, and you shoot lightning from your eyes like the Great Wakinyan. He claims the scar on his cheek came from one of your lightning bolts."

Aki laughed. "The scar on his face is from where I hit him with a rock. How is he?"

"I don't know, I've not seen him for a while."

The bus door opened and sunlight cascaded across the interior as Sarah stepped in.

"I think it's a little cramped for all of us," Sarah said.

"We will talk outside under the awning," White Owl said.

Black Hills – May 24 - 1500 hours

When Aki stepped down from the bus, Gray was gripped by trepidation and confusion at the sight of her. The sunlight cast a halo-like light around Aki's head. Gray flashed back to the woman warrior in his vision—now she was standing in front of him. The same brown eyes with copper flakes were locked on him.

"Let me make the introductions," White Owl said, stepping from the bus.

Gray didn't move or say anything as White Owl introduced everyone. He just stared at Aki, taking in every feature of her face. Her eyes never left his and he couldn't help but stare. She was even more beautiful than in his dream.

"Hey, what's wrong with you?" Sarah asked Gray.

He turned away from Aki and whispered to Sarah, "It's her."

"What her?"

"The woman in my dream."

Angela stepped up next to Gray and said, "You're certain?"

"Positive."

"Would you mind telling us what you're whispering about?" White Owl asked.

"Gray had a vision last night about being attacked by warriors," Angela said. "Sarah had been shot and Gray was about to be killed. He thinks Agent Dawson is the woman who intervened."

"We were supposed to keep that between us," Gray said.

Aki stepped closer to Gray and asked, "You're certain that it was me?"

"No doubt in my mind," Gray replied. "I'd know you anywhere, with or without the war paint. You even have the same scar." He described what she was wearing and the war paint markings on her face. He related that she'd spoken to him in Lakota, and had given him a warning while atop a horse.

Aki's eyes narrowed. "Do you speak Lakota?"

"No, but I understood what you said."

"Interesting. I am Lakota and it's been nearly twenty years since I wore ceremonial paint or buckskins."

"Okay, this is really getting weird," Sarah said.

"I don't think there's any doubt that Gray had a vision," Angela said, with excitement. "White Owl, I was hoping to get your impression, especially now that Gray has met the woman he foresaw."

White Owl rubbed his chin. "It sounds like Gray had a powerful vision. I fear it means a dangerous encounter is coming and Agent Dawson, Sarah, and Gray will be involved. I don't believe Director Sutton or the FBI will care about the warning."

"Probably not," Gray said. He didn't understand his intense attraction to Akicita, and he had a feeling that Sarah knew he was captivated by her.

Aki said, "Perhaps we should seek council with a Waken Iyeska about Agent Holt's vision."

"I think that's a great idea," Angela said. "It may give us a clearer picture of why they were meant to meet."

"What's a Waken Iyeska?" Clay asked.

"A spiritual interpreter," Angela answered, drawing a quizzical look from Aki. "I'm an anthropological archeology professor at Brigham Young University. I've spent time on the Pine Ridge and the Rosebud reservations studying Lakota culture and beliefs. I understand and admire them." Then in Lakota, Angela said, "I also speak Lakota."

Aki nodded and answered, "And you speak it well."

"I don't see why any further interpretation of his vision is necessary," Sarah said.

"Agent Dawson, what do you think?" Gray asked.

"Everyone, call me Aki, and Colin prefers to be called Chase. I can tell you that I've never owned a Winchester, but I did ride a pinto when I was younger, like the one Gray spoke about. Like you said, perhaps his vision was simply a foretelling of my coming here and that we will face an adversary together."

"Aki, you should tell them why you're here," White Owl said.

"Very well. We're after a terrorist that was last seen in this area."

"Do you think the terrorist is responsible for all of the disappearances and homicides?" Sarah asked.

"No, she has nothing to do with what's happened here." Aki went on to explain the connection and a little about Dar. "Now that I've told you why we're here, I'd like you all to tell us what you all have experienced over the last two days, and leave no detail out."

"Let's sit under the awning," White Owl said. "I've already told Aki what I know."

"Aki, do you want to talk to us individually or together?" Gray asked.

"Together is fine."

Thirty minutes later, all of their encounters had been recounted.

Aki's cell phone rang and she answered, "Yes, Sharon. I see. Explain that in more detail, please." Aki motioned to Chase, and they took a few steps away from the group for privacy.

"Gray, what do you think that's that all about?" Sarah asked.

Gray didn't respond. He watched Aki, taking in her every movement and gesture.

"Hey, are you listening to me?" Sarah asked, after standing and stepping in front of Gray.

"No, I'm sorry. I was just thinking."

"I could tell," Sarah said, glancing at Aki.

"That's good work," Aki said as she and Chase rejoined the group. "I'll call you back in a few. We're with some people right now and the information has bearing on the homicide investigation and what they experienced last night." She signed off and addressed the group. "Sharon, one of our analysts, says a NASA advanced Terra Surveyor satellite discovered a large cavern directly below this area yesterday. The satellite's new technology allows for hyperspectral imaging and can detect and map what's deep beneath the surface."

"Why would the mining companies be interested in an underground cavern?" Gray asked.

"Yeah, this area has a lot of caves," Sarah added.

"The satellite detected a large mass which has the chemical signature of gold."

Gray was aware there was gold in the Black Hills, but to find a large deposit would be a secret worth protecting or stealing at any cost, including murder.

"How big of a signature?" Clay asked.

"Very large. Of interest is that the satellite also captured several thermal spikes over this area around midnight last night, which has drawn the interest of several intelligence agencies and classified programs. Sharon is trying to get more information."

"So, there's hard evidence proving we encountered something last night?" Gray asked.

"Yes, but I don't know how much will be released. Anything we discuss, and especially this information, needs to stay between us."

"Whatever is in the mountain belongs to the Lakota and is obviously being protected by the Wakanpi," White Owl said. "This is our land. It is the *wamaka ognaka y cante.*"

"Which means?" Clay asked.

"The heart of everything that is," Aki replied. "It is the Paha Sapa, our sacred land. It's the place where humans emerged from the Black Hills to walk on the surface of the Earth."

Sarah said, "I thought that the Wind Cave was supposed to be where humans emerged."

"Perhaps Darren discovered that the legend refers to the cavern below us and that's the reason he was killed," Angela offered.

"Did Sharon provide any information on where we could find the entrance to the cavern?" Gray asked Aki.

"No. We'll have to wait for Sharon to call us back with more details."

"Aki, are you going to tell the FBI and DCI about the cavern, the gold, and the thermal spikes?" Sarah asked.

"Not everything needs to be shared just yet," Aki said. "Like I said, we need to keep this between us. If the information about the gold was released, word would spread quickly and the ensuing chaos would be unimaginable. I doubt even those in charge of the criminal investigation will be told anything right away."

"They should be," Gray said. "It will clear us and provide a motive for the homicides and the missing personnel."

"Gray, I agree, they should be told," Sarah said. "And you should tell them about your vision and the warning."

"I wouldn't go that far," Gray replied. "Director Sutton already thinks we're crazy. Telling him about my vision may result in us being escorted from the scene or locked up. We need to listen to Aki's advice."

Aki added, "Sarah, telling anyone about his vision will only make things more difficult for all of us. The return of the Wakanpi or the Pte Oyate would give your accounting of the events credibility, and I think with the army of law enforcement present, we'll be fine."

"I've never heard of the Pte Oyate," Clay said.

"Buffalo People," White Owl answered. "Legend tells us that the Wakanpi can take human form when needed. They look like people covered in buffalo hides. It would explain why they got up after we shot them and walked like men. I should have thought of it sooner."

"That is interesting," Gray said.

"What about the thermal spikes?" Angela said. "That should get their attention."

"Even if I told them, I doubt that it would be confirmed," Aki said. "I only told you about that in confidence. None of you can say anything about the spikes. It would compromise our intelligence gathering."

"Maybe you shouldn't have told them," Chase admonished. "Aki, we need to check in with the FBI and DCI. We can determine what they know and what course of action they plan to take, then decide what we want to tell them. We can certainly win a few points by telling them about the cavern before they get the information through channels. I also think that we need to tell them why we're here. Someone could encounter our target not knowing who she is and end up getting killed."

"All good points," Aki said. "Let's go introduce ourselves to the investigators."

"I can walk over with you and make the introductions," Gray said.

"I'll go, too," Sarah stated quickly. "I want to snoop around a bit."

Gray had a feeling that Sarah didn't want him being around Aki without her present.

"Wait for me," Angela said. "Clay, are you coming?"

"Why not," Clay replied.

"Aki, I'm going to see if I can line up a meeting with Chairman Red Elk on the reservation," White Owl said. "We need to tell him what has happened here and about the cavern."

"I'll go with you."

"I'll see what I can arrange."

Hill City, South Dakota – May 24 – 1540 hours

Dar was sitting in a small pizza restaurant in Hill City in the center of the Black Hills. The restaurant had an Italian theme, with posters of Rome and Naples hanging on the walls. She'd ordered a large pizza and the aroma coming from the kitchen was making her hungry. The small restaurant reminded her of a restaurant in northern Italy she often visited.

The private investigators had interviewed a number of people on the reservation but had yet to turn up any leads on the missing mining employees. Carlton claimed he knew an NPS officer who was approachable and could provide information from the scene, if the price was right. She'd told him to make the arrangements.

Dar had spoken to Chief Hagans one last time and he advised that Aki and Chase had interviewed him and that he wasn't going to help her. He also told her that his lines were being monitored, which she'd been counting on. After the call, she'd dropped the cell phone into the back of a pickup truck with Montana plates. Hopefully, Aki's team would waste time chasing after the truck.

Dar had rented two additional four-wheel drive SUVs and had them delivered to two different motels just in case she needed to change transportation. She'd also taken the time to scout some of the back roads around the scene, but she'd been turned away at several roadblocks. She'd have to find a different way to gain access to the area.

Just as her pizza arrived, her cell phone chimed. "Yes," she answered, unconcerned about it being traced. It was new and only Carlton had the number.

"Good news," he said. "The NPS supervisor has agreed to feed us intel. He wants two thousand a day."

"His price is acceptable, providing his information is of value," Dar replied. "Can he be trusted?"

"Yes. I've worked with him before on other cases. He's very reliable. He told me that he's been called in to help with the search for the missing DCI agent. He also said that there are roadblocks restricting access to only those who live in the area and law enforcement. No one will be able to get near the scene."

"I discovered that already. I want updates from him every two hours."

"It may be difficult for him to make contact so frequently," Carlton stated. "There's a problem with cell reception out there. With your permission, I'd like to have him contact us when there's something of value and he can get a signal."

Dar had to temper her ire, which was building. She didn't like people questioning her orders, but at least he'd asked for her permission. "Very well, but I want to know immediately of any developments, even if he has to leave the scene. Why aren't your people getting information from the reservation?"

"The FBI, BIA, and a bunch of other law-enforcement agencies rolled onto the reservation a little while ago. No one is going to get any information now. The feds are always heavy-handed, and the Lakota stonewall them just to piss them off. I'm going to leave one of my investigators on the reservation just in case someone comes forward."

"Find out what kind of questions the feds are asking," Dar directed. "That may give us some insight into their focus and if they have any leads. I'll provide a five-thousand-dollar incentive to anyone with reliable and actionable information about the missing people. That should get them talking."

"We'll have people coming out of the woodwork in hopes that anything they say may earn them some money," Carlton said. "Culling their claims will take time."

"Is that a problem?"

There was a short pause, and then he answered, "No."

"Remember, the key words are *reliable and actionable*. Rumors, gossip and supposition don't count unless it leads me to the missing people. Make sure they understand that stipulation."

"I will."

Dar disconnected and took a bite of pizza. She decided it was by far one of the best that she'd tasted. *What a shame it's in this little town out in the middle of nowhere.*

She glanced at the television on the wall and saw that the breaking news was about two homicide victims and a missing Wyoming DCI agent and mining-company employees. After lunch, she planned to drive out to the area again and see where the news media was assembled and broadcasting. If she could forge a press ID and change her looks, she might be able to gain access to the scene without raising suspicion.

Dar paid for her lunch in cash, left a large tip and walked out of the restaurant into the warm afternoon sun. Out of habit, she observed the pedestrians and vehicles, looking for any threats. Then she walked casually to her black Tahoe. She'd picked up some tourist flyers from the counter at the restaurant, hoping they might give her some additional ideas for gaining access to the area. Once in her Tahoe, she went through the flyers. Two of them caught her interest. There was a scenic train ride through the woods around the area, but after looking at the route, she realized it wouldn't get her near the scene.

Another one advertised an aerial-tour adventure. She checked the map and saw that it was only few miles south of Hill City on US 16. She decided to scout the area by air. She could find the media-staging area and see what other routes she could use to gain access to the scene. Dar was certain that for the right price, the pilot would take her wherever she needed to go.

After a short drive, she saw a yellow-and-white sign atop a tall pole marking the dirt-road entrance to Black Aerial Adventures. Dar pulled in and noticed a red R44 helicopter sitting in a field next to a small building. There were only two cars in the grass parking lot. She assumed one belonged to the pilot.

She parked and as she was walking to the entrance, a bald, overweight man in his fifties walked out and greeted her.

"Hello, are you interested in an aerial tour of Mount Rushmore, seeing the Crazy Horse Monument, or some other sites in the area?"

"Are you the pilot?" Dar asked.

"I am, and I also own the business. Gordon Black at your service. I've been flying people around this area for years, and I can also provide you with a historical tour and point out some things you won't normally see from other aerial tour companies. How many in your party?"

"Just me. I don't care about seeing the normal sites. I want to fly over the Black Hills area to the west of here, around the Wyoming border, and I need to go now."

Black crossed his arms and asked, "Are you a reporter?"

"I could be. Is that an issue?"

"The airspace over that area has a lot of aircraft traffic, and the authorities have been restricting where the media can fly. I take it your news agency doesn't have a helicopter?"

"Correct. Will you take me?"

Black looked back at his helicopter. "The fee to fly that far west and loiter will cost you more. Are you still interested?"

"Your ad says three hundred for a ride to Mount Rushmore."

"It does, but that only lasts about thirty minutes, and I usually take three people."

Dar knew his type. "I'm willing to pay you four thousand, cash, for an extended tour, no questions asked."

He beamed at her and said, "I can give you two hours. It'll take us twenty minutes to get there, so our time in the area will be just over an hour. Will that work for you?"

"I may need more time."

"We run out of daylight in two hours. I can fly you back out in the morning. Flying in the Hills at night isn't a good idea. Terrain is over six thousand feet with higher peaks, and we could fly into the ground. It gets really dark out here, and you won't be able to see anything anyway."

"We better get a move on then," Dar said, pulling five thousand from her backpack. "There's an extra thousand there as a retainer for tomorrow."

Black took the money and quickly counted it. "You have yourself a charter. I'll need you to fill out some forms and then we'll get airborne."

"I'll fill them out when we return. Like you said, daylight is waning."

"I need a name and contact information in case of an emergency," Black insisted. "I have to preflight the helicopter and top off the fuel. While I do that, you can see my associate and get the paperwork out of the way."

Dar decided to acquiesce. She'd use her Cora Zemanski alias and would be long gone before Aki could pick up the bread crumb. "Very well. Is my vehicle safe here?"

"Yes. What's your name and news affiliation?" Black asked.

"Cora, and I'm a freelance journalist. I sell my work to the highest bidder." By the look on his face, she didn't think he believed her. She turned and headed for the building before Black could ask her any more questions.

Ten minutes later they were airborne and headed west.

Dar was pleased that Mr. Black wasn't the talkative type. He'd provided some basic information about the helicopter during his safety briefing and only asked a few questions about the area she wanted to fly over. As they approached their objective, Dar noted a number of helicopters and a few aircraft working a search grid. She listened to the radio chatter between the aircraft as the helicopter approached the scene. Aircraft were being warned to stay away.

"As you can hear, we aren't going to be able to fly near where the law-enforcement aircraft are searching," Black said. "We'll have to circle around them. Will that suffice?"

"Yes," Dar replied. She could see the command post in the distance. "How high can we go?"

"I won't fly above six thousand feet AGL. At that altitude, you should have a great view."

"Circle the area once at this altitude, then climb and circle again."

Black gave the law-enforcement and news-media helicopters a wide berth for the lower-altitude orbit. Then climbed above them and circled again, closer to the scene.

Dar saw where the media was staged. She also noticed the steep terrain and dense foliage. If she went in by foot, it was going to be a tough hike.

"I guess you're the kind of journalist who doesn't like taking pictures," Black commented.

"Not today. I'll take some tomorrow. Too many shadows this late in the day. Make one more circle. I want to see the roads and trails again."

"I don't think they'll let you get very close to the scene on any access road, if that's what you're planning. You saw where all the media vehicles were parked. That's as close as you can get."

"Just do as I requested and then we can head back."

As Black made one more orbit, Dar took note of the numerous law-enforcement vehicles positioned along the main roads and on several of the trail roads. Getting in was going to be difficult. She needed a different approach to breach the security, and she had an idea.

"Ready to head back?" Black asked.

"Yes. We'll need to fly back here early tomorrow."

"I'll have to charge you for tomorrow's flight in advance. Your retainer only reserves your spot on the schedule. I get no-shows every once in a while, and I can't run my business sitting on the ground without being paid."

"I see. In that case, I'll require something else."

"And what would that be?" Black asked.

"The freelance world is competitive and often requires that I remain in the shadows and push the boundaries of lawful activity to be successful. Getting the real story first and negotiating a fee for my work can involve stepping on toes." Dar looked over at Black and added, "I would be most displeased if I learned that you told anyone about my having chartered your helicopter or where we flew today. That includes law enforcement."

"Well, chartering my helicopter is one thing, but lying to the police is quite another," Black said. "We'll need to negotiate a fee for my silence. Where are you from anyway?"

"I'm Belarusian but I live in Quebec, and that's all you need to know."

"I knew that I detected a Russian accent. I'm not buying that you're a freelance writer. Are you a spy or a drug dealer?"

Dar broke out laughing. "You're very perceptive. I'm neither of those. I'm what you would call a problem solver and I don't like people asking about my work." Then in a threatening tone, Dar said, "It isn't healthy for anyone to remember me or discuss my business."

"I see. I don't really care who you are or what you're doing here, as long as I get paid."

"So, you're just a gun for hire?" Dar asked, then smiled. "I could use someone like you to be available when called upon."

"I believe that we could come to an arrangement for whatever you may need in the future."

After they landed, Dar handed Black another five thousand dollars. "This is for the trip tomorrow. I'll give you another ten thousand later so that I have priority access to your helicopter. That could mean cancelling a tour on short notice."

"I can live with that."

"I'll see you in the morning about nine," Dar said.

"Nine it is."

CHAPTER SEVENTEEN

Black Hills – May 25 – 0730 hours

"Unhappy-looking crowd," Sarah said as she and Gray entered the mess tent.

"Let's grab a cup of coffee and find an empty table." He picked a table away from the other diners, sat down, and took a sip of his coffee. He found it was actually quite good.

When the FBI and DCI had set up surveillance in the area last night, he was told that he couldn't participate, which had given him time to catch up on some much-needed sleep.

"Where did you go earlier this morning" Sarah asked, sitting down across from him.

"I went for a short walk. I heard there wasn't any activity last night, which is probably why we're getting the nasty looks."

"I think we're screwed if the warriors don't show themselves," Sarah said.

"It certainly won't help us." Gray took another sip of coffee. "Chase and Aki joined the FBI team last night, but I haven't seen them yet. I wonder where they're being housed?"

"Who cares. Before I turned in last night, I asked Aki if there was any news and she said that there wasn't anything to report, but I don't believe her. Aki was on her phone way too much not to have gotten an update. I don't trust her."

"Don't judge her yet. Were Clay and Angela still sacked out when you left our tent?"

"Yup. Gray, I think you made a mistake, telling Aki about your vision."

"I had to tell her. Aki being here means something."

"But did you have to stare at her like that? It just made her more curious."

"How could I not stare? I was trying to understand how it was possible to have dreamt about her the night before I actually met her. For a brief instant, I thought that I was dreaming again."

"Well, you weren't."

"The good news is, Aki said that White Owl managed to get us an interview with Chairman Red Elk at three today," Gray said. "We'll have to sneak off because we're supposed to stay nearby, but I don't think we'll be missed."

"And when did Aki tell you about the interview?" Sarah asked, sounding indignant.

"When I last spoke to her." Gray decided it was time to confront the issue. "Sarah, what's your issue with Aki?"

Sarah stared at him for a few seconds, then replied, "I saw the way you looked at her and the way she looked back at you. It was more than just a casual greeting or one of curiosity. I knew instantly that you were intrigued by her. I feel something for you and I thought you felt the same way about me."

Gray leaned across the table and took Sarah's hand. "I'm drawn to Aki for reasons I can't explain. But I also care for you and would never do anything to hurt you."

"Please don't say that you just want to be my friend, because my feelings for you run a little deeper than that. I thought I'd made that perfectly clear."

Gray squeezed her hand. "You have. Which is why I'm not going to lie to you. I just need time to sort out what I'm feeling."

She pulled her hand away. "You're joking, right? Maybe it's good that this happened now before we got serious."

"What is going on with you?" Gray said, with a flare of anger.

"I'm jealous," Sarah said loudly. "I have no claim on you, so you can do what you want, but I'm not waiting around while you figure it out. You're either with me or you're not. Decide!"

Gray noticed that their raised voices had drawn the attention of a few people sitting nearby. "Why don't we go for a walk?"

Sarah drained her mug, then said, "Let's go."

Just as Sarah and Gray exited the mess tent, Aki walked out of the female shower trailer. She was dressed in a blue HSI polo shirt, black BDU pants with black tactical boots, and carried a small bag. Aki's hair was still wet from the shower and glistened in the early-morning sun.

"Why don't you go say hello to her?" Sarah said. "We have nothing else to discuss."

Gray stopped and watched as Sarah walked quickly to the NPS bus and met with White Owl and Chase, who were sitting under the awning. He couldn't believe Sarah's reaction. He'd never seen her so upset before.

"Sarah looked angry," Aki said, joining him.

"She is," Gray replied.

"Why?"

"I don't want to discuss it."

Aki gave him a knowing look, then said, "She senses that I'm a threat to your relationship."

"How in the hell could you know that?"

"It's a woman thing."

"Aki, this may sound forward, but I have to tell you that I'm attracted to you. I don't even know you and I'm struggling to understand our connection. Maybe it's because of my vision. I still don't understand how you could have been in it."

"Did you tell Sarah how you were feeling?"

"Yes. A few minutes ago."

"I can see why she's upset. And since we're being open about it, I felt a connection to you when we first met, and it wasn't because you said I was in your vision."

Gray sighed. He had almost hoped Aki would say he was crazy. It would have simplified everything. Now he was even more conflicted.

"Why don't we talk about it over breakfast?" Aki said. "How's the food in the mess tent?"

"It's actually quite good. Breakfast does sounds good."

"I'll brief you on what happened last night and give you the latest updates I received from Sharon this morning while we eat."

Gray glanced back at the NPS command bus. Sarah was staring at him. There was fire in her eyes. If he went with Aki now, any hope of patching things up would be over. Aki must have sensed his hesitancy.

"Or you can go sort things out with Sarah and we can talk later."

Before Gray could respond, he noticed Director Sutton, Commander Littlejohn, and an unknown man wearing an FBI raid jacket walking his way.

"Agent Holt, I need a moment of your time," Director Sutton announced.

"This should be fun," Gray muttered.

"I'll stick around," Aki said, then added teasingly, "Just in case you need backup."

"This is Special Agent in Charge Jeremy Stevens with the FBI," Sutton said. "He's now in charge of all of the investigations. Agent Holt, your services and those of the members on Agent Crawley's team are no longer required. Let me have your DCI credentials, and you'll need to turn over any DCI-issued equipment to Commander Littlejohn as soon as we're done here. Are we clear that you no longer have any DCI investigative authority?"

"Very clear," Gray replied. He handed Sutton his DCI badge and commission. "I don't have any DCI equipment. Our weapons and other equipment were seized as evidence."

"That makes it easy then," Sutton replied. "You also need to contact the Office of Aviation Services and speak to your regional director as soon as possible. Here's the number." Sutton handed him a slip of paper.

"Why didn't he call me? And why in the hell would you be talking to my director?"

Sutton stiffened. "Because your story about Agent Crawley's disappearance isn't credible and I felt it was appropriate to notify your command to express my disbelief and allow them an opportunity to review the facts. We encountered no lights or anything else last night."

"Maybe nothing happened last night because there was an army out there waiting for them," Gray said, his temper and voice rising. "I don't suppose that any of you noticed the lack of animal or insect noise in the area last night?"

"I'm not going to listen to any more of your stories," Sutton said. "You and the other members of Agent Crawley's team are officially under investigation in his disappearance. In addition, all of you will make yourselves available for further questioning and remain here for *our* convenience. You can seek legal counsel if you desire." Then he added in a disgusted tone, "You should never have been allowed to work for us."

Gray took a step forward, ready to strike, but Aki grabbed his arm to prevent him from engaging.

"Not worth it," Aki whispered.

"Listen up, asshole," Gray spat. "We were attacked and we did our jobs. If Crawley had listened to us and brought in additional support, we wouldn't be having this conversation."

"*Mr.* Holt, I suggest you call your regional director, now," Sutton said, with a smug look on his face.

"Agent Dawson, we appreciate the heads-up on the cavern and the potential threat," Stevens said, stepping forward to create a buffer between Sutton and Gray. "Since the FBI is now in charge of all aspects of the investigation, I've been advised by FBI Director Watts to inform you that HSI is no longer required on the scene."

"What's going on?" Gray asked. He'd seen the FBI push their way in on high-profile cases before, but this was uncalled for. "Agent Dawson and Agent Chase have been nothing but supportive. What happened to cooperation and teamwork?"

"This wasn't my call," Stevens responded. "The order came directly from Director Watts. He called Under Secretary Basset to thank him for your agency's assistance and warning about Dariya Novikov. Secretary Basset wasn't aware that you were looking for her and he told Director Watts that you'd gone rogue. He claimed that you are obsessed with capturing or killing Dariya regardless of the cost, and that you and Agent Chase would be a liability if allowed to remain on scene."

"I don't report to Basset," Aki replied coldly. "Agent Stevens, I appreciate the information and I'll inform my superior of the conversation. I can assure you that I have not gone *rogue*. Our mission is fully sanctioned."

"I'm certain that it's just a bureaucratic foul-up," Stevens said. "I'd be pleased to have you assist once the HSI internal matter is resolved."

"Agent Stevens, if you encounter Dar, please notify us immediately," Aki requested. "We have a great deal of time invested in bringing her to justice and we want to be there." She wrote a number on a piece of paper and handed it to him. "That's a secure line, not to be shared. You can reach me at any time."

Stevens sighed, then added, "Headquarters has instructed me that if we do encounter Dar, that we're to engage and apprehend. You are not to participate."

Aki shook her head in disbelief, then said, "Dar is a formidable enemy and she will not go peacefully. You best be prepared for battle and you *will* need our help if you want to keep your losses to a minimum." She let her warning sink in for a moment. "Call me before you engage. May we remain on scene if we stay at the NPS command bus until this is resolved?"

"That's acceptable, and I appreciate your warning and offer."

"Mr. Holt," Sutton said, "I'd appreciate it if you kept to your tent or stay with the others by the NPS command bus. I'll let you give the others the good news about the task force being disbanded and that they're under investigation."

"Director Sutton, am I under arrest or being detained in any way?" Gray asked.

"No."

"Agent Stevens, are you detaining me?"

"No."

"In that case, I'll go wherever the hell I want to after I give the others the news. I have a few days left before I need to report for duty with OAS. If you have any questions, you can call me on my cell or stop by my property in Rim Canyon. Agent Stevens, good luck with the investigation. Director Sutton, you're welcome for my service, and someday you'll understand why." Gray turned and walked away.

Sutton shouted, "You aren't going anywhere! You should really call your director. You may not even have a job."

"What!" Gray said, wheeling around to face him.

Sutton mumbled something that Gray couldn't understand. Gray felt the blood pounding in his temples. He needed to get away from Sutton before he did something that got him arrested. He turned and walked toward the NPS command bus and an angry-looking Sarah.

"Director Sutton, you just lost a good man and made a huge mistake," Aki said.

Sutton bristled but didn't respond.

When Aki caught up with Gray, she said, "I guess breakfast can wait."

"I'm not hungry. I need to tell everyone what's happened and then I'm going to pack up my gear and get the hell out of here." Gray stopped. "Crap, I don't have a car."

"That's not a problem. I can take you wherever you want to go."

"Thank you," Gray replied. "I'm sure that Lt. White Owl can help us out if you have other things to do."

"Do you have a minute to talk with me before you convey the bad news?"

"Sure."

"I want to check on something, and while I do that, I think you have a call to make as well."

Gray looked back and saw that Sarah was still watching as they walked over to Aki's car. He called the number Sutton had given him and the line was answered after the first ring.

"Office of Aviation Services, Director Bartley's office," a male voice answered.

"This is Gray Holt. I was told the director wished to speak with me."

"Hold please."

Gray looked over at Aki and saw that her brow was furrowed as she spoke to someone on her cell.

"Mr. Holt, this is Director Bartley. I have some bad news for you."

"I'm listening," Gray replied, feeling his stomach muscles tensing.

"Wyoming DCI Director Sutton informed me of some disturbing events that have occurred over the last few days and of your involvement. Is it true that you were engaged in numerous gun battles with what you and others have described as 'buffalo spirit warriors'?"

"Yes."

"And you were present when DCI Agent Roland Crawley was kidnapped by these warriors?"

"That's correct," Gray answered.

"And you saw mysterious lights, one of which was a red orb that hovered over you and froze you in place?"

"That is what happened," Gray said. He knew what was coming next.

"Really?"

"Yes. May I provide you with some context as to what happened?"

"Not necessary," Bartley said. "You answered the questions that I needed to confirm. I can offer you two options. You can resign before I ask for a formal internal investigation, or you can report to Rapid City today and meet with Office of Internal Affairs investigators. I would suggest the first option. It will save everyone time and embarrassment. Needless to say, you won't be flying for us, even if you choose the latter option. I'm already making arrangements to fill your position in Custer."

Gray took a deep breath. Sutton had submarined him. He was a new employee and the optics weren't good, especially since he was under investigation by the FBI. "May I have a moment to think about this?"

"If it makes any difference to you, option one gives you an opportunity to find employment elsewhere without negative reviews from OAS or the Department of the Interior," Bartley said. "I will accept your resignation without prejudice, and no official paper trail will follow you. We'll just say that you changed your mind about the position for personal reasons. It's really in your best interest to resign now."

Gray knew that even if he went through the process and cleared his name that the stigma would follow him. Bartley was right, it was better to make a clean break. "Very well, Director Bartley. I tender my resignation. I'll forward a letter stating the same. I was really looking forward to this assignment."

"And I was looking forward to having you in Custer," Bartley said. "I wish you the best."

"Director, when the FBI's investigation clears me of any wrongdoing and they learn that what we've been telling investigators is true, will I have an opportunity to reapply to fly for OAS?"

"I can't make any promises. Your grant position is definitely off the table. If a position opened up, you'd probably have to relocate, and I understand that you have property in Custer."

"Yes, I do."

"Call me when the investigation is over, and then we'll see what options are available."

"I appreciate that, and thank you for the opportunity."

"Goodbye," Bartley said.

Gray put his cell phone in his pocket and stared at the trees, thinking about this turn of events. He should have never taken the job with Crawley.

"Well, you don't look happy," Aki said.

"I could say the same about you."

"Sharon just advised me that my response team at Camp Rapid and the aerial support I was counting on have been recalled."

"That doesn't sound good."

"It's not. Removing a team assigned to an operation could only have been done by Under Secretary Basset. My boss may not even know what he's done."

"If you don't work for Basset, how could he just pull the plug?"

"Good question. My next call is to my boss and I'll be asking her the same thing. From the look on your face, I'd say the conversation with your director didn't go well."

"I may have just set a record. I've managed to lose two jobs in less than fifteen minutes."

"I'm sorry to hear that, but I kind of figured that would happen. In light of what I just learned, I may be able to cheer you up. I have a proposition for you."

Gray jokingly replied, "We only just met yesterday and we never did have that discussion."

Aki smiled. "That's true. Let me rephrase. I'd like to offer you a position on my team at Homeland."

"Doing what?" Gray asked, surprised.

"I asked Sharon to run a background check on you last night because I need another good investigator and a pilot. You have both qualifications. I also know that you're not risk averse and that you won't hesitate to use deadly force if required."

"So, you checked me out."

"Yes."

"But you've been labeled 'rogue agents' by your agency. I couldn't stand to lose a third job in one day."

"Like I told Agent Stevens, Chase and I haven't gone rogue, we're just off the radar. Under Secretary Basset is unaware of our assignments. I can have you on the Homeland payroll by noon today. I'm certain we pay more than the grant position did and we're a lot more fun than being a glorified flying chauffer."

"Are you sure that I'll fit in?" Gray asked. "I don't really know what it is that you do."

"I'm certain that you'll be a great addition to the team and I can assure you that every day will be a challenge," Aki replied. "Our team is considered dark ops. I'm the section chief of TCT, which stands for Target, Capture, or Terminate. We're sanctioned under the Special Projects Division and no one knows our unit exists except my boss, the Secretary of Homeland Security, and POTUS."

"I guess that explains why Under Secretary Basset didn't know that you were here."

"That's correct. We work on assignments that are on a need-to-know basis, and Under Secretary Basset didn't need to know that we were still involved with hunting Dar."

"Well, he found out," Gray said. "Won't that be a problem?"

"No."

"Doesn't your boss report to Basset?"

"Not when it comes to TCT operations. I'll explain it more thoroughly if you accept the position and stay here with me. However, now that I've told you about TCT, disclosure of that information would have serious consequences. Understand?" She raised an eyebrow.

"Yes. I understand perfectly. I am curious about what's happening here and I'd like to see if Crawley turns up. What about Clay, Angela, Sarah, and Lt. White Owl? They all have an interest in the outcome of this investigation. Can they continue to work on the investigation under Homeland?"

"I don't see how. I think that Angela's expertise would be of value to the FBI, but I don't think they'll take advantage of it. They tend to rely on their own experts."

"Yeah, I know."

"Gray, our missions are important to the stability of the United States and to the world. You won't lack for excitement."

"Sounds like a recruitment promo for the Marines. How can I refuse? I'd be honored to join the team."

"Excellent—I knew you would, and your paperwork is being processed as we speak."

"You're pretty sure of yourself."

"I can be." Aki paused. "Actually, we're intercepting all of the transmissions originating from here. I knew about the FBI taking the lead and you being discharged from OAS last night. I couldn't say anything because I didn't want them knowing that we're monitoring their comms. I needed you to respond just the way you did."

"You're spying on our own agencies?" Gray was astounded.

"Necessary evil. We aren't monitoring everything. I didn't know that Basset had been called by the FBI director or that he'd pulled our backup teams."

"Are you still planning to meet with Chairman Red Elk today?" Gray asked.

"Yes. I'd also like to roam around the reservation later and see if anyone knows anything. The agencies doing interviews there now aren't going to learn anything worthwhile. I'll have better luck gaining trust once I speak to Red Elk and get his cooperation. I've also tracked down Makawee, and with Angela's help, she may be able to tell us who Dar has snooping around the reservation. I'm hoping we can track Dar through her operative."

"Does Dar have her own team?" Gray asked.

"No. She's going to need help from the locals. I'll brief you fully on her later."

Gray stopped and glanced at Sarah. "This isn't going to be easy."

"No, it isn't. If you tell her about coming to work for Homeland, don't mention TCT. Just tell her that you've been offered a pilot position, which isn't a lie."

"Okay. Standby for some fireworks. You're certain that Sarah can't stay involved in the investigation?"

"I need a stable team without complications and I know that I'm not her favorite person. Sarah also doesn't have any experience that we can use, and she's going to be suspended and placed under investigation by the NPS Internal Affairs Unit shortly. She hasn't been notified yet."

"You intercepted that call, too?"

"Yes."

"She's going to be devastated," Gray said. "Aki, I'm sure that Sarah could help us on this investigation. She knows people in the area, and if we need to get into that cavern, she's trained in cave-rescue operations and knows the cave systems around the Black Hills. She'd be of value to the team."

"Wouldn't it be easier to end it now?" Aki asked bluntly. "Conflicting careers and distance will certainly kill any relationship."

"You know this from experience?"

"I was married to an FBI agent and our careers got in the way. I lost him to someone who was willing to move when he needed to change assignments and who didn't feel like a competitor. You'll be traveling all over the world and you won't be able to tell Sarah what you're working on or where. You'll also have to relocate to Virginia, and I believe Sarah will want to stay here."

"I hadn't even thought about having to relocate."

"And there's the issue that we'll be working together. I don't think she will be able to deal with that, and she'll eventually demand that you choose between her and the job or me. It'll make for a complication and distraction that I can't have on my team."

"You're right, and I'm sure you know that I lost my ex-wife because of the job."

"I do. I also know that Sarah is strong-willed, possessive, and independent." Aki paused, then said, "I'll let you decide if you want to ask Sarah if she wants to keep working on the investigation, but it would be very temporary and she'd need the approval from NPS before I would agree. With her under investigation, I don't see that happening."

"Thanks," Gray replied. "Let's go find out."

Gray walked up to Sarah.

"What were you both talking about?" Sarah asked, and crossed her arms.

Chase and White Owl stood and joined them.

"Sutton has pulled the plug on the task force," Gray replied.

"We're no longer involved in the investigation?" Sarah said.

"Nope, and I've been decommissioned as a DCI agent. And thanks to Sutton, I was also just forced to resign from the Office of Aviation Services. And, all of us are considered suspects in Crawley's disappearance."

"That's ridiculous!" Sarah exclaimed.

"I agree, but that's the reality of the situation."

"I'm sorry to hear about your job. I know how much you were looking forward to it."

"I was, and you need to know that you'll be getting a call from NPS Internal Affairs pretty soon," Gray informed her.

"How would you know that?" Sarah asked.

"Because I told him," Aki interjected.

"Of course you did."

"The good news is that Aki offered me a job at Homeland and I accepted," Gray said.

"What!" Sarah cried.

"Hear me out. Aki may be able to give you a temporary position with Homeland, if you want to continue working on the investigation and NPS approves."

"Really?" Sarah gave Aki a quizzical look.

A ranger stepped from the bus and interrupted. "Sarah, there's a call for you."

"Sarah, think about the offer regardless of what happens next," Gray requested.

"I'll think about it."

Sarah stepped into the bus.

"I'll need to inform my sheriff," White Owl said. "Excuse me."

"We need to talk in private for a moment," Chase said to Aki.

"Excuse us," Aki said.

When they were far enough away, Aki asked, "What's on your mind?"

"Have you lost yours? Director Canton isn't going to agree to this. We don't know anything about Gray or Ranger Sarah."

"I know what I need to know about Gray. Sharon vetted him for me last night. And, we're going to need him. Basset pulled the response team and our aerial support."

"How in the hell could Basset do that?" Chase asked. "Those were our people. He's not even supposed to know that we're out here."

"Director Sutton called the FBI and the FBI called Bassett. Basset told the FBI that we'd gone rogue. I doubt that Canton even knows what he's done."

"She could go to Evans and get our support retasked."

"I think that would compromise TCT."

"And that isn't going to happen," Chase said.

"Correct. We need a pilot, and Sarah knows the caves around here. If we get a chance to get into that cavern or go underground elsewhere, she could be useful. We can use a few more seasoned people to help us out, especially someone that Dar won't recognize. I believe the director will agree with me."

"Is this temporary or permanent?" Chase asked.

"I want Gray permanently. We could use another field investigator and he's experienced. Sarah's only temporary."

Chase smiled at her and said, "I say this as a friend, but not so long ago you had a discussion with me about my wanting Traci on our team. I've known you a long time and I can tell that you have more than a professional interest in Gray."

"Don't go there," Aki said sternly, but she knew that Chase was right.

"Okay, It's your call."

"Yes, it is. I'm going to have Sharon do some research on the subterranean caverns in the area and have her send us the info from the satellite passes. I know this area but not the cave systems."

"You think that Dar will hear about the cavern and come looking to see if the missing people are being held there, don't you?" Chase said.

"Yes. Like us, she'll try and find a way in, and I want to be waiting for her."

"If the FBI thinks that the cavern holds clues to the missing, they'll want to excavate," Chase said. "It's the fastest way in."

"I imagine they will, but they have a lot of red tape to get through in order to receive permission, and they'll meet resistance from the environmentalists, the Lakota and other tribes."

"Are you planning to tell Chairman Red Elk about the cavern and the gold?"

"I plan to tell him about the cavern if White Owl hasn't done so already. I'm not going to tell him about the gold. Let's see what Sarah has to say about the job and then I'll call Director Canton."

"Whatever became of that cell phone Dar left active after she talked to Hagans?" Chase asked.

"Sharon said Brian tracked it to Montana. It stopped at a residence where the truck was registered. I told her not to monitor it any longer. She just wanted to have us chase a ghost."

"At least we didn't fall for her ruse. It was a pretty lame attempt."

"Definitely not up to her usual standards."

Sarah exited through the rear bus door, and from her pale face, Gray knew that she hadn't taken the news well. "How bad is it?" he asked.

"I've been suspended with pay pending the outcome of the FBI investigation. I was told that Director Sutton notified the NPS regional director and demanded that I be removed from the investigation as I was a 'person of interest' in Crawley's disappearance. If the results of their investigation implicate me in any way, they'll open a formal internal affairs investigation and assist in the criminal investigation. They also weren't happy to hear that I had discharged my firearm and hadn't notify anyone at NPS. I told them at the time, I was working with DCI and communication was limited. They're going to take that under review." She sighed then continued. "I was instructed to cooperate fully with the FBI, as if I wouldn't, and I'm not to discuss what's happened with anyone other than the investigators."

"In other words, you can't run to the media and sell your story," Gray joked. Sarah's dagger stare indicated that she wasn't pleased with his attempt at humor.

"I also have to check in every morning at nine with an NPS investigator. But other than that, I have no restrictions. I was told to keep my truck, so at least I'll have that when the FBI is done with it. They also said I don't have to stay on scene. In fact, they encouraged me to go home. I just have to be available by phone."

"At least you weren't terminated," Gray said.

"True."

"Sarah, are you alright?" Aki asked, sounding genuinely concerned.

"Been better."

"Gray said that you're a caver and know the underground systems in the area," Aki said.

"I do. I've helped map many of the major cave systems here and in Wyoming for NPS and with my grotto."

"What's a grotto?" Chase asked.

"It's a spelunking club," Sarah replied. "The nearest one is in Custer. I belong to the grotto in Casper. Aki, are you offering me a job because you need someone with caving experience?"

"To be honest, yes. Your expertise for the next phase of our investigation will be a big help. I'd really like you to take the temporary appointment I offered."

"I'm tempted, but NPS won't allow me to work with Homeland while I'm suspended," Sarah replied.

"I could make some calls," Aki said.

"Don't do that. I don't need any more trouble."

"I understand," Aki replied. "What if you were to work off-book?"

"What do you mean?"

"If I can provide you with detailed maps of the cavern and the adjoining systems, would you be willing to help us unofficially?"

"I have detailed maps of all the cave systems in the Black Hills at home," Sarah said. "Aki, what exactly do you want from me?"

"I need you to take a look at the satellite images of the cavern and find a us way in before anyone else does, and I want you to see if anyone could gain entry from another cave system. I'll also need you to train us and tell us what equipment we'll need in order to explore the cavern once you find an entry point. And, I'd like you to be our guide when we enter the cave."

"I see."

"You wouldn't be directly involved in any case activity," Aki added. "You'd only be acting as a consultant. If our work leads to answers about the disappearances and homicides, we'll turn it all over to Agent Stevens. He's the Special Agent In Charge on the case."

"Caving I can do, but what you really need is a geologist who can interpret your satellite data to find the best access point. Don't you have experts you can call?"

"We do, but it will take time to find one and get them up to speed."

"I'm not supposed to be involved in the investigation, but I guess consulting on caving would be alright. Aki, just so you know, I only have a basic understanding of geology. When it comes to caving it's nice to know what you're crawling through, especially in tight quarters. I'll look at the information you provide and give you my best guess as to what's down there and if there's a way in, but that's all it will be."

"Sarah, would it be unusual to find an undiscovered cave in this area?" Chase asked.

"Not really. There are caves all through the Black Hills. A lot of them were created by the major geological uplift that gave birth to the Black Hills about seventy million years ago. Most of the passages were formed by ancient shifting faults or carved out of limestone by underground rivers and water erosion." Sarah paused for a moment, then added, "It would be fun to find gold in an unexplored and pristine cave."

"I thought this area was mostly composed of granite," Gray said.

"Mount Rushmore, to the east, is granite. Understand that what's beneath us is mostly limestone and schist. Geologically speaking, we're standing at the northern edge of the Fanny Peak quadrangle. The Black Hills and the Fanny Peak monoclines intersect near here."

"What's a monocline?" Chase asked.

"It's a step-like fold in the rock strata, basically a steep dip," Sarah replied. "They're formed in a number of ways. I'm starting to sound like I'm giving a lecture."

"You are, a little," Gray said. "But it's interesting."

"Why do you need to find more than one way into the cavern?" Sarah asked. "Finding one entry point will be hard enough."

"We may have unfriendly company," Aki replied. "I'll explain further if you decide to work with us."

"What about Clay, White Owl, and Angela?" Sarah asked. "Will they be joining us?"

"I'm not sure yet," Aki replied. "I want to see what you discover first."

"Angela told me that she has spelunking experience," Sarah said. "She could assist me in interpreting the satellite images, and it would be a big help to have two trained cavers going underground."

"That does sound safer," Chase said.

Aki knew that Chase had a touch of claustrophobia. "Chase, I need to have a member of our team focus on geological research and have them coordinate with Sarah."

"Omar would be the best choice," Chase replied. "Sharon has a full plate."

White Owl stepped out of the bus and said, "I talked to my sheriff and it seems that I'm to remain here until dismissed by the FBI. The good news is that I'm not under investigation by my department. Gray, have you told Angela or Clay about the new development?"

"I haven't."

"Now might be a good time," Sarah said, and pointed. "They're headed this way."

"Sarah, I really need to know if you're onboard," Aki said. "Time is critical."

"I'll help you," Sarah replied, raising her hands in mock surrender.

"Thank you," Aki said.

"Sarah, did NPS approve your continued participation in the investigation?" White Owl asked.

"I'm just a volunteer assisting DHS with a caving project on my own time. I'm not involved in the homicide or the missing-persons cases."

"I believe that you're walking a thin line there," White Owl cautioned.

When Angela and Clay walked up, Gray said, "We need to talk."

When Gray had finished telling them what had happened, Angela said, "Isn't that special. I'm a suspect again. I should be getting used to this by now."

"Yeah, it's really special," Clay lamented.

"If it makes you feel any better, I don't like what's happened either," White Owl said. "We've done nothing wrong. They're just being thorough and everything will turn out fine."

"I think that Sutton needed to find a scapegoat," Clay said, pointing at Gray. "We're just collateral damage."

"When the spirit warriors return, that'll change their minds," Angela said.

"*If* they return," Gray stated.

"I better call my sheriff and let him know that I'm a suspect and see what he wants me to do," Clay said. He took out his cell phone and stepped away.

"I hope everything works out for him," Gray said. "He's a good deputy."

"And a good guy," Sarah added.

"Angela, Aki knows where to reach Makawee and wants to interview her," Gray said.

"Any chance I can go with you?" Angela asked Aki. "I haven't seen her in a while and I may be of help."

"I was hoping you'd want to join us."

When Clay returned, Gray asked, "Well?"

"The sheriff said that I'm to stay put and cooperate with the FBI and not to worry," Clay replied. "I'll return to normal duties unless I'm arrested. I think he was trying to lighten the mood. He knew that I was upset."

"Since you are assigned here, maybe you and Lt. White Owl would be willing to give us updates on how the investigation progresses while we're away," Gray said.

"I'd be happy to, but I'm not sure how much I'll be able to find out," Clay said.

"The NPS command bus is monitoring all of the radio channels," White Owl said. "We'll know what's going on. If we hear a juicy tidbit, we can pass it on."

"That sounds like fun," Clay quipped.

CHAPTER EIGHTEEN

As soon as Dar parked in the grass lot, Gordon Black came out of the office, waved, and walked toward her.

When Dar opened her car door, Black said, "We're fueled and can depart whenever you're ready."

"Excellent. Did anyone make any inquiries concerning my activity?"

"No."

Dar's cell phone rang and the caller ID told her it was Carlton. "I'll be just a minute." As soon as Black was a discreet distance away, Dar answered, "Yes."

"I have an update."

"Go ahead."

"Let's start with the bad news. My investigators on the reservation still aren't getting any good information. We spread the word about your financial incentive and had a few people come forward, but it was all nonsense."

"Was there any commonality in the information they provided?"

"No. The latest from the scene is that the FBI has taken over the investigation. My source advised that the missing agent's task force has been disbanded and that the members are now under investigation."

"What's the good news?" Dar asked.

"It seems that they've discovered a cavern beneath the crime-scene area. They're trying to find a point of entry and if there's any link to the missing mining employees. There's also supposed to be something in the cavern, something big, but my source couldn't find out what's being kept secret."

"If it's a secret, how did your source get the information about the cavern?"

"They asked him if he had anyone under his supervision qualified in cave operations. He gave them the names of several people trained in cave rescue. One of them was a woman ranger who was on the task force. The closest cavers are coming from the Jewel and Wind Caves. They're probably already on the scene."

"How many cavers have been requested?"

"I don't know the exact number. It's shaping up to be a major operation and it seems they need quite a few cavers. He said NPS cave-rescue personnel are being flown in from around the country."

"That is really good work," Dar praised. "Can your source get an NPS ranger uniform for me?"

"I can ask. What size?"

Dar told him her size, then added, "I'm going to need some spelunking equipment and NPS coveralls. Can you procure that for me in the next few hours?"

"I believe so. Are you planning to sneak into the scene?"

"Maybe. Call me when you have the gear and I'll give you a delivery point."

"I'll get on it," Carlton said.

Dar disconnected and motioned for Black to rejoin her. "Let's get airborne."

"You got it. What about the extra money for being available anytime?"

Dar leaned in her car and pulled ten thousand from her pack and handed it to him.

"Nice doing business with you," Black said.

Dar locked the car and they walked to the helicopter.

"I need to look further north of the crime scene today," Dar said, as the engine turned over and the rotor blades began to turn.

"No problem. I heard a rumor that a cult is committing sacrifices up there. Is that the problem you're here to solve?"

Dar turned and gave him a hard stare. "I thought you knew better than to ask questions." Then in a softer tone, she said, "I'll let you in on a secret. I'm looking for the missing people. I was wondering if they may have gotten lost in a cave. A friend of mine told me that the Parks Service is bringing in expert cavers."

"There are several major cave systems in the area. Though I don't know of any in the area where they're looking."

"Do you know if you can determine if a cave lies beneath the terrain simply by looking at it from the air?" Dar asked.

"I don't think that's possible, unless the entrance is out in the open or on the side of a cliff." He sounded like he was trying not to laugh at her question.

"Well, maybe I'll see something that looks interesting."

As soon as they reached the area, Black started making wide orbits to the north of the scene.

"Looks like they've brought in more help," he said.

"So it would appear." It looked like the number of vehicles and people in the search area had nearly doubled. She turned her attention to the terrain, and after an hour of looking for depressions or obvious openings in the side of the hills, Dar decided that nothing looked like it could be a cave entrance.

"Seen enough?" Black asked.

"Yes. We can head back now."

Twenty minutes later, they were approaching the field for a landing when Dar noticed a news van parked in the grass lot. "It looks like you may have some additional business."

"I guess so. Do you need my services any longer today?"

"No." Two people were standing near the landing area. A thin man with long black hair was videoing a woman wearing a red dress holding a microphone. The downdraft from the rotors blew the woman's strawberry-blond hair across her face as they touched down, forcing her to stop talking. She gave them a nasty look as she moved away from the helicopter.

"I think you spoiled their shot," Dar said.

"They shouldn't have been standing so close to my landing zone."

Dar's cell phone rang just as she was getting out of the helicopter. "Yes, Carlton."

"I have what you need as far as equipment. I'm still waiting to hear about the uniform. Where would you like to meet?"

"Let me know when you have *everything* I need." Dar hung up. The woman reporter walked up and Dar said, "Mr. Black, I enjoyed the tour."

Black nodded and replied, "Glad to hear it. Come back anytime." He turned to the reporter. "What can I do for you?"

As the reporter started asking Black about his helicopter, Dar walked quickly to her Tahoe and pulled out of the lot.

Black Hills – 1000 hours

White Owl relieved Dawn of her dispatch duties so she could go eat, which allowed the group to have the NPS command bus to themselves. Clay and Angela offered to go get breakfast from the mess tent for everyone. Gray didn't want to go anywhere near Sutton or the other agents, and Aki agreed.

Aki's cell phone rang. "It's Sharon." After speaking to Sharon for a few minutes, she said, "Send all of the images to Chase's laptop." Then disconnected.

"What's she sending me?" Chase asked.

"Everything we need. I hope, so that Sarah can put the pieces together. We'll be receiving updated Terra Surveyor satellite imagery of the substrata around the cavern in a few minutes. Brian intercepted the data in real time as the satellite was sending it to NASA, then snuck onto a USGS computer to analyze it. Apparently, he had access to the computer through an old connection at HSI."

"Satellite imagery usually takes several days or even weeks to analyze," Sarah said.

"Brian was able expedite the process. We're also going to receive new imagery of the Jewel and Wind Cave systems in case the systems are connected. Sharon says the images show a three-dimensional maze of tunnels, and some of the Jewel Cave tunnels extend into the southern Black Hills, toward the cavern."

"So, we'll have all of the new images before anyone else has a chance to examine them," Gray said.

"Yes," Aki replied, "and long before the FBI gets the information."

"I know the Jewel Cave very well," Sarah stated. "I trained and spent many days camped underground in those passages. Hopefully, I'll be able to find something new that hasn't been explored and determine if there are any links to the new cavern. I'll also look for any passageways that are near the surface that could be used as an access point. How deep are the scans?"

"A hundred meters in some places," Aki replied. "The three-dimensional spatial resolution is less than a foot across with a scan swath of a mile."

"That's incredible!" Sarah exclaimed. "With that resolution, we'll be able to see any number of geological layers, cavities, passages, and maybe even some crawlways."

"Sharon's also lined up a geologist from MIT who's cleared just in case we need her assistance, but I would rather keep the information circle tight. So, Sarah, we'll need you to do your best at analyzing the images. If you can't handle it, we'll go to the expert."

"Like I said, I'm not a geologist, but I'll do my best. Just so you know, the images may not have mapped everything. The Wind and Jewel caves are both deeper than a hundred meters in a lot of places. In fact, the Jewel Cave goes down over eight hundred feet in one location and is thought to be the deepest cave in the Black Hills. I wonder if I'll be able to settle the argument over whether the Jewel and Wind Cave systems join as most experts believe."

"You'll certainly have the best imagery available," Aki said.

"How long would it take someone to walk from the Jewel Cave to the new cavern if they're connected?" Chase asked.

"I believe there would be more crawling than walking. Even though the Jewel Cave is the closest major cave system to the cavern, I doubt that there's a direct route between them. The Jasper Cave is actually closer to the cavern, but isn't very remarkable and hasn't been fully explored."

"Is it possible the Jasper Cave is connected to the Jewel Cave?" White Owl asked.

"Unknown. It's estimated that only about five percent of the Jewel Cave has been mapped. It's a huge underground system. If the new cavern has passages leading southeast, it's possible they could connect to a southwest splinter from either the Jewel or Jasper caves. That's why I can't wait to see the satellite images."

"What do you mean by huge?" Chase asked.

"A little over two hundred miles of passages have been explored."

"Two hundred miles would put it in Wyoming, Nebraska, or Colorado," Chase said.

"No, it doesn't work that way. It's not like a tunnel. There are multistory mazes of passages, all at different depths. You could have many miles of channels stacked vertically over a very short distance.

"One interesting feature of the Jewel Cave is what's called the Big Duh. It's a cavernous expanse about two football fields long, over thirty meters wide and ten meters high. It really is something to see."

"How far is it from the Jewel Cave entrance to the new cavern?" Gray asked.

"Straight-line distance is only about ten to twelve miles."

"The new images will give us a better idea of the dimensions of the cavern and maybe we'll see a passageway that we can use," Aki said.

"I imagine it's easy to get lost in a cave system," Chase said.

"It is, if you don't come prepared. There are some simple rules to follow."

"Like?" Chase asked.

"You can make arrows in the dirt or cairns out of stones to tell you which way to go," Sarah answered. "You can use the simple right- and left-wall rule or leave signs at confusing intersections. Experienced cavers use memory tricks to remember how to get back out. If you're near the surface, you may find animal droppings. You can also use finely powdered dust to see if there's an airflow and follow that to the surface. First rule if you're completely disoriented, don't panic. Rescuers will eventually find you."

"Unless you're in an unexplored cave and no one knows that you're there, which is what we'll be facing," Chase said. "I'm not a big fan of dark, confined spaces. The thought of being stuck underground doesn't sit well with me."

"Hey, I've gotten lost in caves before. It's no fun. The worst experience isn't being in the dark when your light fails, it's getting stuck in a crawlway. That's why you don't go caving alone."

"Relax, Chase," Aki said. "Sarah won't get us lost. We'll be fine."

Gray didn't care for confined spaces either, but he'd never admit it. "Aki, did you hear from your boss about the loss of support?" he asked.

"Still waiting. When I spoke to her earlier, her voice sounded a bit strained and I could hear a heated conversation in the background."

"Does she need to give the okay on my position?"

"No, that's a done deal."

Chase's laptop chimed. "The data is downloading. It appears to be several large files. This may take a few minutes."

Sarah slid closer to Chase at the conference table in the back of the bus.

"Don't worry, I'll share the images," Chase said.

"You bet you will," Sarah declared.

Aki, White Owl, and Gray chuckled. Gray was pleased to see that Sarah and Chase were growing friendlier.

"Why don't you put the laptop where we can all see the screen?" Gray suggested.

Chase pushed it back and said, "Sarah, open the first file. It's queued up."

Sarah opened it and toggled through the images, zooming in and out. "Amazing detail," she finally said. "The main cavern is enormous. I'd say nearly three-quarters of a mile wide, a mile long, and a hundred feet high. It makes the Big Duh look small. There are two adjoining caverns about a quarter of the size of the main cavern." Sarah zoomed in again. "Take a look at this."

The others moved closer as Sarah pointed at the screen.

"What are we looking at?" White Owl asked. "Are those buildings?"

"I think so," Sarah said. "They're symmetrically shaped and appear to be arranged side by side. I've never seen a natural formation like that in any cave system. And look, these passages leading to the other caverns run in a straight line. That's very strange."

"You're saying that these structures were carved out of the limestone," Gray said.

"It appears that way," Sarah replied.

"Where's the entrance?" Aki asked.

"I don't see one."

"Open the other files," Aki ordered.

Sarah scrolled through the file folders. "There's one labeled hydrological imagery, there's a geologic remote-hyperspectral deep-penetration imagery file, a LIDAR and ASTER imagery file, and another with an acronym I've never seen before. Let's start with the file that's labeled 'geo-hyperspectral and deep-penetration imagery.'"

A moment later, a vividly colored map appeared. The structures in the center were displayed in red. The surrounding area was displayed in green, yellow, and black.

"This is a spectral three-dimensional image of the entire cavern," Sarah said. "The quality and detail are incredible."

"What do the different colors mean?" Chase asked.

"Minerals and elements have unique spectrum wavelengths and software assigns different colors to them," Sarah replied. "There isn't a legend to explain what the colors represent, but my guess is that the expanse of the green-and-black images is limestone or schist. I don't think the structures in red were carved from the limestone." Sarah zoomed in. "Whatever the red denotes, there's a lot of it." She paused. "I wonder if the structures are coated with or made of gold?"

Aki said, "A city made of gold would certainly look like a large gold deposit on conventional scans."

"But who built it and why?" White Owl asked.

"And how long ago?" Chase added.

"Aki…you know Angela could help us answer those questions," Sarah said. "Her expertise in archeology is a given, and like I said, she also has caving experience. There's a lot of information to analyze and I'm certain she'd be able to help. It could expedite our finding an entrance into the cavern. You should ask her to help us when she gets back."

"I agree," Gray said. "Maybe she can tell by the architecture who built it and how old it is."

Aki leaned back and pursed her lips. "I think we're going to need support if we do find a way underground. White Owl, would you care to join our ad hoc group?"

"Certainly. What about Clay? He told me that he wished he could be more involved in solving this mystery than listening to radio traffic."

"I don't have an issue with him participating," Aki stated.

"I guess the team is getting back together," Sarah said.

"Temporarily," Aki cautioned.

"Angela's a civilian and needs to be told about the risks involved and understand that her role is voluntary," Chase added.

"I'm certain that she knows the risks," Gray said.

Just then, the rear bus-door opened and Angela and Clay entered carrying their breakfast. A smell of bacon quickly permeated the room and Gray suddenly realized he was hungry.

"Perfect timing," Aki said. "We were just talking about you two."

The Styrofoam plates with their breakfasts were put on the table.

"They're all the same, so dig in," Angela said.

Once the seven of them were seated around the table, Aki explained what was happening. Without hesitation, Clay and Angela agreed to join the group. Aki emphasized the need to keep everything discussed classified.

"If that is a city of gold, it could be the reason the buffalo spirit warriors are protecting it," Angela said. "And why Darren was killed. I want a look at those structures."

"Angela, we also need you and Sarah to find a way into the cavern to get an up-close look at them," Aki said.

"Give us some time to study all the files," Sarah said. "If people once lived there, we'll find an entrance."

Just then, Aki's cell phone rang. "It's the director. Chase and I will need to take this. Let's go outside."

As soon as Chase and Aki left the bus, Sarah turned to Gray and said, "I'd like to speak with you in private."

"Was it something I said," Clay joked. "I took a shower and everything."

They all laughed.

Gray and Sarah went to the front of the bus. Gray slid the partition door closed and noticed that Dawn hadn't returned yet. There were several radios and two computer monitors against one side that made up the two dispatcher stations. Gray sat in one of the chairs and Sarah took the other.

"What's on your mind?" Gray asked.

Sarah leaned closer and spoke quietly. "Did you really think about what the job you've been hired to do entails before you agreed to take it? Or was your ego so damaged by losing your other jobs, and your vision so clouded by Aki, that you just grabbed at the first offer?"

Gray could tell Sarah was concerned about his decision. He had mixed feelings about Sarah, and what Aki had said about conflicting career paths had resonated. He didn't want to alienate Sarah, but he also didn't want to lead her on.

"I knew what I was getting into. Besides, most of what I'll be doing is just flying."

Sarah sighed. "I think she wants more than that from you. Even if I get to keep my job, how could we have any kind of a relationship with you living in Virginia?"

Gray wasn't sure if he should even respond. He had feelings for Aki that he couldn't explain, but he also liked Sarah and didn't want to lose her friendship. Sarah was adventurous, fun, and direct, which were qualities he found attractive, but he felt a stronger connection to Aki.

"I don't know," he finally answered. "If Aki were to offer you a permanent position, would you take it?"

"That isn't going to happen. I don't have the investigative experience. I'm a ranger and that's what I like to do."

"I understand." Gray heard the back door open. Aki and Chase were back. "Let's go see what she's learned from her director."

"That's all you have to say?" Sarah asked, without getting up. She shook her head and said, "I guess that means you want the job more than our relationship."

Gray looked at her and replied, "I think that works both ways."

"I guess it does."

They rejoined the group in the back and Gray asked, "What did the director have to say?"

"Nothing good. I'll brief you later."

Sarah said, "Angela and I need to get started on those files and see if we can find an opening near the surface. So, unless it's important, leave us alone." She grabbed the laptop and went back to sit in the front of the bus.

Angela took a last bite of bacon and a sip of coffee, then said, "I better go see what we can find."

After the partition door was closed, Aki asked softly, "Everything okay?"

"She's adjusting," Gray replied.

"I see."

"Aki, what's our next move?" Gray asked.

"It depends on whether Sarah and Angela can find a way into the cavern. If they come up empty, then I'll have Sharon consult with the MIT expert. Remember, even after they find one opening, they'll need to keep looking for more."

"Are you all still meeting the chairman at three?" Gray asked. He'd been surprised to learn that he wouldn't be attending the meeting. Aki had told him Chase needed to get him up to speed on TCT operations while they were gone.

"Yes," Aki replied. "White Owl will drive us to the reservation."

"Chairman Red Elk and the new Oglala Sioux Tribe police chief, Brian Tate, want to meet us at a church near Oglala Lake," White Owl interjected. "They thought it best to meet off the reservation because the FBI and the increased law-enforcement presence is stirring up the community."

"Which is what I knew would happen," Aki said.

"How long of a drive is it to Oglala Lake from here?" Gray asked.

"About two hours," White Owl answered.

"White Owl, how long can we use the bus?" Aki asked.

"For as long as it's here. Clay and I offered to help with dispatch when Dawn needed breaks during her shift. Even Sutton seemed okay with us helping out. I think he wanted us out of the way. The evening and midnight shifts are being covered by other dispatchers or rangers. There really isn't much communication traffic being handled from here since the original call-up. The FBI is taking care of most of the coordination with the local law enforcement, and DCI has their own people. I think we need to keep a presence here to monitor the investigative activity."

"I agree. Clay, you'll need to stay here while we're gone."

"No problem." The phone rang and Clay answered. After a brief conversation he said, "The FBI has finished processing Sarah's truck. It's going to be brought back here late this afternoon."

"Gray, when her truck is delivered, you all need to go buy whatever gear Sarah recommends for spelunking. Hopefully, she'll have located an entrance by then."

"You really think that we'll have to go underground?" Chase asked.

"I want to be ready if we do."

"We're also going to need a place for all of us to stay and work," Chase said.

"Custer will be the best location," White Owl offered. "I know a place that should work."

Black Hills - 1240 hours

Aki left Gray and Chase sitting under the awning after briefing them on what Director Canton had said and providing Gray with insights into TCT and backgrounds on the rest of the team. She entered the rear of the bus, where Sarah and Angela had moved to keep working after Dawn returned.

"We're getting tight on time," Aki said. "Sarah, are you and Angela any closer to finding an entrance?"

Sarah looked up from the screen and rubbed her eyes. "The only thing we've found is a shallow dead-end passage near the area where we encountered the spirit warriors."

"How shallow?" Aki asked.

"About twenty-five feet beneath the surface. There's no visible access or any sign of a vertical shaft, so it's not useful unless you want to dig. The passage doubles back on itself as it ascends from the city until it stops at a large boulder-size node. The spectral image shows the node in red."

"Interesting. You're sure that there's no way to reach the structures without digging?"

"Based on the images we've examined, that would be the only option," Sarah replied. "I'll keep looking for a passage that's closer to the surface, but I don't think it'll be nearby. Your geological expert may see something that we've missed, but I doubt it. The FBI will be told the same thing once they receive the data. I imagine that they'll want to dig a small shaft to put a remote camera down."

"How long would that take?" Aki asked.

"That all depends on how readily available the equipment is and whether they can get permission," Sarah replied. "The quickest way to get a look in the cavern would be to bypass the passageways and bore the two hundred feet to the cavern ceiling. That's easier than trying to dig an opening over the node and sending in cavers. The NPS has been an advocate for preventing excavation on sacred lands for years. But if the FBI guarantees the area will be returned to pristine condition, it could happen soon."

"I'll let Chairman Red Elk know. The FBI may try and claim exigent circumstances and bypass getting tribal approval due to the ongoing criminal investigation. Telling Red Elk will allow the tribes a chance to voice their concerns and stop them before they dig."

"How well do you know the chairman and the police chief?" Angela asked.

"I believe Red Elk will remember my family. I don't know anything about Chief Tate other than that he came over from the Bureau of Indian Affairs."

"I hope that Makawee will be willing to provide some information," Sarah said.

"I'm hoping Angela's friendly face will put her at ease," Aki replied.

Sarah nodded. "You might be interested to know that I did find a descending passageway that runs southeast from the cavern in the direction of the Jewel Cave. I couldn't follow it because it dropped below a hundred meters. I'll keep looking and see if it comes up anywhere."

"Why didn't you say something about that earlier?" Aki asked.

"Because you were interested in finding an access portal for the cavern."

Aki sighed. "What's so interesting about it?"

"Like many of the passageways, it's straighter than it should be for a natural channel and it has a constant fifteen-degree descending grade. It's also high enough for a human to walk through without having to stoop. Aki, none of the passageways seem to have been made by nature."

"I need you to determine if that passage comes back up before you work on anything else. Since there doesn't seem to be an opening over the cavern, that may be our key to getting in."

"Aki, from what I've seen, those structures could have housed anywhere from a hundred to three hundred people," Angela said. "I have a strong feeling that this ancient city is what Darren suspected was there. I just wish I knew how he could have known." She wiped a tear from her cheek. "I thought I was done crying."

"It'll take time," Aki said. "Do you think he found a way in?"

"I don't see how," Angela replied. "You have to understand that the craftsmanship needed to create an underground city of gold is unimaginable for any ancient civilization. This place is of significant historical value and must be considered sacred."

"I agree," Aki said.

"We can't let anyone enter the cavern until it's protected," Angela stressed. "The cavern must be kept pristine so that archeologists and historians can examine it."

Aki nodded, then called out, "White Owl."

The partition door opened and White Owl stepped in. "Yes?"

"We need to go. Sarah, call me if you find anything else."

"Will do."

Gray stared at Sutton, who was watching them from the DCI command bus. He desperately wanted to beat the arrogance out of his vindictive ass.

Aki stepped from the command bus and said, "I don't think he likes you."

"The feeling is mutual," Gray said. "He's been staring at us for the last few minutes."

"I think you need to take a drive," Aki said. "Chase, follow us out and park down the road. You can continue briefing Gray on operations and monitor the traffic. Maybe Sutton will lose interest."

"Will do," Chase replied.

"Gray, you need to let go of the anger," Aki said.

"Easier said than done, but I'll work on it."

CHAPTER NINETEEN

Hill City – May 25 – 1430 hours

Dar was keeping watch on the newly rented Chrysler Voyager minivan she'd left unlocked across the street from her favorite pizza restaurant, which offered a perfect vantage point. She'd finished eating a half hour ago and was still waiting for Carlton to deliver the equipment and uniform he'd promised. Frustrated and not liking having to wait, she absently drummed her fingers on the table while she took a sip of her cola.

A few minutes later, a grey Chevy Blazer pulled up behind her rental. Carlton got out and looked around, checking to see if anyone was watching him. Dar thought that his many furtive glances only drew attention as he loaded several boxes into the minivan. Carlton locked the minivan, went back to his vehicle, and pulled away.

Dar paid her bill and left a generous tip, and she had just walked outside when her cell phone rang.

"Yes, Carlton?"

"Everything you asked for has been delivered. Do you want me to stick around to watch the van?"

"No. I'll call you if I need anything else."

"Just before I dropped off your gear, I received some new information from the scene. My source didn't have access to the specifics, but he advised that the FBI had just received new satellite imagery of the cavern and the surrounding area. It's got everyone excited. He hopes to learn more later."

"That's good intel. Anything new from the reservation?"

"I heard that Chairman Red Elk and the new OST police chief are scheduled to meet with an agent from Homeland Security and a local deputy sheriff. Both are supposed to be Lakota. The meeting is at three today at a secret location away from Pine Ridge."

Dar smiled, knowing the agent was Aki. "That is interesting. Any chance we can find out what's on the agenda?"

"I was lucky that one of my people got this much, but I'll see what we can learn when Red Elk returns from the meeting. The source may be more talkative, especially if we offer a little more incentive."

"Do it."

"I'm headed for the reservation now and I'll take care of it personally."

Dar hung up and walked across the street toward the minivan. With Aki away from the scene, she decided to see if she could breach the perimeter.

Oglala Lake, South Dakota – 1500 hours

Aki, White Owl, and Angela were seated at a large table in a small church-annex office. At exactly three, the church pastor led Chairman Red Elk and Chief Tate into the office and greetings were exchanged. Aki addressed Red Elk in the traditional Lakota manner.

Red Elk was slightly taller than Aki, in his sixties, and had a thin build with long gray hair and weathered features. In contrast, Chief Tate appeared to be in his thirties and was short and overweight, with cropped black hair. Tate's appearance and his casual attire was not what Aki expected.

Red Elk sat across from Aki and addressed her in Lakota. "Akicita, it has been a long time since you were last on the reservation. I believe you left to stay with your Aunt Kimimela after your parents walked on. How is she?"

Aki thought that was an interesting question. "She is well and still lives in Virginia with her husband. How did you know my aunt?"

"We were friends. I was disappointed when she left the reservation. I had my eye on her—she was very beautiful."

"She still is beautiful," Aki replied.

"How old were you when you left to live with her?"

"I was sixteen."

Red Elk smiled, then said, "I seem to remember as a young girl you were often defending someone's honor and clashing with young men. Does that warrior spirit still burn inside of you?"

"It does."

"Lt. Takoda White Owl, I see that you are still fighting crime—just not on the reservation, where we continue to be plagued with criminal activity." He gave Tate a disdainful glance.

"It is difficult to reduce crime when poverty is so prevalent," White Owl stated.

"That is true," Red Elk replied, then in English said, "Dr. Kingman, I understand that you spent time on the reservation years ago."

"I did. I admire your people and culture and made a number of friends while I was here. I hope to meet one of them after our meeting. I also speak Lakota if you'd prefer to converse that way."

"Chairman, we should get down to business," Tate interrupted, drawing another look of disdain from Red Elk.

"Akicita, I was told that you need our help with the ongoing investigation in the Black Hills," Red Elk continued in English.

"I wanted to meet with you out of respect and to request your permission to speak to those who may offer information about the killings. I understand the hesitancy of people not wanting to come forward."

"I think that you've been gone too long to hope anyone will trust you any differently than any other federal agent," Red Elk said candidly.

"I admit that I'd hoped I would be able to obtain information that would help the FBI in their investigation, but there are other reasons and events that have occurred in the Paha Sapa that I wanted to talk to you about as well. I'm searching for a terrorist who's in the area."

"A terrorist?" Red Elk said. "Chief Tate, were you aware of this?"

"No."

"We didn't want local law enforcement knowing about her. She's incredibly dangerous if cornered. She can't operate openly on the reservation without drawing attention. I believe that she'll have someone else asking questions for her, perhaps a security officer from a mining company or someone local that she's paying."

"There are two private investigators offering large sums of money for information about the missing, but I don't think they've learned anything," Tate said. "I was told by one of the investigators that they'd been hired by a mining-company representative."

"That would be her," Aki said. "Did the investigators provide a name?"

"The one I spoke to said that it was a woman named Cora, but I don't remember the last name," Tate replied.

"Cora Zemanski is an alias the woman I'm trying to apprehend uses. I'll need the names of the investigators so that I can speak to them."

"I'll get those to you as soon as I get back to the office."

"Why would a terrorist be looking for missing mining employees?" Red Elk asked.

"In addition to finding the missing, she was hired to kill those responsible. The woman is a professional assassin. If anyone from the reservation is involved, they will be hunted."

"I don't like the sound of that," Tate said. "Do you have a photo of her that I could distribute?"

"Several, but I'm not going to provide them. If she does come onto the reservation and any of your officers stop her, it's better if they don't show any sign of recognition."

"My people can handle themselves," Tate replied defensively. "They can certainly apprehend her."

"No, they'd most likely end up dead. She's highly trained and will not hesitate to kill. A little over a week ago, she was in Germany and managed to incapacitate three GSG 9 special operators, wound another one, shoot up a town in Poland during her escape, and shoot down my helicopter."

"She does sound dangerous," Red Elk said, then turned to Tate. "I think you should heed Akicita's warning."

"Chief Tate, I'd think of her as a rattlesnake," Aki said. "Just leave her alone and she won't strike. If any of your officers see a new face, just call me."

"I don't like it, but I'll play along."

Aki pegged Tate as an arrogant, incompetent fool.

"What other things did you need to tell me?" Red Elk asked.

"Chairman Red Elk, a large cavern has been discovered over two hundred feet beneath the surface where the FBI is investigating the agent's disappearance. So far, no access has been found. We have obtained detailed images that were taken by a satellite that show what could be structures within the cavern. It could be an ancient sacred city."

"No one has mentioned a cavern or structures," Red Elk responded indignantly.

"And they may not tell you until after they excavate," Aki said. "The FBI and other agencies will want to get into the cavern as part of their investigation to determine if the missing mining employees are being held there."

"A sacred city on our land will not be violated," Red Elk said emphatically. "I will not allow it."

"I was hoping you would feel that way. There's more that leads us to think that the city is sacred. Dr. Kingman, Lt. White Owl and others were attacked by buffalo-clad warriors on two occasions at the site."

Red Elk sat straighter. "Warriors?"

"Yes," Angela answered. "Three warriors covered in buffalo hides attempted to kidnap me and a deputy three nights ago. The following night we were attacked and Agent Crawley was kidnapped, and more buffalo-clad warriors shot at us."

"Tell him everything," Aki directed White Owl and Angela.

For the next few minutes, Angela and White Owl related what had happened during their encounters, including how the mysterious lights appeared and disappeared.

When they'd finished, Red Elk took a deep breath, and asked, "Akicita, did you see the spirit warriors?"

"I did not. I hadn't yet arrived. Nothing has happened since the agent was taken and the FBI set up camp."

"Spirit warriors clad in buffalo skins who are impervious to bullets? Tate questioned. "And four of these warriors had red eyes and floated across the ground. It sounds a bit far-fetched to me."

"The FBI and the other agencies who are investigating didn't believe us either, but it happened," White Owl stated forcefully. "I think they are Wakanpi who are protecting the city."

"Red Elk, we must prevent them from excavating or drilling anywhere above the cavern, no matter what claims are made," Aki said. "This cavern may hold proof of our ancestorial origins and provide additional evidence that will prevent any further government acquisitions of our lands."

"Perhaps provide us grounds to retake them," White Owl added.

Red Elk sat quietly for a moment, then asked, "How old are the structures?"

"We don't know," Aki replied. She was tempted to tell him that they were made of gold, but decided against it. "We are searching for a natural access point so that none of the land is disturbed. We would like your permission to access the cavern if my team finds one."

Red Elk sat back and looked at each of them in turn. "This discovery will have major implications for our people, our culture, and possibly our beliefs. We need to proceed slowly. If you find an entrance, I will give you my decision then. I need to think about this further and consult the other tribal leaders."

"I appreciate your cautious approach," Aki said. "I will inform you as soon as we find an entrance."

"Considering the number of agents that are asking questions on the reservation, I believe a visit to the site is appropriate," Red Elk said. "I will give the authorities an opportunity to tell me about the cavern."

"And if they don't tell you?" White Owl asked.

"Then I will know where we stand and act accordingly. Akicita, thank you for telling me about the cavern. Is there anything else?"

"Not at this time," Aki said.

"I will let you know when I decide to visit the area."

"Please don't disclose how you came by this information," Aki said.

"It will be our secret. Now, Dr. Kingman, who is the friend that you wish to speak with while you are here?"

"Her name is Makawee. She's a teacher at the Oglala Lakota College in Pine Ridge."

"I know her. She's one of our best teachers and mentors. She has given many of our children hope and has kept them from a life of crime and alcohol."

"She taught me about the customs, culture, history, and legends of the Lakota many years ago," Angela said.

"To avoid any potential conflict, I suggest that you give me the contact information and I'll have her meet you here," Red Elk said. "Under the circumstances, I believe it would best that she not be seen speaking with any of you."

"I believe that would be wise," Aki agreed.

Angela jotted down Makawee's number and Red Elk called her. After a brief conversation, he said, "She will be here in thirty minutes."

"Thank you," Angela said.

"Akicita, I hope that someday you will return to the reservation," Red Elk said, and then he stood, signaling that the meeting was over.

"Thank you again" Aki said, standing and passing him a business card. "That's a phone number where I can be reached at any time."

He gave a slight nod as he pocketed the card and said in Lakota, "Go well."

After Red Elk and Tate had left, Aki said, "Do you think that he'll forgive me when he discovers that I didn't tell him everything?"

"I think so, providing you explain your reasons," White Owl said.

"I need to call Chase and let him know what's happened here while we wait for Makawee."

"Is anyone else getting hungry?" Angela asked.

"I could eat," White Owl said. "There's a general store just up the road. Angela and I can get something to go while you make your call."

"Just bring me back a sandwich," Aki said. "I'll let the pastor know that we're going to need the office a little longer."

After White Owl and Angela left, Aki called Chase to check on Sarah's progress.

"Hey, Boss," Chase answered. "I was just going to call you. We've had some developments in the last few minutes."

"I keep telling you not to call me that," Aki said. "What developments?"

"First, Sarah called and said that she's found where the deep tunnel you wanted her to follow comes back up near the surface."

"That's good news."

"It continues on a direct line, which Sarah emphasized had to have been constructed. It approaches the surface near Sled Canyon. Sarah wants to verify a few things, then drive out there and see if she can find an entrance."

"How far away is Sled Canyon from the cavern?"

"About four miles. The tunnel descends again on the other side of Sled Canyon and disappears in the direction of the Jewel and Jasper caves."

"How close does the tunnel come to the surface?" Aki asked.

"About fifteen feet. The terrain looks rugged around it and the access roads into the area don't look all that great. I think the closest we'll be able to get to it by vehicle is about a half mile. Sarah thinks there could be an opening there."

"Excellent work."

"Also, Sarah said her truck was delivered, and I think that'll be the best vehicle for us to use to get into Sled Canyon."

"Isn't her truck marked?"

"Which will help us blend in," Chase said.

"Where are you now?"

"We're sitting off the main road on a trail a little over a mile from the command site. There's been a lot less traffic than expected. I booked us a number of rooms at a lodge in Custer for a week. Clay and White Owl will be staying at the command site. I figured that you'd want the rest of us to stay together. You and Angela will need to have White Owl drop you off at the lodge when you're finished."

"Text me the information and directions."

"Will do, but it's the lodge White Owl recommended. He'll know where to take you."

"Alright. How long will it take for us to reach Sled Canyon from the lodge?" Aki asked.

"It's about thirty miles away, but like I said, the roads aren't great, so we'll need at least forty-five minutes to get there."

"Okay, anything else?"

"Clay advised that three badly decomposed bodies have been found in Wind Creek, just south of Interstate 90 near Moorcroft, Wyoming. Several

FBI and Wyoming DCI vehicles drove by us a few minutes ago, followed by a forensic van."

"It sounds like they've found some of the missing mining employees."

"That's what we think," Chase said.

"Call Sharon and let her know what's going on and update her on the tunnel," Aki directed.

"How'd the meeting go with the chairman?"

"It went well. Dar has hired some PIs to do her snooping on the reservation. We'll need to track them down."

"Private investigators, huh? She's never used them before."

"I know, it surprised me, too," Aki said. "And she hired them using the Cora Zemanski alias."

"If she used a known alias to hire the PIs, you know that will be a dead end. She wants us to expend time and resources chasing after them."

"I'm not so sure," Aki stated. "From what I was told, she's offering a substantial reward for information on the reservation, and the PIs have interviewed a number of people looking for leads. Chief Tate is supposed to provide me with the PIs' names and contact information. I want to track them down and interview them. I'll check in with you when we leave. Stay safe."

"You too."

CHAPTER TWENTY

Dar was driving along a narrow road toward the command site when she saw several emergency vehicles with flashing lights speeding toward her. She pulled her gun from the holster as her heart rate jumped. She checked the rearview and didn't see anyone behind her. She pulled onto the grass shoulder just as vehicles sped by, then took a deep breath. *There must have been a development.* She put the gun on the seat and continued toward the site.

She'd had no difficulty getting through the checkpoints with her fake ID and new disguise. Dar was wearing a short blond wig, sunglasses that hid her green contacts, and an NPS ranger uniform. She rounded a blind corner as she neared the command site and caught a glimpse of a car nestled amongst some trees on a trail road. She slowed and recognized Agent Chase in the driver's seat. As Dar passed, she gave a casual wave and he stared as if he recognized her. She checked the rearview mirror and watched until she went around a bend. He wasn't pursuing, but she still squeezed the handgrip on her Glock. *He couldn't have recognized me.*

Had Carlton given her bad info about the meeting? Was this a trap? Aki wasn't in the car and the man with Chase didn't look familiar. Her senses, honed from years of dangerous encounters, were on high alert. She needed to avoid any close contact with Chase at the scene.

When she arrived at the command site, she parked on the grass behind a truck and positioned her Tahoe for a quick escape. She noted the only other access road out of the area was now a parking lot, blocked completely by at least fifteen cars, a slew of trucks, and large buses. She'd have to drive back the way she had come, past Chase.

She exited the Tahoe and stayed close to the trees to avoid contact with anyone. It appeared that most of the people on scene were in groups and seemed to know each other. *Perhaps this wasn't the best idea.*

She reached the ridgeline and followed a well-trampled trail through what had to have been dense brush at one time. Dar stopped and listened to a small group of people discussing where to cut a path for a long-reach excavator. If they were bringing in an excavator, it meant they were going to dig to the cavern, and that would shorten her window of opportunity to gain access.

Dar had grossly underestimated the complexity of this mission. She wondered if she should risk meeting with Carlton's source. Maybe for the right price, he'd provide her with a cover that would make her less conspicuous. She decided that infiltrating a caving team wasn't going to be possible. She'd have to find another way into the cavern.

She surveyed the scene, taking in as many details as possible. As she stood there, she realized there wasn't any sign of wildlife in the area and the only noise she heard was coming from the people near her. *This is a strange place.*

"Hey, are you with cave rescue?" a man wearing coveralls asked, walking up behind her.

"Yeah, I was just getting the lay of the land," Dar replied, using a southern accent.

"They're assigning people to search teams up by the FBI command bus. You might want to get up there."

"Thanks." Dar moved up the ridge toward the command area. When she reached the ridgeline, she moved away from the command bus and the rangers congregating there. She walked past an FBI forensic truck where two men were working. She heard them talking about three bodies having been found. *Probably where the units that passed me were headed.* Dar stopped and pretended to check her phone while she listened to them grumble about the expected increase in their workload. Dar heard enough to surmise that the three bodies were from the first group of mining employees who had disappeared. She'd expected them to be killed. After a quick look around, she saw that a few people were looking her way. It was time to leave.

As she walked toward her Tahoe, Dar saw Chase's vehicle drive up and park next to the NPS command bus and a marked NPS truck. A deputy came out of the bus to meet them. From their interaction, it was obvious that they knew one another.

She walked quickly behind a truck and knelt down. She peeked around the back bumper and saw that Chase was looking around. He was probably trying to spot her Tahoe. Then the group went into the bus.

Dar hurried to her vehicle, started the engine, and pulled past several parked cars to get back on the road. She saw Chase and the other man run out of the bus, headed for their car. She punched it and flew down the winding road, leaving a dust cloud behind her.

When she reached the first checkpoint, she didn't even slow down. She drove onto the grass and around the two cruisers that were blocking the road. As soon as she was around them, she stomped the accelerator. The deputies weren't pursuing, but they'd certainly radio ahead to the next checkpoint to let them know what had just happened. They'd also tell Chase which direction she'd gone. She worked out an exit route that would avoid further checkpoints. There were plenty of places to hide, provided she had enough of a lead. She could also stop and make a stand.

She flew past the first side road she passed and turned onto a rutted forest-service road. She followed the road through the woods until she reached Custer Limestone Road and turned east. She didn't see any sign of pursuit, but she floored it anyway. Her biggest concern was that Chase would call in air support and she couldn't outrun a helicopter. She smiled, knowing that she could shoot it down with the rifle in the backseat.

Black Hills – 1605 hours

"Are you sure it was her?" Gray asked, as they jumped into their car.

"I wasn't until I saw her moving toward the Tahoe," Chase said. He'd been watching from the bus window. "I know the way she moves, and her speeding away sealed it. Call Aki while I drive."

They headed off at high speed as Gray dialed Aki's cell number and put his phone on speaker.

"Yes," Aki answered.

"Chase and I are in pursuit of Dar," Gray announced. "She came to the command site wearing an NPS uniform. She's driving a black Tahoe."

"She was also in disguise, wearing a short blond wig," Chase shouted.

Suddenly, Chase veered off the winding road, cut the corner, and just missed hitting a tree.

"Shit!" Gray cried.

"What is it?" Aki asked.

"We almost hit a tree."

"It wasn't that close," Chase said. "The shortest distance between two points is a straight line."

"Hey, the tree was on my side. Just stay on the road."

"Knock it off," Aki commanded. "Do you have backup?"

"Just us right now," Gray replied. "Sarah's at the command center and will be following shortly, but she'll never catch up. Wait a sec, we're coming up on a checkpoint."

"I think it would be better if you let her go," Aki said.

"What?" Chase replied. "She's out in the middle of nowhere. We can catch her. Wait a second." Chase screeched to a stop at the checkpoint. "Did you see a black Tahoe come through here?" he asked the deputy.

"It went that way," he replied, pointing north.

"Thanks."

"We're northbound on Summit Ridge Road," Gray told Aki.

"Stand down. She'll suck you into an ambush."

"Aki, we can get her," Chase said emphatically.

Gray knew that Chase wanted to capture Dar, but he couldn't believe how recklessly he was acting.

"Chase. I said, stand down. That's an order. I'll call Sharon and see if we can get a drone to follow her."

"Basset probably pulled those, too," Chase said.

"Chase, I can tell by the sound of the engine and the wind blowing past the open window that you're still in pursuit. I said, stand down!"

Chase pounded the steering wheel and slowed to a stop. "Standing down."

Gray knew that Chase was furious. "Aki, I have an idea," Gray said.

"Hold that thought while I talk to Sharon about a drone." She put him on hold.

"She's really pissed me off," Chase said. "We could have had her."

"I understand your frustration, but Aki has a point," Gray said.

After a minute, Aki reconnected and said, "There won't be any air support."

"We just let her get away again," Chase spat.

"Chase, I know you're angry with me, but I also know Dar well enough to know that if she determined you were the only pursuers, she'd ambush you. I can't take that chance. Drive on into Custer, and I'll meet you at the lodge."

Chase mumbled something that Gray couldn't understand.

"Gray, what's your idea?" Aki asked.

"Get me a helicopter. Now that I know what she's driving, I'll find her. You did hire me to fly."

"Yes, I did, but she won't be in that vehicle for very long. I'll have Sharon check recent car rentals in the area." Aki paused, then added, "I'll also find you a helicopter."

"An AS350 or Bell 206, preferably."

"I'll see what I can do."

Chase said, "Sarah's coming up behind us."

Sarah pulled up and Gray went back to talk to her.

"What happened?" Sarah asked.

"We were ordered to discontinue our pursuit," Gray replied. "Aki couldn't get us air support."

"That woman has balls, coming into the command area," Sarah said.

"Dar's not afraid of much," Chase said, joining them. "She was probably gathering intelligence and getting a good look at the scene."

"How did you know it was her?" Sarah asked. "You only got a quick glance at her from the bus."

"Aki and I have been trying to catch her for a long time. The profile fit, but not the hair. That's why I wasn't sure when I saw her on the road.

Wearing a ranger uniform and driving an unmarked Tahoe didn't look right. When I saw her moving behind the vehicles, I knew it was Dar. We could have had her. Aki should have let us continue the pursuit."

"He's a little pissed off," Gray said.

"I can tell," Sarah said. "Sled Canyon is our best bet for finding an entrance into the cavern without having to dig. We need to go get our gear. I know a store in Custer that should have everything. If not, there's a small store in Hill City. I already have my gear stowed in the lockbox in the back of my truck. Where are we going to meet the others?"

"Aki and Angela are going to meet us at the lodge."

"Where is this store?" Chase asked.

Sarah gave him the directions, then said, "Why don't you just follow me?"

"I have something I want to check. We'll meet you there."

Oglala Lake – 1620 hours

Angela greeted Makawee with a hug. "It's so good to see you again. Let me introduce you to everyone."

Makawee was a small woman with glasses. Her black hair was braided in a traditional style and hung to the center of her back. She was wearing blue jeans, and her white t-shirt had the Oglala Lakota Sioux flag on the front. Once the introductions were complete, they sat down at the table.

Aki said, "Makawee, I understand that federal agents have been asking questions, so you may already know about the murders and the missing mining employees."

"Yes, I've heard."

"There is much more to the story, and some of what we are going to tell you cannot be shared. It could endanger you. May I continue?"

Makawee nodded. "I trust Angela, and you and Lt. White Owl are from the Nation. I'm not sure what help I can provide."

Aki knew that Makawee would be uncomfortable discussing the investigation, so she took care to leave certain details out as she explained what had happened in the Black Hills over the last week. Angela related her experiences with the buffalo spirit warriors and told her about Darren.

Makawee appeared stunned and shook her head. "This is most disturbing."

"What we'd like to know is, have you heard anyone discussing a cavern or spirit warriors around campus or on the reservation?" Aki asked.

Angela added, "We think that Darren may have been killed to protect the location of the cavern."

Makawee sat in silence for a moment, then said, "Angela, I'm sorry to hear about Darren. I didn't know that he was one of the people killed. I know you two were close."

"Yes, we were."

Makawee took a deep breath. "I wasn't going to say anything, but since it may have bearing on Darren's death, I will tell you what I overheard a few weeks ago in the parking lot of a restaurant. I had just parked when two men came out. It was late and they were arguing, so I decided to stay in my car until they left." Makawee paused and looked down. "They didn't know I was there."

"They won't know that you spoke to us," Aki assured her. She saw that Makawee was frightened.

Makawee continued, "One of the men asked the other why he wouldn't join the Guardians. He said the Guardians are committed to keeping the Paha Sapa safe and that his being offered this opportunity was an honor. At the time, I'd never heard of the Guardians and didn't know what he was talking about."

Makawee paused.

"Go on," Aki encouraged, seeing that Makawee appeared hesitant to continue. "I believe what you heard is related to our investigation."

Makawee nodded, then said, "The men got in a truck, which was parked next to me, and I could hear them talking because the truck windows were down. I heard the big man say that the Guardians needed to recruit more warriors and that they needed to bring the people into the light. The other man became angry, telling the big man that he wasn't interested and to leave him alone. Then he called the big man a fool and said something about Wi Can and Gnas."

"Star people and a demon," Angela said.

"Yes. I thought the big man was going to fight the other man, but instead he became quiet and they sat without saying anything for a minute. I was really frightened when the big man spoke again."

"What did he say?" Angela asked.

"That the Wakanpi had killed many *wašíču* intruders who were trespassing on sacred land. He claimed that a war was coming and Guardian warriors were needed. The Waawanyanka, the guardian spirit, would see that more wašíču intruders died if they didn't leave the Paha Sapa. Darren must have been one of the people killed."

"Did the big man say anything else?" Aki asked.

"No, they left. I don't know how they didn't see me."

"Do you know either of the men you saw?" White Owl pressed.

Makawee hesitated, swallowed hard, and said, "I know the big man. When I saw him last week, I marshalled my courage and asked him about the Guardians. He became angry and demanded to know where I'd heard about the them. He was very menacing."

"What did you tell him?" Aki asked.

"I lied to him. I told him that I was sitting in on a class at the college and a student had asked if anyone had heard of them. The big man demanded that I tell him the name of the student. I claimed that I didn't know it because it was a one-day seminar about Lakota gods and legends, and I didn't know any of the people attending. The man became enraged and threatened to kill me if I didn't give him the student's name."

"What did you do?" Angela asked.

Makawee's hands began to shake. "I told him that the student wasn't from the Nation and that there was no way that I could identify him. Then I begged him not to hurt me."

"And he believed you?" White Owl asked.

"Yes. He apologized for scaring me and we talked for a while. Eventually, he told me that knowing about the Guardians was dangerous and that I must never mention them again. If anyone else asked about them, I was told to tell him immediately. I promised that I would. He demanded I give him my telephone number.

"He called me the next day wanting to meet. I was afraid, but agreed. We met in the parking lot at the hospital and found a tree to sit under. We talked for over an hour. He questioned me about the gods, and many other things concerning our history and the other Plains tribes. It wasn't what I was expecting. It sounded like he was disturbed by what had happened in the Paha Sapa."

"Did he say anything else about the Guardians?" White Owl asked.

"He said that the Guardian warriors come from many different tribes. For most, there was no choice but to serve. It was their duty, because the honor is passed down from father to son. It has been that way for many centuries. When there aren't enough legacy warriors, they recruit the best and biggest men to join them."

"Like the encounter you witnessed," Aki said.

"Yes. He never said how many warriors there are, but he told me that when called upon, that they must protect a sacred city."

"He said that there was a sacred city?" Aki asked.

"Yes, but I have never heard of a sacred city in the Paha Sapa, other than what has been described in legends. When I asked him where it was, he only said that it was buried deep underground. The more I questioned him about the city, the angrier he became, and he told me never to speak of it to anyone."

"What happens to the men who don't join the Guardians?" Aki asked. "What prevents those people from disclosing their existence?"

"I don't know, but occasionally, people do disappear from the reservation under mysterious circumstances. That's why you can't disclose what I have told you to anyone."

"Like I said before, no one will know about our discussion," Aki said. "Red Elk and Chief Tate think you are here to catch up with an old friend. You said that you know this man, but you have been careful not to mention his name."

"I don't want to tell you."

"It would be helpful," Aki replied.

Makawee crossed her arms and remained silent.

"How about a description of him?" White Owl prodded. "You said that he was big. How old do you think he is?"

Makawee hesitated, then answered, "I think that he's about forty. He's very large, with a thick chest, and has black hair to his shoulders."

"Does he wear glasses or have any distinguishing features?" White Owl said.

"He has a jagged scar on his left cheek."

Aki froze, turned to White Owl, and said, "That sounds like Mato."

"You know him?" Makawee asked, sounding alarmed.

"Yes, he's a childhood friend of mine. I gave him that scar and he gave me mine." Aki pointed to her brow.

Makawee appeared stunned. "You can't tell him I told you anything."

"I won't, but I'm certainly going to speak to him," Aki said.

"Do you think Mato is one of the men who tried to kidnap me?" Angela asked Aki.

"Mato is a huge man, incredibly strong, and in buffalo hides he would be a formidable sight. When I punched him, it was like striking a brick wall."

There was silence in the room for a few moments, and then Angela said, "Makawee, you once told me about sacred star maps. You said that they'd been protected for thousands of years. Do you think the Guardians are the keepers of the maps?"

"I don't know. I have told you what I know and I would like to leave now."

"Certainly," Aki said. "You have been a great help."

"Makawee, it was good to see you," Angela said. "I hope we can talk again sometime."

"Yes. I would like that, but we will never speak about any of this again." Makawee said her goodbyes and hurried out of the office.

Aki said, "She's scared."

"Definitely," White Owl said. "I guess we need to talk to Mato. I'm not looking forward to that interview. We may need to bring something bigger than a rock with us if he decides to fight."

"Let's wait a day or so, just in case anyone followed Makawee here. Chase and I have other matters to attend to anyway, and then I'll talk to Mato, alone."

"Do you think Mato was there when Darren was murdered?" Angela asked.

"It's hard to say. The cavern must be the sacred place the warriors are protecting, and the structures within are the remnants of a city. I thought it was interesting that Mato seemed disturbed by what had transpired. He may talk to me about it, if I approach him the right way."

"The pieces are starting to come together," White Owl said.

CHAPTER TWENTY-ONE

Custer – May 25 –1730 hours

What should have been a leisurely hour-drive, turned into a forty-minute harrowing experience for Gray. He was starting to think that Chase had a death wish. Sarah was nowhere in sight and had obviously given up trying to stay up with them. *Smart woman.*

When they rolled into Custer, Chase said, "While we wait for Sarah to arrive, I want to check out the motel parking lots in the area and see if we get lucky."

"I figured that was what you had in mind," Gray said.

"Yes. Without air support, we'll have to track her the old-fashioned way."

"I was surprised to hear that air support wasn't available," Gray said.

"Very strange, actually. There seems to be some infighting between our director and the under secretary, and we're on the whipping end."

After twenty minutes of searching, they'd found no sign of Dar's Tahoe. They pulled into a sporting-goods store parking lot off Mt. Rushmore Road and parked next to Sarah's truck.

Sarah got out and angrily asked Chase, "Are you crazy? You drive like a madman."

"And you drive like an old lady," Chase countered.

Sarah was about to say something and Gray interjected, "Have you been waiting long?"

"No, only a few minutes. Where were you two?"

"We checked a few places hoping to spot Dar's Tahoe," Chase answered.

"Without anyone knowing where you were. Not smart."

"You sound like Aki," Chase said. "Have you shopped here before?"

"Many times. We're going to need rope, climbing gear, gloves, helmets, headlamps, and two backup flashlights for each person. You'll want some good waterproof boots, coveralls, and extra-warm clothing, freeze-dried meals and power bars. Most importantly, you'll also need kneepads. It's all on the list I gave you."

"Yes, it is," Chase said, holding the door open for her. "This is a lot of stuff. Is all of it really necessary?"

"I wouldn't have put it on there if it wasn't," Sarah replied. "I hope you have a high-limit credit card."

"I do. It's under a bogus business name, so don't tell anyone that we're with Homeland."

"What about water?" Gray asked. "I didn't see that on the list."

"Waterproof containers are on there, and every person will need at least a half-gallon of water per day. And since Chase has a government credit card, we'll buy only the best of everything for the team. Like I said, I have my gear in the truck, so I'm good to go."

"Sarah, lugging that much water is going to slow us down," Chase said.

"First lesson in caving; there is no going fast, so lugging the water won't be a factor. From the images I've seen, I expect that we'll be underground two days, maybe three, so buy accordingly."

"Do you really think that we'll be underground for two to three days?" Gray asked.

"I don't know what we're going to find. The passageway from Sled Canyon appears to be a straight shot, making it a four-mile hike…but there's several miles that aren't visible, and that section could turn out to be a slow crawl that takes us a day to get through. I think we should be prepared for anything. Do you have everyone's sizes?"

Gray and Chase exchanged flummoxed looks.

"That's what I thought," Sarah said. "You two get the gear and your clothing, I'll pick up Aki's and Angela's things. I'm pretty good at guessing sizes."

Twenty minutes later, they had assembled what they needed, checked out, and headed for the lodge.

The Custer Lodge – 1900 hours

The group was gathered in Aki's room, except for White Owl, who had driven back to the command center to relieve Clay. Sarah and Angela had provided the basics on caving and how best to wear the gear in a confined space. They were as ready as they could be for their expedition.

"Angela, how did the interview go with Makawee?" Sarah asked.

"It went well. There's a lot we need to tell you."

Aki's cell rang and she answered. "Sharon, I see that you're working late. I'm going to put you on speaker. Gray and the rest of the team are listening."

"Hello everyone. Can they all hear the updates?"

"Yes, go ahead."

"Brian advised that the FBI has identified the three bodies found in Wind Creek. They're Carlos Marino, Ivy Cullen, and Nicolas Easton, all from Universal Mining. The bodies were badly decomposed and each of them had three stab wounds to the chest, just like the other two victims found in the Belle Fourche River. The FBI hasn't notified Ketterhorn yet."

"That means only Crawley and two others are still missing," Sarah said.

"Yes. Also, you won't be getting any air support from Homeland any time soon. Omar discovered that Basset ordered all aircraft and UAVs grounded in your area unless he approves their use."

"I figured Basset was behind it," Aki said. "I'll call the director and find out what's going on with him."

"Now the good news," Sharon said. "Omar was able to secure a Bell 206 for Gray to fly."

"That's excellent," Aki replied. "Where is it?"

"It's in Cheyenne. It belongs to an acquaintance of Omar's uncle. The one in the Kidon."

"What favors will this cost me with the Mossad?" Aki asked.

"None," Sharon replied. "There were no questions asked and no mention of a quid pro quo. If you want it, it's going to cost us twenty thousand per day for unlimited use. He threw in the repositioning fee for free. I told him we needed it flown to the Custer airport. That is where you wanted it, right?"

"Perfect," Aki replied.

"If we accept his price, the guy will deliver it tonight."

"Make the deal," Aki said. "Wire him the money. What time will he be at the airport?"

"He said he could get there around 2300 hours. Gray will have time to meet with the guy and check it out. Omar vouched for Gray, so he better not crash it."

Everyone in the room chuckled.

"How long do we have it?" Aki asked.

"As long as we need it. We pay by the day."

"I'm okay with that, but see if Omar can get us a lower weekly rate," Aki directed. "Anything else?"

"Field-operations chatter indicates they don't think Crawley or the others are still alive," Sharon said. "We also confirmed that Dar has rented two vehicles using the Cora Zemanski alias. One of them matched the Tahoe that Chase and Gray pursued. The other one is a white Voyager minivan she rented in Hill City, which is just north of where you are now."

"She wouldn't be caught dead in a minivan," Aki said. "What about the Tahoe?"

"Omar hacked into the traffic-camera feeds around the main intersections in Hill City and Custer, but so far there's no trace of it. He did spot a white minivan parked in downtown Hill City, but it's too far away from the camera to confirm if it's the one Dar rented. No one has been near it since he started monitoring."

"She's ditched the Tahoe and is using the minivan as a decoy," said Aki. "Sharon, if Sarah's right about there being an entrance at Sled Canyon, we'll be underground for a while starting tomorrow. I'll check in before we drop out of communication range. Critical updates can go to Lt. White Owl." She provided his number. "In your spare time, I'm going to need any information you can dig up on a Lakota by the name of Mato, and on a group known as the Guardians."

"Got it. We're getting a bit ragged out and need to grab a few hours of sleep. Can we hit the rack at midnight?"

"That'd be fine. We'll be resting up for tomorrow as well. I'll check in with you at six."

"Sounds good. Stay safe."

"The Guardians?" Gray asked, after Aki was off the phone.

"I'll tell you all about them and about what we discussed with Red Elk and Makawee over dinner. Let's all grab a quick bite at the restaurant across the street."

"That sounds good," Gray said. "I'm starved."

They were seated at a large table at the back of the restaurant and had ordered dinner. Once the waiter had left, Aki briefed them.

"Aki, isn't Mato the guy you knew on the reservation?" Chase asked.

"Yes. I'm going to talk to him, but I need to pick the time and place. I want to see if we can get into the cavern and capture Dar before I interview him."

"I advise getting him alone and away from the reservation," Gray offered. "You could always get White Owl to have some deputies box him in on a traffic stop."

"That would only piss him off," Aki replied.

"You could always just pass the intel on to Agent Stevens and let him deal with Mato and the Guardians," Chase said.

"Not a bad thought," Gray said.

"I want to talk to him," Aki said. "We also need to make contact with the private investigators before we go underground. If we could turn one of them, we might get information that could help us trap Dar."

"Time is short if we're going underground tomorrow," Chase said.

"Chief Tate said he would provide the names of the PI's working on the reservation, but I haven't heard from him. I'll go call him now." Once Aki was outside, she dialed Tate's number and he answered on the first ring. "Chief Tate, this is Agent Akicita Dawson."

"I was just getting ready to call you. Sorry for the delay, but I had a situation to deal with here. The private investigators work for the Discreet Investigative Agency out of Rapid City." He texted her the investigators' names and their contact numbers. "I just learned that one of them, Loni Abraham, was sniffing around trying to get information about our meeting with you. She offered one of our staff a large sum of money if she would tell her what we discussed."

"Someone told her about our meeting? Do you know where Abraham is now?"

"No, but you should be able to reach her at the number I sent you. I'm looking into who told her about our meeting. How was the reunion with Makawee?"

"It was nice for her and Angela to reconnect." She sensed that he was fishing for information. "I won't keep you any further." Aki signed off before he could say anything else.

She had just returned to the table when her dinner arrived. She sat down and took a sip of the merlot.

"Well?" Chase asked.

"Chief Tate sent me the two private investigators' names and the name of the agency Dar hired. One of the investigators, Loni Abraham, knew about our meeting with the chairman."

"That's not good," Chase said.

"I'm going to call her after dinner." Aki paused, then added, "I have an idea."

"That's always dangerous," Chase stated, then took a bite of his filet.

"Usually," Aki replied. "Dar is no doubt growing frustrated, which is evident by her risky infiltration of the command site. She likes challenges, but she relishes being in control, and she doesn't have that now. She can't operate on the reservation through intimidation, and her financial incentives don't seem to be working. I believe she's also figured out that even in disguise, she can't blend in with the federal and local law enforcement. The only other option she has is to cultivate a source within the law-enforcement community to provide her intel about the investigation. So, I propose we give her a source."

"And who would that be?" Gray asked.

"I'm thinking I'll have White Owl call Abraham. He gives her a fictitious name and tells her that he has information about the Guardians and the location of a secret tunnel where there's a lot of activity."

"You want to tell her about the entrance to the cavern?" Chase asked.

"That's crazy," Sarah blurted. "It'll be tough enough finding it and getting in without a killer trailing us."

"Relax," Aki said. "I'll have White Owl mention that the Guardians are using a tunnel to reach a sacred city and are going to perform a ritual sacrifice tomorrow."

"I'm not sure that will that work," Gray said. "Dar would expect that he'd want to get paid before he gave a location. Plus, White Owl is too well known around here. Odds are that the investigator will know him if she wants to meet."

"What if I made the call?" Angela asked. "I could say that my boyfriend is in the Guardians. That he's going to participate in a sacrifice tomorrow and I'm afraid of him. I can claim that I don't want to be involved and I need money to leave him."

"I like that better," Gray said.

"I do, too," Aki said. "You speak Lakota, know the reservation, and could pass as a local over the phone. We'll have you tell her that the sacrifice is happening tomorrow morning."

"I would think that after sunset would be a better time for a sacrifice," Chase said.

"Under the cover of darkness, Dar would have an advantage, and we can't afford giving her any chance to escape this time," Aki said. "She needs to think that she has to move quickly if she's going to get there in time to save any hostages. Mr. Santos told us that she was being paid to recover them and kill those responsible. She may feel this is an opportunity to do both. She'd like nothing better than to accomplish her mission, collect her paycheck, and thwart us from catching her."

"Doing it at sunrise would force her to move quickly," Chase agreed. "She just might take the bait, but how do we trap her?"

"We need to find a place with only one access road and somewhere that she can't go off-road to escape."

Sarah shook her head. "From what you've told us about Dar, you're going to need more people to capture her than just our small group. Didn't you say that you had a whole response team?"

"That won't be possible now. Besides, she'd spot a response team. I think the fewer people involved, the better."

Sarah leaned forward and said, "Just for the record, I think this is a bad idea."

"Your objection is noted," Aki replied. "We don't have a great window of opportunity here. Sarah, from your research, is there a place that provides the cover we need, is absent of people, and is where we can seal off any escape routes?"

"There's a location that meets those criteria, but it's still a bad idea." Sarah brought up a satellite view with a road-map overlay of Sled Canyon on her cell. She passed the phone to Aki and slid her chair closer. "When I was looking around Sled Canyon, I noticed it had limited access by trail or road." Sarah pointed at the map. "This is Red Bird Canyon Road, it's south of Sled Canyon and near the place we suspect there's an entrance to the cavern. There are a number of fire trails and dirt roads to the north around Custer Limestone Road, but once she passes this intersection, there is only one way out to the south. The area has several ravines and a small box canyon with steep walls on both sides of the road. There's no way out of there by vehicle if you block the road from the north and south."

After studying the map, Aki said, "I think the location is perfect. There's an arroyo on one side and trees on the other near this turn. We can stop her here." Chase moved so he could see the satellite view.

"I agree," he said. "This cluster of trees where the road bends will block her view until she's in the trap or kill zone. If we block the road, there won't be enough room for her to turn around, but she can still back away."

"Not if we block her in before she can get turned around," Aki said. "We pre-position Sarah's truck, wait until she passes, and then block her escape. Chase, we'll need to get camouflage netting for Sarah's truck."

"I have some netting in my truck that I use when doing surveillance," Sarah said.

"Great. Sarah, I want Clay to ride with you. The fewer the vehicles the better."

"Gray, we'll have you airborne, and you'll monitor her approach from the air," Aki said.

"Just so you know, the Bell 206 has just under three hours of flight time," Gray said. "The long-range version has about four hours. Do we know which one is being delivered?"

"No," Aki replied. "How long of a flight is it from the airport to Sled Canyon?"

"Once airborne, I can be there in twenty minutes."

"Okay, so you can stay on station for about two hours."

"That's correct," Gray said.

"I can work with a two-hour window," Aki said. She looked at the map. "Dar will use this fire road coming in near Gooseberry Springs." Aki pointed at the road. "It's the same route we'd take to get to Sled Canyon. If she does manage to escape to the south, her only exit is near Route 16, and that's a long drive.

"We'll block the road where it curves with a large vehicle. We'll just need to procure one. When she comes around the bend, she'll have to stop, since there's no room on the shoulder. Sarah, once she passes you, you'll have to wait a bit and then come up from behind in your truck. She'll be looking for anyone trailing her, so don't come screaming in. We don't want to spook her."

"I'll be in a marked unit," Sarah said. "You don't think that'll spook her?"

"You're a ranger. I have no doubt that she's seen lots of those trucks out here. If you are a lone vehicle, driving normally, she won't suspect you and rabbit."

"That puts Sarah and Clay in the line of fire if this turns bad," Gray warned.

"Dar has a bolt-action Remington hunting rifle and Glock with her," Aki said. "We'll take her down before she can engage. Chase and I will challenge her from cover once Sarah and Clay arrive. If Dar opens fire, it will be at us. Sarah, you and Clay just need to duck."

"I don't like the sound of that," Sarah said. "I'll definitely wear my vest."

"Gray, we'll need White Owl to fly with you. You'll need to call him." Aki took another sip of her merlot. "Also, see if he can have marked units available to assist to the south, just in case she manages to get by us."

"What time is all of this going to happen?" Gray asked. "Sunrise is about five-thirty."

"Let's make it six," Aki replied. "That'll give us time to get in position."

"I suppose you want me to call Clay and ask him to join me?" Sarah said.

"Yes," Aki replied. "I know that White Owl and Clay are supposed to stay at the command site, but at that time of morning, they should be able sneak away without too much trouble."

"Where will I be?" Angela asked.

"Once you make the call to Abraham, your work is done," Aki replied. "You'll stay at the lodge. It's safe and I've already endangered you enough."

"I shouldn't use my cell phone when I call the investigator," Angela said. "Too easy to trace."

"We'll get you a cell phone that we can clone to a pay phone that I saw in Oglala. If they track the number, it'll come back to that location, which will add credibility to your cover."

"There are still working pay phones?" Gray asked.

"There are a few around the reservation," Aki said. "Angela, I'll need you to make the first call as soon as we get the phone ready. I'll prepare your talking points. You'll need to tell Abraham that you'll try to find out exactly where your boyfriend is going tomorrow morning and that you'll call her back."

"She'll want to know where to meet me to give me the reward," Angela said.

"Don't give her a location. She'll have it watched. I don't want to give Dar any specific information about where the sacrifice is going to occur until after we're in place. She'd scout the location and I don't want to give her any time to prepare. Your second call will be critical."

"I can handle it," Angela said. "I still want to make entry into the cavern when this is done."

"When we capture Dar tomorrow, I'll make sure that you're the first into the passageway."

"Are you forgetting that we still have to contend with the FBI, DCI, and the spirit warriors?" Sarah asked.

"No, I haven't forgotten, but I won't have to worry about Dar then, and right now, that's *our* primary mission. Chase, after we finish dinner, I want you to call Sharon and have her monitor signals traffic in real time starting at 0430 hours. We need to get a new burner phone and have Brian clone it so Angela can use it at the lodge and still have it register to the pay phone."

"That won't be hard for him to manage," Chase said.

"Tell Sharon that I'm sorry that their sleep cycle will be shorter than expected. I want the whole support team ready no later than four."

"Will do," Chase said. "Now, can we finish dinner?"

The Custer Lodge – 2230 hours

"Angela, you sounded very convincing," Aki said, after Angela had spoken to Abraham.

"It sounded like she bought it."

"I believe she did. We'll be on our way to Sled Canyon when you make the next call at four-thirty. Keep to the script. Just tell Abraham that your boyfriend just left. That you overheard him telling another guy where they were headed and that there's going to be a sacrifice at six this morning. Include something about other Guardians attending, but if asked, you don't know who they are. Act concerned, as if your life is in danger and emphasize that you need the money to get away, but don't give her a meeting place. Just tell her that you will meet with her later."

"Do you think she'll grow suspicious if I don't want to meet her right away?"

"Tell her that you don't know her and you want to make sure that your boyfriend is in custody before you meet with her."

"Easy enough," Angela said. "Would you mind if I drove out to Sled Canyon after everything is over?"

"Make sure you don't leave until after seven," Aki instructed. "Everyone, check your gear and be ready to leave no later than four. I want to leave nothing to chance. Gray, you and White Owl need to be ready to fly by five."

"We'll be ready," Gray said. "White Owl and I will leave shortly after you do. That'll give me time to do a preflight."

"I thought you were checking the helicopter tonight," Chase said.

"I am, but I don't like surprises. Things can happen in a few hours."

"I want White Owl armed with our Ruger Mini-14 just in case," Aki said.

"I'll have him ride in the back. It'll give him a better field of fire and I won't have to worry about hot shell casings hitting my neck."

Three Forks S.D. – 2230 hours

After renting a light-gray Suburban under a new alias, Dar transferred her gear, then drove the Tahoe to a wooded area just outside of Hill City. Dar needed another way into the cavern and since her rapid departure from the command site, she was sure that the park-ranger disguise was a bust. She walked a mile back to where she'd left the Suburban and drove the short distance to a small inn in Three Forks that offered cabins to await an update from Carlton. His call came in just as she arrived.

"Yes," Dar answered.

Carlton took his time relating the graphic information he'd received from his source about the bodies, and at the end provided their identities. She decided not to call Ketterhorn just yet. If her call was intercepted, Aki would know that she had an inside source at the command site.

Carlton said, "I have something else that will interest you."

Dar was growing tired of his saving-the-best-information until last routine, but she understood his reasoning. You never end a conversation with a client on a negative. "Go ahead."

"My source has indicated that they received some new information about the cavern and a particular passageway. A rather large one, from what I was told."

"Where is it?" Dar asked.

"He didn't know, but the cavers and geologists at the site are excited about the find. I'll get you updates as he provides them. Some scattered rain is forecast until early morning, so I doubt they will be working through the night."

"I don't need a weather report. I want to know if they find an access point into the cavern and where it is. Make sure your source understands that. Are we clear?"

"Yes."

"What's happening on the reservation?"

"Nothing. I'm on my way there to relieve my two team members. They're hitting dead ends and need some rest, but if anyone calls with information, I'll interview them myself."

"Just get me what I need." She hung up. She felt the frustration building and started to wonder if she'd missed something.

Dar sat down on the worn quilt that was covering the bed. Pictures of horses were sewn onto its blue fabric. She shook her head in disgust. If there was another way into that cavern, she knew that Aki would know about it. She needed a new plan.

Carlton called her back just as she was closing her eyes. "What is it?"

"One of my investigators just received a call from a Lakota woman. The woman said that her boyfriend is going to be involved in a human sacrifice tomorrow morning at six."

Dar bolted upright. "Where is the woman?"

"She wouldn't say, but my investigator traced the number to a pay phone on the reservation. She doesn't have an exact location, but she's working on it. She said that the woman sounded frightened and claimed that her boyfriend admitted to killing someone a few days ago as part of a ritual."

"Did your investigator believe her story?"

"Yes."

"Did she provide your investigator with the name of her boyfriend or any other information that can be confirmed?"

"No. She said that if her boyfriend was arrested that he'd know it was her who had turned him in."

"I'm not sure I believe her," Dar said.

"She spoke Lakota and claimed she needed the financial incentive you offered to get away from the reservation. It's the best lead we've had so far. She said that she'd call again as soon as she knew the location."

Dar felt something was off. Aki spoke Lakota and she could have made the connection that Carlton had people asking questions on the reservation. "You said she'd call back?"

"Yes. I assume before six."

"I want to listen in on that conversation. Who's the investigator that took the call?"

"Loni Abraham. She's the best I have and I trust her."

"Can Abraham conference me in on the call?"

"I'll have her connect with you as soon as she receives the call."

"Good. I don't want the woman to know I'm listening," Dar cautioned.

"I'll make sure that Abraham understands."

"And confirm the pay phone's location and have someone watch it."

Dar hung up and thought about whether she could have been compromised. Her gut was telling her that she was being suckered into a trap. But as Carlton pointed out, this was the first solid lead that she'd gotten, and time was running out. If there was to be a sacrifice, then one of the hostages was still alive, hopefully the tycoon's niece. She needed to be ready just as soon as the woman called in the morning with the location. She'd have to wait and see if she recognized Aki's voice and whether the story rang true, and then she'd decide what action to take. Carlton's investigator could confront the informant at the pay phone, take a picture, and text it to her to make sure Aki wasn't involved. There wasn't anything else she could do tonight, so she decided to grab a few hours of sleep.

CHAPTER TWENTY-TWO

Custer Airport – May 25 - 2300 hours

The Bell Jet Ranger 206B helicopter was on the tarmac when Gray and Chase arrived. They met the delivery pilot, a short, thin man in his fifties, who insisted that no names be exchanged. Gray suspected he was with the Mossad.

Gray took a moment to admire the midnight-blue paint job and knew that it would be tough to spot the helicopter from the ground during night operations. A light-blue accent stripe was the only civilian marking on the aircraft. A quick check of the Hobbs meter indicated it had low hours, especially for a 2010 model, and it appeared well maintained.

"She's one of the last 206Bs to be produced," the pilot commented.

"Looks to be in pristine condition," Gray announced, after his thorough preflight inspection. "I'd like to get the feel of the helicopter and do a few landings to get current in night operations."

"That's smart."

"Chase, do you want to come?" Gray asked.

"I'll wait here."

Gray climbed into the right front, pilot-in-command seat. Once the delivery pilot was buckled in the copilot seat, Gray went through preflight checks, noting the altimeter was already set to the airport elevation, which was over a mile higher than the airports he flew out of in Florida. He checked the emergency engine-system caution lights and the movement of the flight controls. He then went through the start-up procedures, ensuring the turbine-outlet temperature was at a safe start temperature. He held the starter button and listened to the increasing whine of the turbine until it fired up. As the two blades rotated faster and faster, he watched the instruments while waiting a minute for the engine temperatures to stabilize.

"You ready?" Gray asked, after one final check of the gauges.

"Whenever you are."

Gray radioed his intention to stay in the pattern on the UNICOM channel, checked that Chase was clear, and then gently raised the collective. He felt the skids leave the ground and he hovered. It felt good to be back at the controls as he air-taxied to the runway and took off.

Gray felt a sense of elation every time he flew. His worries seemed to fade away as he focused on his flying. The glow of the lights from Custer stood out in the distance against the darkness of the surrounding area.

The Jet Ranger handled beautifully as he maneuvered. He circled the airport several times, staying in a left traffic pattern, then made three landings at the end of the runway before air-taxiing back to the ramp. He touched down softly and went through the engine shutdown procedures.

"Well done," the other pilot said.

"Thanks. How do we contact you when we're done here?"

"I'm sure that whoever requested the helicopter can call when you're ready, and I'll come pick it up."

Chase joined them. "Are we good to go?" he asked.

"All except for taking on fuel," Gray replied.

"Can we drop you somewhere?" Chase asked the pilot.

"I'll get a rental." He walked off toward the FBO building.

"Strange little guy," Chase said.

"I'll need your credit card for fuel," Gray said.

"Of course you do."

After the Jet Ranger was fueled and the blades tied down, Gray called Aki.

"Everything satisfactory?" she asked.

"Very good. We should be back in a few minutes."

"Okay. Let Chase know that I found us a truck that we can use to block the road. Sharon called, but there wasn't anything to report. Don't bother checking in when you get back. Just get some rest."

"I'll give Chase the message," Gray said.

Custer – May 26 – 0430 hours

Angela dialed Abraham's number from the burner phone. She knew what she needed to say, including a description of the old truck Aki had procured. When Abraham finally answered the phone, Angela heard a faint change in the background noise that was quickly muffled. Someone else was listening in. Aki had told her to expect it.

"This is Loni Abraham."

"It's me, my boyfriend just left with another big man," Angela said, sounding scared.

"Do you know where they're going so that we can alert the authorities?"

"I heard my boyfriend tell the other man to drive out to Sled Canyon off of Red Bird Canyon Road. He said something about the Guardians needing to be at a cave before six. I think they saw me listening as they pulled out. I shouldn't have gone outside, but it was the only way I could hear them. Please, I need the money you promised. If they aren't arrested, they are going to kill me."

"Tell me who your boyfriend is and where you are, and I'll call the tribal police," Abraham said.

"No. I can't. I'm going to go back to my house and pack my things and leave. I'll call again when I'm able and tell you where we can meet so I can get my money."

"What's the make and color of the vehicle they left in?"

"It's an old green pickup truck. I've never seen it or the other man on the reservation before."

"What does your boyfriend look like? What's he wearing? Does he have any weapons with him?"

Angela hesitated, then said, "I told you what he looked like last night. Why are you asking me all of these questions?"

"The police will need to know exactly who he is, what he's wearing, who's with him, and if they're armed."

Angela waited a moment before she responded. "I don't trust the tribal police and I don't know you."

"You can trust me. I need you to answer my questions or you won't get the reward."

Angela sighed, then said, "I need that money, so I will tell you what I can, but not where I am. My boyfriend is wearing blue jeans, a red shirt, and a green military jacket. He had a large duffle bag with him. I don't know what's inside it. He always carries a large knife with him. I will call you when I find a safe place to meet."

"Any idea how many of the Guardians are going to the cave?" Abraham pressed.

"I don't know."

"I already know that you're calling from a different number than last time," Abraham said. "We had someone at the store waiting to protect you. Please tell me where you are."

"I knew you couldn't be trusted. *Tókša akhé.*" Angela responded, and hung up. It was good that Aki had Brian change the number on her cell just in case Dar had traced it to the payphone location. There was no word in Lakota for "goodbye," and Angela hoped her farewell would cement her as a Lakota.

Dar called Abraham's burner phone immediately.

"What do you think?" Abraham asked Dar.

"I'm not sure. She sounded scared and her answers seemed genuine." Dar paused as she thought for a moment. "I want you to call Carlton and have him go to Black Aerial Adventures in Hill City. I'll call Mr. Black and have him meet Carlton there in an hour. Tell Carlton to call me when he gets there."

"Yes, ma'am. What do you want me to do?"

"I want you to find that woman."

"You do realize how large the Pine Ridge Reservation is, don't you?" Abraham asked.

"Yes. Just do what I tell you. While you're there, find out about the Guardians."

"I'll do my best."

"Yes, you will," Dar said in a threatening tone and disconnected.

Dar knew that the woman on the phone wasn't Aki, but the woman could have made the call for her. She quickly changed into a pair of camouflage pants, boots, and a black t-shirt with a Lakota flag on the front that she'd bought in Hill City. She put on a black braided wig, then grabbed a pair of dark-rimmed sunglasses from her case. With a little makeup, she'd pass for a Native American.

She felt that everything was unfolding too quickly and she didn't like it. She opened her laptop and reviewed the satellite images of the area. After a few minutes, she found the area where the woman claimed the Guardians were going to meet. "A perfect place for an ambush," she muttered.

Dar saw that there was only one road leading south away from Sled Canyon and there was no room to maneuver. She didn't like this at all, but with Carlton as her eyes in the sky, it would be worth the risk. He'd surely spot any vehicles in the area and the one the Lakota woman had described. The urge to abort was strong, but she knew this could be her last chance to save a hostage. Dar made sure she had what she needed and left the room.

South of Sled Canyon – 0530 hours

Aki and Chase were standing together in dense brush beneath a ponderosa pine tree. Both were wearing their tactical vests, fatigues, and hands-free headsets linked to their walkies.

Aki radioed Sarah, "Are you and Clay ready?"

"Yes," Sarah replied. "No one will spot us under the camouflage netting and we can see the road. We'll be able to give you a heads-up if anyone passes us. That old truck Chase was driving didn't look like it was going to make it."

"I didn't think it would either, but Chase nursed it along. He was able to position it in the middle of the road with the hood up. No one will be able to get by."

"How's our air support?" Sarah asked.

"Gray and White Owl are airborne and should be over us shortly. Sharon and Brian monitored Angela's call, and Sharon said that she was convincing. Brian confirmed that a third party was listening."

"Then Dar bought the story?" Sarah asked.

"I hope so, but she's very cagey and I'm certain she'll have some stratagem that we haven't counted on. She won't go peacefully, so you and Clay need to be ready. Stay alert for any other vehicles. She could have hired some local muscle or someone to act as a decoy."

"Wish we knew what she was driving," Sarah said. "But there won't be much traffic up here at this time of the morning."

"Let's hope not."

"White Owl to Aki, radio check."

"A little rotor noise in the background, but readable," Aki replied.

"Gray advised the comms in the helicopter aren't compatible to our radio frequencies, so the walkie you gave us is all we have besides our cell phones. Be advised, I have two marked units waiting at the south end of Red Bird Canyon Road, just in case she gets past you. I'll give them the description of her vehicle once we know it."

Aki's cell phone pinged. "Chase, Sharon's calling. Monitor the comms."

"Got it," Chase replied.

Aki answered. "Sharon, what's the latest?"

"We intercepted a call made to an encrypted cell phone owned by Carlton Safir about fifty minutes ago. We captured the call, but it took a little while for Brian to crack the encryption algorithm and listen to the call. The caller was Investigator Abraham, and she told Carlton to be at Black Aerial Adventures in Hill City within an hour."

"Pretty sophisticated equipment for a PI," Aki said. "What do we know about Black Aerial Adventures?"

"It's owned by Gordon Black and he's a pilot. There's only one helicopter registered to the business, a small R44. We're still running the background on the owner, but so far, he looks clean."

"I knew she wouldn't come alone. They could be airborne by now and scouting her route. Any other intercepts?"

"Not yet. We're now monitoring Black's and Carlton's phones. Thanks to Brian's wizardry, we're also able to monitor your radio communications."

"We just overflew a light-gray Suburban hauling ass along Custer Limestone Road heading in your general direction," White Owl radioed. "Do you want us to stay on it or begin orbiting the area?"

"Stay on the Suburban," Chase replied.

Aki heard White Owl's transmission and felt the tension building. "Sharon, I have to go." Getting back on the radio, she said, "Listen up, everyone. I just received information that Dar hired an R44 helicopter. White Owl, I'm going to need continual updates as the vehicle approaches. We're blind until she makes the curve. Any chance you can see who's driving?"

"If Gray would keep this bird steady, I might."

"Also, Dar's air support will probably have two aboard."

"We'll be looking for it," White Owl said.

"White Owl, be aware that if you're spotted, Dar will abort," Aki added.

"Gray says we look like a news helicopter. There's one of those to the north of us that's circling. It's still a little overcast from the rain earlier, so we'll be hard to spot."

"Aki, we just had a red helicopter overfly us at a fairly low altitude," Sarah announced.

"Copy," Aki replied. "White Owl, do you see it?"

"Just spotted it. It's at treetop level and flying without navigation lights. Gray says that it's an R44. It looks like the Suburban has slowed and is allowing the chopper to scout ahead."

"That has to be Dar. Any chance for an ID?"

"Not unless we get lower."

"Stay at altitude," Aki directed. "Are there any other vehicles in the area?"

"No." A few seconds later, White Owl radioed, "I can see the driver through the binoculars. Hard to say if the driver's male or female. Black hair, possibly Native American, and wearing sunglasses."

Chase turned to Aki and said, "Dar may want us to think she's a Native American. No need for sunglasses yet. I have a feeling that's her."

"I agree. You better get across the street and in position before her helicopter flies over us. I can hear it coming."

Chase bolted across the road and dropped down behind a large birch tree. A few seconds later, the helicopter flew over the disabled truck and made an immediate turn for a second pass.

"The helicopter is over the truck," Aki radioed. "They're circling it. We believe that the person in the Suburban is Dar, but we need to confirm before we close the net."

"The Suburban is slowly approaching the fork," White Owl announced.

"It just passed by us at Gooseberry," Sarah radioed. "The driver is female and she's doing a lot of rubbernecking, and she appears to be Native American. She could be the decoy you mentioned."

Aki knew that was a possibility. She needed to get eyes on.

"The vehicle's stopped just before the fork," White Owl radioed. "She's getting out."

Aki said, "I'm going to reposition and try to make a positive ID."

She crept toward a small break in the trees, using the tree canopy to cover her movement. The R44 continued to make tight circles over the truck, then suddenly changed altitude and began to make a wider orbit. Aki lowered herself to the ground and crawled to a small opening in the brush to where she could see the front of the Suburban, which was about a half mile away. The woman was standing by the driver's door. She brought her rifle up and looked through the scope, focusing it at the highest power. Aki's heart started to race. "It's Dar," she radioed. "She has on a long black braided wig and a black t-shirt with a red emblem on the front."

Sarah advised, "Aki, we could block the road here and prevent her from coming back this way."

"No, stay where you are. She'll hear the truck and bolt. She's hyper-vigilant right now. She can't see the truck from the fork and is relying on the helicopter to be her eyes. I'll tell you when to move. White Owl, don't get any closer—she's talking on a cell phone, and looking up and around now."

"Copy," White Owl replied.

"The R44 has come back and is now hovering about a hundred feet above the truck," Chase radioed. "It's moving slowly around it. I think they're trying to see inside the cab."

Aki's phone vibrated and she answered. "What is it, Sharon?"

"It's Brian. Carlton is in the helicopter and is on the phone with a woman. He told her that the truck appears disabled. He also told her that she wouldn't be able to get around it, and she acknowledged."

"Thanks. The woman is Dar. Stay on the line."

"Be advised, I have Brian on the line and he's monitoring comms between Carlton and Dar," Aki radioed. She watched Dar get back in the Suburban, but it remained stationary.

The R44 gained some altitude and began making wider orbits again.

"Dar told Carlton to check the tree lines," Brian relayed. "If there's no other traffic, she plans to push the truck out of the way and start a search of the area on foot. Carlton just said that the vehicle matches the description the woman gave of the boyfriend's truck."

"Copy," Aki said. She relayed the update and watched as the R44 made several more passes over the road.

A few minutes later, Brian said, "Carlton said that he doesn't see anyone and that there are no other vehicles on the road. Dar said that she's moving up."

"Dar's going to be moving toward us," Aki radioed. She watched as Dar drove toward her at a very slow speed, then added, "Don't anyone underestimate her."

"She's just making the left at the fork," Sarah radioed. "When do you want us to move onto the road?"

"With her helicopter up there, our blocking maneuver will be hard to set up like I planned," Aki replied. "I'll let you know when to move. When you do start this way, drive like Chase."

"Copy," Sarah replied, with a nervous chuckle.

"Helicopter making another low-level pass," Aki announced.

Brian said, "Dar wants the helicopter to check the area further south of your position."

"Looks like she's picking up speed," Aki radioed. "I need to get back to the sniper hide. White Owl, you're my eyes now."

"Roger."

Aki left her position and crawled back to the hide that she'd set up earlier. She had a limited view of the road, just beyond the rear of the truck. "In position. Everyone stand by. Contact in less than one minute." She could hear the Suburban coming closer as it crunched along the gravel road.

"About thirty seconds out," White Owl announced. "The R44 is slowly headed back toward you."

When Aki saw the front bumper of the Suburban, she radioed, "White Owl, start closing in. Sarah, move, now!"

Dar stopped the Suburban about twenty feet behind the truck, just past the sharp curve, and got out with rifle in hand. *Damn her senses.* Aki whispered into the radio, "Be advised, Dar has an M4 assault rifle."

"That wasn't on the list of weapons she brought," Chase radioed.

Aki didn't dare respond, as Dar was looking in her direction. She wondered if Dar had heard her transmission. She watched Dar sweep her rifle slowly back and forth looking for any threats. Then she aimed at the disabled truck and quietly moved closer.

Aki didn't even want to breathe. Dar was only about fifty feet from her. Aki sighted in, her finger going to the trigger. Dar continued cautiously to the truck, stopped, and checked the cab with a quick glance, then pivoted in several directions. Dar reached for her phone and stood, then suddenly ran to the front of the truck and took cover.

"R44 has spotted Sarah and Clay," Brian reported.

As the R44 flew over her, Aki radioed, "Sarah, you've been spotted. Chase, I don't have a shot. She's on your side of the truck."

"I have her in my sights," Chase radioed.

"Chase, it's your call," Aki said.

"Dariya Novikov!" Chase shouted. "You are under arrest. Put your weapon on the ground."

Multiple shots instantly rang out.

"Shots fired!" Aki radioed, scrambling from the sniper hide and running toward the rapid exchange of gunfire, which was moving deeper into the woods. She took cover behind the truck, then worked her way around to the front. Suddenly the shooting stopped. "Chase, where is she?"

There was no response.

"Chase, respond." Aki scanned the area around her. She couldn't afford to have Dar get behind her. She heard Sarah's truck slide to a stop on the gravel. A quick glance and she could see that the road was blocked. Dar wasn't going anywhere in the Suburban. Dar was trapped, which meant that she would kill anyone in her way.

The R44 continued to orbit above them. "Sarah, Dar is to the west in the trees," Aki radioed. "Use the truck as cover and watch our west flank."

"Copy."

"Chase, answer me!" Aki yelled.

The squelch on her radio broke, and then Chase's weak voice said, "I'm hit."

Aki didn't wait. She ran to Chase's last position, but he wasn't there. She took cover behind a tree and listened. The tree bark above her head exploded from a rifle round hitting it. Aki threw herself to the left and up against another tree. The dirt around her flew up, and more pine bark blew from the tree above her. She thought back on her first encounter in Germany with Dar. *Move!* Was her only thought.

Aki scrambled as more rounds hit near her. Then she saw Chase on his back, and a dark stain was spreading from the side of his tactical vest. His pistol was lying loosely in his hand, and his rifle was on the ground.

"Aki!" Dar cried out. "You set a good trap. Sorry about your partner, but it was him or me. Now I must take care of the rest of your team. Then we will face off. Our game ends today."

Aki heard the sound of rounds hitting metal.

"Taking fire from the air!" Sarah screamed over the radio.

"Bring that chopper down," Aki ordered. She jumped up and ran to Chase. He was breathing, but it was labored. She saw where numerous rounds had hit the front of his vest. She felt the vest and could tell the ceramic ballistic plate had been shattered. She checked Chase's side where she saw the blood oozing and knew that at least one of Dar's rounds had found the gap at the side of Chase's vest. "Don't you dare die on me."

"Open the door and hold on," Gray told White Owl. He pushed the nose of the Jet Ranger down into a power dive. "I'm going to cut in front of the R44. Fire on the gunner."

"I'm ready," White Owl acknowledged, then slid the rear door open.

As Gray approached, he could see the R44 moving to get a better angle on Clay and Sarah, who'd taken cover beneath the truck. He couldn't cut in front as planned.

"Move to the left side and pop the other door. I can't get the angle I wanted." Gray felt the weight shift in the back and the whoosh of the air as the left door opened. "Five seconds."

Gray flew past the R44, nearly clipping the rotor blades, and then he heard White Owl open fire.

"Too fast, I missed them!" White Owl yelled.

Gray pulled back on the cyclic and performed a high-performance turn. "Right side."

White Owl moved to the other side.

The R44 spun so that the shooter could get a shot at them. A second later, two rounds blew through the acrylic windshield and hit the copilot seat.

White Owl didn't even flinch. He opened fire, with his Mini-14 peppering the R44.

Gray saw the pilot slump as blood splattered the windshield. Then the shooter jerked several times and the R44 went nose down and slammed into the ground. The airframe crumbled as the rotor blades tore through the tail boom, sending shards of metal flying in all directions, igniting the fuel tanks and engulfing the wreckage in flames.

Gray spun back just in time to see Dar standing next to a tree. She was aiming at him. He jerked the cyclic hard to the right and felt the sting of the round crease his left forearm, followed by what felt like a powerful punch to his head.

Aki heard the crash of the helicopter and prayed it wasn't Gray and White Owl. Then came the report of more rounds being fired from Dar's rifle and the sound of a helicopter turning away, followed by the clank of bullets hitting metal.

She had a moment of indecision as she looked down at Chase. He was unconscious and he wouldn't be able to keep pressure on his wounds if she left him. He'd bleed out. If she didn't help Gray and the others, they'd be killed and Dar would escape. "Chase, I'm sorry."

Aki ran toward the gunfire. As she cleared the trees, she saw that Sarah and Clay were on the ground behind Sarah's truck. Neither were firing. Clay was struggling to reload his Glock. Sarah's pistol was on the ground next to her and she was trying to retrieve it. Aki could see that Sarah had been hit by the way she was moving.

Dar was stalking in for the kill from behind the truck and was almost on them.

"Dar!" Aki yelled as she ran toward her, bringing her rifle up for a snap shot. As expected, she missed, but it had drawn Dar's attention.

Dar spun around and smiled at her. Dar's rounds split the air just above Aki's head as she dove for the ground. Aki rolled and took aim again, but Dar was protected by the back of Sarah's truck—only the top of her head and the M4 aimed Aki's way were visible. Aki fired again. The round hit the side of the truck by Dar's face, driving her back. Dar fired multiple rounds, forcing Aki to slide deeper into the gulley.

Then the sound of the Jet Ranger coming closer echoed through the trees. Aki saw White Owl firing from his door position behind Gray.

Maybe. Aki stood, not caring if Dar saw her, and took aim at where she hoped Dar would appear.

The side of Dar's head popped up as she pivoted to fire at the helicopter. Everything slowed down. Aki pulled the trigger and Dar's head exploded in a red mist.

Aki ran to where Dar was lying, her rifle ready to fire again, but no more shots were needed. Dar was dead, and Aki felt a sense of relief as she realized that it was finally over.

The helicopter blew dirt and dust into the air as it bounced across the road and skidded to a stop. *Not the best landing.* Aki went around the rear of the truck and noticed that Sarah was holding her left calf and there was blood on her left shoulder. Sarah had her gun aimed at Dar's body.

"Aki, is she dead?" Sarah asked.

"Yes." Clay was on the ground and wide-eyed at the front of the truck. "Clay, are you hit?"

"Yes, but thank God for ballistic vests." Clay rubbed his chest and tapped on the steel plate. "Ribs hurt like hell, but I can move. Sarah, how bad is it?"

"I'll live," Sarah replied.

White Owl, had jumped from the Jet Ranger and was running toward them. Gray stumbled from the pilot seat as the rotors wound down.

"White Owl, Dar is dead and Chase is critically wounded," Aki said. "Call for medical support, then tend to Clay and Sarah. Gray, we'll need a trauma airlift. Get the chopper ready to fly." Then she saw the blood covering the side of Gray's face as he staggered forward.

"You'll need another pilot," Gray said, and he fell to his knees.

Aki was torn. Did she go to Gray or leave him? He was vertical, but Chase wasn't. She ran back into the woods.

When she reached Chase's side, he was conscious, but he was having trouble breathing and his face was pale. She knelt next to him and took his hand. "Chase, medical is on the way. You're going to be okay. Hang in there."

He smiled up at her. Blood painted his teeth. "You're a lousy liar, Boss. Did we get her?"

"Yes. She's dead."

Chase nodded and closed his eyes for the last time.

"No!" Aki wailed. She sat by his side and wept.

CHAPTER TWENTY-THREE

Custer – June 8 – 0830 hours

Gray was sitting in a lawn chair under the RV's awning, sipping a cup of English breakfast tea. Chase had recommended that he try it. Gray found that he preferred adding sugar and a squeeze of lemon to the brew.

He didn't understand why Chase's death had hit him so hard. He'd thought highly of him, but he hadn't known him very long. Maybe his grief was amplified because he knew Aki had been devastated. Gray knew from experience that losing someone on your team was difficult. Time spent second-guessing yourself only compounded the grieving process.

Aki's plan to capture Dar had been a good one, but trying to foresee and account for every possibility that can happen during a battle is impossible. There's always an element of risk in any confrontation and sometimes fate doesn't go your way. Aki needed to come to terms with that fact. Gray took a deep breath and exhaled slowly as he focused on the vista before him, allowing the tension in his stomach muscles to release.

A loud bang came from inside the RV. "Damn!" Sarah cried.

"Do you need help with something?" Gray called out. He knew she wouldn't accept it even if she did. Sarah was still hobbling around, refusing to use a crutch, and she'd tossed her shoulder sling in the garbage two days ago.

"I got it," Sarah replied. "Just having an issue making my coffee. My shoulder is still a little stiff this morning."

After they were released from the hospital, he'd asked Sarah to stay with him. White Owl and Clay had driven the RV to his property from the Devils Tower campground. He wasn't sure who'd delivered Sarah's truck, but it was there when they arrived. It was nice to have a vehicle other than the RV to drive.

White Owl had brought them back from the hospital after their release. They'd stayed in the hospital for only two days and Gray thought that was a day too long. Clay and White Owl had connected the RV's waterline to the well, the sewer hose to the septic, and the power to the electrical outlet on the power pole next to the pad. They'd made sure that there was extra fuel for the generator in case the power went out. They'd also brought an extra tank of propane for the stove and stocked the food pantry and refrigerator. Both of them had gone above and beyond to make sure everything was ready for them.

Both Clay and White Owl were still officially assigned to the command site as the investigation continued. Clay had suffered only a few bruised ribs and had returned to full duty. White Owl's shootdown of the helicopter was deemed justified by both Homeland and the Department of Justice. There had been no formal review by either of their departments, since HSI and DOJ had conducted the investigation. The operation had been classified for national-security reasons. The downing of the helicopter had been reported as an accident, and the NTSB preliminary report indicated that the cause appeared to be pilot error. None of them would be able to discuss what really happened.

White Owl had advised that Tyra Stathopoulos's and Tucker Ryan's car had been recovered from a wooded area near Silver City and that the FBI had expanded the search area for Crawley to include most of the Black Hills and eastern Wyoming. Gray knew that none of them would be found alive.

No one had yet entered the cavern. OST Chairman Red Elk had managed to raise enough publicity that the excavator at the command site wasn't allowed to start digging. No one had mentioned anything about Sled Canyon to the FBI yet.

Gray hadn't heard from Aki since Chase's funeral in Virginia. He'd wanted to attend, but Director Canton had instructed him not to make the trip. His doctor had also directed him to stay at home while he recuperated. So, he'd followed orders.

When he spoke to Canton, Gray had made it very clear that Aki's order to shoot down the helicopter was the only option to save Sarah and Clay. She'd agreed with Aki's decision. Canton had informed him that Carlton Safir's Ruger nine-millimeter pistol caliber carbine had been recovered in the wreckage. It was determined that Safir was responsible for shooting Sarah and Clay.

Canton also related that Chase had died from a 5.56 round fired from Dar's rifle. It was determined that the rounds that struck Chase's tactical breastplate had fragmented, forcing him back and causing him to twist, which exposed the seam between the front and rear ballistic plates. One of Dar's rounds had found the opening and pierced his liver and a lung. The wound was fatal. He wouldn't have survived even if he'd been near a trauma center.

Canton had told Gray that his two wounds had also come from Dar's rifle. She emphasized how lucky he had been. The bullet that creased his skull would have taken his head off if it was a smidge more to the right. He already knew that he was fortunate to be alive.

Their investigation also revealed that a fund-transfer request was made from one of Dar's accounts to both Gordon Black and Carlton Safir the morning of the aerial dogfight in the amount of fifty thousand dollars each. That information, combined with Carlton's and Black's actions, justified Aki in ordering the downing of the helicopter, and the case was closed.

Gray heard a vehicle approaching. He stood and saw a black Ford Expedition headed up the limestone road toward his property. "Sarah, we have company coming."

Sarah appeared at the door. "Friend or foe?"

"Not sure."

"I'll grab a gun."

The Expedition pulled up and parked about fifty feet away. "There's two of them," Gray shouted.

Sarah walked to the doorway, dressed in loose-fitting black pants and a gray t-shirt. She held a Glock 26 at her side. "Wonder why they're just sitting there?"

"I don't like it," Gray said. His head wound started to throb.

The doors opened and two men got out. The driver gave a friendly wave.

"You can relax," Gray said. "It's Littlejohn. I wonder if he's here to arrest us."

"Maybe I should keep the gun handy," Sarah joked, then put it on the counter.

As Littlejohn walked up, he said, "Morning, Gray. We need to talk. I know whatever you were involved in with Homeland is secret." As he approached, he added, "I wasn't told how badly you were injured. It appears that you had a close call."

"Just a graze." Gray felt a tingle by the elongated scab under the stubble on the side of his head where the bullet had torn away the skin. The nerve endings were starting to grow back together. The doctor had to shave that side of his head to suture his scalp closed. He was going to have a scar, but eventually his hair would cover it. "What brings you all the way out here?"

"Can we sit?"

Gray took his seat and the two men sat down next to him.

"Hello, Sarah, you're looking well," Littlejohn said, as she stepped gingerly down from the RV.

"What do you want?" Her tone wasn't at all friendly.

"This is DCI Agent Tom Rain. He'll be taking over Agent Crawley's cases and will work the Devils Tower and Sundance area. I thought I should introduce him since you'll be seeing him around."

Gray nodded without replying, noting the agent was young, maybe twenty-five, short and thin, with a full head of brown hair. He was wearing black cowboy boots, blue jeans, and a sportscoat. A little different look than what he'd seen other agents wearing.

Sarah continued to stare without saying anything.

Littlejohn shifted uncomfortably in his chair. "We've also come to ask for your help."

Gray was dumbstruck. "Our help? I thought we were suspects."

"Things have changed. Agent Crawley's body was discovered around eleven last night in the Belle Fourche River near Devils Tower."

"I'm sorry to hear that," Gray said.

"Me too," Sarah said. "How in the hell did he get up there?"

"I'll get to that in a second. I wanted you both to hear the news from me before the FBI releases any information to the public about his death."

"We appreciate that," Gray said, his suspicion growing. "Now, answer Sarah's question."

Littlejohn hesitated before responding. "Well, several witnesses noticed a red ball of light circling the river near the campground. When the orb disappeared, some of the campers walked to the river's edge and found Agent Crawley's body. He had three stab wounds in the chest, just like the other victims."

"Were his hands bound?" Gray asked.

"No."

"We also recovered two more bodies," Rain said. "They were in the river downstream from where Agent Crawley was found."

"Were they the other two missing mining employees?" Sarah asked.

"Not a hundred percent certain yet, but the descriptions and clothing match," Rain replied.

"I'm betting that Director Sutton was too chickenshit to come and tell us that he was wrong," Gray said. "That's why he sent you."

Littlejohn smiled and said, "That's one way of putting it. On behalf of the Wyoming DCI, we apologize."

"Kiss my ass," Sarah spat. "You put us through hell and now you're sorry. Sutton screwed Gray out of a job and his meddling caused us to lose a good man. Without Homeland tactical support, we all nearly died."

Agent Rain looked like he wanted to hide.

"I'm sorry," Littlejohn said. "I really am."

"What help could either of us provide the DCI or the FBI now, and why should we?" Gray asked. "It sounds like you've recovered all of the victims. Now all you need to do is find the killer or killers."

"Finding the killers is where you two come in," Littlejohn said. "You've encountered these red orbs and other lights before, and you've dealt with the buffalo-clad warriors. White Owl called some of them 'spirit warriors.' We'd like you to walk us through everything again. We could have missed something earlier."

"You're joking, right?" Gray said. "We told you about the lights and the warriors two weeks ago."

"You did, but we'd like a better description of the warriors and the lights. Not only what you saw, but any opinions you may have about what happened or what these lights are, no matter how insane they may sound. Since what you encountered has been verified, another accounting from those who saw these things up close, several times, could save another agent's life."

"Did you think we were lying about what happened?" Sarah asked.

"I wasn't sure. If it means anything, I believe that Director Sutton calling the NPS and OAS was premature."

"You think?" Sarah asked.

"We need to come up with a plan to deal with whatever we're facing so we can prevent any further abductions and deaths," Littlejohn said. "We think a group briefing will save time."

"You want us to hold a group discussion session?" Sarah scoffed.

"In a manner of speaking, yes," Littlejohn replied.

Gray shook his head slowly in disgust, then said, "Has the FBI officially cleared us of any wrongdoing?"

"Yes. Agent Stevens would have come and told you in person, but they are incredibly busy working the homicides."

"You could have led with that news," Sarah said. "Have you discussed this with Dr. Kingman, Lt. White Owl, or Deputy Gurley?"

"I spoke to Lt. White Owl and Deputy Gurley early this morning," Littlejohn said. "They said that if the two of you agreed, they would participate. The FBI is reaching out to Dr. Kingman. She's gone back to Utah."

Gray huffed and felt the side of his head. It was starting to itch and his head hadn't stopped throbbing. "Agent Littlejohn, I'm currently on medical leave. I can't commit to anything without my boss's approval."

"And I'm still under investigation by NPS," Sarah added. "My having been involved in two firefights, one where I was shot, coupled with Sutton's accusations, has landed me in serious trouble. The NPS is conducting a formal inquiry into my actions. Plus, I've been advised that if I'm not terminated, I'll need to undergo a psych review, and then they'll have to determine if my injuries are career ending. I think the writing is on the wall."

Littlejohn nodded, then said, "I spoke to the NPS Office of Professional Responsibility and your regional supervisor on my way to see you. They've been informed that you're no longer under criminal investigation. I can't speak to any policy violations they may choose to pursue, but I think participating in the meeting will go a long way to getting you back in the field."

"I'll wait to hear from them before I decide," Sarah said.

Littlejohn said, "Look at the big picture. We need to know exactly what we're facing and time is critical. Can't you put this pettiness aside?"

"That's enough," Gray said forcefully. "She's not being petty. You have no idea what we've been through."

"I know that it's been hard and I'm sorry," Littlejohn said.

"You have an army of agents at the site, and I'm certain that experts from many fields are being consulted about the lights," Gray said. "I'm not sure our retelling what happened will be of any value to anyone at this late date. We were as complete and thorough in what we told you before. Just read our statements. I don't believe there's anything else of value that we can provide."

"There's still something or someone out there who will kill again if we don't stop them," Littlejohn said. "Something new may come to light during the Q&A."

"Sarah and I will discuss it and call you later with our decision."

"I guess I'll have to live with that. We won't put you back in the field if that's a concern."

"Not a concern at all," Gray said. "Tell Director Sutton that I want a personal apology delivered to the FBI, the Department of the Interior, NPS, the Director of OAS, and any other people or agencies where he made false statements. We'd all like to have our names publicly cleared. Not that I expect he will comply, but let me know what he says."

"I'll convey your message," Littlejohn said. "Agent Rain, I think it's time we go."

Once they had left, Sarah said, "You know that Sutton won't admit that he was wrong."

"I know. I just want Littlejohn to deliver the message and drive Sutton's blood pressure up a few points."

"I think it would be a waste of time for us to reiterate what we've already told them. We could tell the FBI about the possible entry point at Sled Canyon."

"No."

"With all of their geologic specialists, the FBI will eventually discover what we have found. I'm surprised that they haven't already checked out Sled Canyon."

"I'm not going to share any information with them. All of the missing people are accounted for and we can't do anything without Aki's approval anyway. I'd like to see the cavern before anyone else does, and I know Angela will also. It's why Darren died. We can always call the FBI once we know what's there, and if it's what I think it might be, then we owe that to the Lakota as well."

Sarah took a deep breath, then said, "Alright then. Let's call the others and talk this through. I'd like everyone to agree."

"Fine by me. Start making the calls while I contact my office and see where we stand."

Sarah went back inside the RV and Gray called the TCT office. Sharon answered.

"It's Gray. I wanted to check in and see how everyone is doing. Is Aki still on leave? I haven't spoken to her since the funeral."

"No, and we're all still in shock. Losing a member of the team is hard, but it comes with the territory. How are you and Sarah doing?"

"Healing nicely, thank you. I'm looking forward to meeting all of you. There's no doubt that you guys are the best of the best. Is Aki in the office? There's been a development here."

"No," Sharon replied. "Aki left early this morning. She's flying out to see you. It was supposed to be a surprise visit. She should be at your place around noon."

"Interesting. How's Aki *really* doing?"

"She's heartbroken. Aki and Chase had worked together for two years and were more like brother and sister than partners. She blames herself for his death, even though we've all stressed that she wasn't at fault."

"Deep down she knows that, but it's difficult to accept," Gray stated.

"It's going to take her some time to get past the grief."

"I'll see if she'll talk to me about what she's going through," Gray said.

"Just so you know, we're still monitoring the FBI signals traffic, and I think the latest development is one of the reasons Aki wanted to talk to you in person."

"What did you intercept?"

"I've said enough. You guys stay safe out there."

The line went dead.

Gray felt he was in for an interesting afternoon. He took a few minutes to look out on the landscape. *Virginia won't have these views.* He went into the RV and sat down at the dinette.

When Sarah finished her call, she said, "White Owl and Clay have been ordered to speak to the FBI and DCI agents tomorrow morning. They have a concern. Not telling about Sled Canyon or the gold could cost them their jobs."

"They have a point," Gray said. "I also think that if they mention it tomorrow, they'll be in trouble for not having said something earlier."

"That's what they thought, too."

"What did Angela have to say?" Gray asked.

"She had a visit from an FBI agent about the same time Littlejohn spoke to us. She agreed to cooperate but won't make the meeting tomorrow morning. It's a nine-hour drive from Utah, and she has some things to do this evening at BYU. She plans to leave early tomorrow and meet us here around two o'clock. She also doesn't want to disclose what we know about the cavern and emphasized the need to keep the cavern pristine."

"Any disclosure about Sled Canyon or the gold should come from Aki," Gray said. "If there's any blowback on Clay or White Owl, she can fix it by claiming it was classified and they were directed not to say anything. I can't believe the FBI hasn't discovered what we did already."

"What's new at Homeland?"

"Sharon said that Aki is flying out to see us today and should be here around noon. Did you check in with NPS?"

"Not yet. I think I'll wait for them to call me."

Custer – Gray's Property – 1150 hours

Gray went to meet Aki as she parked her red Jeep Wrangler next to the RV. When she got out of the Jeep, Gray couldn't help but stare. She was stunning even in her tan BDU pants, blue HSI polo, and tactical boots. Her hair was braided and it shimmered in the sunlight. He realized that he'd really missed her.

"Hey there," Gray greeted her, trying hard to keep his excitement at seeing her in check.

Sarah waved to her, not bothering to get up from her chair.

"You don't seem surprised to see me," Aki said.

"We were given advance warning," Gray replied. "Come and sit. We have some things to discuss."

"Yes, we do. I heard you had company this morning."

"We did," Gray answered. Once they had settled, he told her about their meeting with the DCI. He also told her about White Owl's and Clay's concern and the need for her to run interference for them.

"I'll take care of it. Sled Canyon must remain a secret for now. I know that Chairman Red Elk and several of the other tribal leaders have been successful in preventing the FBI and NPS from digging at the site. All of the bodies have been recovered and none of them were found near the cavern. There's no need for them to expedite entry into the cavern now.

"I have no issue with you and Sarah briefing the FBI and DCI. They have eight unsolved homicides, so it might buy us some goodwill when they find out what we've kept secret."

"Agreed," Gray said.

"How soon can you get back in the field?" Aki asked him.

"The arm is nearly healed and I've been cleared by the doctor to resume normal activity when I feel up to it, so I'm ready to go. I look like shit with the side of my head shaved, but the surgeon did a nice job sewing the skin back together. Stitches will come out in a few days."

"It gives you a rugged look," Aki said. She smiled at Sarah and asked, "And how are you doing?"

"Shoulder is tender, but I refuse to wear the sling. The calf muscle is healing nicely and there wasn't any nerve damage. The doctor said I could resume light duty. I get around fine, just a little gimpy."

"That's good news. Let me get to the reason for my visit."

"Before you do, we want to know how you're doing," Gray said.

Aki clenched her jaw. "I'm hurting, which is why I needed to get back in the field. I've been cleared to resume all duties by the director and DHS Secretary Evans. They've both told me that my decisions and actions were appropriate, but it doesn't feel that way."

"I understand," Gray said. "If you want to talk, I'm a pretty good listener."

"We both are," Sarah added.

Aki stilled, looked at the ground for a moment, then looked back at them. "I left Chase." Her voice cracked as she fought back tears.

"You did what had to be done," Gray said. "It was the right decision. Chase's wound was fatal. Nothing could have saved him."

"I know that," Aki said. "But I left him alone."

"You saved us," Sarah said, "and you went back to him as soon as you could."

"He wasn't alone at the end," Gray offered. "Chase died knowing that the mission was a success and that you were safe."

Aki wiped a tear from her cheek. "I can't seem to stop crying and I'm not the crying type. I should have shot her before she made it to the truck."

"Aki, no one could have foreseen what was going to happen," Gray said. "Chase was behind cover and he had the best shot at her. It was his decision to challenge instead of shooting her. There was no way you could have known that one of Dar's rounds would find the seam in his vest. Sometimes, things just happen."

Aki took a deep breath, then said. "Chase did shoot Dar, but she was wearing concealed body armor. Several rounds hit a metal plate covering her heart. Damn, he was a great friend. I'm going to miss him."

"I know," Gray responded solemnly.

Aki wiped her damp cheeks and cleared her throat. "Now, back to business. I started thinking about ballistic armor and the lack of blood after your encounters. Based on what Makawee told us, the Wakanpi may not have acted alone. I had Brian search ballistic-armor purchases in the area to see if we could get a lead on other Guardians besides Mato. He found several deliveries had been made to a number of people on several of the reservations over the last year, including Pine Ridge."

Sarah said, "A data search of all the ballistic vest sold would be incredibly tasking. How would you even get that data?"

"All I can say is that Brian McFee is very good. He sent me a list of the purchasers, and Mato's name was on the list."

"You might want to share that information with the FBI," Gray said.

"I plan to, with the condition that I be in on his interview. I'm also going to offer our assistance on the homicides again. I'll approach Agent Stevens at the briefing tomorrow morning."

"You're going to offer to help work on the homicides again?" Sarah asked. "I thought the cavern was the priority."

"It is. Everything happening here is linked. Our team has no other current missions, so I can dedicate my resources to finishing what you started. Plus, it will give us a reason to stay in the area. Are you interested?"

Gray looked at Sarah. "How about it?"

"I'd like to help, but there's the matter of the NPS internal investigation. I'm not sure that they'll authorize it, and then there's the FBI and Sutton."

"I think the internal investigation will be wrapped up *very* soon," Aki said. "They won't have an issue loaning you to Homeland."

"You know something, don't you?" Sarah said.

She nodded. "Secretary Evans called the DOI secretary and conferred his appreciation for your contribution in stopping Dar at great personal risk. The internal investigation is closed. You'll be notified that you've been exonerated and can resume normal duties when medically cleared."

"Thank you," Sarah said. "That's a relief."

"The FBI and Sutton won't be an issue," Aki added. "Agent Stevens called me and told me that they discovered a mole at the command site. Carlton Safir left a paper trail detailing payments made to an NPS supervisor. The information was given to the FBI and the DOI. He was arrested yesterday evening. It hasn't been made public yet."

"Who was the supervisor?" Sarah asked.

"Your boss, Jim Holden."

"That's unbelievable. He was great to work with and he has two kids." Sarah shook her head in disbelief.

"They'll get to visit him in prison," Aki said. "This wasn't the first time he'd received money from Safir."

"Did he know who the information was going to and how it would be used?" Sarah asked.

"No. He wasn't aware that he was putting anyone in harm's way. Stevens told me that he's confessed to all of his misdeeds and he seems contrite about what has transpired. He's already working on a plea deal."

"What happened to the Jet Ranger?" Gray asked.

"It was returned and DHS is paying for the repairs. Considering your wounds, I believe that you landing it in one piece was miraculous and a credit to your piloting skills."

"Thanks. What's up next?"

"As soon as you two are up to it, I want to explore Sled Canyon. I believe it would be appropriate for Angela to join us."

"She's in Utah, but she'll be here tomorrow afternoon," Sarah said.

"We could go check out Sled Canyon after the briefing," Gray said. "Sarah, what do you think?"

"I'm up to looking, but I won't be able to do any caving."

"That's okay," Aki replied. "We just need to see if an entrance is there." Aki paused. "Sarah, after seeing you in action, I'd like you to join the team, permanently."

"Well, I certainly wasn't expecting a job offer," Sarah replied. "I'll need to know more about the position, and you have to know that I really like working for the NPS and living here."

"To be honest, I do, too," Gray said.

Aki scrunched her brow. "I see."

"Don't get me wrong, I'm looking forward to the job, just not the move," Gray said. "This feels like home to me."

"I understand," Aki said. "I'd forgotten how special this place is." She paused, then said, "I wasn't going to say anything until it was approved, but since it has bearing on our conversation, I will tell you that I've proposed an operational change to Under Secretary Canton that may work for all of us."

"I'm intrigued," Gray said.

"I'll tell you more after I speak to the rest of the team."

"You said that Canton is now the under secretary?" Gray asked.

"Yes. It turns out that we had a mole of our own. Under Secretary Basset was providing information to his girlfriend, who, it turns out, was a Russian agent. He lawyered up as soon as he was confronted and hasn't said a word since. It doesn't matter, his girlfriend rolled over on him after her arrest. She's cooperating to avoid prosecution and being sent back to Russia to face execution."

"How did you determine Basset was the mole?" Gray asked.

"Canton told me that she had suspected Basset was leaking information. After our ambush in Germany and having our support team and drones pulled from our operations here, she dug deeper. Too many operations had been compromised over the last six months, and only a small group knew about them."

"So, Basset was providing information to Dar?" Sarah asked.

"Indirectly. Dar knew too much personal information about Chase and me. We're certain that she was aware that Chase and I had tracked her to her safe house in Germany."

"I hope they execute him," Sarah said. "Do they still do that?"

"Not since 1953," Aki replied. "I checked, hoping execution was an option. In addition to all of his other charges, Secretary Evans is asking the Attorney General to look into prosecuting him for abetting in Chase's death."

"That's a start," Gray said. "Do you still report to Canton?"

"Yes. Canton was asked by the president to fill Basset's position until confirmed."

"So, no more problems getting the support we need?" Gray said.

"Nope, and we're getting an additional position added to our staff. That's the position I want Sarah to fill."

"Aki, tell me what the job entails," Sarah said. "I also want to know if you're only offering me the spot because you think Gray may change his mind and stay here if I don't accept."

"Sarah, I want you on my team because I like what I see in you. Look, when I heard you two were living together, I figured you were a couple. Sarah, you don't have to worry about me."

Sarah sighed. "Aki, Gray and I have only known each other a short time and we were just getting to know one another. I would have liked to have seen where our relationship was going, but we've decided that we'll be better off as friends. We're staying together because Gray thought it would be easier to look after each other while we recuperated."

"Sarah, I'm sorry if I caused you any pain."

"We're good. No need for any further discussion."

"I'm happy to hear that."

"I need to exercise my leg a bit. Can we walk while you tell me about the job?"

"Certainly."

"The position is unique," Aki began. "It involves some field work, but mostly research and analysis. I know that you have a Bachelor of Science degree in forestry from the University of Kentucky, with a focus in geographical information systems and research."

"I guess you had Sharon check me out."

"I did. It's clear that as a ranger and from your background in caving, you're comfortable in nature. Sarah, I need a field agent who can work in less-than-hospitable environments. I can also use your GIS expertise for mission planning into those areas. I know that you're cool under fire, and most importantly, you need to know that I respect you."

Sarah nodded. "Thank you. Is that all you can tell me about the position?"

"You'll be working with the best team in the world on assignments that are critical to national security. It will be very challenging and travel will be involved. You'll also get a substantial increase in pay over what you're making now. You already know that we're a covert arm of DHS. I can't get into any mission specifics unless you accept."

"I see. Aki, I'm not financially motivated, and unlike Gray, I'm going to need time to think this through."

"I figured you would."

After a moment, Sarah said, "I believe that working with you would be very dangerous. I'm no coward, but a steady diet of being under fire isn't for me."

"I understand, and it really isn't that way most of the time. We are intelligence gatherers until we need to act, and then there's some risk involved in apprehending our targets. I'll be staying out here for a few weeks. That'll give you some time to decide."

"Don't you have other matters in Washington?" Sarah asked.

"I told Canton that solving the homicides and looking into the Wakanpi, the mysterious lights, and the Guardians was a matter of national security and needed to be investigated. She agreed and also liked the idea of my interacting with the FBI…you know, building inroads for future cooperation on covert missions."

"Which will be negated when Agent Stevens finds out you've been holding out on them," Sarah said. "Where are you going to stay while you're here?"

"I'll find a place in Custer."

"Stay here tonight. I plan to move back home after the briefing."

"Do you think Gray will mind?" Aki asked.

"Actually, I believe he would like you to stay here. You need some personal time together."

Custer – Gray's Property – June 8 – 1500 hours

Gray's cell phone had rung several times in the last hour. He knew it was Littlejohn.

"Why don't you get that this time?" Sarah said. "I think you've made them wait long enough."

Gray answered and put it on speaker so Sarah and Aki could listen. "Yes."

"This is Justin Littlejohn. I need an answer."

"We'll provide you with whatever you need."

"That's excellent. Be at the command site tomorrow morning at eight. We're going to meet at the mess tent."

"We'll be there," Gray said. He caught Aki's attention. She smiled and nodded. "My new boss, Homeland Security Special Agent in Charge Akicita Dawson will also be there."

"She's welcome to attend."

"Will Sutton be there?" Gray asked.

"Yes."

"Good. I'll expect that apology."

"That isn't going to happen," Littlejohn replied firmly, and disconnected.

"This is going to be fun," Gray said.

"Gray, I think you should wear an HSI uniform tomorrow," Aki said.

"That'll be difficult, considering I haven't been outfitted yet."

"I brought two shirts, two pairs of BDU's, and tactical boots in your size. Sarah, I brought a uniform for you, too."

"Thoughtful, but I haven't made my decision yet."

Aki's cell phone pinged, and she checked the text. "Sarah, you'll be getting a call from NPS any moment now."

"How would you—" Sarah's cell phone rang.

"Magic," Aki said.

"I'll take this in private." Sarah limped away and answered. After a brief conversation, she came back and plopped down in her chair.

"What happened?" Gray asked.

"I've been officially cleared and can resume normal duties when I'm ready."

"That was expected, so why the puzzled look?"

"I was offered two promotional opportunities. I can take my old boss's position and stay here, or take a special-agent slot in the Investigative Services Branch. I have to let them know by tomorrow afternoon." Sarah looked at Aki and asked, "Did you set this up?"

"No. I knew that you'd be cleared of any criminal or policy infractions, but not that you'd be offered a promotion. I guess you need to decide whether to accept my offer by tomorrow."

Gray's Property – 2115 hours

Twilight cast a purplish hue on the western sky as the stars began to appear. The last vestiges of the sun's rays had gone and a chill had descended. Even in the summer, the evening air was cool, which Gray enjoyed over the ever-steamy Florida weather. Aki didn't appear to mind the cold as she sat near the small fire that was contained by a ring of rocks.

"Can I get anyone anything?" Gray asked, getting up to get a sweatshirt from the RV.

"I'm good," Sarah said.

"Me too," Aki said.

Gray went into the RV and picked an old green sweatshirt from a pile of clean, unfolded clothes on the pullout. Then he made a cup of Chase tea, as he'd started calling it. He went back outside and noticed both women were gazing up at the stars.

Gray sat down between Aki and Sarah and said, "Sarah, you look deep in thought."

"I'm just thinking about how much I love it here."

Aki said, "When I was young, my parents and I would sit around a fire like this one. My father would tell stories of our ancestors' exploits and speak about their courage, their love for our people, and the land. I plan on living here again, soon."

Gray turned and asked, "Does this have anything to do with the operational change you mentioned earlier?"

Aki smiled, then said, "I found an eighty-acre estate near Pringle that would be perfect for a new operations center. It's secluded, bordered by a hundred-foot-high cliff along the east side of the property, and it is surrounded by dense forest. The nearest neighbor is over two miles away. I spoke to the other team members earlier and they're looking forward to the move, except for our newest member, Traci Long. She's getting married."

Gray sat back in his chair. "Don't we need to be near headquarters in Washington?"

"No. We can operate from anywhere. In fact, it may be better not being around there. The space we occupy at the NGA building isn't working out as hoped. Too many inquisitive people in the intelligence field. Our cover won't hold up much longer. Canton has already approved the move and she has plans to use the NGA offices for another HSI group."

"You said the land is near Pringle?" Sarah asked.

"Yes. It's an old estate. I've been authorized to purchase the property through a bogus real estate holding company. The estate home is large, but it will need some updating to be operational while we wait for the site to be developed. I envision building a secure underground facility and some homes, maybe a clubhouse to make it look like a small, exclusive gated neighborhood. Our team members can live there for free if they want, or they can stay off campus and commute."

"That's great news, but won't that require serious funding?" Gray asked. "And keeping what we're building a secret will be difficult, probably impossible. I thought that we were supposed to be covert."

"A black-fund account has already been established for the initial purchase of the property through the dummy holding company. Burrowing into the base of a cliff or canyon wall has been done before without drawing suspicion. The main operational facility will be concealed. The whole complex will be away from any other homes and main roads and it will be secure, so no one will know what we're doing. Sarah, you won't have to leave and you'll have a new home."

Sarah took a deep breath. "Aki, I've decided to stay with NPS. I'm taking the ISB investigator position. I've invested ten years of my life in NPS and I'll have new challenges. I was told that if I accepted the posting, I would be assigned to this region."

"You're really sure that this is what you want?" Gray asked.

"Yes. I believe this is what's best for me. I'd like to drop by once you all get settled, if that's permitted."

"You'll always be welcome," Aki said.

CHAPTER TWENTY-FOUR

Black Hills – June 9 – Command Site – 0100 hours

Two FBI agents were talking outside the command bus when a blue light flashed through the trees, drawing their attention. A red orb appeared at treetop level and slowly circled the command site.

"What the hell?" one of the agents cried. Then he opened the bus door and said, "We have activity."

A moment later, four Wakanpi drifted out of the tree line and stood shoulder to shoulder. Their eyes glowed red.

The agents drew their firearms and one of them shouted, "Stay where you are! Let me see your hands!"

Other agents heard the commotion and ran from their tents to assist. Some were half-dressed, but all had their weapons drawn. The Wakanpi stood like statues as the orb made another circle around the site.

"Get on the ground!" another agent shouted as he advanced on the Wakanpi.

A few more agents joined the advance. The red orb stopped and hovered above the Wakanpi and cast a shimmering red light over the warriors.

When Agent Stevens saw what was happening, he recognized that these were the lights and buffalo-clad warriors Gray and the others had encountered. "Don't get any closer to them!" he ordered.

Sutton emerged from his tent, wearing only his slacks and a white t-shirt. "What in the world? Agent Stevens, arrest those men."

Stevens felt compelled to walk toward the Wakanpi and the red-light barrier. As he neared them, their eyes began to pulsate. When he reached the barrier, he felt a tingling sensation creep over his body. He had to force himself to stop as the light was pulling him forward.

Just as quickly as they had appeared, the Wakanpi withdrew into the dark forest and the red orb shot off into the sky. A moment later, an intense flash of blue light lit up both the trees and the command site for a second.

"After them," Sutton yelled.

"No, I want a head count on our people," Stevens instructed. "Make sure no one has been abducted."

The light towers came to life, revealing the faces of confused and disbelieving agents.

Once Stevens was satisfied that everyone was accounted for, he and Sutton led a group of agents into the woods. After nearly an hour of searching, nothing was found.

"You should have chased after them," Sutton said accusingly. "Then they wouldn't have gotten away."

"I don't think it would have mattered," Stevens said. "We need to rethink our position about what's happening here. Those things looked just like what Gray and the others described."

"It has to be a trick," Sutton countered. "They're just messing with us."

"Really?" Stevens said. "Blue lights, a red orb that cast a glow over the red-eyed warriors and then flew away. I also felt a tingling sensation when I approached the warriors. That was no trick." Stevens shook his head in disbelief and stated, "I need to make some calls. This is no longer just a criminal investigation."

Black Hills – June 9 – 0730 hours

Aki drove Gray and Sarah to the command site and parked next to the NPS bus. Clay and White Owl were waiting for them. Gray noted the increased presence of agents standing along the tree line.

Aki's phone rang. "It's Sharon. I need to take this call."

"Good morning," White Owl said. "Gray, that uniform suits you well."

"Morning," Gray replied, watching Aki walk away. "This was Aki's idea."

Sarah said, "I guess last night's events got everyone's attention."

"It did," White Owl replied. "I think that they are all believers now. How did you hear about what happened? We were instructed not to make any calls."

"Aki was notified about the encounter earlier," Gray replied.

Sarah said, "I doubt we're going to need to conduct a briefing."

"The blue glow came from the same area where we first saw it," White Owl said. "The FBI has declared the event a national security threat."

"Just before you arrived, I overheard an FBI agent saying everyone is going to have to sign a lifelong nondisclosure agreement concerning what we've witnessed," Clay said. "They're locking the site down. Like I've been saying, we're dealing with aliens. Why would they do that if it wasn't aliens?"

"Good question," Aki said as she joined them. "Sharon advised that an FBI special-response team is headed this way. The National Guard in Rapid City is deploying to secure the area and establish a restricted zone. The FAA has been directed to create a twenty-mile-wide prohibited airspace zone, which the Air Force is going to enforce. The special team should arrive shortly."

"What type of special-response team?" Clay asked.

"The kind that investigates unexplained events. This will only be the first of several teams that are coming."

White Owl asked, "They think we encountered aliens?"

"They're not sure of anything, so they're covering all of the bases."

"So, what do we do now?" Sarah asked.

"Not sure," Aki replied. "Gray and I have to stay since there's a Homeland Security interest. They may want the rest of you to brief the special teams as they arrive."

"Perhaps it would be best to leave them and the cavern alone," White Owl said.

"This doesn't make any sense," Gray stated. "Why would an alien species dress up in buffalo hides and kill people in a ritualistic manner?"

White Owl pointed down the road at a group on horseback that had suddenly emerged from the woods. All of the warriors wore buffalo hides and hoods, except one. "Maybe they can tell us what's going on here."

"Oh, shit," Sarah said, putting her hand on her sidearm.

"Clay, they don't look like aliens to me," Gray said.

"White Owl, you and I should greet them before anyone does something stupid," Aki suggested. "I'm betting they're the Guardians. The rest of you stay here and keep those idiots from shooting at them. Sarah, find Agent Stevens and have him join us, but only him."

Gray said, "Aki, I'm going with you."

As the approaching warriors grew closer, Gray could see that the man leading the group of fifteen warriors was huge. The warrior riding next to the leader had blue, white, and black lightning-bolt stripes of war paint across his face from forehead to chin. He carried a Winchester lever-action rifle in his right hand, as did the other warriors. Their advance was slow and measured as they rode toward the command site. All of their horses had buffalo hides decorated with ceremonial paint draped across their chests and sides, some with the Lakota Kapemni symbol of the sun and earth.

Gray remembered that the symbol meant. *'What is below, is what is above.'* It also represented a portal or doorway between the physical and spiritual worlds. A chill crept up Gray's spine when the painted warrior locked eyes with him. "Aki, the warrior to the right of the leader is who I saw in my vision. I'll never forget those cold eyes."

"You're certain?"

"No doubt in my mind."

Aki looked more closely at the warrior wearing the warpaint. "I know him. That's Mato." Aki took her keys from her pocket and tossed them to Gray. "Change in plans. There are two rifles in the trunk of my car. You and White Owl bring them up quickly, but keep them pointed at the ground." Then she turned to face the warriors, locked her jaw, stood tall, and continued walking toward them.

Gray ran to the car and pulled the rifles from the trunk, handing one to White Owl. They each charged their weapon and took two extra magazines. Gray slammed the trunk and saw Sutton and Stevens leading a group of agents toward them. They all had their weapons pointed at the warriors. Sarah and Clay were doing their best to keep them from advancing, but they weren't having any success.

Gray looked back at the warriors. The warriors had stopped their advance and were taking positions on both sides of their leader, forming a line that blocked the road. Aki was steadfastly facing the warriors. He hoped Aki had a plan to prevent a bloodbath.

Sarah and Clay ran to join Gray and White Owl.

"They won't listen," Sarah said. "Sutton wants them all taken into custody. The way he's acting reminds me of Crawley. Hardheaded and impulsive."

"What does he want to arrest them for?" Gray asked. "Dressing badly? We don't know which, if any, of those riders are responsible for what's happened here. White Owl, go join Aki. Sarah, you and Clay are with me. Follow my lead."

White Owl nodded and quickly walked toward the warriors.

"Sutton!" Gray shouted, as he moved to block Sutton and Stevens from advancing. "Stay where you are or I will arrest you for interfering with an HSI investigation."

"Go ahead and try," Sutton spat.

Gray brought his rifle to his chest and stepped in front of Sutton. "Listen to me. Last night, you encountered the Wakanpi. The men approaching are not them. However, they are a part of a classified HSI investigation. You will not be allowed to go any further."

"Have you lost your mind completely?" Sutton bellowed. "Those savages are responsible for the deaths of eight people, one of which was Agent Crawley. I don't give a crap about what I saw last night or about your investigation. They killed my friend and they're going to pay. Now, get the hell out of my way."

"Not happening," Gray replied. "If you persist, I will enjoy arresting you. Clay, I need your handcuffs." When Clay unsnapped his handcuff case and stepped forward, Gray noticed a smile creep across Stevens's face.

"What's wrong with you?" Sutton asked. "Deputy, put those damn handcuffs away. Agent Holt, why are you taking *their* side?"

"I'm not taking anyone's side," Gray replied. "I'm stopping a firefight and probably saving your life. Those are warriors, not savages. Clay, stay here. If he moves, arrest him on my authority. Agent Stevens, I need you to accompany me. Aki and White Owl will interpret if needed." He raised his voice and said, "The rest of you stay here. Do not advance or take any action that will be considered a threat or you will face dire consequences." He thought his challenge rang hollow, but no one moved.

"Agent Stevens, I thought the FBI was in charge here," Sutton said.

"We are," Agent Stevens replied, holstering his weapon. "Stand down, people. Let's see what the warriors have to say." As he passed by Gray, he whispered, "You better be right about this."

"I am."

When Gray and Stevens joined Aki and White Owl, Gray asked Aki, "Who are they and what do they want?"

"So far, no one has said anything. I think they were watching you. That was a bold move. I'm impressed, and like most warriors, they admire strength."

"It was all I could think of to keep a lid on the situation," Gray replied.

"It was effective," Aki said. "You three stay here. I'm going to go talk to them."

As Aki started toward them, the leader of the warriors urged his horse forward to meet her. The other warriors held their ground.

"*Háu*, I'm Homeland Security Agent Akicita Dawson."

"I am Ohanzee, the seventh-generation chief of the Guardians of the Sacred City," he replied in Lakota. "Akicita, you don't look like the ferocious giant Mato described."

Aki smiled, uncertain of how to respond. It seemed everyone on the reservation knew about their fight.

"You and White Owl stand with those who take our land and threaten the sacred city," Ohanzee said. "Do you speak for the intruders?"

"We're not here as your enemy," Aki replied. "I represent the government of the United States and the interests of Homeland Security. I am here to help the FBI solve the murders of eight people. Like you, I want the Paha Sapa protected. It belongs to all of the Oceti Sakowin Oyate, the people of the Seven Council Fires, and the other Plains tribes. It is the heart of everything that is. The *wamaka ognaka y cante*."

"Mato," Ohanzee called.

Mato rode up, dismounted, and handed Ohanzee his rifle.

"What the hell is going on?" Gray asked White Owl.

White Owl related what Ohanzee had said in Lakota.

Mato was an imposing sight. Aki watched Gray tightening his grip on his rifle as he caught the daggered glance Mato shot his way before the warrior stopped in front of her.

"It is good to see you again," Mato said in Lakota. "I have often thought of you and have seen you in my dreams." He touched the scar on his left cheek and smiled. "I tell everyone about what a great warrior you are and that we once met in battle. Of course, I defeated you."

"I have missed you," Aki replied, in Lakota. "We seem to be on two different paths."

"We are here together now. But are we friends or enemies?" Mato's posture stiffened.

"I will always consider you my friend."

"Then friends we will remain," Mato said. He embraced Aki, lifting her up.

Gray started to move forward, but White Owl stopped him.

"They're friends," White Owl said.

Mato held Aki for several seconds. When he finally let her down, she turned and motioned for Gray, White Owl, and Stevens to join her. Ohanzee dismounted, summoned another warrior to take the horses, and gave Mato back his rifle. Ohanzee was even taller and heavier than Mato.

"These are my friends and colleagues," Aki said. "We have many questions."

Ohanzee nodded and replied in English, "Then we will sit and talk."

Aki introduced everyone and they walked into the shade under the ponderosa trees and sat on the ground.

"What the hell is going on here?" Sutton cried. "Ranger Goodson, are you really just going to stand there and prevent us from doing our duty?"

"I'm going to prevent you from getting another agent killed," Sarah replied. "Your ugly ass is staying right here."

"I didn't get anyone killed. Don't you dare try and blame that agent's death on me. I'm going to get you fired for that remark."

"No, you're not," Sarah said defiantly.

"Agents, rally up!" Sutton shouted. "We're going to go have a chat with the *warriors*."

"With all due respect, Director Sutton, we shouldn't interfere with the FBI investigation," Littlejohn said, taking a position in front of him. "The FBI is in charge and we were directed to stand down."

"Maybe I need to find a new supervisor," Sutton said. "One who's loyal and follows orders."

"Or the governor needs to appoint a new DCI director," Sarah said, coming to Littlejohn's defense.

Sutton turned a deep shade of red. "I can't believe this. We're standing here while they have a powwow under the trees. What kind of sissy-ass law enforcement is going on here? Ranger Goodson, Deputy Gurley, stand aside."

"We won't do that," Clay said. "You heard what Agent Holt said. I will put you on the ground and handcuff you if you try and get past us."

"Do you really think that you two can stop all of us?"

An FBI agent came forward and stood beside Sarah and Clay. "They won't have to. If you attempt to interrupt SAC Stevens while he's investigating, I will help them arrest you." Some of the other FBI agents came forward.

"This whole thing is a travesty of justice," Sutton lamented. "You're all a joke."

"Take your people back to the mess tent or to the command bus and relax," the FBI agent instructed.

Sutton glared at all of them. His pupils were pinpoints. "I'm going to make some calls and heads are going to roll. What's your name, agent?"

"Special Agent Ken Barnes."

"Go make your calls, Sutton—it's the only thing you're good at," Sarah chided.

Sutton slowly raised his middle finger as he walked away. "You're through, bitch. DCI agents that want to keep their jobs, follow me to the mess tent. Now!"

"I guess I finally got to him," Sarah said.

"I believe you did," Clay replied. "What do you think they plan on doing?"

Littlejohn said, "Nothing. They'll listen to his tirade until Agent Stevens returns. I guess I better go see if he meant what he said. I may be out of work, or at the very least, suspended."

"Thank you for standing with us," Sarah said.

Littlejohn glanced at the group of warriors, then back at Sarah. "Don't thank me. I disagree with your methods. Agent Crawley deserves to have those responsible for his death imprisoned or dead. If those warriors aren't the ones who killed him, then they know who did. You're lucky we aren't in Wyoming or all of you would be under arrest." He turned and walked away.

Sarah turned to Barnes and asked, "What do you think? Did we overstep?"

"SAC Stevens said to stand down. I trust him. Let's see how this plays out. I have to say, you have conviction."

Aki sat between Mato and Ohanzee with her back against a tree so that she could watch the other warriors on the road. Ohanzee removed his buffalo hood. His face was also ceremonially painted. White stripes ran across his forehead. Blue and red stripes adorned his cheeks and chin.

"You look apprehensive," Ohanzee said. "You have nothing to fear."

Gray said, "We've been fired on by warriors, twice, and we were forced to shoot several of them." Gray paused, then added, "So, it's out of an abundance of caution that we are hesitant to trust you."

Mato smiled, then said, "You did not harm anyone. Your weapons are no match for the protection spell given by the Wicasa Wakan."

"Who?" Gray asked.

"A medicine man," Aki said. "Mato, did he also bless your ballistic armor?"

"Yes," Mato replied, smiling at her. "How did you know?"

"Because it's my job to know what I'm facing when protecting people."

Mato nodded. "Still standing up for the weak."

Gray's brow furrowed. "Mato, were you one of the warriors who shot at us?"

"No," Mato replied. "But it appears that someone did." He pointed at Gray's head wound.

"That was from an adversary who's now dead."

"Aki, wherever you go, trouble follows," Mato said.

"It seems that way," Aki replied. "Ohanzee, we're here to learn the truth about the kidnaping and murders of eight people."

"I know why you're here. The Guardians haven't killed anyone."

"I watched as buffalo-clad warriors, big men like yourself, shot at us and carried Agent Crawley away," Gray said.

"The Guardians were not involved," Ohanzee stated firmly.

"None of your people were involved in any of the kidnappings?" Stevens asked.

Ohanzee remained silent.

"Ohanzee, why are you here and dressed as Pte Oyate?" White Owl asked.

"We were summoned by the Wi Can."

"Who's the Wi Can and Pte Oyate?" Stevens asked.

"Star People," Aki answered. "The Pte Oyate are Wakanpi. They're beings superior to humans and have power over everything on Earth. They are spirit warriors and are *wakhán*, magical."

"You're saying that *star people* told you to come here today?" Stevens asked.

"Yes."

"And I suppose they killed and kidnapped everyone," Stevens said. From his tone, it was evident that he was growing aggravated.

Ohanzee took a deep breath and looked at the sky, then said, "From time to time, the Guardians are summoned to assist the Wakanpi. We do various things for them. Occasionally, we are asked to track and monitor intruders. If they pose a danger, their fate is determined by the Wakanpi."

"Seriously?" Stevens said. "Are you saying that the Guardians are abetting the kidnappings?"

Again, he didn't reply.

"Who killed all of these people?" Aki asked.

"The Wakanpi took them into the light, where they suffered the death of the three knives."

"Did you witness these murders?" Stevens asked.

"I did not."

"But you knew that some of Guardians were involved in the kidnappings and knew about the murders," Aki said.

"We have not killed anyone," Ohanzee replied.

"You didn't answer Agent Dawson's question," Stevens said.

"There is nothing more to say."

"How do you know the victims were killed by the Wakanpi?" Aki asked.

"The Wi Can told me."

"I want to make sure I understand you correctly," Stevens said. "You're saying that the star people told you that they killed them."

"Yes. They were deemed a threat to the Wi Can and the sacred city."

"And you didn't report it?" Stevens said.

"No."

"Ohanzee, Dr. Kingman and Deputy Gurley were abducted by three men in buffalo hides," Gray said. "Were they Guardians?"

"No. They were Wakanpi in Pte Oyate form."

"What happened to the one I shot?" Gray asked.

"Nothing. When the Wakanpi take the Pte Oyate form, they are temporarily vulnerable to earthly weapons. It takes a few minutes for them to recover. You didn't harm any of them."

"Were the Guardians present when Agent Crawley was taken?" Gray asked.

Ohanzee hesitated, then answered, "Some of the Guardians were on the ridge when the agent was taken by the Wakanpi. None of them shot at you or were involved in him being taken."

"Why were you there, then?" Stevens asked.

"Because we were summoned."

"I found 44-40 shell casings the first night we made contact and again when Agent Crawley was taken," Gray said. "Why would the Wakanpi use Winchester rifles?"

"The Winchesters are ancient weapons that have been in their possession for over a century. The weapon was used by the wašíču to subjugate the Plains tribes. Some of the rifles taken in battle were given to the Wakanpi as gifts by our ancestors."

"I think you're lying," Stevens declared.

Mato went to stand, but Ohanzee motioned for him to sit.

"Agent Stevens, that's enough," Aki said, seeing the fire in Mato's eyes.

"Ohanzee, why weren't Ranger Goodson and I considered a threat?" Gray asked. "And the night Agent Crawley was killed, only he was taken. Why?"

"I don't know."

"Ohanzee, I need the names of all the Guardians involved," Stevens demanded.

Ohanzee stared at Stevens, then finally responded, "Agent Stevens, the Wi Can don't wish to kill anyone, but a warning had to be sent. The four Wakanpi in the form of Pte Oyate that came to you last night was a warning. They could have easily killed all of you. The Wi Can and the city must be left alone."

"Why is the city so important?" Aki asked.

"The city is where the Wi Can and the Wakanpi reside. It is the most sacred of all places in the Paha Sapa, and one of the few things that hasn't been taken from our people. All of you must respect their sanctity."

"I can't do that," Stevens said. "I have an obligation and a duty to bring those responsible to justice."

"The Wi Can and the Wakanpi can't be taken into custody," Ohanzee stated.

"I can arrest you and anyone else who aided the Wakanpi."

"The Wi Can will not permit you to arrest any of the Guardians," Ohanzee stated. "We are needed here and they will protect us."

"Ohanzee, you already admitted to knowing about the homicides and the Guardian involvement in tracking people who are then kidnapped by the Wakanpi. That makes you and those involved accessories at the very least. I will be taking you into custody." Stevens went to stand.

Ohanzee bristled with anger.

"Agent Stevens, sit down," Aki said. "We have more to discuss. If you attempt to take him into custody, you will start a fight that you won't win."

"Whose side are you on?"

"I hope you're not questioning my allegiance because I'm Lakota?"

"To be honest, it crossed my mind," Stevens admitted. "You gave Mato a big hug."

Aki shook her head and said, "We don't have all the answers yet, and until we do, it would be premature to take any action."

"Agent Stevens, we all need to take it down a notch," White Owl said. "We must respect and accept that the city is sacred and should remain untouched. If Ohanzee would provide us with more details about the Wi Can and the city, that may clarify their role and culpability in the crimes."

"Ohanzee has already admitted to being involved," Stevens said. "I don't believe any further clarification is needed. Agent Dawson, do you think we should just let him go?"

"Like White Owl said, we need to understand how they were involved," Aki said. "We also need to understand why the city is considered sacred and defended."

"I can't believe this," Stevens said.

Aki sighed, then said, "I'd like to continue my questioning."

Stevens capitulated. "Go ahead."

"Ohanzee, our satellites have detected a large deposit of gold in the city. That's what brought the mining-company representatives here."

"Wait, the city is made of gold?" Stevens said, sounding exasperated. "And you didn't bother to tell us about it? That was an important detail to omit, don't you think? Gold would be a great motive for killing people."

"The mining companies know that there's gold here, as do many other federal agencies, including yours," Aki replied. "It was detected by satellite some time ago. I can't help it that your command didn't enlighten you. Agent Stevens, I also told Red Elk about the cavern and the Guardians, hoping that he would stop you from excavating."

Ohanzee gave a quick snort and said, "So that's how Chairman Red Elk knew about us."

"Yes," Aki answered.

"How did you learn about the Guardians?" Mato asked Aki.

"Like I said before, it's my job to know things." She had no intention of telling him about Makawee.

"Agent Stevens, the city *is* made of gold and it nourishes the Wi Can when they visit," Ohanzee said. "The gold must remain pure and untouched by human hands. That is one of the reasons it is defended."

"How could gold nourish the Wi Can?" Gray asked.

"All I can tell you is that the Wi Can take nourishment from the power of the Earth. The gold acts as a conduit. It energizes them. I don't know the technical aspects."

"I think these homicides were committed so the Guardians could keep the gold," Stevens stated.

"Agent Stevens, the Guardians have known about the golden city for millennia," Ohanzee said. "It's not ours to take, but there are others who wished to do so. The city may no longer be a secret, but we are still duty bound to protect it."

"Have you seen the city?" Stevens asked, more calmly.

"Once, after I was chosen to lead the Guardians. No one, not even another Guardian, is allowed to enter the city uninvited. I am the only one entrusted with the knowledge of how to enter without passing through the light and suffering the death of the three knives." Ohanzee paused, then gave Stevens a hard stare and added, "The Wi Can wish only to be left alone."

"Well, that isn't possible now that they've killed people," Stevens said. "I'd say that if what you've told me is true, they need to be held accountable. They could very well be a threat to our existence."

Ohanzee straightened and said, "They are not a threat if left alone."

Stevens rubbed the back of his neck, and said, "Ohanzee, just so that I'm clear, are the Wi Can alien beings?"

"I was told that they were here when Man first walked on the Earth. I believe that we are all of this universe."

"I see," Stevens said. "I'll need proof of these claims."

"You have seen the Wakanpi and the red orb. That is proof enough."

"No. It is not."

After a moment, Aki asked, "Ohanzee, how did you become chief?"

"I inherited the duty from my father, but not all chiefs are chosen that way. The Wi Can select from those of us who are pure of heart. The same is true for becoming a Guardian. Those selected must pass a test. It has been this way for thousands of years."

"The chiefs are selected from different tribes?" Aki asked.

"Yes."

"You said that the Guardians have been around for thousands of years, but the Lakota didn't arrive in this area until after seventeen hundred," Aki stated.

Ohanzee nodded. "That is true. The Lakota are newcomers to the Guardians, but many of those who serve are descended from ancient tribes. The first Guardians were nomadic plains people who interacted with the Wi Can and learned from them. They were peaceful until disagreements over material things arose and splintered the people. Tribes were formed over time, like the Mound Builders, the Mandan, and the Arikara, and so on until present time. The Guardians have remained steadfast, putting aside their differences, even when the tribes made war against each other."

"How do you know this?" Aki asked.

"My father told me. Our connection and duty to the Wi Can and this land has been passed down through the generations. Nothing has ever been written down. I imagine that will change now."

"Aki, Dr. Kingman could help us understand all of this better," Gray said. "Ohanzee, she's an academic who is an expert in Native American lore."

"I'm just not sure how she'll feel about the Guardians having known about Dr. Waters' death," Aki replied.

Ohanzee regarded them for a moment, then said, "As I have said, we were not involved in any killings. I will speak to Dr. Kingman if you like. Do you have any further questions?"

"What threat did Dr. Waters pose?" Aki asked. "I can understand how the mining-company employees could threaten the city, but not a BYU professor just doing research."

"If he tried to gain entry into the city, the Wakanpi would have considered him a threat. He could have disclosed its location, which I presume he did, since you knew to come here."

"Dr. Waters left the coordinates, but we didn't know about the city," Gray said. "We were only following a lead. Ohanzee, he was interested in Native American history and ancient cultures, like Dr. Kingman. Neither are interested in gold." Gray paused, then looked at Mato. "From what I know, Dr. Waters was a defender of the Lakota. He even carried a Lakota bone-tooth-handled knife in a red-and-blue beaded sheath."

Neither Ohanzee nor Mato replied, but Aki saw a spark of recognition in Mato's eyes when Gray mention the knife.

"Mato, you know something about the knife, don't you?" Aki said.

"Yes."

Ohanzee looked at Mato and asked, "What do you know?"

"I walk through the sacred land to feel closer to the Wi Can. I have never seen one, but I know they are here. I saw the Wakanpi carry a man into the light once. It was the first time I had witnessed the death of the three knives. I was disturbed by what I saw. The following day, I returned and found watches, jewelry, and other items scattered on the ground. I gathered them and buried them in a box as a sign of respect. I found the knife and kept it, since it was Lakota."

"Do you still have it?" Aki asked.

"Yes."

"Dr. Kingman would like the knife back," Aki said. "It means something to her."

Mato nodded, reached beneath his hides, and gave the knife to Aki.

"Did you keep anything else?" Gray asked.

"No. Everything that I found went in the box."

"You said that the man who was killed was the first time you'd seen the death of the three knives," Gray said. "How many other times since then?"

"That same night I saw a woman suffer the same fate."

"That had to be Tyra Stathopoulos," Gray said.

"And you told no one about what you'd seen?" Stevens asked.

"No."

"Mato, your admission gives me probable cause to arrest you for being an accessary after the fact," Stevens said.

"As I said, that can't happen," Ohanzee stated. "We are the spear tip of the seventh generation, as Crazy Horse and Black Elk foresaw."

"What the hell are you talking about now?" Stevens asked.

Aki nodded, then explained, "Crazy Horse prophesied that the Lakota would have to wait seven generations before all people would gather under the sacred tree of life, no matter their heritage. Black Elk had a similar vision."

"I'm not sure what bearing this has on the investigation," Stevens said.

Ohanzee gave a snort, then said, "All humans are linked and living under one sky. The Wi Can will see that happens and nothing can be done to stop it, which is why they must be left alone." Ohanzee closed his eyes, and a moment later, a red orb appeared in the sky above the group. "More armed invaders are approaching."

There was a commotion amongst the warriors. Several of them broke from the group and rode into the woods on both sides of the road.

"I think the FBI special team has arrived," White Owl said.

Mato and Ohanzee stood, taking up their rifles. The remaining warriors tightened their ranks to protect Ohanzee from the threat.

"Ohanzee, that's going to be an FBI special team," Aki said, standing and stepping up beside him. "They are here because of what happened last night. Do not engage these men."

Ohanzee stared at her. "I will do what the Wi Can wish of me."

CHAPTER TWENTY-FIVE

Black Hills – June 9 – 0815 hours

Two black vans and an armored vehicle screeched to a stop a hundred yards away from the warriors. A dozen men dressed in black tactical gear exited and took cover in the trees at the side of the road and behind the vehicles. An unmarked Black Hawk helicopter flew over them at treetop level, spun around, and hovered over the command site. Aki could see a door gunner aiming an M240 machine gun at the warriors.

"Ohanzee, your ballistic armor will not protect you from their weapons," Aki declared.

"They cannot harm us." He and Mato jumped on their horses. The warriors who had ridden into the woods reappeared, taking up positions behind the vehicles, blocking the road.

"The tactical team will treat them as a threat," Gray warned.

"Stay here," Aki said. She walked past Ohanzee toward a tall man standing by the front passenger door of the first van. "I'm Homeland Special Agent Akicita Dawson. Do not fire on the warriors."

The man shook his head and said, "Stay where you are. This is now our scene. Stand aside, Agent Dawson."

Aki stopped when she saw she was being targeted by two members of the special team. "You need to withdraw immediately."

"That isn't going to happen. Where's Agent Stevens?"

Aki turned and shouted, "Agent Stevens!"

Stevens walked up and stood next to her. "I'm FBI SAC Jeremy Stevens. Who are you?"

"I'm FBI Special Agent Burke, and by order of FBI Director Watts, you are relieved. I'm now in command of the scene."

A second later, a stunned expression crossed Burke's face as an intense blue flash split the air and at least thirty red orbs materialized in the sky above them. Several of the orbs surrounded the Black Hawk, boxing it in. There were shouts of alarm from the command site as several dozen armed Wakanpi emerged from the woods, dressed in buffalo hides. They formed a line along the ridge. A moment later, several more Wakanpi walked from the woods and joined the Guardians who were on the road behind the FBI tactical team.

Ohanzee spoke loudly in a language that Aki had never heard before and two red orbs bracketed him. He raised his rifle over his head and was bathed in a red glow. Several of the orbs hovered above the Guardians, and a red wall of shimmering light appeared, surrounding them like a protective barrier. A red beam struck the Black Hawk and it was frozen in place. Only the helicopter rotors continued spinning.

Ohanzee shouted, "Respect those who dwell here and never return! This is sacred land. You will have safe passage if you leave now."

Burke shouted into a radio, then frantically punched in numbers on his cell phone.

"Agent Burke, you need to leave before this gets ugly," Aki urged. "You're facing an ancient force of unbelievable power which you can't possibly fathom. Agent Stevens, tell him."

"Agent Burke, listen to her. Move the tactical team back."

Burke looked at Ohanzee, up at his Black Hawk, and then jumped into the van and spoke to someone on his phone.

"Agent Burke, we need to deescalate the situation!" Aki shouted.

The agent stepped out and took pictures of Ohanzee, the Wakanpi, the Black Hawk, and the orbs with his phone, then went back in the van.

"If he does something stupid, a lot of people are going to die," Aki said. "I'm amazed no one has fired a shot yet."

"My people are disciplined," Stevens said. "I'm more worried about Sutton or some of the other local law enforcement starting something."

After a few tense minutes, Burke emerged from the van, glared at Aki, and said, "Agent Stevens, we've all been ordered to vacate the area. Advise your team and the locals that they need to evacuate the area immediately. Agent Dawson, that goes for your people, too. We will escort you out. This area is now a restricted zone and will be under military control shortly."

"I'm not going anywhere," Aki said.

Stevens sighed, glanced at Aki, and said, "Agent Burke, my team and the Homeland team will remain here. I'll give you a full report as soon as the investigation is complete."

Aki watched Burke as he made another call and then issued an order over the radio and made a circular motion with his arm. The tactical team moved slowly back to the vans and the armored vehicle, then boarded.

"Agent Dawson, I don't know what's going on here, but I've been directed to withdraw without you," Burke said. "Agent Stevens, you need to contact Director Watts immediately. The safety of the locals is now your responsibility."

"I'll call him after you've left and things stabilize," Stevens said.

"I want those red orbs to release my Black Hawk."

Aki half turned and shouted, "Ohanzee, release the helicopter. They're leaving."

Ohanzee spoke in the strange language again and the red orbs surrounding the Black Hawk withdrew. The helicopter wobbled momentarily as the pilots resumed control.

"Agent Stevens, I wouldn't want to be in your position." Burke took one more look around and got back in the van. The vehicles turned and drove toward the warriors blocking the road with the Black Hawk hovering over them. As they approached the line of warriors, the red shimmering light receded, and the Guardians and Wakanpi parted to allow the vans to drive past. A single orb followed them as they headed south.

Aki looked back at Gray. He was smiling and nodding in obvious admiration. Ohanzee said something in the strange language and all of the orbs withdrew to the ridgeline and hovered above the Wakanpi. Aki looked down the road again, and only the Guardians remained.

When Aki and Stevens rejoined Ohanzee, Ohanzee said, "You know who is responsible for the deaths of the people. You have witnessed the power of the Wi Can. There is nothing left for you to do here."

Stevens asked, "Are the red orbs the Wi Can?"

Ohanzee just stared down at him as Mato edged his horse closer to Stevens, forcing him to back up.

"Agent Stevens, I suggest we leave," Aki urged. "We'll have to wait for the answers to our questions until later."

"How the hell do I explain this to Director Watts?" Stevens said. "Ohanzee, Mato and several of the other Guardians have broken federal and state laws. They have to be charged."

"I would suggest you explain the exigent circumstances to the director," Aki said. "This isn't like a normal criminal case. I'm not sure how you could arrest or prosecute any of the Wakanpi or the Wi Can. I need to call my boss and tell her what's happened." She turned and looked up at Ohanzee. "I was informed that a twenty-mile-wide no-fly zone is going to be enforced by the Air Force. The military is already headed this way."

Ohanzee closed his eyes. The red orb that had followed the special team returned and hovered above him. When he opened his eyes, he said, "There are fighter jets approaching us now. Since the Wi Can sacred city is no longer a secret, this land will need to be defended. The Guardians will remain."

"I'll see if I can get the military to erect a physical barrier to keep people away. Agent Stevens, the curious may get through the National Guard's cordoned-off area. I have an idea on how to keep them away and offer an explanation into the deaths, but I'll need your cooperation."

"What do you need?"

"Release a story about chemical munitions being found buried in the hills. Tell the media that the victims were in the area surveying and accidently stumbled across an old shaft to an abandoned and forgotten World War II secret facility. Several canisters inside were disturbed and leaked, releasing a poisonous gas. All of the victims died from exposure. The shaft has been temporarily sealed, but it will take time to dispose of the chemical munitions. That should keep most people away, including the mining companies."

"How do we explain the victims being found in rivers or tributaries with knife wounds?" Gray asked.

"Booby-traps and an underground river that feeds into them," Aki replied.

"Did you just come up with this cover story?" Stevens asked.

"Yes."

"Impressive. It could work and buy our bosses some time to decide what they want to do next."

"We need to make it clear that there's no danger to anyone living in the area, but anyone coming near the site will be arrested," Aki continued. "Agent Stevens, I suggest you get everyone out of here as soon as you can and make sure they understand the importance that the cover story be maintained. What's happened here must be kept secret. It must remain highly classified."

"I don't think that will be a problem. When I'm done talking to everyone, no one will want to say anything. Sutton won't dare utter a word."

"Excellent."

"Ohanzee, I'm certain there will be many more questions that my superiors and others will want answered," Stevens said.

"I will answer all of your questions once you and your people have left."

"How will I get in touch with you?"

Ohanzee looked at Aki and said, "Akicita will be my ears. She will know how to reach me. She is one of us."

"Wait a minute," Aki protested. "I'm not a Guardian."

Ohanzee spoke in Lakota. "Akicita, you have been judged to be pure of heart." He appeared to go into a trance for a few seconds, then added, "The Wi Can have invited you to join with them. This is a rare honor that they offer."

Aki wasn't sure what Ohanzee meant and asked in Lakota, "They want me to go into the city?"

"Yes."

"When?"

"Once the others have left. I will guide you through the secret passages."

"Can I bring my team?" Aki asked, pointing at Gray and White Owl.

"The others must leave. Only you are invited."

"Aki, what's going on?" Gray asked.

"I've been invited into the city."

"Hey, I'd like to see this city and get a few photos," Agent Stevens said.

"Akicita is the only one who is invited," Ohanzee said forcefully.

"Aki, I'm not going to let you go in there by yourself," Gray said.

"I won't be alone. Ohanzee will be with me. You and White Owl need to help Agent Stevens get these people out of here."

Gray and White Owl exchanged looks of concern.

"Move it!" Aki commanded. "Agent Stevens, I hope to work with you again sometime."

"I'm not sure I feel the same way right now, but I'm certain that we will meet again to sort this all out."

As White Owl, Gray, and Stevens walked back toward the group, Aki wondered if it was a good idea to go with Ohanzee.

"Mato, you and the others need to watch the roads," Ohanzee said. "I will join you later."

Mato nodded, then said, "Akicita, you are one of us. The Wi Can will embrace you." He turned his horse and led the Guardians quickly away.

Agent Stevens dreaded calling Director Watts. He wasn't sure how this was going to play out. He dialed the director's direct number and Watts answered.

"Agent Stevens, I understand from Agent Burke that we're dealing with a unique situation."

"Yes, sir."

"Tell me about it."

Stevens walked him through what had transpired, and told him about Aki's idea on how to keep the encounter secret.

"I like the cover story," Watts said. "So, are we dealing with first contact? We have protocols in place if that's the case."

"I never received an acceptable answer to that question. Ohanzee said that the Wi Can have been here since humans first walked on the face of the planet.

I can tell you that neither the Wi Can or the Wakanpi are human. They don't appear to pose a threat unless their city is threatened. We didn't encounter any of them until the city was endangered. If we blockade the area, there shouldn't be any more problems while determining what we're dealing with here."

"This seems impossible to believe," Watts stated.

"I've experienced two encounters with these entities, and I'm still unsure of what they are."

"You said that the Guardians were involved in some of the killings?"

"Not directly," Stevens replied. "The homicides were allegedly committed by the Wakanpi and the Wi Can. There are charges we can bring against some of the Guardians, but Ohanzee made it clear that the Wi Can won't allow that to happen. Even if we were able to arrest some of the Guardians, I'm afraid that this whole event would become public. The area would be flooded with alien-seekers and news media. It would be a zoo and cause more problems for us while we try and put the pieces together. I don't think it's worth the risk."

"I see. Did you see one of these Wi Can?"

"No. Only the Wakanpi in Pte Oyate form. I'm still not sure what the red orbs are, but they are obviously under some type of control."

"And you can't convince Ohanzee to take you into the sacred city with Agent Dawson?"

"No chance at all," Stevens replied.

"What do you recommend for our best course of action?"

Stevens knew that he'd be blamed if anything went wrong, so he replied, "I say we go with the cover story, classify the whole event, and observe the area from a distance. Have the president direct the military to blockade the area but make no attempt to enter."

After a moment, Watts replied, "I concur. Wrap it up and head back to Rapid City. The military can secure the area. I'll confer with the attorney general about our options concerning the Guardians. I'm certain that under the circumstances, President Benchley will have questions, so be available. I'll see to it that all of these cases are classified, so you know what you need to tell the local law enforcement and others who are aware of these events. Limit any discussions with other agents."

"Yes, sir."

"I'll be in touch."

Stevens took a deep breath and rejoined Gray and White Owl.

"Well?" Gray asked.

"We're going to go with the cover story, and the whole matter is now classified," Stevens said. "Let's deliver the news to the others."

"Agent Stevens, what in the hell is happening?" Sutton asked, as Stevens, Gray, and White Owl approached.

"We're leaving," Stevens replied. "Everyone, pack up the gear. Leave nothing behind."

"You're just letting them ride away?" Sutton said, waving his hands in the air. "They murdered eight people."

"No, they didn't." Stevens nodded toward the few Wakanpi still standing by the ridge. "They did, but we can't arrest them."

"Why not?"

"Because they aren't human. What you've seen here is now classified, a national-security matter, and is not to be disclosed."

"What!" Sutton cried. "Did you smoke something you shouldn't have at the powwow or have you just lost your mind?"

"You saw what happened when the Black Hawk and the special team arrived." Stevens took an aggressive step toward Sutton. "Do you really think I would leave it like this if I didn't have to? FBI Director Watts has ordered us to leave. We'll talk about this further at the DCI office in Cheyenne. None of your people are to breathe a word of what has happened here." Stevens motioned for Agent Barnes to join him. "I want all of the cell phones, pads, and laptops seized. You will accompany Director Sutton to Cheyenne. Inform the other agency heads who are present that what has occurred here will not be disclosed or they will face federal charges and long prison sentences."

"Yes, sir."

"Director Sutton, this area is under government control. Get your people out of here. Now!"

Sutton stormed off and spoke to Littlejohn and Windward for a moment, then turned and stared back at Stevens and the others.

Sarah and Clay walked over and stood beside Gray. "What *is* going on?" Sarah asked.

"You all have to leave," Gray said. "Aki is staying here with Ohanzee."

"I take it the warrior next to her is Ohanzee."

"Yes. Aki's been invited into the city by the Wi Can."

"Seriously?"

"Yes. I need you and Clay to go back to the RV and wait there with White Owl. He'll fill you both in on what has happened. I'll call you when we're on our way back. Clay, Sarah, no one at NPS or at the Sheriff's Office can learn about what has really happened here. White Owl will explain everything and provide you with the cover story."

"I hear you," Clay replied.

"I know that I made the right decision, to stay with NPS," Sarah said. "This is some weird stuff. Agent Stevens, I guess this is goodbye."

"For now, anyway."

"Gray, you can't stay here with Aki," White Owl cautioned.

"I'm not leaving her."

"She told you to leave," White Owl stated. "So did Ohanzee. You aren't welcome and you know what they do to intruders."

Gray glanced at the Wakanpi, then replied, "Yes, I do, but I'm not a threat to them, so I'm staying. Get going and take all of your deputies with you. Reemphasize to Captain Hunt and the other Pennington County deputies that they can't say anything about what has happened here. Stick to the cover story."

"That cover story won't last long," White Owl said. "There are too many witnesses and a leak is bound to happen."

"Let's just hope it's not anytime soon," Gray replied.

"If it does and we identify who leaked the real story, I'll make sure that an example is made," Stevens said. "Well, I wish I could stay, but I took Ohanzee's warning to heart. I wish all of you the best and I'll be in touch. I have some calls to make before I head for Rapid City."

"I thought you said you were going to Cheyenne," Gray said.

Stevens smiled, then said, "I only said that to shut Sutton up. Agent Barnes will explain the cover story to Sutton and his people. I've had my fill of him." He headed for the FBI command bus.

"Sarah, come on," Clay said.

Gray looked into Sarah's eyes and said, "I'll be alright. Go with Clay. I'll meet you back at the RV."

"You better be careful," Sarah said, swallowing hard. She leaned in and kissed him on the cheek. "And don't do anything stupid. I want you and Aki to come back safely."

"That's the plan."

Fifteen minutes later, all of the command buses rolled past him, followed by a parade of cars and trucks. All that was left of the once-bustling command site was beaten-down grass, Aki's car, and the Wakanpi who still stood watching from the ridgeline. He looked back where Aki and Ohanzee had been standing, but they were gone. Ohanzee's horse was grazing, the reins lying on the ground.

Gray felt a sense of panic begin to take hold. He walked over to the horse and patted its neck, then faced the Wakanpi. A blue flash appeared and all of the red orbs disappeared. The Wakanpi withdrew into the woods like a well-trained military unit.

Gray relaxed.

After another flash of blue light, a sole orb appeared and drifted toward him and suddenly he was enveloped in a red glow. There was no pain associated with the light and he could still hear the wind whistling through the trees. His heart raced as he stood frozen in place.

Aki followed Ohanzee for nearly twenty minutes through thick brush and down a slope into a small rocky ravine to the east of the command site. The direction they traveled seemed to be following the underground passageway that Sarah had shown her on the satellite images. Ohanzee stopped by a rock overhang and Aki noticed a triangular indentation in the ravine wall.

"We are here," Ohanzee stated. "You cannot speak of this place to anyone."

"I understand."

Ohanzee stepped in front of the indentation and said a few words in the strange language.

A blue light emerged from the ravine wall and surrounded them. A moment later, Aki was standing in a golden chamber. She looked around and saw a soft blue light illuminating a passageway.

"That was different," Aki said, taking an unsteady step forward.

Ohanzee grabbed her arm and said, "Wait. We must be escorted to the city. Remember, do not touch the walls or anything encased in gold. It must remain pure."

Aki nodded and looked around in amazement. There was a large golden node behind her, like the one she had seen in the satellite image beneath the command site. "The node is a transporter?"

"Yes. It allows us to pass through the rock."

"That's why Gray and the others couldn't find an entrance." Aki noted a faint smell of ozone in the air, and then a Wakanpi wearing buffalo hides appeared at the entrance to the chamber.

Ohanzee nodded and said, "We must follow. Do not deviate from the path."

Aki stepped from the room into a passageway. There were only two ways she could go. Another Wakanpi was standing in the passageway blocking one direction, so she could only follow Ohanzee and the Wakanpi escort. She was certain that the passageway running to the east would connect to Sled Canyon. As her eyes adjusted to the reduced light, she noticed that the walls and ceiling were composed of a gray-white, smooth stone, which was emitting the light. The floors were smooth, but dark.

They walked quickly uphill for at least a mile, maybe more. It was hard to get a fix on the distance. Each time Aki had glanced back, the other Wakanpi was following. When they walked into the city, she was stunned to see several wispy ghosts of light floating across golden rooftops. "What are those?" she asked.

"Wakanpi in their natural state."

They continued to follow the escort deeper into the city, walking between the structures that she'd seen on the satellite images. The buildings were beautiful and glowed amber as if illuminated from within. The buildings were single and two-storied with no windows. Some of the buildings were larger than others and they were all symmetrically oriented. She heard the sound of a river in the distance. "Is there an underground river nearby?"

"Yes. It runs deep beneath the city."

At least the river part of the cover story will hold up.

A powerful orange ball of light materialized in a courtyard between two structures. Streaks of purple and red electrical lightening-like bolts discharged from the top of a golden building into the orange light. A humming and crackling sound echoed around her and she felt a deep vibration running through her. Aki stumbled into Ohanzee as the light grew more intense. She shielded her eyes with her hand and squinted. She could see a ball of energy that was about three feet in diameter. It floated above the floor in her direction, radiating a shimmering light.

"We can go no closer," Ohanzee cautioned, holding her arm firmly.

Aki stood beside him as he bowed and spoke in the strange language. The ball of light decreased in intensity and an iridescent blue entity emerged from it. The ethereal being approached, stopping a few feet in front of her. She felt the presence of the entity.

Ohanzee continued to converse with the entity, but Aki never heard a response. After several minutes, the blue glow flickered as it appeared to be studying her. Aki was mesmerized. The entity suddenly withdrew, reentering the orange ball of light, and it blinked out.

"Ohanzee, I assume that was one of the Wi Can?"

"Yes."

"Where did it go?"

"Back to where it belongs. It is time to leave."

"Wait. That's it? Can't we explore the city?"

"No. We are only permitted to know a small portion of the city. I was told that much more lies beneath, but that is not for us to see. We must go now." They walked back the way they had come with an escort in front and one behind.

When they reached the opening to the passageway, she said, "What did you talk about? I only heard your side of the conversation, which I didn't understand."

"We discussed you. I was told that you would make a great Guardian chief."

"I'm not interested," Aki replied.

"I know that is how you feel now, but someday you may not have a choice."

"I always have a choice."

"The future is uncertain now that the city and their presence has been revealed. You must convey a message to your superiors that the city remains untouched. Tell them what you have seen and convince them to stay away or more will perish."

"I'll convey the message, but I can't make any promises that it will be heeded."

"It must be, or the power of the Wi Can will fall upon the Earth."

"That sounds ominous."

"It would be," Ohanzee replied.

They walked in silence until they reached the chamber. Aki pointed at the passageway that continued on and asked, "Ohanzee, how far does that go?"

"I can't say. I've never been past this point."

They entered the chamber and the escorts remained outside. Ohanzee approached the golden node and spoke a few words in the Wi Can language. It took Aki a moment to realize that she was back in the ravine.

She shook her head. "How does that work?"

"I don't know. It just does."

They hiked back to the command site and Aki couldn't believe that Gray was still there. He was encased in a red beam.

"Your friend needs to listen better," Ohanzee stated.

"I'll work on that with him."

Ohanzee mounted his horse and said, "*Tókša akhé.*"

"Later," Aki replied. She walked over and stood next to Gray.

When the orb winked out, the sun was higher in the sky than it was a few minutes earlier and the horse was gone. "What the hell," he muttered, checking his watch. It was almost noon. He didn't understand what had happened.

"You shouldn't have stayed," Aki said.

Startled, he turned toward Aki, and relief poured through him at seeing her. "I couldn't leave you." He glanced around. "Where's Ohanzee?"

"He rode off. Gray, you need to learn to follow orders, but I'm glad you're here. I saw the city and I met with one of the Wi Can." Aki's beautiful face appeared to glow. "Our lives have just become very complicated." She took his face in her hands and kissed him gently on the lips. "*Cantecikiya.*"

"What does that mean?"

"My heart is inspired by you," Aki replied.

"And my heart is yours." Gray took her in his arms and kissed her deeply.

Aki stepped back and took his hand. "It's time to go. I'll explain everything when we get back to the RV. I'm sure the others are going to want to know about what I've seen."

"Do I have to wait to hear about what happened until then?"

"I'm still digesting everything. I'll need to call Canton and tell her what has transpired and about the warning."

"I don't think that the military will leave it alone regardless of any warning," Gray said. "I wouldn't be surprised if they drop a GBU57 MOP bunker-buster bomb on the site."

"For everybody's sake, I hope they give this place a wide berth. From what Ohanzee has said, the Wi Can are monitoring activity and have issued an ultimatum of sorts. Any perceived threats will be met with a powerful response. From what I saw, the Wi Can have a lot more capability than they're using, are very advanced, and have abilities that we can't begin to understand."

They left the site and Gray listened to her story as he drove. What she related seemed surreal, and her experience scared him more than their previous encounters with the Wakanpi.

"The node where you made entry was like the one that we saw on the satellite images over the cavern?" Gray asked.

"Yes, but much deeper."

"We can't use the nodes for entry, but can we reach the city from Sled Canyon like Sarah thought?"

"I believe so, but I don't think we should tell anyone about that possibility or even try."

"What will happen if the military takes an offensive approach?" Gray asked.

"Nothing good. They need to leave the Wi Can alone."

"Aki, what if the Wi Can do have hostile intentions? Ohanzee said that they are nourished by the Earth. What if they are depleting our resources and setting the stage for a cataclysmic event?"

"You've seen too many science fiction movies. They've been here for thousands of years. If they wanted to destroy us, they would have done so already. No, my sense was of a benevolent species that took drastic measures to keep their city hidden. I was only allowed to see a small portion of the city. Ohanzee said that there is much more beneath the structures."

"Ohanzee is connected to the Wi Can and can communicate with them. I'm certain that Agent Stevens will pass that information along, which means that he will be sought."

"I know that, and I'm sure he does, too. The Wi Can will protect him."

"Do you think the cavern and the city are what's referenced in the Lakota creation story?" Gray asked.

"I think it's possible."

"I better call Sarah and let her know that we're still alive. I'm certain they are growing concerned."

"While you talk to her, I'll call Sharon and Canton," Aki said.

"Sharon, it's me," Aki said.

"Well, I hear that you created a firestorm out there."

"Just a little brushfire," Aki replied. "What's the latest?"

"First, Under Secretary Canton has been calling us about every half hour wanting to know if we've heard from you. She said she hasn't been able to make contact. You're to call her immediately."

"I will."

"Brian says that signals traffic at the highest level has exploded. We're monitoring, but a lot of it doesn't make sense. There's talk about red orbs, Native Americans wearing warpaint, and an alien encounter. What happened out there?"

"I can't discuss it now."

"Well, whatever happened, the FBI isn't happy with you. In fact, you were mentioned in unflattering terms when Director Watts spoke to Secretary Evans."

"Not surprising," Aki said.

"The president has called an emergency meeting at 1600 hours this afternoon at the White House with all of the national intelligence community directors and the joint chiefs. DHS Secretary Evans and Under Secretary Canton will be attending, as well as a select group from the National Geospatial-Intelligence Agency."

"Sharon, continue to monitor and report, and see if you can snag us a feed of the meeting."

"I'll take care of it. I guess it's probably good that we're leaving Virginia. We still are, aren't we?"

"I'll let you know after I speak to Canton," Aki replied.

"Well?" Gray asked, after Aki hung up.

"The president has called an emergency meeting."

"I imagined he would."

Aki's conversation with Under Secretary Canton had gone better than she'd expected. Secretary Evans liked having his people on the front lines when events unfolded, and according to Canton, it seemed she was developing a reputation for being in the right place at the right time. She believed Canton was actually proud of the way she'd handled everything. Canton had advised her to stay in the area and to wait and see what action the president decided to take.

CHAPTER TWENTY-SIX

Ohanzee rode back to the Guardian ranch on a hidden, tree-covered trail. The ranch was six miles east of the sacred city and where the Guardians met, away from prying eyes. The spread encompassed six acres of grassland and trees with a shallow creek running through the center. It was accessible by vehicle only from forest service roads. Two old doublewide trailers were nestled beneath the trees, adjacent to a corral. Several trucks were parked haphazardly on the grass next to the trailers. As he approached, he noted that the rest of the Guardians had already groomed their horses and were feeding them in the corral adjacent to a large barn.

As Ohanzee rode up and dismounted, Mato approached and asked, "Did Akicita make a good impression?"

"Yes. Have everyone assemble. We have much to discuss." Just then Ohanzee froze as he felt the Wi Can connect with him.

After a moment, Mato asked, "What is it?"

"The Wi Can have summoned me again."

"I'll gather the others."

"No," Ohanzee stated. "I was instructed to come alone and to meet them at the city portal."

When Ohanzee reached the now-abandoned command site, he left his horse by a tree and walked down to the portal. He offered a greeting in their language as he felt the Wi Can presence. A blue light shone brightly from the open portal. Ohanzee moved closer to it, realizing that he had never seen it left open before. As he peered over the edge, he felt the ground begin to shake and grow in intensity. He watched in amazement as hundreds of red orbs shot out and formed a ring above him. Then hundreds of Wakanpi in ethereal form flew into the sky and hovered with the orbs as several Pte Oyate emerged and took positions around the open portal. Ohanzee moved away from them, uncertain what was happening.

Then he felt a stronger connection to the Wi Can. Dozens of orange balls of energy materialized and he could see the Wi Can inside. He'd never seen so many. Ohanzee couldn't believe what was being conveyed to him. A wave of guilt and anger swept over him. The Wi Can were leaving and he felt responsible, even though he was assured that he was not to blame. Some of the Wakanpi would remain in the city to maintain it, but the portals would be sealed until they retuned. Ohanzee, felt a sense of relief, knowing they would return one day.

The Wi Can instructed him that the Guardians were to stand vigil over the land as they had done for millennia. It was now up to Ohanzee to decide what sanctions would be imposed against those who sought to intrude on the city. He was directed to increase the number of Guardians, and to his surprise, he was also instructed to seek counsel with the newcomer, Akicita Dawson. Ohanzee acknowledged the directives and they bid him farewell.

The Wi Can energy balls rose slowly into the sky. Then the ethereal Wakanpi joined with Wi Can and the balls of energy expanded until they merged, glowing as bright as the sun. The red orbs surrounded the large sphere, and together they vanished in a flash, skyward. He shook his head and watched as the Pte Oyate surrounding the portal disappeared into the ground and the portal closed.

Ohanzee felt an emptiness he'd not experienced since before he became the Guardian chief. A part of his being seemed to be missing. He knelt down and took some soil into his hand. As he released it, he watched it blow in the wind. The high-pitched whistle of an eagle announced its presence as it landed high in a tree near him. He'd never seen an eagle over the city before. It was a good sign. The eagle looked down at him and extended its wings, taking flight. As it circled, an eagle feather floated down and Ohanzee snatched it from the air. He would wear it with pride, knowing that it was a symbol from the Great Spirit, granting him the strength and power to carry on until the Wi Can returned.

Gray's Property – June 9 – 1545 hours

Aki watched Angela pull up and park.

"Sorry, I'm late," Angela said as she walked up.

"How was the drive?" Gray asked.

"Long."

Sarah said, "Angela, it doesn't look like we're going caving anytime soon. The city is off limits and Aki said that going through Sled Canyon isn't an option. I'm sorry."

"Well, that's too bad. I really wanted to explore the city."

"I know you did," Aki said. "I'll tell you all about it after the conference call."

Just then, Aki's laptop chimed. She looked at the request. Canton wanted her to be included in the president's meeting. In five minutes, she was to join the conference call. "Well, that's short notice," Aki muttered.

"What is it?" Gray asked.

"They want me to participate in the conference call and I'm to be prepared to provide a firsthand accounting of the events. Agent Stevens will also be participating."

"This should be good," Sarah said.

"I don't know about that," Aki said. Her stomach growled.

"The FBI wasn't happy that you stood up to them," White Owl said.

"No, they weren't. I'm going to make sure that Sharon and the team are monitoring through my laptop feed."

When she finished speaking to Sharon, Aki said, "Here we go, guys. You all need to be quiet."

The group huddled on the other side of her laptop. She pressed the key and said, "Homeland Security Agent Akicita Dawson is on line."

Several other people checked in via secure teleconference over the next few minutes, including Agent Stevens, who checked in from Rapid City. A number of military personnel from the Pentagon joined in at the last minute. Aki had a clear view of the meeting room and the people around the table in the center. She could see Canton sitting with several others along a wall behind Secretary Evans. Once everyone had checked in, there was a moment of silence, and then all of the people in the room stood as President Benchley, the vice president, and the secretary of state entered and took their seats.

"Thank you all for coming or attending remotely on such short notice," President Benchley said. He was in his sixties, bordering on being obese, and Aki noted that his usual jovial demeanor was absent as he looked around.

"A lot has happened over the last few hours," Benchley began. "I want options on how best to deal with this situation and how to establish contact with these entities. General Sanchez, I understand that there was activity over the site a little while ago."

"Yes, sir." Sanchez explained what had been observed by satellite and from the pilots flying over the city, then played a drone video of the event.

Statements of disbelief spread across the room.

Aki was caught off guard as well. It appeared that several of the Wi Can, red orbs, and ethereal Wakanpi had materialized over the portal and then disappeared. She hadn't heard from Ohanzee since he'd left her at the site, and she wondered if he was aware of what had happened.

"Director Watts, didn't you have an agent in the field who made contact with Ohanzee and witnessed these beings?"

"Yes, sir," the director of the FBI replied. "SAC Jeremy Stevens. He's online."

"Agent Stevens, have you ever witnessed any activity like this?" Benchley asked.

"No, sir. The blue light was never sustained and I've never seen those wispy beings or the orange balls of light. I have only encountered the red orbs and the Wakanpi. Ohanzee, the leader of the Guardians, could tell us what they are. I'll track him down."

"Mr. President," Director Evans interrupted. "This is a Homeland Security issue. My people need to take the lead. It was Agent Akicita Dawson who made direct contact with the Wi Can and knows some of the Guardians."

There was an immediate cacophony of protests and comments made by some of those in attendance objecting to Homeland taking the lead role. Benchley raised his hands and said, "Before you all get into a turf war, I can tell you that I've already decided to have Homeland take point, at least for now. Director Watts, in light of Agent Stevens having worked with Agent Dawson, the FBI will assist."

"Yes, sir," Watts grudgingly replied.

"Secretary Evans, I want it understood that you will work closely with all the agencies involved, including the military. There will be no secrets. We need to know exactly what we're dealing with and how to keep it from the public."

The CIA director, the secretary of defense and the chairman of the Joint Chiefs of Staff and several others shook their heads in disagreement and again protested.

"I understand that some of you believe that this is a military operation, and it may very well be, eventually," Benchley said. "But I've been informed that these beings have been here for thousands of years. I want to make contact with them to determine if an aggressive posture is warranted. We don't really know what they're capable of doing."

"With all due respect, Mr. President," Army Joint Chief General Musgrave began, "that's exactly the point. We don't know what their intentions are now that they've been discovered. They may feel threatened and attack. What we detected earlier could be a prelude to a strike." All of the other military officers present nodded and offered supporting comments agreeing with Musgrave.

"I understand all of your concerns," Benchley said. "But I will not authorize military action until I know exactly what we're dealing with here."

"Mr. President, I suggest at the very least that we raise our threat level to DEFCON 4," Musgrave insisted.

"Very well. General Sanchez, you will maintain the no-fly zone. General Musgrave, I want a secure perimeter maintained around the underground city. I don't want anyone getting within three miles of the portal, with a two-mile buffer. I want a barrier in place to prevent any accidental incursion as soon as possible, and I want it monitored and patrolled. There is to be no encroachment within the restricted area, and that includes the military. Have I made myself clear?"

"Yes, sir," the military officers responded in unison.

Benchley continued, "Position whatever forces you think are necessary should peaceful efforts fail or these beings become aggressive. Any activity around the site must be made to appear like we are dealing with a chemical leak. I don't want the Chinese or the Russians elevating their threat level in response to ours. I want this to look like we're dealing with an internal issue and that we are only taking precautions."

Benchley leaned back in his chair. "We also need to keep in mind that the city is considered sacred by the local tribes. I don't want a confrontation with the locals to complicate matters. Secretary Evans, I understand that Agent Dawson is Oglala Lakota. I believe having her as a liaison will be beneficial."

"Yes, sir. I believe that she can also assist in establishing a dialogue with the Wi Can."

"Good."

"Her team is best suited to take point, and as liaison, she will gain the cooperation of the Lakota and the other tribes involved," Evans added.

Aki hoped that her expression didn't show her surprise.

"Agent Dawson, tell us what you witnessed in the city and give us your opinion on what we saw on the video."

She provided them with a detailed accounting of what she'd seen in the city and about her encounter with one of the Wi Can and the Wakanpi, explaining that the wispy beings they saw on the video were actually Wakanpi in their natural state. She had no explanation for the Wi Can exiting the city. She also didn't mention the second portal to the group.

"Agent Dawson, you said that you only saw one Wi Can and one energy ball when you were there," Benchley said.

"Yes, sir."

"Do you have any idea what they were doing?"

"I don't know, sir," Aki replied. "I will contact Ohanzee and see if he can provide any additional information."

"Do that," Benchley directed. "Agent Dawson, you said that Ohanzee speaks the Wi Can language, I want you to get him to establish contact with the Wi Can as soon as possible."

"I will do my best to make that happen."

"Thank you for your report and assessment. I know all of you have questions for Agent Dawson and Agent Stevens."

After an extensive Q&A round that Aki thought would never end, the president finally said, "I believe that we've heard all that we need to for now. Direct any further questions to Secretary Evans or Director Watts. We'll continue to use the cover story. Now, I want options for how best to proceed when we do make contact."

Aki sat patiently listening as a number of different opinions were proposed. All of them required Ohanzee to act as an interpreter with her oversight. As the discussion wound down and the meeting appeared to be concluding, she said, "Mr. President, I'd like to suggest something."

"Yes, what is it?" Benchley asked.

"Creating an advisory board composed of the members of the military and other agencies, including representatives from the Guardians, would help prevent misunderstandings and reduce suspicions in the tribes as we move forward."

"I can't support that idea," General Musgrave interjected. "We don't want the Guardians or the world knowing what we're doing until we have completely explored and understand what we are dealing with here. Hell, if this gets out, the Russians or Chinese may decide to nuke the site so we can't obtain their technology."

"General, the Guardians are composed of members from many tribes and they have kept this secret for thousands of years," Aki stated. "They know more about the Wi Can than we do and will be of assistance in keeping the area secure."

"I agree," Benchley said. "The Guardians don't want people knowing about the Wi Can or the city any more than we do. Secretary Evans, assemble a board."

"Yes, Mr. President," Evans replied. He cast a quick smile at Aki.

After a few more questions and further discussion, the meeting was concluded and Aki signed off.

"Aki, you did good," Gray offered.

"Thanks, but I need to convince Secretary Evans that I'm not a diplomat or a scientist, and that I wouldn't have anything of value to offer as a liaison."

"Are you kidding me?" Sarah said. "I think it would be exciting and an honor to work with the Wi Can. You'd be interacting with beings from the stars, and what could be more exciting than that?"

"Exciting, yes, but it's not what I want to do for the rest of my career."

"Aki, is there any chance I could fill that role?" Angela asked. "I have the background and I'm not a government agent or affiliated with any agency, so I wouldn't be considered a threat to any of those involved. I'm a scientist and an academic with a passion for studying ancient cultures. Plus, I speak Lakota. I think that I'd be perfect."

Aki smiled and said, "I believe you would be. But the Wakanpi were responsible for the death of Dr. Waters. Can you put those feelings aside?"

"I understand your concern, but I realize that they were protecting their way of life. Their actions were in response to a perceived threat. Darren would want me to continue his research and determine what they mean or have meant to humanity. Aki, I wouldn't have volunteered if I couldn't deal with them."

"I'll run it by Canton," Aki said.

Gray sat back in his chair, steepled his fingers, and said, "Perhaps we can make this work to our advantage."

"How?"

"If the president would fast-track building our new facility on the estate in Pringle, you'd be close to the sacred city and could offer to supervise Angela. You'd be available to attend meetings with Ohanzee and the board when not on a mission. It might make it easier to sell the president and Secretary Evans on Angela being the liaison."

"That's not a bad idea. I need to contact Ohanzee. Maybe he'll know what the Wi Can were doing. Angela, I'd like you to join me for that conversation and make sure that he's open to working with you. Then I'll call Canton."

"If Canton approves my appointment, I'll start looking for links to the Wi Can in other ancient cultures," Angela said. "Who's to say that this is the only sacred city the Wi Can have on Earth?"

"Angela, if you find another city, don't call me to go explore it," Sarah chimed in. As everyone chuckled, she added, "I'm serious."

Angela and Aki stepped away from the group.

Gray looked at the others sitting around the firepit as they talked, as close friends do. Their friendships and bond had been forged in battle. He reminisced about the events that had brought this unusual assortment of people together, and of the two people they had lost.

He smiled when he thought about meeting Sarah for the first time and his first impression of her. If not for Aki, he wondered where their relationship would have ended up. Sarah's dedication and interest in the NPS had kept her from coming to Homeland, which was probably for the best.

Clay laughed at something Sarah said, and he remembered when Clay had been assigned to the task force. Gray was certain that Clay had no idea what had been in store for him—none of them had—but Gray knew that those experiences would serve Clay well in the future.

Gray noticed that White Owl was sitting quietly, listening to the others. He was a quiet man who seemed to like working behind the scene. He'd been steadfast during their encounters with the Wakanpi and the firefight with Dar. Gray wondered what was in store for him. Hopefully, a promotion, but Gray wasn't sure that was what White Owl wanted for his future.

He looked over to where Angela and Aki were standing and recalled meeting Angela for the first time. If her interview hadn't turned out like it had, he wasn't sure that they'd have ever found out about the Wi Can or the Wakanpi, and he never would have met Aki or Chase. He'd still be employed by the Department of the Interior and flying, while the homicides would remain unsolved. It also occurred to him that Agent Crawley would still be alive and making everyone's life miserable.

Fate is a funny thing. How different their lives would have been if they hadn't all come together in the Black Hills.

As Angela and Aki walked back to join the group, he knew by Aki's demeanor that something wasn't right. Aki motioned for him to join them.

"Did Ohanzee have an issue with Angela?" Gray asked Aki.

"No. That's the least of our problems. Ohanzee said that the Wi Can have left the city. What we saw on the video was their departure. He doesn't know when they'll be back, but he said he was directed to protect the city until they return. It could be days or years."

"Which means that you won't be able to open a dialogue with the Wi Can anytime soon."

"Correct. I want this development kept to the three of us. I'm not even going to tell Canton yet."

"That's a big risk," Gray said.

"Yes, but if the president and others know that the Wi Can have left, they'll descend on the site. That will force Ohanzee and the Guardians to confront the military, and you know how that will end."

"Yes, I do, but I don't think the others would say anything."

"I'm not going to risk it."

They walked back to the firepit and Aki said, "Gray, Angela and I have some things we need to discuss and a few more calls to make. I need to tell you that this operation is officially at an end and your services are no longer needed here."

Gray thought that Aki's announcement was a bit brusque, and from the reaction of the others, it was obvious that they felt that way too.

"You all are welcome to stay and talk, but we have work to do," Aki added.

"I think now is a good time for us all to leave," White Owl stated.

Gray knew White Owl perceived something had happened and that they weren't going to be included this time.

"I have to say that you all have done great work here and I thank you," Aki said in a softer tone. "It will not be forgotten. It's been an honor."

"Are we done?" Clay asked. "I mean, really done?"

"Clay, you are free to return to Sundance and go back to your regular duty. Sarah, I know that you are looking forward to your new job and I wish you the best."

"Thank you. I'll stop by from time to time."

"White Owl, what are your plans?" Aki asked.

"I was thinking of taking a vacation before returning to duty. I want to spend some time on the reservation and reconnect with some old friends."

"That sounds like a good idea," Aki said. "You know that you are all welcome here anytime."

They all exchanged hugs and handshakes with promises to get together again soon.

Gray watched as Sarah, Clay and White Owl drove away. He had grown closer to this group of people than any others he'd ever worked with in the past. He hoped that they would remain close.

Aki took his hand and said, "We'll get together with them as often as we can."

"I know. I just feel like we aren't finished here."

"Maybe we're not."

Gray's Property – June 12 – 0700 hours

Gray sat drinking his 'Chase' tea as he watched the low-level white clouds drifting past in the quiet morning. The air was cool and he took a slow, deep breath. Aki appeared serene as she gazed at the vista.

Under Secretary Canton, Secretary Evans and the president had all approved Angela as the Guardian liaison. They all agreed that she was better suited for the job than Aki. Gray had also spoken to Clay last night and was pleased to hear that he had been assigned to investigations and was going to be promoted when his sergeant retired next month. Clay actually sounded relieved to be back to a more normal routine.

The area around the ridge had already been secured. The only sound over the area was an occasional fighter jet on patrol or a UAV dropping down for a closer look. Gray was amazed that there hadn't been any leaks about the Wi Can encounters, which he thought might be in part due Director Sutton being replaced by Justin Littlejohn.

"Are you still meeting Ohanzee at the Wi Can city portal at one?" Gray asked.

"Yes. I know the intelligence community and the military are getting antsy since there's been no contact with the Wi Can."

"How long do you plan to keep Canton and the others in the dark?"

"For as long as I can," Aki replied, then took a sip of her coffee. "Telling anyone now would derail the economic incentives the president has promised the reservations."

"Do you think the president will buckle to pressure and attempt to enter the city if contact isn't made soon?"

"I hope not."

"You do realize that deceit through omission is just as bad as telling a lie. We can't keep the charade up for much longer."

"We'll see." Aki smiled at him. "Don't you go soft on me. We're in the intelligence business. Not revealing information is part of the job. I will eventually tell Canton and let her decide what happens next. By the way, she's authorized relocation assistance for the team and they'll start the moving process shortly. Until the team has relocated, Canton has pulled us from active assignments."

"Is Traci still staying behind?" Gray said.

"Yes. She told me that she thought the job would make having a normal married homelife difficult."

"That's probably why Brian, Omar, and Sharon are single. When are you going to start teaching me Lakota?"

"We can start anytime you want," Aki replied. She went to him and kissed him softly.

"*Cantecikiya*," Gray said.

"It seems you already know the most important word."

EPILOGUE

Aki stood next to the compound's new helipad. Gray was flying Under Secretary Canton in from Rapid City in the new AS565 MBe Panther helicopter the team had acquired. Canton was coming to officially open the hardened TCT command center. The center and adjacent hangar had been built in record time and were protected by the most sophisticated camouflage system ever developed. The eighty-acre campus was already fenced and gated, and the advanced electronic security measures were continuously monitored. The security and defense systems were state of the art and low profile.

In addition to the updated estate house, four additional homes would be ready for occupancy in another month, and three more homes would be built, giving the campus the appearance of a small subdivision.

Sharon planned to move into one of the homes on the property. Brian was still undecided, while Omar had chosen to live off campus in a cabin he'd purchased. His cabin was just south of Custer and only a fifteen-minute drive away.

Angela, now officially a member of the team, was going to move into the home that had been slated for Omar. Over the last two months, Angela had spent most of her time with Ohanzee, learning the Wi Can language and doing historical research on ancient world sites to determine if the Wi Can had appeared in any other location. BYU had granted her an open-ended research sabbatical at President Benchley's request. Aki didn't think Angela would go back to teaching anytime soon.

The house reserved for Gray and Aki would remain unoccupied, but Aki planned to move her furniture and some of her personal items into it just in case they needed to stay on campus for any reason. She preferred living with Gray on his property. She'd grown accustomed to the RV's smaller living space, and the serenity the open space offered was worth the commute time. She enjoyed the breathtaking sunsets.

Over the last month, Sharon, Omar, and Brian had been busy making all the final preparations to get the center operational, while Gray had been spending time in Texas receiving advanced training on the Panther. The helicopter had been purchased with funds seized from two of Dar's hidden accounts discovered in Australia.

The Panther was equipped with the latest advanced avionics systems, including a harpoon system to assist in anchoring to a ship's deck in foul weather. The two Saffran Arriel turboshaft engines would provide operational capability at high altitude, with a max speed of one hundred and sixty-five knots and a four hundred fifty nautical-mile range. It could operate in the worst weather conditions imaginable.

The armor-shrouded tail rotor provided additional safety from ground fire and with the thirty-four-foot diameter main rotors, it fit nicely in the hangar that had been built into the cliff next to the operations center. The civilian white-over-blue paint scheme hid the military configuration and its real capability.

Sarah had stopped by the campus a few times over the last two months. Her new investigative position was a great career fit. On her last visit, she'd told them that she was dating another NPS agent and hoped that would develop into a serious relationship.

When Aki and Angela had lunched with White Owl a few days earlier, Aki inquired why he hadn't come by the campus yet. White Owl explained that he didn't want to intrude during construction. He promised that he would stop by soon.

The newly promoted Sergeant Clay Gurley had visited the week before and was surprised at how quickly the campus had been constructed. Gray had asked him about his new role as sergeant and Clay told him he was enjoying it and that he wouldn't have the job if it hadn't been for his time on the task force.

The no-fly zone over the Wi Can city was still being enforced and Gray was amazed that no one had tried to breach the barrier. The hazardous-materials and toxic-gas placards on the fences, combined with the original and updated news-media reports about the victims and hazards, seemed to be keeping people away.

Aki and Angela had accompanied Ohanzee into the restricted area on several occasions, walking near the portal, to keep up the appearance that the Wi Can were still present. Aki wasn't sure how much longer she could keep up the charade. She kept telling Canton that the Wi Can weren't responding. Perhaps it was time to tell Canton that they had left. The president, intelligence community, and the military were increasing their pressure on Secretary Evans. The longer she kept silent, the harder it would be to explain when the truth came out. Aki secretly hoped that the Wi Can would return before she had to tell anyone, but time was running out.

The Panther rotors made a distinctive sound as the helicopter approached. Aki watched as Gray flew in low over the treetops and performed a quick 180-degree turn as the retractable gear descended. She shielded her eyes from the fine gritty particles that blew off of the pad as Gray landed. Canton waved from the copilot's seat after the wheels touched down. Once the rotors stopped turning and Gray had shut down the engine and avionics, he got out and Aki helped Canton from the passenger seat.

"This is one nice machine," Canton said, then added, "Take care of it, Aki. You have a tendency to lose aircraft."

"I do at that," Aki replied. "Welcome to the TCT operations campus."

"That's not what it's called anymore. Secretary Evans has decided to give the facility a code name. When you go live today, you will be known as *Ghost Sentinel*."

"I like it," Aki said, feeling a chill creep up her spine.

"Me too," Gray added.

They walked along a compacted pine-bark trail, that was adjacent to the cliff wall and stopped at the concealed entrance to the operations center. As they went through a holographic cloak that mirrored the trail, a recessed door suddenly materialized in front of them.

"My goodness, that is very cool," Canton said.

"It doesn't get any better than this," Gray said.

Aki faced a retinal scanner and placed her palm on the biosecurity pad next to an oversized steel door. The seal on the door hissed as it unlocked and opened.

"The automatic door is a nice feature," Canton said.

"The door is very heavy," Gray offered. "Opening it manually is an effort. The armor plating will withstand anything thrown at it, except a direct hit from a nuclear bomb."

"I'm aware of the facility's hardened design features, Gray," Canton stated. "Eventually, this facility will be enlarged and used as a strategic relay and communications center. It will also serve as a presidential safe site. Construction won't begin on phase two for a few years."

"Let's go in," Aki said. "The door is on a timer."

"Lead the way," Canton replied.

The large door closed behind them as they walked along the hallway to the operation center. They'd passed a number of offices and other passageways that went deeper under the cliff. One of the passages led to an underground hangar for the Panther. Aki put her hand on the security pad and the operations center door opened.

"Welcome," Aki said, motioning for Canton to enter.

The center was impressive. There were a number of offices ringing a hub, with massive monitors positioned on the high walls for easy viewing from six workstations in the center of the room. Sharon, Brian, Omar, and Angela greeted Canton, and after an exchange of pleasantries, they all went into a large conference room. Aki took her usual chair at the circular table and the others settled into their seats. Canton remained standing, catching Aki off guard. She stood back up, thinking she'd slighted Canton. The others did the same.

"Please, that isn't necessary...sit down," Canton said.

When everyone had resettled, she said, "I'm not here just to see the facility. We have a couple of things to discuss." Canton's tone became serious. "Aki, the president is tired of waiting for you to establish a dialogue with the Wi Can. It's been too long. He's wants Ohanzee to press the issue and get the Wi Can to the table. You need to tell him that if a dialogue isn't established by the end of next week, the military will take action."

"As I've explained, Ohanzee can't gain entry without being summoned." Aki paused, then added, "And that isn't going to happen."

"And why is that?" Canton asked, taking a seat, casting her an inquisitive look.

Aki sighed, knowing the moment had come. "The Wi Can have left the city."

"What!" Canton exclaimed. "When?"

"A while ago," Aki admitted.

"We thought it best not to tell anyone," Angela added.

"You all knew about this?" Canton asked, looking around the room.

"Only Angela, Gray, and I knew," Aki said. "Ohanzee doesn't know when they'll return. We've periodically checked the city, but Ohanzee says that he still doesn't feel their presence."

"You kept me in the dark about this?"

"Yes. The city is still under Guardian protection. If the president decides on taking military action, the Guardians will be forced into a fight to protect the city. The Wi Can left a directive forbidding entry into the city by anyone, including Ohanzee. They will return and I thought it best not to inform anyone, hoping that the Wi Can would come back before now and we could establish communications with them."

"I see." Canton leaned back in her chair. "You wanted to prevent unnecessary bloodshed and give me plausible deniability."

Aki shifted uncomfortably in her chair. "That's correct. As I said, I had hoped the Wi Can would return before my ruse was discovered."

Canton nodded and stared at her in silence.

Aki braced for Canton's wrath, but to her surprise, Canton smiled and said, "Considering everything, I believe you made the right call."

Aki felt an immediate sense of relief. "When will you inform Secretary Evans and the president?"

"I don't know." Canton took a deep breath. "Probably by the end of next week. This isn't going to go well if the Wi Can don't return before then."

"You could tell them that the Wi Can refuse to speak with anyone and that they will respond with force if any intrusion is attempted," Gray offered.

"I don't believe that will work," Canton replied. "Any other ideas?"

"Why not tell the president a version of the truth?" Angela offered. "I'm attempting to locate other cities where the Wi Can may have lived on Earth in the past. Inform him that I believe that may be where they've gone until things return to normal here."

"That's a start," Aki said. "You can add that you just learned of the situation and that Ohanzee claims that they didn't leave anything behind except empty structures. So, there's nothing to see in the city and it isn't worth risking a war and public disclosure. Convince them that our best course of action is inaction. We need to wait for them to return, or attempt contact if Angela discovers where they've gone. Emphasize that there isn't any threat."

"The president should take the noblest kind of action," Gray said. "Follow the Taoist philosophy of Wu Wei."

"The what?" Aki asked, giving him a puzzled look.

"The Taoist belief that there is action within inaction," Gray explained.

"That could work," Canton said, then remained silent for a moment. "Dr. Kingman, from now on, you'll report directly to me. Clear?"

"Yes, Ma'am," Angela said.

"Now to our next order of business. Ghost Sentinel has an assignment. You'll receive the complete mission package at noon. But in a nutshell, there were several well-coordinated assassinations and attacks against oil, coal, and power-company executives and CEOs in Texas, Wyoming, West Virginia, and Tennessee yesterday. All of them were killed within hours of each other. Additionally, several high-voltage transmission lines across Europe were destroyed in an attempt to disrupt the power grids. Wind farms, nuclear and other power-generating facilities around the world have also come under attack. The FBI is putting together a task force and is working with law enforcement and intelligence agencies worldwide."

"Someone is targeting energy generation and transmission capabilities," Gray said.

"That was the thinking until late last night. We also learned that a number of agricultural, logging, and mining-company executives and cattle-ranch owners were murdered late yesterday in South America. The companies are responsible for the latest encroachment in and destruction of the Amazon rainforest. And oddly enough, two Chinese fishing fleets, one off Chile and the other off Ecuador, were fired upon. They suffered casualties and the loss of one vessel."

"It sounds like a well-funded and organized group of ecoterrorists with up-to-date intelligence capability and global resources," Gray said. "What are they demanding?"

"No one has claimed credit and there haven't been any demands as yet. We're still piecing it all together, but intelligence believes that there will be more attacks based on signals traffic."

"How do we fit in?" Aki asked.

"This will be a multiagency operation, and Ghost Sentinel will be the tip of the spear for Homeland. Your orders are to identify the group responsible and its leaders, then capture or terminate them."

"That's what we're here to do," Aki said. "We'll get the job done."

On to the next mission

FROM THE AUTHOR

This is the first book in the Holt and Dawson Ghost Sentinel series. I wanted to write something that was a little different from my previous science fiction novels. Because of my law enforcement background, I decided to write a crime and mystery adventure story, but I couldn't resist adding a science fiction component. To add a sense of realism to the story and characters, I incorporated real locations, criminal investigative procedures, and the disputed control of the cases between the state and federal law enforcement agencies involved.

I had the most fascinating time doing research for the book. I found myself being drawn to the mystique and history of the Lakota, the Black Hills, and how important the Black Hills are to the Native American people. I have the utmost respect for the Native People.

I hope that you enjoyed this first adventure with Grayson Holt and Akicita Dawson. I always appreciate reviews. If you would be so kind, please leave a review on Amazon, Goodreads, BookBub, or your favorite review site. You can connect with me at my website, www.gbholley.com or on Twitter at gbholley1, or at gbholley on Facebook and Instagram.

ACKNOWLEDGEMENTS

I wish to thank everyone who took the time to read this novel. I hope it gave you hours of enjoyment.

I have many people to thank for their contributions to the book. First, my wife Terry, who read and reread, reviewed, edited, provided the title, and offered suggestions to enhance the story. Your advice, perspective, support and encouragement were invaluable in this endeavor. I can't thank you enough.

A big thank you to Susan M. Grossman of Narwhal Editorial for the great editing and fact-checking work on this novel. The time you spent researching the small details, and the corrections you made, really honed the work. I appreciate all of your notes and edit suggestions.

My sincere appreciation and thanks to Darlene and Richard Kingas for their continued support, comments about the book, and your friendship. You both are the best.

Thanks and appreciation to Kimberly Martin and her team at Jera Publishing for the exceptional interior design work, book cover, and getting the book ready for release. This is the fifth novel you and your staff have prepared, and it's always a pleasure working with you.

A NOTE ABOUT THE AUTHOR

G. B. Holley is the author's pen name. He has published three novels in the ARKLIGHT Ancient Alien Adventure series, and an alien abduction thriller, Quantum Arrow. He is a native Floridian and retired law enforcement commander who spent more than three decades serving with the Pinellas County Sheriff's Office. He's a pilot, a former high liability trainer and adjunct instructor at St. Petersburg College. He earned his MPA and BA degrees from the University of South Florida, Tampa, Florida. He has also instructed and consulted on leadership and organizational development topics to many organizations and agencies around the country.

He loves reading science fiction and adventure novels and enjoys researching unknown phenomena.

He is currently writing ARKLIGHT Kyla, the fourth book in the ARKLIGHT series and doing research for the next Ghost Sentinel novel.